LITTLE HOMETOWN, AMERICA

Other books by CG FEWSTON

A TIME TO FORGET IN EAST BERLIN

A TIME TO LOVE IN TEHRAN

VANITY OF VANITIES

THE MYSTIC'S SMILE ~ A PLAY IN 3 ACTS

THE NEW AMERICA: A COLLECTION

A FATHER'S SON

LITTLE HOMETOWN, AMERICA

A Look Back

An Original
American Novel
Inspired By
True Events

CG FEWSTON
2020

This book is a work of fiction. Names, characters, places, and incidents are the product of the author's imagination or are used factiously. Any resemblance to actual events, locales, or persons, living or dead, is coincidental.

The book uses American spelling. The book took five weeks to write, five years to publish and forty years to live. A huge thanks to the Hemingway Society, to Fraser Place, and to everyone who gave their support at the American Academy in Rome (Italy) while the author worked on this book.

If you purchase this book without a cover you should be aware that this book may have been stolen property and reported as "unsold and destroyed" to the publisher. In such cases neither the author nor the publisher has received any payment for this "stripped book."

Copyright @ 2020 by CG FEWSTON
All rights reserved. Excepted as permitted under the U.S. Copyright Act of 1976, no part of this publication may be reproduced, distributed, or transmitted in any form or by any means, or stored in a database or retrieval system, without the prior written permission of the author or publisher.

ISBN 978-1656908872

Printed in the United States of America

For You
For Americans
For America

For Thor, my son

Looking back is just as important as looking forward.

"You found the earth too great for your one life, you found your brain and sinew smaller than the hunger and desire that fed on them — but it has been this way with all men. You have stumbled on in darkness, you have been pulled in opposite directions, you have faltered, you have missed the way, but, child, this is the chronicle of the earth."

From *You Can't Go Home Again* (1940)
Thomas Wolfe (1900-1938)

LITTLE HOMETOWN, AMERICA

A Look Back

There's so much I haven't told you and there's so much more I don't even know where to begin. One could say the end was the beginning when the ferry bore me to Discovery Bay all those years ago, because it was then I first considered the idea for the book. In truth, however, I'd been looking back my whole life and seeing a world apart from the one I'd been living. It would be then, as I looked back over the long steady years of my life, I wished for the ability and power to turn back time to the good old days, but even then, those days hadn't been all good and I'd been far too young to know better. When I think back to those moments which have haunted me all my life, I tell myself I hadn't meant to look back, but I did and that changed everything. I'm not sure how old I'd been but I was old enough to remember my mother's wet hand and her finger that had no ring. A dream, a scar, a memory, an angel. A circle, a unicorn, a beginning and an end.

Among the oak and pecan forests of Texas, in my old hometown of Brownwood, the memory or dream begins with rainclouds rolling in after church on a late Sunday morning. On a highchair I sat while my family ate lunch in a country restaurant called Pass the Biscuits near a river that fed into a spillway, boiling over in the rainy season beneath the restaurant's bay windows. With a napkin dipped in water, my mother attended to me by wiping my lips and chin clean while I glanced over at my father's face, usually soft with a grin, and noticed he had grown firm and complacent as he stared out the window and into the spillway below. Something had been said between my father and mother and I still wasn't sure what it was or whether it was good or bad. My big brother Chadwick leaned next to my father and asked if we could go down to the river after lunch. My elder sister, the middle child, contested and wanted to return home afterwards. My mother agreed with Cassandra and said, 'Henry, let's just go home. It's been a long day.' And when all four of my most beloved family members turned to me — the child, the babe, the innocent — as the deciding vote, I had only begun to enter the age when numbers meant something and I could distinguish that my say, the youngest of the family, meant a clear tiebreaker. Over the years, though, I would gradually lose respect for my father, but when I think about him when he was then in his mid-thirties, a bit younger than I am now, I can respect how he believed in fairness and the democratic way of solving a dispute, and in this way was how I learned what it was to be a Texan and an American. 'I want to go with Chadwick,' I said to my mother, and she returned with, 'If that's what you really want,' and I shook my head that it was. My father had written a check for the meal and what I could tell from his expression and the words shared between my parents, I guessed it had not been a good thing. But at that age money held too many vague abstractions and I soon forgot the sad look on my mother's face as I ran out of the restaurant, down the steps, into the parking lot and next to my family's worn-blue station wagon, the one we had nicknamed 'Old Blue,' where I often rode sitting happily on the armrest between my father, the driver, and my mother, the passenger.

Once we were nestled in the car, my father drove up the incline, turned to the right out of the parking lot, drove onto the highway and across the bridge. He made another quick right and descended our family into a small park and rest area situated alongside the river and down below the restaurant we had left a minute prior. Chadwick, the first out of the car, bounded out and down to where the rising river tore over the concrete wall, creating a furious waterfall a few feet away. When the river ran low, my brother and I could walk out on to the concrete barrier two or three feet above the stagnant and harmless waterline. Then, however, the rainy season had come and I stood amazed at the power of the water hurling itself over and down the spillway and beneath the bridge off to my right. My mother, last out of the car, walked by herself in the opposite direction of where my brother and father and I had congregated. My sister often tortured me so I tried not to pay too much attention to her. But my mother I still loved and as my father and brother skipped rocks over the rushing river, I watched my mother hold herself, head down as if counting her steps, and after she reached a desired number she stopped to stare out over the river.

As a family we'd made coming to the river a ritual after eating our Sunday lunch, but never in all that time had I seen my mother so sad. My sister had joined my father's side as the sky began to drizzle rain. When my mother lifted her palm skyward, I decided to run to her side so she would not be alone.

'Mom, what're doing?'

'Nothing.'

'I saw you looking at the ground. Why?'

'Oh, baby. I was just looking for seashells.'

'Can I help?'

I should've known there'd be no seashells on the riverbank, but I began helping my mother look anyway. We never found any. Even after all this time, I've never found any. After a time by the raging river — where I'd find myself looking out over the same rushing waters some twenty years later before leaving America to go teach in South Korea — the rain increased from a light shower to a heavy downpour. Down at the opposite end, my brother and my sister had already run to Old Blue and my father, now at the driver's side door, waved his huge paw of a hand and yelled, 'Cody! Gwendolen! Come on!' He then fell into the driver's seat and slammed the door. The engine turned and the wipers slapped the rain hitting the windshield.

I imitated my father. 'Mom, come on,' I said.

'Go ahead, son,' she said. 'I'll be there in a minute.'

The rain poured harder, hurting my little head, so I obeyed my mother and ran towards Old Blue. But then I thought of my mother all alone in that rain getting all soaked and I stopped, wanting to go to her, hold her hand in mine, escort her to the car and back to our family.

I stopped running and looked back. My hair, fully wet, leaked water into my eyes. Through the haze and thick veil of rain I watched my mother stare out across the river with a determination I'd never seen from her before. And with the cool grace of a giant bird lifting itself out of the water to take flight, my mother slipped off her wedding ring and threw it hard into the river.

The rain continued all around me and I told myself how this was the stuff of dreams and how I should not believe my young eyes. I'd return to the car, take my perch dripping next to my father and wait until my mother returned so I could check her left hand. If there was still a ring, I'd been a fool. I had imagined it all.

'Where's your mother?'

'She'll be here in a minute,' I said.

'God, Gwendolen.' My father turned to look for his wife in the rain.

Chadwick and Cassandra grumbled and waited in the back seat as the rain pelted the roof harder. After all this time I can still hear the rain hitting the roof above me in a flotilla of notes as if from a typewriter. Outside the front windshield I could barely see the lone figure of my mother cross in front of Old Blue and I felt relieved she was safe.

My mother opened the door and backed into her seat before sliding her legs in and shutting the door, 'Okay, Henry. Let's go.'

Then I did what I should not have done. Positioned high on my perch, I leaned down to be doubly sure of what I'd seen five minutes before. My mother's left hand — I'll never forget — rested on her left thigh. Blue veins lined her hand as though they were rivers on a worn map showing a land that had been forgotten long ago. There I saw the wetness of her bare finger glisten.

'Where's your wedding ring, mom?'

My father had just put the gear shift into reverse when I spoke up loud enough for my brother and sister to lean forward over the front seats to check for themselves. My father touched the brake, looked over at my mother's hand, which she now held with her right hand out of some fear of its discovery, and my father pushed the gear shift up and back into park.

'God, Gwendolen. What did'ya do now?'

'Let's go, Henry. Forget about it.'

'I'm not going to forget about your wedding ring. I bought you that ring. My sweat paid for that ring. What did you do with it?'

'Maybe,' her voice trembled, 'maybe I left it back at the house.'

'No, mom,' I said. 'You had it on at lunch. I remember.'

'Quiet, Cody.'

My father knew I was on his side and he waited for my mother to respond.

She bowed her head. 'Maybe it slipped off in the rain.'

My father turned his head to stare out the window and into the rain that consumed the landscape, and I knew my father was thinking what I was thinking: that ring could be anywhere out there.

'God, Gwendolen.'

No one moved. No one seemed to breathe. I could smell the rain and that was it. As a family we could not move forward and we could not go back. And then I did a stupid thing.

'I'll be your hero, mom,' I said. 'I'll find that ring.'

I spun around and exited out the back door on my brother's side before he could stop me and as I did, I heard my father say, 'Come on. Let's look for that damn thing.'

Once again, my mother was last out of the car. As my father, my brother, my sister and I searched the ground seeping into mud, my mother sat in the car alone. It rained and we looked, and the whole time I waited for my mom to save us from the rain, from the useless attempt at trying to find what would forever remain lost. I waited for my mother to come and tell us — to tell me — the truth. After about ten minutes, my mother switched off Old Blue and joined us in the hunt for her lost wedding ring.

'God, Gwendolen. Where were you when you last had it?'

The rain came down in large clumps and stung my head.

'Yeah, mom,' Chadwick said. 'Where were you?'

'I don't know.'

'She was over here,' I said. I led my father and brother to the area where I knew my mother to be standing when she threw her ring into the river.

Even now at forty years old I dream about the rain wetting my hair, my face and the mud down by my little boots, and in some dreams, not all, I spot the gold band and diamond half-covered in wet grass and mud. I pick up the ring from the muck, hold it high over my head, and feel I have saved my family from the path that unfolded before us years later. But on that day, I never found my mother's wedding ring, and she never came to tell me the truth of what I had seen.

My father eventually called off the search because my mother didn't seem to care; for most of the time she held herself on the riverbank and looked into the river's oblivion and mystery, and if she were crying, no one could distinguish between the raindrops and the teardrops when she wiped her face with the tips of her fingers. The rain even seemed to give up as it slowed and lightened while everyone trudged back to Old Blue wet and sad. Inside, looking straight at the river, as was I, my father said, 'Guess we'll have to buy you a new one, Gwen.'

'There's no need, Henry. We don't have enough money anyhow. There wasn't even enough money for the check you wrote for lunch.'

The memory or dream ends when my father backs Old Blue out of the parking spot facing the spillway, uses the butt of his palm to spin the steering wheel into position, shifts the gear into forward to drive us out of that little park and to take us children home.

I have a bad habit of looking back when I'm not supposed to, and I'm not at all sure why I even do it. But I was older, much older in the spring of 1999, and I knew enough to turn and walk up that grassy slope when the time came for the pastor to do his work in a pond out on my father's Pine Creek Ranch.

After university class one morning, I drove home by the back roads, where Dead Man's Curve can be found by the rock quarry and where my mother, years later, would return from her late shift at the hospital at three in the morning to see in her headlights an overturned truck and a young college man's body and brains splashed across the macadam — she later told me that she thought it was me lying there dead on the road.

Unlike that night or that day full of clouds when I would, years later, find my sister's dog Gator dead by the roadside, the sun warming the dog's motionless body along with the quiet and good earth, and unlike those days I knew to enjoy days like this as a freshman because when I became older such freedoms and trouble-free days would be hard to come by.

Once I entered my father's land and closed the cattle guard so the horses couldn't get out, I drove slowly up the gravel to a motley crew of dogs: Gator with his classic brown spot over one grayish-blue eye and a silly, playful expression slapped across his face as his tongue hung to one side; Samson, a cross between a Golden Retriever and a Rottweiler, lagging in the distance beneath the shade of my father's giant oak which had stood for my entire life some nineteen years and more in front of the house; and Angel, my dog since she was a pup and Samson's Hellenistic, fair-haired mother.

Cassandra's horse, Patches, thinking it time for lunch clip-clopped up the gravel road behind my car as I parked. I could see Jedi with his black coat and mane up by the weeping willow my father planted on a small southern hill next to a pond half-surrounded by a grove of trees on the opposite bank.

But all of this and more is gone now, having been sold by my father a few years back to the rock quarry, which — if it has not done so already — will dynamite the land and memories to harvest the rocks within, leaving holes the size of lakes with collected rainwater to come and fill the empty spaces with cool, crisp artificial seas.

On that day, though, Patches and Jedi roamed Pine Creek Ranch with an ease of retired colonels and Gator bounced alongside me as I walked over to Cassandra, who lazily swung on a white swing built for two and hung from chains attached to a limb on the great oak. She had just smoked a joint and the marijuana tickled my nostrils as I approached and joined her on the swing. Ironically, despite all the peanut butter and barbecue sauce she had put in my hair as my younger self slept dreaming of my first crush, Winnie Cooper on *The Wonder Years*, my sister and I grew to become more than best friends; we grew to become soulmates.

'What's wrong?' I asked. Jedi moved away from the weeping willow and the pond and made his way into greener pastures.

'Something's wrong with Twilight.'

Twilight, Samson's younger sister and my sister's second dog, had not been among the others when I drove up and I hadn't noticed. Sometimes Twilight and Gator would scout the distant lands in search of wild game, but as my sister and I swung in the shade and peered out into a bright, sunny day I felt an awful gloom descend upon me.

'What's wrong?' I asked.

'I don't know.' Cassandra turned to me with fear in her eyes and her pale lips trembled. 'I called for her all morning and found her standing in the pond. She wouldn't come. I called to her but she wouldn't come. Something's wrong with her, Cody. I can't bear to look.'

'Wait for me by the house. I'll go check.'

I didn't hesitate, didn't need to. I figured on a hot day like that one in the Lone Star State, where temperatures could easily get to over a hundred, that a smart dog like Twilight would find comfort in the cool waters of our pond.

I walked across the slope among the bluebonnets, those ancient buffalo clovers, that separated the oak tree and the pond and stood next to the weeping willow on the grassy slope leading down into the water, and there, sure enough, was Twilight standing belly deep in the brown muck. When I called her name, she did not budge nor did she twist her head, but her right eye that already faced me swiveled all by itself to meet my gaze. Her brown and black combination of fur, from her father's side, glistened from the water and sun.

I called her name. Nothing. Just that odd, lone eye staring back at me in a fixed torment she waited for me alone to discover. I turned and saw my sister now sitting on the steps of the back porch waiting for me to come and tell her about Twilight. But nothing was doing and I couldn't be sure until I pulled Twilight out of the water and placed her on dry land. After all, she might only be stuck in some mud and need a little help. I pulled off my T-shirt, kicked off my shoes, slipped out of my socks, rolled up the bottoms of my jeans, and waded into the pond. I gently poured water over Twilight and tried to ease her out. She didn't budge. I reached down below her belly and lifted, but her body transformed into an immovable object weighing something like a ton. Whatever was wrong with Twilight, she didn't want out of that mud and water. *Swamp of sadness.*

Then I froze, thinking of snakes and perhaps she had been bit and she was trying to warn me the whole time. I scanned the water. Nothing.

After a solid minute of standing with my hands on my hips and the water to my knees and looking down at that small, beautiful dog, I splashed around to her front because I had noticed she never lifted her lower jaw out of the water.

'Oh, God.'

Twilight's jaw had been shattered and dangled, held on by shreds.

I brought a hand to my mouth and bent lower and double checked. The lower half of Twilight's jaw had been mutilated, kicked off, and I believed I knew who the culprit was.

'God,' I said. 'I'm sorry.'

I rubbed Twilight's head and back with more water and coming from that right eye of hers I believed I saw tears. She hadn't meant to do anything wrong, Twilight seemed to say to me. I'm really sorry. Really sorry. Can't we go back to the way things used to be?

I trudged out of the mud and water, up the grassy slope and picked up my T-shirt, shoes and socks, and headed to the house. Only then did I realize that Angel, Samson and Gator had been watching me and Twilight the whole time.

Crashing to the steps beside my sister, who sensed it was bad, I just sat for a few minutes with my arms on my knees, my hands clasped, and I looked from oak tree to weeping willow near the pond.

At that moment I wasn't thinking of Twilight, but of how Cassandra and I had been on these steps before and how she cried and wailed and moaned and broke my heart. In my mind, Time and Space were abstractions and ever collapsing upon themselves.

A month or so before, I had arrived home just as I had done that day after class to find Cassandra crying on the back steps. She smoked a cigarette and let her head rest on my shoulder as I looked from oak tree to weeping willow thinking how awful it was for my sister to be so extremely sad.

Even at my age, I have nightmares where I can hear nothing but my sister's despair as she wails her lament into the Universe.

On those steps, a month or so before Twilight decided to wake up and play with Jedi, my sister cried and told me how she had been to the doctor's office and how the doctor had told her she would likely never conceive any children. Too much scarring, my sister had said. I kept it to myself but I told myself, yes, we all have too many scars and this was how we determine the length of our lives: by the number of our tears and the severity of our scars.

I kept my thoughts quiet and instead I said, 'Don't listen to those doctors.' I wrapped an arm around her and stroked her head. 'Doctors make good guesses, that's all. But in the end, the doctors make guesses and they can't be sure.'

'You don't know what you're talking about. I can't have kids. Ever!'

What does a man say to that? What does a baby brother say?

I raised my head to feel the sunshine on my face and heard the Universe, the Super Logos within, speak to me. She'll think I'm crazy, I said to myself. *Tell her.* I'm crazy. *Tell her.* And so, I told her what I'd heard from a universe as old as Time. I told Cassandra how God, or the Universe or Allah or Super Logos or whatever you want to call a Higher Power, knows more than human doctors and how in the Bible there were similar stories of barren women giving birth in their old age, and then I told her the Universe, or what I now call Super Logos, wanted me to tell her that, one day, she was going to have a baby boy.

Cassandra became hysterical after that. 'Magical, immaculate conception,' she said, and though she listened to me with sincerity in her heart I knew she didn't believe in what I was saying. But I had grown to trust the Universe through my monthly fasts and I believed and wanted more than anything for her to have her baby.

A few years later, Cassandra did have a baby boy and she named him Brighton, after our cousin who died, like Keats, far too young at the age of twenty-five from cystic fibrosis, a genetic disorder affecting the lungs and other internal organs. In some ways, but not all, we were able to cheat death. But here my sister and I were once again on the back-porch steps. I didn't want to tell her what had happened to Twilight.

'What's wrong with her?' Cassandra asked.

'One of the horses must've kicked her face off.' I'm not sure why I phrased it that way but the words came nonetheless.

My sister began wailing, that long mournful cry that rips into my soul and my dreams late at night and heard out across the moors in *Wuthering Heights*, and that sound haunts me to this day.

'I think it was Jedi. I've seen Twilight barking and pestering those horses. It was bound to happen.'

'How could you be so cruel?'

'What?' I said. 'I can't help what's happened. What's happened has happened. I wish to God it hadn't happened, but it did.'

'Should we take her to the vet?'

'Do you have money for that?'

'Henry can pay.'

'You know better than I do he won't do that. He'll take the shotgun….'

Cassandra knew I couldn't finish that sentence any more than I could pull a trigger. 'We can't just leave her there. Suffering,' she said.

'No. I suppose we can't.'

I got up and went inside and made a phone call to Pastor Hiddleston, a preacher of a church my Grand-Daddy, Reverend C.G., used to preach at, and in a time before the church was built, where my father and mother, pregnant with my older brother Chadwick, lived in a trailer house on the exact spot the Assembly of God Church would be built and remain to this day.

'I'll be out there as soon as I can, Cody. God bless you, brother.'

'God bless you too, Father.' I wasn't Catholic but I had a habit of calling all priests and preachers and pastors 'Father' out of respect for the clergy. But the way Pastor Hiddleston said 'God bless you,' it sounded more like a bad omen or a final gasp and sigh before death, and goosebumps crawled across the flesh on my arms as I hung up the phone.

I didn't get Henry's twelve-gauge out of respect for another man's gun. I had my own 4.10 shotgun I never used but maintained out of another respect for my father's gift. I had shot the gun only once or twice, and I recalled the last time I pulled the trigger, aiming at two bobwhite quails nestled in a mesquite tree, the blast resounding, the leaves and limbs splattering the air, and the two birds flying away untouched, unharmed. I told myself then and there I was no hunter, no killer; I could not murder what God and the Universe had created. My sister and I spotted Pastor Hiddleston in his sedan driving up the gravel road and we greeted him out in the front yard. I had left the gun on the kitchen table, and the pastor and I walked in silence over to the weeping willow at the pond where Twilight waited for us to come. Pastor Hiddleston's face often held a spiritual joy of unquestionable depth to it, and I hated myself for having called him to come and do what I could not and for having to see that supreme joy go out of his face.

'Let me see what's wrong,' he said.

Even as he pulled off his shoes and socks, I believed in miracles. Maybe he could lay hands on Twilight and all would be well. Pastor Hiddleston treaded into the water and patted Twilight's back with more sympathy and love I have ever seen a person show a dog.

'Go get the gun.'

I did as he instructed, walking briskly up the grassy slope, across the pasture, up the back steps and into the kitchen. I did not load the gun, and when I returned with the 4.10 in one hand and a few cartridges in the other, Pastor Hiddleston treaded back out of the water and met me on the grassy slope near the weeping willow. Clouds drifted in front of the sun and a breeze rattled the pecan trees on the opposite side of the pond.

'Go keep your sister company.'

I paused for a moment looking at him and then at Twilight waiting in the water before returning back to the house. But like I've done many times before, I stopped and turned to look back. On the crest of the hill I looked back and saw the pastor, slacks twisted up around his knees showing the fatty whites of his calves, descend the grassy embankment and enter the water as if headed to a sacred baptism.

I didn't stay to watch. Couldn't. I like to think I knew better by then. I turned and retreated down the hill to my father's home and went inside to join my sister, who paced throughout the house.

'I can't go out there,' she said.

The pastor must've said a long prayer because my sister and I waited but heard only the thin layer of silence anticipation creates. My sister was in the middle of a sentence, saying something trite and mundane, when we heard the blast from the gun echo out across Pine Creek Ranch. She jumped and shook. We held our breaths. We waited with eyes fixed on one another. Then the second and final blast came.

After a time, Pastor Hiddleston eclipsed the top of the hill and made his path to the back door. I don't remember what was said between us but we must've agreed to have my father bury Twilight later that day when he returned home from work at the cable plant. My sister ignored the pastor and I thanked him for doing what I was too much of a coward to do and his only reply was, 'I'll see you in church,' and he got into his sedan and drove back down the gravel road he had traveled an hour or so before.

Cassandra had called Henry who returned home after work to bury Twilight in the corner lot where many of our old dogs were buried, including Shenandoah, a great white beast I had first loved and first known as a baby. One of the last things I remember from that day was my father, shovel in hand, heading to the pond as the day dimmed into twilight.

There were times, like the episode with the peach pits, I looked back for a reason, and I suppose most people know what that reason was: not out of fear but from a curiosity wanting to know what the future days held for the both of us. To hold a moment in the mind long enough to vivify the memory into its own captured eternity.

I'm exhausting myself telling you all of this, and my head begins to hurt from remaining too long on the arm of the sofa, much the same way I imagine Holden's did when confessing to *his* psychoanalyst. But I don't mind being exhausted anymore.

Besides, the world tires me even more than sharing a few memories from my life. Where should I begin?

Begin at the beginning, you reply.

I can't begin at the beginning because I no longer remember where the memory begins or ends, and I can't be trusted. But I do know the day must've been Saturday and I had convinced my mother to take us to our church in Early for an outdoor day of festivities and fun.

My mother had been divorced — how long? I can't be sure — for some time and we were no longer attending my father's Assembly of God Church in Brownwood. Whether our new church was Baptist or Protestant I can't be certain either but I remember my first Sunday service well. The church, actually a large house built in the early part of the 1900s, held its weekly services in the front most living room. My mother dragged me to a pew and with head held down I opened the hymnal on my lap and flipped page after page to determine how different this new church was from my old church — like a taste test between the new Coke and old Coke — and to find my favorite gospel: 'Victory in Jesus.'

A makeshift choir of the young and old clamored to the back of the room, or the front of the congregation depending on how one looked at it — after the pastor had led us in prayer and summoned the singers. There she stood. An angel with blonde hair and red dress — the pastor's daughter, I came to find out later — took her position in the center of the choir as the pastor, her father, called for any and all to come and share in the joy of the Lord and participate in the choir. I wrestled with myself much the same way Jacob must've wrestled with God. I had never been in a choir and I had never actively, knowingly chased a girl before.

Last chance.

I slipped the hymnal back in its place on the back of the pew in front of me and told my mother to move over, I'm going up there.

Less than a minute later I maneuvered myself into and around the choir members until I squeezed next to —

This is where I have to say I can't recall her name, despite the impact she had on me over the years.

Any name will do, you say.

No. No it won't. Names have meanings and her name meant something but I've lost both her name and its meaning to the sharp edge that cuts a broken memory, the first traces of history wiping what little there was of me away into oblivion and mystery. So, let me call her 'the pastor's daughter' because that's who she was, though I didn't know it then as I took my place beside her in the choir. The pastor asked if I had ever sung in a choir before, and I replied no I hadn't but I had the fire of God to do just that. Then the audience, including my mother somewhere in the back, laughed and laughed. The choir, including the pastor's daughter, laughed too.

The pastor made some joke of his own but I was busy asking the pastor's daughter for her name, and when the pastor chose a song and the choir rustled the pages of their own hymnals to find the song, I leaned over and asked the pastor's daughter if we could share because I had forgotten to bring mine.

She agreed with bright twinkles in her blue eyes and blushing in her cheeks, and I held the hymnal as she turned from one song to the next.

At one point, I do recall, the pastor commented on my remarkable — or unremarkable, as it were — singing abilities and asked if I would best serve the choir in one of its back corners.

I politely declined saying I was comfortable and that I was only getting warmed up. The audience laughed even louder than before.

Very well then, he said after the audience calmed and we continued singing our praises to God, the Almighty.

Every Sunday night I joined the pastor's daughter to sing in the choir. So you can see why I urged my mother to go that Saturday when the church would be filled in almost every corner with lime-colored grasshoppers and how the pastor's wife served platter after platter of mint Oreo cookies and I kept thinking to myself: what did they do to those poor grasshoppers? I declined to partake of those grasshopper cookies.

Out in front of the church, a wiffle-ball game started up and at one point my younger cousin Ronald attempted to hit a homerun but he struck out.

Even at such a young age I had already won a minor-league state title with the Tigers under Coach Finbarr — may to God he rest in peace, because he was one of the nicest men I've ever met — but none that day could convince me to play ball. I had other things, or someone, on my mind.

Turning the corner of the church, I made my way to its back yard where a trailer house had been parked and where the pastor lived with his family. I continued on around to the back where a small orchard of peach and pear trees lined several acres onward. I stood as Adam must've stood in the Great Garden and felt pleased at how God could create beauty out of such simplicity. I could live here, I told myself.

'Cody, I'm over here.' The pastor's daughter's voice called out to me from beneath the back porch attached to the trailer house. I ducked my head under and found her sitting on dirt she had smoothed to create a comfortable floor for the both of us.

'Look, children, daddy's home.'

'What?' I crossed my legs and sat beside her in the underbelly of the back porch and the cool shade it created around us. 'Children? What children?'

'Why? Don't you want children?'

'Why, I never thought about it. I'm only eleven.'

'I'm thirteen; that makes me older, so we should start thinking and talking about having children right now.'

I nodded and thought and played with sticks I found in the dirt. I broke a stick and tossed the halves into the grass in the sun.

'This is all so fast. I just came to see what you're doing. They're playing baseball up there.'

'We're playing house. Don't you want to play with me?'

'I do. I really *really* do. But let me go and check on my cousin and let him know I'll be away for a while. I'm a man now and it's only proper.'

'Oh, all right, but give me a kiss before you leave.'

I had never kissed a girl other than my mother and my sister, and even that was becoming torture, and I wasn't at all sure how to kiss correctly. I had stood up to go and without thinking too much more about it, I leaned down and kissed her on the cheek.

'No, silly. A husband kisses his wife here.' She placed a finger on her lips.

She had me cornered but I was too much in love with her to back out, and so I leaned down and kissed her on the lips.

I remember the kiss being wet and soft and enjoyable, but I hurried away — as my older self would come to do many times with many more women — and waved as I told her I would return for her.

I checked on Ronald then ran back.

The pastor's daughter had a tea set spread out and she waved when I ducked under the back porch and reclined beside her once more.

'Are you hungry?' I asked just as soon as I had found a twig to play with.

'A little.'

'If I'm going to be the man of the house, I need to bring home the bacon. I can't let you starve.'

For some reason girls wanted to play house with me and I was never at all sure why. One time, a year or so later at the Assembly of God Church located at 1910 Indian Creek Drive, an Hispanic girl named Desiree led me by the hand into Pastor Hiddleston's spare room near the front door, and when I entered that room for the first time I was shocked at having never known how the pastor had a bed some fifty feet from the altar. The spare room contained all the comforts of a hotel room and Desiree wanted to play house.

'I'm the mother and you're the father.'

I kept thinking that I was too young to be a father but if a father I must be, a father I would be. I told her I would need to try and go make a living, bring home the bacon, that sort of thing. She lay on the bed and asked me to join her. You should take a rest, she said, you've been at work all day and now you should rest. I left her in the room to roam the church halls for a few minutes before returning out of a silly fear another boy would find my pretend wife on the pastor's bed — or God forbid, the pastor himself.

Desiree leaned on one elbow when I entered and closed the door and locked it as quietly as I could have done. At that time, she was fifteen or sixteen, my sister's age, and I was only twelve, and when

I lay next to her on that bed and she began to rub me in places no one ever did, I never once thought of sex.

I kept feeling the stress of being the husband and a father at such a young age, and though we touched and kissed what stopped me was ultimately the fear of God and eternal damnation if I did relinquish to my throbbing arousal and fuck that fifteen-year-old on the pastor's bed where he took naps inside the church.

My fear of remaining a virgin lost to the supreme fear I held for God, the Almighty, and I did not have sex then, nor for many years after that, and now as an aging man in my late thirties I can tell you true that I've never once regretted my decision.

I would leave the pastor's daughter, however, several times throughout the course of that Saturday afternoon only so I could kiss her as I left and kiss her upon my return. On one such excursion to the front of the church where the wiffle-ball game played on, I spoke to my cousin Ronald as he waited next in line to bat. The batters used a red-plastic bat, quite heavy, to hit the wiffle-ball and I pulled Ronald several times back towards me.

'You're too close,' I said. 'Come stand by me.'

Ronald shrugged me off. 'Go play with your girlfriend.' He stepped forward waiting his turn.

I stepped back, trying to pull him towards me. Ronald stepped closer to the batter, who swung and missed the ball and struck Ronald below his right eye, where a gash instantly formed and gushed blood.

'I told you not to stand so close.'

'Shut up.' Ronald held his face with a bloody hand.

The adults running came and Ronald would later return to the party boasting fresh, blue stitches beneath his eye. But as the adults, my mother I'm sure was one of them, escorted Ronald off to surgery, I rushed to the pastor's daughter to tell her all about the swing, the hit and the blood.

When she and I had calmed a bit from all the excitement, I looked out from the shadow of the shade into the orchard lit by the sun and decided to get some food. If God feeds the mockingbirds, then why not us? I kissed the pastor's daughter goodbye and walked into the orchard. The pears did not taste right, a little too sour for me, but the peaches to the touch seemed ripe.

I waved back to the Pastor's daughter and she waved in return. I grabbed two peaches and joined her in our home beneath the back porch. She ate in a pleasure knowing her pretend husband could provide for her, and I ate in a pleasure knowing I could feed my pretend wife. I just had to trust God, that's all.

With one knee bent, supporting one arm, I ate the peach next to my pretend wife and looked out at the good earth and the Great Garden before me and felt pleased with myself for the first time in my life, because I figured I was finally becoming a man — though it would take me a short lifetime to understand what 'being a man' meant. At the age of eleven life was simpler, wants to be, needs to be, and I made it so.

'Let's throw the seeds away,' I said. 'We can't have trash and ants in our home, can we?'

'How about we bury them?'

'Where?'

'Here, silly.' She pointed to the dirt between us. 'Then the two pits can grow into a single tree.'

I joined her in her story. 'And then thirty years from now, when we come back here to this very spot, we can see how our love has grown, and we can eat peaches from our peach tree.'

'You love me?' she asked.

I kept digging a hole with my stick and thought of how I had never told a girl that I loved her. 'Yes,' I said. 'I love you, and let these two seeds represent our love for one another. Let them grow and be strong and always bear fruit.'

'Amen,' she said, and then she kissed me on the lips.

We buried the pits and poured a little water over the spot of dirt. We kissed once more before I got up to leave, what seems to me and my slipping memory, for the last time. Like the dozen or so times when I'd left the pastor's daughter before, I pulled myself up out of the dirt and out of the dark shade beneath the back porch. I wasn't going to turn — I hadn't done so any of the other times — but as I told you before, I have a bad habit of looking back.

Maybe I was supposed to — I was supposed to see the pastor's daughter in the shade beneath the back porch on her knees blowing me a kiss goodbye, because shortly after that Saturday, the pastor of that church in Early moved the trailer house and his family out of Texas and to a city I never could quite learn.

Some years later — who knows correctly the timeline of one's childhood? — I do remember I had my driver's license then, and I spent thirty minutes or more driving up and down the highway looking for that old house that had once been a church. Then, quite suddenly and unexpectedly, I found the house. I pulled into the driveway and imagined a wiffle-ball game being played in the front yard. The house, vacated and left to ruin, warmed my soul.

While walking to the back, I half expected to see the pastor's trailer house still parked there, but it wasn't. The back lot remained empty. The orchard trees looked sickly and old. The fallen fruit, rotted.

For a time, I walked in search — much the same way I held my head down in the rain looking for my mother's lost ring — but this time I was looking for a young peach tree. Who is to say that our peach tree wasn't there, or is still there, much larger now after two and a half decades of uninterrupted growth?

I searched and searched and searched for the proof I was looking for, but — like my mother's ring — I never found it. I'd like to tell you that everyone you're going to hear about were all made happy and lived to a good old age. But that wouldn't be the truth, now would it?

At times I didn't even need to look back; things happened right in front of me whether I liked it or not; whether I had any control of the situation, of fate, was also not up to me: much like the time I waited for my turn at bat in a playoff game beneath heavy stadium lights with the mad crowd in the stands cheering and jeering to 'win it! win it all!' But most of my memories about baseball remain pleasant ones.

Which ones, you ask?

You ask a lot of questions, I reply as I adjust my back on the sofa, and you sure know how to ask them.

Go on, you say.

Okay, then. What I remember most about those American summers as a child were my friends — names lost to the illusion of time — dressed in uniforms and cleats, running to the concession stand to get a snow cone in exchange for a foul, stray ball. When we won the state title with the Tigers under Coach Finbarr, all that season we crunched on Tiger's Blood snow cones as our victory treat, but my favorite flavor had been pickle juice. Fresh nachos with sliced jalapenos had been among my favorite snacks as well — unlike the time my older brother Chadwick fed me spicy *chili con carne* right before an afternoon baseball game in the dead heat of summer; *Chili con carne* had long ago been a trail stew for cowboys who used dried beef and dried chili peppers. My mother never let Chadwick feed me again.

I'm an old man now; over the hill.

Forty isn't that old, you tell me.

Age can't be a number and the oldness I feel wets my bones.

I know how that feels, you say.

Before I was interrupted, I was going to tell you how I do have better dreams than the ones I've told you about. When I close my eyes, sometimes I can smell the leather from the mitts before I see the dugout strewn with empty glass bottles of Gatorade, half-eaten sunflower seeds and helmets on the cracked concrete. The chalk marking the batter's boxes and the foul line has its own smell, mixed with the freshly turned dirt I'd kick up to set my cleats in place. I can almost feel the starched uniform and the baseball in my grip as the umpire in his bulky pads and wired mask, revealing beady eyes that shouldn't be trusted nor debated, peered out over the catcher's helmet and glove and home plate. As I dug my cleats into the batter's box, I waged the distance to the pitcher's mound ahead. From that small mountain, like Zeus raining thunderbolts down on mortals, the ball came hurling down at nearly eighty, sometimes ninety, miles per hour.

The selection of the bat — wood was outlawed — had to be precise in relation to the length and weight and feel to meet its needs to the design of your personal destiny: a base hit or a homerun.

I'd take the call sign from the coach at third base and he'd instruct either to hit or to bunt, and if the latter, I'd curse myself and him for having to sacrifice myself when I knew I could hit anything the pitcher threw at me. Pull of the ear. Swipe of the forearm. Touch of the nose. Pat of the head. Palm against neck. I've forgotten now what all the signs meant but back then I knew them well and which one meant hit and I was going to hit. In all truth, I never swung for the fences. I'd swing for the gaps, either between third base and short stop or between the second and first bases. Patiently, I'd move the runners around the bases as best I could.

The pitcher would stretch while an announcer over the loudspeaker called the surnames of players: Smith, Jones, Ledbetter, Gerald, Christian, Aventine, Thomas, Marks, Barron, Holland, Chandler, Coffee, Reyes, Steptoe, Lancaster, Mills, Yonnie and Pierce. The smell of my sweat became a kind of perfume as I gripped the bat steady over my right shoulder. My father, I know, stood at the side of the left outfield fence and I wanted to hit a double or a triple to his side to make him proud.

I could hear the other baseball games being played in the complex, and teams mimicking the professionals with their own fitted caps: the Yankees, the Giants, the Marlins, the Rangers, the Braves, the Cubs, the Mariners, the White Sox, and on and on, all becoming lost to the cheers and boos of the parents and siblings and relatives in the stands. Earth, sky, grass, lights, parking lots in the distance with trails of dust, the high school football stadium looming large out over the back fence and I knew I could never smack the ball that far.

Clinking of aluminum bats, slaps of the mitts, the thud of a bat hitting a ball foul, the smaller boys chasing the lost ball down for hopes of a free snow cone, the crack of the bat signifying a clear homer, round the bases to the parents' cheers and from the opposing dugout taunts, and even your own team screaming at the top of their lungs, run! run! run! And you do run, run like you've never ran before, the wind at your hips, and stop to stand one foot firm on second base, stop to catch your breath as you look at what you've accomplished with your own two hands, as young as they may be, but soon you get ready again, check the third base coach to steal or to stay, because you know deep down what you've done doesn't matter until you make it home. Home, they cried.

The stadium lights would flicker on as the sweltering Texas sun set over the pecan trees in Riverside Park, where the high schoolers ventured to smoke joints or blunts — but you didn't know that then — settling in the breeze as evening came cooling down the ballpark at dusk and twilight, your teammate who stepped tentatively to the plate as the opposite dugout taunted: hey-batter-batter! hey-batter-batter! swing-batter-batter! swing!, or more severe chanting, choke! choke! choke!, reserved for those batters who were faint of heart.

Chokechokechokechokechokechokechokechoke, never bothered me when I stepped to bat. Instead, I absorbed the rhythm, making the voices my own, feeling the Universe open up before me, the energy being pulled into me from all around until I swung and felt-heard the crack of the bat in my hands.

I miss the paper cups we used to get drinks of iced Gatorade from a large orange jug placed over in the corner by the dugout's exit, and how we drank like raw huntsmen and smashed the paper cups in our hands and tossed them away down by the Snicker wrappers to pull ourselves back to the action over on the field and behind the chain-link barrier protecting us from wildly hit balls.

Those were the best of times and they were the worst of times. I can never get those times back, can I?

Would you want to? you ask.

Maybe. Maybe not. Maybe I'd like to coach my son; he's just a baby now though, but I'd like very much for him to know some of the experiences — both victories and defeats — that I had known as a child playing baseball. I would want him to know about the Ten Run Rule or how to steal a base by taking a grand lead, usually two steps out away from the bag — about one's body length — just enough to dive back, stretched out, get up and dust off the uniform just so you could step away from the bag to take that risk all over again. I wouldn't want him to know about the slaps on the butt or for him to know about the laps around the field as punishment or for him to know how destiny could be stolen away while he was looking back at the dugout.

Like the time in the third game of a triple-header where I had been drafted from the Giants to play for the Yankees and we played for the privilege to go to state playoffs, and how that last game dragged on, point for point — each team trying to break the tie — and midnight had come and gone and we played on into the summer night, and I waited my turn to bat while little Neal West stepped inside the batter's box while one of our guys took a safe lead off second base. We were down by one, that much I knew, and we were in extra innings and we were the last to bat with only one out. I kept thinking to myself: I've been hitting this pitcher all night and all Neal has to do is walk or hit and get on base and I can bring them home. One out left me room to stay calm and compose myself. I'd been in this kind of situation a hundred times, or more.

A few pitches had been thrown and two strikes piled up against Neal. I yelled to him not to swing for the fences, to play it safe and to get on base. I'd do the rest. One of my friends from the dugout said something to me and I turned to say something when I heard the famous, the infamous CRACK!

I turned in time to see the ball fly high over right field and then over the fence. We had won the game. Just like that the long night came to an end.

Our dugout cleared out and rushed to home plate while the guy who had been on second touched home and everyone waited for Neal to round the bases, and to officially claim our victory.

I didn't run nor rush nor cheer nor shout. Like a professional, I pulled off my helmet, returned the bat to the dugout, undid my left batter's glove and tucked it in my back pocket, retrieved my Yankees fitted cap out of my bag and by the time I joined the rest of the team Neal had just touched home.

What're you thinking about? you ask.

I leave the sofa and go over to the great windows that look down over New York City in the rain. It's been raining since I started talking to you and the rain seems to want to burst into a sad song, the kind of song a grieving lover hears when lost along the steady path of life.

I'm not a great writer, I reply, not even a good one. But you know that, don't you? Maybe I should give up and work in a factory like my father.

Now that's not true. I've read your —

But it's not that exactly. For the longest time I expected better from the world, from my America. I believed if I could write well enough, anything'd be possible, but we both know that's not true. The American Dream is dead for us Americans. Why do you think I had to leave?

Why did you leave? you ask. You never told me.

I had to leave because I found myself in a vicious cycle that would've only ended in my failure. There's a fear about white Americans I don't quite understand, and that fear rests at the top of the publishing industry.

Perhaps if you were of a different race or of a different gender, do you imagine, you would've been more accepted as a writer? What do you think?

I don't want to believe in the sad-gruesome reality of the American publishing industry, which is mostly foreign owned: egoless individuals as fabricated products created by highly-educated-London-swayed editors who want to present fuck-toys at swanky literary parties, and to influence voters by holding these celebrated few above their heads and in front of their noses like juicy, fat carrots — or perhaps I should've been born British or Canadian my literature would be celebrated here at home in America. Perhaps I'm too white. Perhaps I'm too masculine. Too American. Too Texan. Perhaps I don't even know the right kinds of people to *guanxi*-up to. Kiss ass. What do most people want? Sex or money. That's what people want. But when you start making money, the hands come out. They want a slice of the pie. They want their cut. Publishers, most of the big ones are foreign owned — not even American — and these non-American publishing companies want to shape American culture, American politics, American ideals. They ignore you until you do what they fear, what they hope you don't do. Write from the heart and make money doing it. Because they think it's their money. That it's their industry. No

Americans allowed. Perhaps, perhaps, perhaps. What difference does it make?

Perhaps, you say. Perhaps you're right. I know what you mean, but you can't say what you want to say. Isn't that what you want? What you really wanted from your writing? To say what you can't say? Like Salinger did?

I don't think what's in one's soul matters any longer. My life has been determined by when and where I was born and to whom I was born to, and nothing will ever change that. Nothing. Nepotism and guanxi are cheap, but there's a reason for everything. Even racism and discrimination against whites. You don't believe that and I don't believe that, but many Americans do believe that. Tell me I'm wrong. Tell me that true-born Americans don't feel left out in the cold-fucking rain and flat-out abandoned. Go ahead and tell me. I'll believe you. Or I'll try and believe you. But you know it's all rot and garbage.

Do you feel cheated?

I do not turn to look back to see you because I want to look at the rain falling in Central Park for a moment longer in silence.

Do you feel America has let you down? Betrayed you?

I keep my back to you because what I have to say isn't for you but for the rain, for New York, for my little hometown, for all of America.

A long time ago, when I was a young writer in Korea, I once believed my writing would save me, but I'm not so sure of that now. I know I was wrong.

Tell me about South Korea.

That was years ago, and God knows how I've changed, but a part of the writer I am now still feels the writer I used to be on Christmas Day in 2006. As I headed north by train from Daegu to Seoul then east to Namchuncheon, the lake city. At ten at night, I stepped off the train and onto the platform half-engulfed in white clouds of steam billowing out into the empty streets below. I was alone, then, heading up into Jipdarigol Natural Forest and Valley to a cabin to write for a week. It turned out to be one of the worst, yet fulfilling, experiences of my life, and it changed all my days ever after. But it seems more legend than real now, and the young writer who was an idealist has grown old and cynical and in love.

I stay by the window. There's something about the rain....

I'm reminded of the taxi I hired to drive me up the winding mountain road until the forty-five-minute trip ended outside a two-story restaurant which looked more like a cabin from my childhood vacations in Santa Fe, New Mexico.

Dropping my duffle bag on the floor of the antechamber and removing my toboggan, a Korean family paused from their dinner and chatter to stare blankly at the white foreign ghost who had materialized between shots of soju and wild laughter. A man picked himself up from the low table where the family ate and came over to speak broken English, a sort of Konglish. We determined I needed to go further up the road some twenty meters to the main office, where I'd find a man asleep and who'd wake to give me the key to my cabin and who'd show me the way up the rest of the mountain.

Later, I followed the attendant up an icy road into a vacant community of cabins. I'd find out later Koreans came there only during the summer months and how the attendant thought me to be a journalist. As we approached midnight and the end of the road I'd been travelling, a bridge lit with white Christmas lights spotted the dark landscape of snow.

After waking early that Christmas morning, still suffering from the poisonous effects of bad chicken served to me by a pizzeria for my Christmas Eve meal, I kept thinking how nice it was to have traveled all day to arrive to white Christmas lights reminding me of my childhood and to the holidays I had shared long ago with a family too distant from me now I do not know the way back to them. Such was my life at the time.

Just after midnight, the attendant unlocked the one-room cabin, flicked on the light and floor heating. He explained in Konglish as best he could how I was to return the key and where I was to go to shower, and that there was no hot water at that time of year. But they did have a bucket and I could wash up with cold water down near where I had first disturbed his Christmas rest.

He left and I unpacked what little I had. A thin mat lay on the floor and I set up the rice pillow and blankets for a bed. Then I pulled back on my boots and headed out into the darkness to smoke a cigarette and admire the bridge lighting the snowy landscapes in the valley below and on the mountains above. By then, however, the attendant had unplugged the white lights on the bridge and I smoked a cigarette beside a tumbling stream located some ten yards from the front door of my cabin shaped like a small pyramid.

The Marlboro cigarette felt good in the freezing cold air and I still had a little nausea, but overall, I felt stronger and more alive than when I'd left my apartment in Daegu earlier that morning. I came to escape the city, honor the writer within, and to spend a week isolated from people, from society, from the world. Back then I could stand out in the cold and be alone for hours, and after a few more cigarettes, I returned to my little cabin, removed my coat, and dropped beneath the blankets on the floor still wearing my flannel shirt, jeans and socks. All that night the cold bit into me and the floor heater could not match the fangs of a brutal winter as I listened to the falling, rolling stream outside which caused me to dream loosely of my life as it was, as it had been and as I hoped it would one day be.

The next morning I found the only restaurant in that vacant cabin community to be closed for the winter season despite having been told a month before it would be in service. For the next three or four days I drank chalky coffee from a tiny paper cup dispensed from a vending machine posted outside the door of a grocery store open between the hours of ten and two each day. I ended up dining on sun chips and canned spam for lunch and one bowl of hot ramen soup for dinner, but on that first morning I slipped coins into the vending machine and out spurted my instant hot coffee, making me feel like I was possible again.

Being a Texan I had quickly recovered from the food poisoning from the day before, and though I felt a little weak, I was happy to be among the snow and quiet of a place so far removed that the cabins seemed to sit at the edge of a world ready to be forgotten. North Korea lay just over the mountains from me, and just as the morning sun broke over the mountains in the east valley, I scrambled up the snowy trails and the trees and rocks hummed and echoed to one another in a polyphonic-choral music that warmed me beneath the light of a new sun. I can't tell you what I was thinking when I went to a place I found at the top of one of the mountains in the east. I can only tell you that I wanted to be alone, to hear my soul communicate with the soul of the world, of the Universe, and to feel the good and strong earth as it had been hundreds of thousands of centuries ago.

It wouldn't be a lie to say that I found an iron staircase with a flat lookout point where I would sit on top of a mountain and think to myself, to the Universe, about how I didn't really fit in with this world. I'm too moral and the world, most of its people, come off as too immoral, too corrupt, too broken, and they didn't seem to give a damn. I didn't fit in to that broken world back then and I don't fit in to this broken world now. I may have changed but the world hasn't. It's just as broken and morally bankrupt as it's ever been. Years later I would write clearly of this 'broken morality' in the final chapter of my novel *A Time to Love in Tehran*, but that would be years away from the writer on top of that Korean mountain near the border of North Korea. But as I do now, at the top of Jipdarigol Valley I knew myself to be isolated, at odds with humanity for some strange reason I couldn't quite put my finger on — why was I made the way I had been made? The sun rose into the morning sky with me sitting for hours at the top of that mountain all alone each day for a week.

One afternoon I came down the mountain and from the trail above the bridge I spied a father pulling a sled with his daughter riding, and how she wore one of those winter caps that resembled a Husky-dog's head. For some reason, I'm not sure why, I believed I couldn't have, didn't deserve, such a life as beautiful as the one the father and daughter shared, and I wasn't at all sure why. It was just one of those feelings, I'd have to say.

After five or six days of going up and down the mountain, I returned the key to the cabin to the attendant at dawn, hiked to the nearest bus stop, became disoriented as the bus drove into town and heard the Universe or Super Logos tell me to get off at the next stop. I did so and luckily, by pure chance, found the train station around the nearest corner to my right, took the slow train west to Seoul, bought a first-class ticket via KTX back to Daegu, and ninety minutes later I'd returned to civilization all grungy and wearing a scraggly beard. I entered the little coffee shop I frequented on the corner of my neighborhood, dropped my bag by the cash register and said, 'Martini, please.'

Ever since my earliest and fondest memories, I've always admired the story of Scrooge in *A Christmas Carol*, and Tiny Tim had been the first fictional character I could ever relate to — more so for the crutches he and I wore than for any other reason. We were one and the same.

From Scrooge to Tiny Tim, I compared the vastly different character types and, despite being crippled like Tiny Tim, I knew money would never hold power over me. But when Tiny Tim died and his crutches leaned abandoned in one corner of the Cratchit home, I feared, even at the age of two or three, the same might happen to me.

My sister had been the one to teach me the word 'crippled' and for as long as I walked and ran with my favorite pair of wooden crutches, I thought of myself as crippled, but you might be surprised to learn my definition of being crippled wasn't an entirely negative one. After watching Tiny Tim, I learned a cripple was someone who had a good heart, a good soul, and it was only one's body that was broken, and to tell you the truth: I didn't mind being crippled one bit.

Do you still have the scars? you ask. Can I see them?

I don't need to answer your questions. The pain has been a reminder since the day I was born when I was rushed into surgery before the doctors even weighed an ounce of me. My mother still has the metal pin that held my heel and ankle straight for many years beneath a cast my mother had to change at home every six weeks or so.

Please have a seat, you say.

The rain is falling heavier now with bursts of songs I've never heard before and I can no longer see Central Park as cloud cover blocks out the sun. I hesitate for a moment longer, trying to find the

Empire State Building, then return to the sofa where I'd be more comfortable.

Go on.

The time I'm telling you about had to have been in the early eighties because my family lived on Vine Street across from Mrs. Beaman. My mother had taught me how to go check on the old woman by holding my hand, looking both ways before crossing the street, knock three times, then and only then could I turn the knob and open the door to go inside.

I soon learned why I was checking on the old woman who was of no relation — back then neighbors were just that friendly — and I was afraid I'd open the door and find poor Mrs. Beaman dead.

But, thankfully, that never happened. Most times she greeted me after my second knock with a pat on my head, a pinch on my cheek and would say I was such a good boy and ask if I wanted any candy. I'd say that'd be nice and she only had one kind of candy, these old-fashioned butterscotch candies, and even to this day I can't eat butterscotch without thinking about Mrs. Beaman.

Once, after there was no answer to my little knocks, I twisted the doorknob, the iron kind they used to make, and entered her house all alone. In all my years her house had been the only one that held a floating mist of dust and sunlight and this always felt to me that I was entering a memory or someone else's dream. I found the bowl of butterscotch candies full and decided against taking any. Sure, she'd want me to have a few but without her there it felt a bit like stealing; I wanted no part of that. She trusted me, even as young as I was, and I respected her for it.

I did stay for a while checking the back kitchen near the laundry room overlooking an overgrown back yard, and her bedroom with a quilt tucked in to all four corners of the bed remained undisturbed since she woke that morning.

Many times, after checking the whole house for her dead body and coming up empty, I'd usually rush out of there as fast as I could go with my little leg and crutches. But on this occasion, I stayed for a while longer and returned to the living room to look at every single photograph she had framed and hung on the walls and placed on her tables. Most of the photos, if not all, were in black-and-white and very old and spoke to me of past generations.

Mrs. Beaman lived alone and I saw who must've been her husband, once upon a time, and her children as babes, then teens, and later as mothers and fathers. Her whole life had been lived before I had ever been born and that was how I came to discover history. Her life was ending as mine was starting.

One day after not finding Mrs. Beaman home, I stood on her porch facing my family's yellow house with bushes around the edges and white window trimming and a picket fence off to the side, and I tried to absorb every last detail of my first home, and to this day I can still see that house from Mrs. Beaman's porch in my head, there on the corner of Vine Street. I had loved that house as a child because — if I were to call that time anything before the divorce which came later — that yellow house represented the golden age of my family.

In that house one year, my mother baked us all birthday cakes: Chadwick an R2D2, my sister Cassandra a Strawberry Shortcake, and for me a He-Man. After that house, I don't remember my mother ever making us special birthday cakes like that again.

The living room of the house would've been on your left as you entered the front door and I bunked with my brother in a room to the right of the living room, and from there you could take a left to travel down a short hall and in the middle, to the right, was the bathroom. My sister had her own room while my parents had a room at the end of the hall, at the far back corner of the house. You could take a left out of the hall and find the kitchen which led to the right to the back door or to the left back into the dining room and living room.

I had been going to pre-preschool since I was three years old because my mother started working at a doctor's office and later, I attended kindergarten at South Elementary some five or six blocks from my home on Vine.

One night I snuggled in the bottom bunk, Chadwick occupied the top, and I heard my father get up to pee in the bathroom next to my sister's room. I pulled the covers around my face but could still see the bathroom light stretch down the hall and into my bedroom down by my feet.

A few minutes later a flush came and the light switched off. I nestled into a warm spot in my bed and closed my eyes ready for sleep when I heard what sounded like my father stepping on one of my toy cars or trains and a banging against the wall, finished by a loud thud. A picture crashed to the floor.

'Oh, God.' There's no mistaking my father's voice. 'Oh, God, Gwendolen. Get out here!'

'What's wrong, Henry?'

The light to my parents' bedroom switched on and lit the edges of my bedroom and bunk bed. I pulled the covers completely over my head and listened.

'My knee. Oh, God, Gwendolen. It's my knee.'

I heard my mother give a nervous laugh as she sometimes did.

'It's not funny.'

'You should see yourself.'

'Something's wrong with my knee.'

'What'dya do that for?'

'I stepped on one of Cody's toys.'

'That's not his fault. You stepped on it.'

'Help me up for Christ's sake. I need to go to the hospital.'

'Who'll watch the kids?'

'Call my mother.'

'Come to the kitchen Henry and sit down.'

'I can't sit down.'

'Quit complaining.'

'When I get home, I'll teach Cody not to leave his toys lying around.'

'Now hush up. You'll do no such thing. He's just a baby.'

'No, he's not.'

Out of fear of getting whipped by my father's belt and buckle, I fell asleep hoping the moment was nothing more than a bad dream.

I remember once my Grand-Mommy, my father's mother who played the organ in church and was wife to the Reverend, came to nurse me when my neck became creaked and I couldn't even move my head. My neck — which I came to find out later had a crick and not a creak — twisted to the right and had become stuck, locked in place, and Grand-Mommy spent the day icing my neck down, heating it up, massaging it with oils, feeding me hot tomato soup with grilled cheese sandwiches, which I could hardly eat due to my neck being stuck to one side the way it was. She would read to me that day, just as she did time and time again at bedtime, the story of Louis Pasteur and how the doctor never-never-never gave up and how he had cured rabies despite people mocking his failed attempts and laughing at him for years.

One Christmas in Texas it snowed and I hobbled out with my crutches onto the front porch to see my Uncle Gerard and Aunt Catherine unloading a Shetland pony into our front yard. My father had bought Smokey from Gerard, one of my mother's many brothers. Chadwick and Cassandra and Brighton, I think he was there too, got to ride around on Smokey as I limped my cast over the beautiful snow and watched. I had never seen snow before that time — which was probably closer to Thanksgiving now that I think about it since my Uncle Gerard and Aunt Catherine never spent the Christmas holidays with us in Brownwood. And to think of it: I never really saw it snow in Texas like it did that year my Uncle Gerard brought Smokey into our front yard, which soon filled with a crowd of strange children from the neighborhood.

I never got to ride Smokey on the account of the cast on my foot, but I was just so happy to see my big brother Chadwick and my big sister Cassandra and my cousin Brighton, if he was there at all, just so happy at being happy.

Weeks later my family sat in the back of the kitchen around a table with a warm Christmas dinner before us and my father gave a lovely speech, and then Chadwick said something nice as well. My father prayed to bless the meal and as my mother picked up my brother's plate to pile on some turkey and stuffing, I did what I had seen in the movies and tapped my glass with a fork, which didn't quite make the sound I had hoped, but I got everyone's attention none the same and stood up. Cassandra said something rude and I lowered my head and waited for her to finish. Chadwick laughed at what Cassandra said and mother told them to be quiet and to let me speak.

'What is it, Cody?' My father said, 'Get on with it, boy.'

I waited for the silence to draw in the effect I needed. I wanted everyone to clearly hear what I was about to say. My crutches rested in a corner behind my father and the sight of those precious crutches gave me the courage to say what I had to say to the only family I had ever known and loved. I raised my glass for the toast and said,

'Mother, father, I love you.'

'It's mom, dork,' Chadwick said.

I lowered my head and waited for Cassandra to stop laughing.

'Go on, son,' my mother said. 'We're listening.'

'Brother, sister, I love you. I hope we stay like this forever. I love all of you so much. I wish all of you a Merry Christmas and a Happy New Year.'

Chadwick and Cassandra snickered but composed themselves beneath my father's stern look. 'Are you done, boy?' he said.

I didn't want to finish but I saw my crutches in the corner and I knew that if a boy who was born with a clubfoot could learn to walk, never giving up like Louis Pasteur, I could do anything. I held my glass even higher and looked to my father, to my mother, to my brother, and to my sister and said as happily and as honestly as I could,

'God bless us, every one.'

I've wasted the best years of my life in the senseless struggle every artist faces at the beginning of his life, and I can't make heads or tails of the damn mess. Either way, those years are gone and I'll never get them back.

Back then the media broadcasted that the end of 1999 would bring with it the end of the world. Computer experts predicted and warned the ones and zeroes needed to grease the software which kept society running would automatically reset to zeroes across the board. Even though we know the numbers kept on spinning, erasing the data might've been better than watching the economic crash unfold eight years later.

But at twenty years old I waited, like all of America and the rest of the world, for the great reset button to be pushed when the clocks struck midnight, ushering in a new millennium and a new age more glorious than the one before — another big, fat lie the world tells you when you're young — and all the while the radio disk jockeys and car stereos played the 1982-hit by Prince — or the artist formerly known as Prince — 'Party Like It's 1999.' Most, including my elder sister, would be doing just that.

In January of 1999, I entered Howard Payne University, Brownwood's local Baptist institution where my Aunts Patricia and Judy — from my father's side — attended in the 1970s, and I began to major in English. At the time I held only the passion, or obsession, for reading and writing, and so studying literature appeared the obvious choice. I would graduate in four years — the real typical student — in December 2002, more focused than ever to become a writer.

On July 17, I returned from a morning swim class at the university to my mother's home on Durham Avenue and to my sister's shrill cry,

'Oh my God, Cody. They killed him. They actually killed him.'

I immediately thought of the president until I began watching the news report on television citing how John F. Kennedy Jr. crashed his Piper Saratoga into the Atlantic the night before. John Jr. had been a likely contender for the next presidential election, and there had been a buzz around him to follow in his father's footsteps, but that never happened.

My sister Cassandra turned from me to the television she had obviously been watching all morning long.

'God, Cody. How could they do that?'

'Don't know.'

Some reporters explained how a late fog had drifted in and disoriented the young pilot. Others said a malfunction of some sort. Either way, he never made it to Martha's Vineyard.

Cassandra got up from the couch and walked out the front door, which we usually kept open while we were home. Big Mama, our black-and-white Boxer bulldog, followed Cassandra out onto the front porch. When I came out behind them, Big Mama stood, as she often did, confidently at the edge of the porch near the steps leading down to the front yard shaded heavily by pecan trees. Big Mama sniffed the air, gave a few guttural barks. Finding her domain safe, she came over to lay at my sister's feet. Cassandra sparked a joint on the porch swing.

'That's fucked up,' she said.

'It is,' I said. I stood at the edge of the porch listening to the wind and the rushing of the leaves.

My sister exhaled clouds of marijuana smoke. 'They just killed him like that and nobody's going to do shit about it.'

'I can't believe it,' I said. 'Why would anyone want to do that?' I felt the summer ease around me and drift down the lazy neighborhood street.

'People are fucked up, Cody. Don't be so naïve.'

'I'm not being naïve. None of it makes any sense to me, that's all.'

I joined her on the porch swing. Through the open door I could see the television still reporting on John Jr. and the search vessels not giving up on their manhunt or for the crashed plane. Cassandra passed me the joint and said,

'It's not supposed to make sense, little brother.'

I nodded and for a time we smoked the joint in silence secretly hoping that day, or many more like it that might follow, would remain suspended in Time and Space. To never end.

Later that summer I began working as a busboy cleaning tables and stocking the salad bar at the Golden Corral Steakhouse and Buffet. At the time I hadn't wanted much responsibility because at university I loaded myself with nineteen hours of coursework. I just needed to pay $250 for my car each month and to have some extra gas and pocket money.

But soon my work ethic proved to be more than what the manager expected and I was promoted to team leader, organizing and writing up the shifts for my friends and coworkers. I was honest and diligent and that seemed to work against me as well. The harder I worked, the higher the manager promoted me. In less than six months I had been a dishwasher, a cook, a waiter and a cashier. After my experience at the restaurant, it dawned on me that the area manager had groomed me in to becoming the manager of the night shift. To be clear, I didn't mind the promotions nor the added responsibilities. With each new job title, a pay raise came. My friends remained happy at being waiters and waitresses and I stayed happy at improving myself to be better than what I was the day before. And for this reason, more than most other reasons, was how I found myself as the closing shift manager on New Year's Eve, 1999.

At nine o'clock I locked the two front doors to prevent any new customers from arriving and at odd intervals, while I drank my free cups of coffee, I strolled over to let diners out who had finished and wanted to leave. The waiters and waitresses wiped their tables clean and added salt or sugar where needed. The cook closed down the kitchen as the dishwasher, a sixteen-year-old runt who often asked for rides home — some twenty miles or more outside the city — scrubbed like a madman to try and finish by eleven. I had told him I was leaving at eleven and he'd better be finished or there'd be hell to pay.

By ten o'clock most of the staff had clocked out and left and I had finished counting the money and locking it in the floor safe of my office. At five after ten, I poured myself a fresh cup of coffee, went around the deserted restaurant in the dark, straightening up here, straightening up there. At the front of the restaurant the lights had been switched off and I stood drinking my coffee in the dark watching the cars with their yellow headlights pass by in the night — reminding me of other headlights from the time my sister became sick and had to be taken to the hospital — and I tried to imagine where each person was headed, and what they'd be doing when the end of the year arrived in less than two hours.

I thought of my own daughter, Alicen Beth, who had just turned a year old a few weeks before, and what her night would hold in comparison to all the other nights before her. Then I briefly thought of her mother Karolina, but quickly shook the thoughts away.

I checked on the dishwasher to find he was done with stocking the dishes around the restaurant and was washing down his workstation. He clocked out. Then he asked me for a ride home but I said I couldn't. He said he'd have to wait or worse, he'd have to walk home. I answered by telling him to be more responsible and arrange for his own rides home and a little exercise never hurt anyone. It scared me to hear how much I sounded like my own father, but I got in my car and left. The dishwasher would quit a month or so after that night. He said it was because of school, but I knew better.

With the windows down, I drove to Pine Creek Ranch where Twilight had been shot by the pastor out in the pond earlier that year. I tried to avoid the memory as best I could.

Texas winters, snowless, were far more refreshing than bone freezing back then, but now I hear it's a bit different. The night was cool, not too cold, as I pulled up and parked to find my father's home dark and empty. He and my mother had likely gone off to visit my Uncle Gerard and his family in Andrews, out in West Texas that smells of crude oil and sand and money.

I walked for a time around the house checking each room until I finally decided to turn out all the lights and head back outside. If the end of the world came, I wanted to meet it head on in Mother Nature and beneath the stars.

With the dogs — Angel, Samson and Gator — at my heels, I walked in the dark out to the small southern hill where the weeping willow overlooked our pond. The dogs watched me sit facing away from the pond before chasing after wild armadillos and noises hidden in the dark crevices of the countryside and alongside the rock quarry where I used to swim naked as a kid.

I didn't have a watch then and I figured if the end of the world came crashing down, none of it would concern me as I sat beneath a canopy of stars out on Pine Creek Ranch.

I guess I figured the telephone would start going off like crazy and that, for me, would signal the beginning of the end. But for the last hour of 1999, the December night was silent, the stars were beautiful and endless, and I sat there thinking how little my life mattered — compared to the end of the world that is — and how if it all did end, what would happen? What would it be like? Would the end be quick, like an atomic blast? Or would it be slow, as in starvation?

I wondered most about my life and if I'd ever make it out of that crummy little town called Deadwood, a black hole in the heart of Texas that sucked people in and never let them leave. I wondered if I'd ever see the world and live to achieve my dreams at becoming a novelist. I wondered if my parents would live to see it all too. I wondered if I'd grow to disappoint my sister or if she'd grow to disappoint me. I wondered, most of all, if I'd ever find true love, and how at that very moment, somewhere in the world the woman of my dreams, very likely a child herself in China, looked at the universe and galaxy above her and thought of me ten thousand plus miles away.

I thought of all these things and more and as I did the clocks struck twelve, the end of the world did not come, and out over the rock quarry I told you about, the largest most beautiful display of fireworks boomed and blossomed and magnified the spectrum of colors, lighting the night sky in front of me as if the show was for me alone and I was the last man living.

Who is to say when or where things began to go wrong with my family? My brother Chadwick, a senior in high school, readied himself for college the following year, and I believe then on some level with my parents they believed their work on their firstborn golden child was done and once Chadwick left for Kansas that would be the beginning of the end to our tight little compact unit called a family. My sister, the next year, would be attending high school, and prepared herself to leave childhood behind and follow Madonna into womanhood. Years apart, we three would all end up attending Brownwood High. And to think that the Brownwood Independent School District was incorporated on June 3, 1883, over a century ago. Notable alumni from Brownwood High had seen the likes of Bob Denver of *Gilligan*'s *Island*, Robert E. Howard who was the creator of Conan the Barbarian, Larry D. Thomas who was the 2008 Texas Poet Laureate, and Larry Elkins of the AFL's Houston Oilers. In the end, we are all so very small and insignificant, aren't we? What do you think?

In the year of the divorce, my family and I lived in another yellow house located on Vincent Street, about twelve blocks from

East Elementary where I attended the fourth and fifth grades. Most mornings I biked to school alone down a straight set of neighborhood streets filled with lush flowerbeds sprouting from green yards beneath trees that had been there for a hundred years or more, and in the hour between seven and eight those most mornings, I came to love the honeysuckles and morning glories which instructed me in an education unable to be found inside the classroom.

My father had bought me a speedometer for my bike on my birthday in October and all that year I raced against myself to and from school at thirty-five miles per hour, but at some point I asked my father to remove the speedometer because I felt things were going too fast and I wanted to slow down a bit, cherish the here and now and to enjoy the ride as much as one child could.

Then came the separation and the divorce. At some time during my fifth-grade year we moved into a white house three blocks down, located on Durham Avenue, where my mother would live alone for the next decade or more.

My father and mother called their children into the living room — where many years later I'd watch the reports of JFK Jr.'s death on the television — to have a formal family discussion. Right away I knew something was at odds against the normal routine of no news was good news. My family never handled communication well and immediately alarm bells began going off inside my head as I entered to a living room where my father and mother sat side-by-side on the sofa while my brother and sister sat side-by-side on the love seat — which now seems ironic since how much these two siblings have grown to loathe one another. Still a child, I found my place on the floor next to Big Mama, who occupied herself by chewing on her special pillow my mother had made for her. Big Mama was one of the family and she needed to hear what would be said.

'What's going on?' One of three children said, or we all said.

'We should go around the room,' I said, 'and share about our day. Wouldn't that be fun?' I tugged at Big Mama's pillow to tease her. She angrily snatched her prized pillow back and settled into a rhythm of constant chewing.

'Good idea, Cody,' my mother said. 'But that's not why we're here.'

'Don't be stupid, punk,' Chadwick said.

Of all the things I had been most disappointed about my family on that night it had little to do with the news that each one had somehow expected would one day come, but more to do with the fact that no one wanted to share a part of themselves to me and to one another, and I suppose that was how I learned at an early age how to keep my mouth shut and not share myself with another. My sister, however, would always be the one to break the illusions of life to me and she did not disappoint that day.

'They're getting a divorce, Cody. How could we be so blind?'

'I don't know,' I said. Now that I think about it I had been the focal point for most of my family discussions; through me my family spoke to one another and that seemed to make communication easier for them.

'That's right, Cody,' my mother said. She held her hands together in her lap and looked down at me with pity filling her eyes. 'Your father and I are getting a divorce and we want you children to know —'

'How could you do this to me?' Chadwick said. He stood up and walked to the other side of the living room. 'I'm going to be a laughing stock at college.'

'Sit down, Chadwick,' my father said.

'Yeah, Chadwick,' I added, 'sit your butt down.'

My brother looked to me and then to our father. 'I'm not a child to be told what to do anymore. You're leaving us anyway.'

'The golden boy,' Cassandra said between fits of hysterical laughter, 'is losing it. He's freaking out.'

'Shut up, Cassandra.'

'Make me.'

'Yeah, make her, Chadwick.'

'Children,' my mother said in the calmest voice I've ever heard her use to address her three warring children. 'Your father's not leaving anyone. He'll still see all of you.'

'Yeah, right,' Cassandra said. 'That's what they all say.'

At that time, I had no idea who 'they' were or who my sister had meant and I didn't even know families got divorced, but I did know what she meant.

'Your father and I mutually agreed that the best thing to do for the family was to live apart, and who knows: we might get back together again.'

Chadwick paced the room and Cassandra sulked and leaned back on the love seat alone. I picked myself up and sat down beside my sister. I had had enough playing the child and to be completely honest with you I was never able to play the child again. I had observed enough and I was tired of how my family behaved and spoke in half-truths.

'Is this true, dad,' I said. 'Tell us the truth. We have a right to know. Did you both *mutually* agree?'

My father hesitated and looked to all three of his children with what seemed to me like a frustration he was tired of swallowing his whole life. 'It is.'

'Get out of my seat,' Chadwick said. 'I want to sit down.'

'No.'

'I said, get up, punk.'

'Or what,' Cassandra said, coming to my rescue, my defense for the first time in my young life. 'Or you'll do what to my little brother, you dork?'

Defeated, Chadwick gave a half-hearted snarl to my sister before spinning around to return to the other side of the room. I felt sorry for the golden child as his perfect little world started crashing down around him, but I kept silent. We were all going through this together.

'Tell me the truth,' I said once more to my father. I leaned forward on the love seat. We waited for his answer.

'We've already told you, Cody,' my mother said.

'I'm not asking you, mother.'

My father, the strongest man I had known growing up, broke and a release of emotions flooded his face. 'No, Cody,' he said, 'we didn't mutually agree. This is your mother's idea.'

'What?!' Chadwick said. He raised his hands above his head in ignorant shock. "Mom, how could you do this to me?'

'Henry?!' my mother said, turning to him an eye full.
'It's the truth, Gwendolen. They have a right to know.'
'I know, but they're only children.'
'I'm not a child,' Chadwick said. 'I'm not. I'm not.'
'Thank you, dad,' I said. 'Thank you for being honest with me.'
'I knew it,' Cassandra said, 'it's because of Dr. Bovary.'

The living room instantly exploded into a multilayer argument among the five of us. My mother told my sister to shut her face because she didn't know what the hell she was talking about; I defended my sister and she thanked me; my brother defended our mother and attacked me; Cassandra defended me and scolded Henry for not being man enough to keep his family together; my mother defended our father and attacked, once again, my sister, who I in turn defended; then the cycle repeated itself many times over. At some point all three children begged for their parents to stay together, to not get a divorce, and all three asked if the divorce was because of them, the children, and what each could do to stop the breaking of our family.

Nothing could be done. The divorce would happen.

In the heat of the argument I left the living room and my family to finish ripping one another to shreds and ignored my father's request to return and sit down. Something had changed in my father; before that night he had been a giant in my eyes, but the world broke him to pieces and I didn't know how to accept that from him. And something had changed in me, and I left my family to their own twisted devices. I walked down the hall, through the kitchen and out the back door. I kept walking out the back yard, down the street and around the neighborhood for an hour or more until I was good and calm and at peace with the world and my family, but when I returned home, the house was quiet and empty, and from that day on all the houses I would later enter would be an echo in time and space, an eerie reminder of the night my family divorced.

At school, still in the fifth grade, I had become quiet and empty as well. My teacher, a fair-haired beauty I had a crush on before the divorce, noticed my inattention to her charm, to her lessons and she noticed my lack of enthusiasm for all things related to school, to life, to the world around me. She suggested I read a book: *Hatchet*, a 1987 Newbery winner by Gary Paulsen. I came back to class one day and told her how much I enjoyed the book which had a young boy like me also going through a divorce — is that so? I had no idea — yes, and how the boy had survived a plane crash to live alone in the Canadian wilderness; it wasn't quite like me or what I was going through at home, but I told her how I understood the deeper meanings of the young adult novel.

I didn't quite improve my outlook on life after reading that book though. If anything, I became tougher by picking on my fellow classmates, usually the strongest ones who attacked the weaker ones, and I began winning fight after fight. Students chanted 'Rocky!' as I jabbed and ducked and bobbed and weaved and swung and fought my way to victory after victory. The girls shyly looked on as they stood outside the ring of boys who gathered around me and my opponent, and I feared no one and no retribution. I became a Paul Bunyan with fists, and I defended the defenseless boys and girls with an unchecked violence that eventually scared my teacher and landed me into the chair opposite the principal.

'Do you have anything to say for yourself, Cody?'

'I'm guilty.'

'Guilty?' The principal, an ugly woman who had not aged well into her fifties, a Mrs. Ragsdill or something. 'Guilty of what?'

'All of it,' I said. 'Lock me up and throw away the key.'

'Not sure about that, but we'll have to find a proper punishment for you.'

Back then isolation in East Elementary must've been a new concept because the principal had nowhere to put me. She could not send me back to class; she didn't believe in spanking children, and that kind of physical abuse had already started to become taboo; and there was no additional room to separate me from the other schoolchildren. Eventually, the principal cleared a spot in the supply closet, squeezed in a desk and left me to my own designs.

Once, though, the secretary forgot to bring my lunch — it was on a Friday because I remember it was hamburger day — and she begged me to let her go buy McDonald's. I enjoyed the cafeteria burgers much more and politely declined. I wasn't hungry, I said. I lay my head on my desk in the supply closet and fell asleep. On Monday morning my mother walked me into the principal's office and gave them hell. The secretary and the principal apologized profusely and both neither forgot my lunch after that.

But by then I enjoyed isolation from my classmates, from all others. The teacher I told you about would come in around 8:30, first thing in the morning, with a stack of papers for that entire day's lessons, from math to history to reading to writing, it was all there on my desk and I soon learned I could do a full day's work in about two hours. As soon as she brought it in, explained a few particulars, I'd get started and be done by ten. After that, I'd take a short rest for thirty minutes and have the time before my lunch was brought to me to read my books I brought from home. One such book, *My Teacher's an Alien* by Bruce Coville, I must've read a dozen times before I graduated to the mysteries of Edgar Allan Poe and Sir Arthur Conan Doyle's genius detective. After lunch, with my schoolwork done, I'd nap for an hour and still have plenty of time to read and write before the end of the day at 3:30, and for several weeks several times that year it was in this way I spent the better part of my schooldays, and it was how I came to learn that much of school was a waste of my time. In isolation, I could get all my work done in a third of the time and have the rest of the day to myself.

When the principal released me from the supply closet and asked me if I'd fight again, I told her the truth: how should I know what would happen in the future, and I told her how I thought such a question was silly and illogical and in need of rethinking. With contempt, she sent me back into the folds of a society and classroom that hadn't missed me one bit and maintained the eight-hour workday illusion.

The penultimate moment of that year came in gym class. Coach Seamus, an angry drunkard depressed into teaching wild hooligans in his forties, hated me, and so our war of attrition grew to epic heights. He forced us into obedience by sitting in rows and seats marked with an X made from black electrical tape, and there the students would wait ten to fifteen minutes for Coach Seamus to come in to the gymnasium to start the lesson. I grew tired of waiting, and to this day I'm just as impatient. But the blind obedience from my fellow classmates bothered me most and I attempted to free my peers from the illusion of Coach Seamus's control. In the end, I'd fail. I failed them all.

As we waited, I'd get up from my X and stand at the head of the class and tell my peers how eight hours of work could be cut down to two. They would look at me like lost sheep with a haze in their eyes that suggested my words sounded much more like a fantasy than reality, as though I were telling them of how I had found Atlantis or El Dorado. Then I'd play Duck, Duck, Goose with each seated child by walking around and tapping them on their head, and when I shouted Goose! and touched one boy or girl on the head and started to run, none would follow. They were far more passive and obedient than I had realized.

One day Coach Seamus opened the door and I sprinted to my X without him the wiser. He said something. I returned with my own words in jest.

'I'm tired of you, Cody.'

'Good,' I said. 'I'm tired of you.'

My classmates laughed. Coach Seamus grew red and blew the whistle he wore around his neck. He always carried a mug of water and he thrust it in my direction, 'You want some of me?'

'I'm not gay, Coach.'

Once again, my classmates erupted in laughter, much to Coach's chagrin.

'I've had enough of you.'

Coach Seamus strutted in his tight little shorts over to the front doors which led to a large hallway and to the classrooms. Next to the door a black button, a switch to activate an old intercom system linked to the principal's office, was located. He hovered a finger over the button.

'Say one more word and I'll push it.'

'One more word.'

'I mean it, Cody.'

'I don't think you mean anything.'

The class didn't laugh; they held their breaths, waiting.

'I *will* push *the* button. I *will* do *it*.'

By that time, I had heard those words a hundredfold and had never once seen Coach Seamus push that button, and for the life of me I didn't believe the button worked at all. Out of curiosity and less of anger, I did what I did.

'I'm tired of this.'

'Tired of what?' Coach Seamus said. 'You sit down, young man.'

By that time, I was already walking in his direction. 'If you're not going to push that button, then I will.' I walked up and pushed the button just below Coach's finger. The class hushed and waited and gripped their legs as they remained seated. I walked back to my spot marked with an X and waited, thinking the button had always been broken.

'Yes, Coach Seamus?' the Principal said over the loudspeakers. 'What do you want? I'm busy.'

The class awaited his reply, the next move in the mental chess match.

'Uh, nothing, Mrs. Ragsdill,' Coach Seamus said. 'I hit the button by accident, by mistake. Sorry.'

'Don't let it happen again. I'm very busy up here.'

'Yes, ma'am.'

The entire class, myself included, cheered and shouted and laughed and slapped one another on the back and knew that today, of all days, a lone student had taken Coach Seamus head on, called his bluff, and had won. That was how I came to realize I was meant to do greater things than to blindly follow orders.

I'm reading *Daniel Martin* now —

I haven't read it, you say. Who's the author?

John Fowles. In his novel, he writes, '*Genius forgives all* is a dubious proposition at the best of times.'

I like that, you say. What do you think it means?

I don't and can't agree.

Why not?

Genius can never forgive all. Regardless of 'dubious propositions' and 'the best of times' there's no forgiveness for what an artist puts in his art, especially if it's the truth. You're damned if you do and damned if you don't. Forgiveness is for religion, not art.

Which one are you?

I'll let you be the judge of that, but what I'm trying to tell you is that I published a short story several years ago called 'My Side of Damascus' and how much the fiction masks the truth behind that story. I tried to tell people back then what happened to my sister Cassandra but I could never quite get it down right or I could never get the right kind of people to listen.

I'm listening….

I don't expect to be forgiven for what I'm about to tell you, but when I saw her lying there on the back driveway beside the car with its open door and I knelt down to see what was wrong and to see if she was okay and she couldn't give me a clear answer, couldn't even answer me, I felt my stomach drop out from under me because I thought I was going to have to watch my big sister die, and I just wasn't old enough or ready enough for that to happen.

Maybe I was being selfish but I loved my sister and I wasn't ready to let her go. Sure she teased the shit out of me but that's what big sisters were for, and then and there, kneeling beside her with one hand on her shoulder as she moaned and writhed on the driveway and held her stomach, I told her how I'd forgiven her for all the terrible and mean things she ever did to me and I meant every word.

'Milk,' she said.

'Okay,' I said. 'I'll get you some milk.'

'Bleach,' she said.

'Bleach?'

I need to stop there and go back to earlier that night if I'm going to tell this story and if I'm going to tell it right.

The divorce happened, or at least the visible effects of the divorce happened. All I can remember from that time was that in one instant I went from a happy, boisterous home and in the next instant to a broken shell of one. My father moved out, to where I knew not. Chadwick seemed to have vanished as well. My mother worked longer hours at Dr. Bovary's office and over the next few years I rarely saw her home before eight, so I can't blame anyone for what would happen that night which started out like most other school nights.

Cassandra and I watched television in the living room while our mother shut the door to her bedroom and spoke low to someone over the telephone. During commercials Cassandra would go to the kitchen and refill her glass of milk and after the fourth or fifth glass I thought to myself how strange it was for my sister to be drinking so much milk because I'd never seen her drink a single glass of milk before that time.

At one point, Cassandra began complaining how we were out of milk, and I said that was about right since she drank it all; I didn't even get one glass. Cassandra managed to razzle my mother enough to hang up the phone. Our mother told her to wait until tomorrow and then she'd go get some milk. That made sense to me. But Cassandra kept at our mother and finally she convinced her to go to the supermarket that night so we could get more milk.

I didn't want any milk, so why would I need to go? You're going, we're all going, my mother said, now get in the car.

I got off the sofa and turned off the television and walked down the hall to the kitchen, where I saw the back door wide open. Big Mama must've gotten out, so I shouted her name and waited while I noticed the passenger door to the car was ajar and the interior light was on, but no one sat inside.

I shouted again for Big Mama and she sniffed at the back of my leg to let me know she'd been inside the whole time and to quit shouting her name.

'Good girl,' I said.

I stepped outside, closed the back door to the house, and walked around the car to close the car door and wait. That was when I saw Cassandra on the driveway holding her stomach. I yelled for my mother but no reply came. I knelt down beside my sister and touched her on the shoulder as though one attempts to wake a beloved. An odd eye, lonely and in pain, stared back at me, and the fear from that look trembled through my body.

'Are you okay?' I said, touching her arm gently. 'What's wrong?'

'Milk,' she said.

'Okay,' I said. 'I'll get you some milk.'

I thought it strange for her to be craving such large quantities of milk. Once upon a time I'd come home after school and drink gallon after gallon of milk, but not anymore and I never acted the way my sister was acting that night.

'Bleach,' she said.

'Bleach?' I thought to myself, what the fuck is she talking about?

Then thousands of years of evolution bit into me and my instincts kicked in. I did not offer any sincere words of hope or encouragement to my sister — I left her lying there in the driveway because if my instincts were right, then she did this to herself and she'd have no pity from me. I opened the back door to the house and yelled for my mother to get her ass outside, Cassandra was dying.

'Don't talk like that to me — what?'

'She's out by the car. Go help her.'

My mother must've rushed out the back door as I walked around the dinner table to the kitchen sink and opened the bottom cabinet where we kept the cleaning supplies. Sure enough, I found the extra-large bottle of Clorox bleach my mother used for washing whites, and I was startled by how empty the bottle was. I put the bleach back inside and closed the cabinet door. Near the sink I found Cassandra's empty glass of milk and when I smelled it my nose detected a hint of bleach and to myself, I said, Shit. She drank the whole bottle of bleach. I left the bright kitchen and returned into the night to see Cassandra sitting in the passenger seat and our mother coming around the back of the car.

'I think she drank bleach,' I said, disbelieving the words as they came out of my mouth. 'At least four or five glasses full.'

'She needs milk,' my mother, the nurse, answered.

'Cassandra drank all that too.'

It dawned on us at about the same time as we both turned to look at Cassandra's pale face in the car. We paused thinking how we were headed to the supermarket to get the very elixir which would save my sister from death

'Stay here and watch the house,' my mother said. 'She needs to have her stomach pumped.'

My mother lowered herself into the car and shut the door. When she did, the interior light flicked off, shrouding my beautiful, sickly sister in darkness. The headlights flipped on and blinded me as I remained standing at the end of the driveway watching the car back into the street. Soon the car turned and with it its headlights fell away from me and in less than ten seconds the car turned right at the end of the street and was gone.

I stood for a few minutes in the driveway in the dark all alone, and found myself unable to go back inside to a brightly lit house — which for many years after, I'd find myself walking into that same empty, quiet house without the solace of companionship, of joy, or of laughter, and all of that emptiness would be mine, mine alone, but on that night I feared I'd never see my big sister again and I feared how I never told her how much I loved her.

Corn and flies: that had been the day my family traveled far into the countryside to those farms in my father's old yellow Ford truck, the same truck my sister fell out of and cracked her skull in the front driveway of our house on Vincent Street. By the time we reached the cornfields I had fallen asleep in my mother's lap.

'Leave him,' I faintly heard my father say.

'Henry, it's too hot.'

'Yeah, leave him,' Chadwick must've said from the back seat.

'Roll down the windows.' My father concluded, 'We have work to do and you can't carry him all day.'

'Why can't I stay with him?' I recognized the voice as my sister's.

Then I heard the windows being rolled down, the engine settling off, and my mother stretching me out on the front seat. Being so young, I quickly slipped into a deep sleep. For a time, I dreamed of vast cornfields. As I flew above the endless rows of cornstalks, I could see my father, my mother, my brother and my sister down below in one row after another filling buckets with ears of corn.

In the real world down in the yellow truck, flies began buzzing my ears and face as the summer morning heated up. I'd slap and swat the flies away from my sweaty neck and hair until I awoke half-aware of my surroundings.

I let the daze of a heavy slumber ease from me, and when I felt restored to my full mental acumen, I knelt beside the open window to find myself swallowed and lost inside the belly of a cornfield. Part of me knew my family sweated out there in the vast, dusty green but another part of me feared I'd lost them forever; they had become separated and lost just as I had become separated and lost from them, and I half-believed we'd never find one another again. I unlocked the door by pulling up on the small knob, and with both hands managed to squeeze the bar inside the armrest to open the door. Then I tumbled down and out.

First, I made my way to the back of the truck and climbed up on the bumper and peered over the tailgate. Inside the truck bed two or three baskets of corn had been placed near the front. I held the tailgate and stayed standing on the bumper to look in all four directions, but all I could see were the hairy tops of corn endless and far reaching.

I leaned my ear up into a passing breeze and thought I heard my father or brother off to the field to my right. I hopped down from the yellow truck and marched into the cornfield by slowly parting the first two giant stalks I came to. I walked straight for a time admiring the immense height of the corn. In all that giantness, for a moment at least, I knew what it was like to be Tom Thumbling. On the bottom most leaves I stopped to observe ladybugs and crickets resting in the shade. A lizard darted near my sneaker and I loved how alive my surroundings were. But after several more minutes of searching, I could not determine where my family was located. They had to have been there somewhere.

For a few minutes more I played with the corn. I grabbed a stalk and began shaking it fiercely and thought perhaps my family would see this. But when the thrashing sounds ceased, no one came. Next, I peered inside an ear of corn and touched the kernels one by one and thought of how this very corncob would one day end up on someone's plate, quite possibly mine. Growing bored, I walked straight back the way I came, with a tenseness and anxiety I'd never known before that time. It was all for naught. After a minute or so I came out of the cornrow I'd dedicated myself to and almost smacked into the side of my father's yellow truck. I opened the door and stood on the inner edge, then on the front seat, straining to see some signs of my family. Nothing. Not even a sound. The remarkable cornfield overpowered my senses and I gave up. I stepped down inside the truck, knelt on the seat and shut the door. I lay back down on the front seat, where for several more hours I would sweat, swat the flies away and dream of the endless rows of corn.

For many years after that episode in my life, I'd dream of sleeping in the front seat of my father's old, yellow truck — Old Yeller, we called it — swatting flies away from my face, remembering the smell of dust and corn and sweat as I waited for my family to return. The dream, however, was not a peaceful one, and only came to me when I was anxious and unable to get comfortable and I still associate that dream with being unable to rest well.

Over the first ten years of my life, I had two additional recurring dreams.

The second and least prominent dream of the three I had would be the one with King Kong, and I must've seen clips of that old black-and-white film at some point. Though I haven't dreamt the dream in a decade or more, I can still remember the water and the giant gorilla well.

The dream begins with me walking down Austin Avenue, a main artery of Brownwood two blocks from Vincent Street and Durham Avenue, with Austin smack in the middle. No traffic stirred and, in the background, ongoing reports warned of a 'disaster flood' soon approaching Brownwood, much like the flood on September 24, 1900 when the Pecan Bayou received the heaviest rain since 1873 and drenched the land in ten feet of water. The trepidation I feel at this point of the dream was minimal and I enjoyed how quiet and empty the streets were.

Then King Kong's epic roar startles me, but I see him in the distance across the town where he's atop the coliseum. He beats his chest and roars again and I grow more afraid. When I look back behind me on the empty street, a wall of water, a hundred feet or more high, builds and rolls towards me. I turn back to run but realize I'd be running back towards King Kong, but when I look to the coliseum King Kong has vanished, but I grow more afraid because I know he's out there and I can't find him.

When he roars, I jump because I sense it's coming from right behind me. My body trembles as the first signs of water rush around my ankles, making it quite difficult to run faster. I'm trapped and I know it. I swivel to check and see how much time I have before I'm drowned beneath the tidal wave. And when I look back, no matter how many times I have the dream, the wall of water has grown higher but reaches to King Kong's knees as he charges towards me.

The dream ends. I wake up. Every time.

The final dream which marked — or marred — my childhood was a far stranger, and more surreal dream than the others.

My family and I still lived on Vine Street because in the dream I'm crawling on the orange-brown shag carpet in the living room of that yellow house I told you about with the white window trimming. I'm crawling toward the television my sister left on before she darted out the front door. Like most dreams in my childhood, I'm alone and my surroundings empty.

The television plays the gameshow *The Price is Right* — for decades after, whenever I saw old reruns of this show, I'd instantly recall the dream — and I crawl to touch the television screen with all the wonderful, bright colors. But when I touch the screen, my hand continues forward until my whole arm is inside. Next comes my shoulder and head and slowly I'm swallowed by the television, by the gameshow, and I leave my house behind. I tumble head over heels, like Alice entering Wonderland, and land upright on my feet in one of the aisles surrounded by the audience, anticipating their names to be called as a contestant for *The Price is Right*. Then Bob Barker, the host of the gameshow, calls my name and says,

'Come on down!'

I begin running down the aisle to the stage and the audience cheers and applauds me, and I feel the energy of the room, of the moment growing as I approach the stage.

The dream ends. I wake up. Every time.

Oh spacious mountains majesty....

Or is it,

Purple mountain majesties above the fruited plane?

When I first learned 'America the Beautiful' in pre-preschool at the age of three, I had a hard time reconciling the adjective 'fruited' with the noun 'plane.' I kept thinking how could an airplane be 'fruited' or made of fruit, and this eccentric play on words made me love the song even more, and that was how I came to learn my first official song, next in line only to the ABC and Happy Birthday songs.

Our teacher taught 'America the Beautiful' to us every morning right after we stood beside our desks, held a hand over our hearts in the direction of a crisp American flag, stars and stripes and all, and we pledged our allegiances to the flag and to one nation under God and said in unison our 'God bless America.'

The teacher would then have us take a seat, switch off the lights, and place on the overhead projector a transparent sheet with the song 'America the Beautiful' and we'd take notes analyzing the individual words like 'spacious' and the grouped phrases like 'to sea from shining sea' and I sat in awe of how my fellow students could hold a pencil and write and how there were so many new vocabularies for me to learn, and that was how I came to know that I was at the beginning of my life and how I had a long, long way to go.

Then we were asked to stand once more, the stereo playing in the background the music along with the lyrics, the teacher pointing with a marker to each line on the overhead projector, and we would sing our hearts out, myself included, though I didn't know all the words, my heart sang full and proud:

For spacious skies....

For amber waves....

For purple mountains....

America! America!
That last part came out the loudest as:
Ah-mare-ree-ka! Ah-mare-ree-ka!
We all lowered the register of our voices to continue,
God shed His graces….
From thy good….
To sea from shining sea!

We sang the song two more times before the stereo and overhead projector switched off. The lights came on and we were allowed to take our seats to begin the morning lesson. One such lesson I remember well. The teacher turned off the classroom lights, got out her beloved overhead projector and instructed us in the art of stippling.

The first few shadow figures placed on the luminescent screen we had to guess and I had no clue as to who these people were, but I recognized Abraham Lincoln's hat and beard, and the teacher painstakingly displayed the method of using our pencils or black-coloring pencils to dot the paper a hundred, a thousand times if necessary to create the illusion of a shadow effect.

Then one by one she called us up to the front to sit in the light from the overhead projector and she traced the outline of our head onto a sheet of paper; after that, we were instructed to go back and fill in the sketched head with as many dots as we could until the next activity. At the time constantly holding the pencil upright and steady to apply all those dots to my face on the paper was intense, hard work.

One day though the teacher got into an argument with me and for the life of me I can no longer recall why I'd been the one to blame, but she sent me to the principal's office — where this strange person's office was I had no idea but I wasn't going to ask for directions — and so I ended up exploring the entire school grounds. I walked along the hallway where immediately another teacher spotted me and asked where I was going. I lied and said the bathroom and how I was new to the school, which was true, and she politely escorted me to the bathroom and left me to be on her way. I washed up and proceeded back to my exploration before I had been interrupted. I climbed the stairs to the second floor and discovered that the school had many more classes than the one I was in and with much older students. Once again downstairs, I exited a back door and walked down the ramp and around the cars parked there and walked to the end of the parking lot to the street. I turned to my right and went on up the sidewalk to the front of the school, and soon recognized my surroundings.

Out front where a concrete birdbath had been placed was where my mother dropped me off on the first day of school and I cried, I bawled great deep tears because she was leaving me in a strange, new place I'd never been before. I climbed the small ledge of the birdbath and looked down inside to see dry leaves and twigs, and I recalled how near that very spot I had met an older black boy spinning on his head. School had ended and we all waited to be picked up and I saw this kid upside down and spinning on his head. I thought his moves neat so I introduced myself and since I didn't know what else to say I asked if he wanted to be my friend.

'What?' he said with a playful shock in his eyes. 'What's this crazy white boy want?'

'Who's the white boy?'

'Mother of God,' he said. 'A white boy that doesn't know he's white.'

I looked at the skin on my arms and had to agree that I was white. 'And you're black,' I said.

'Now yous catchin on.' He spun like Michael Jackson and kicked his feet up in similar moves as if his knees were made of jelly. 'You know what?'

'What?'

'I like you,' he said. 'I can dig your groove.'

'My groove?'

'Boy, you are white aren't ya?'

The little black boy laughed and I laughed and he danced and I watched on in innocent amazement. I wished then I could do what he could do.

'What do you call that?' I pointed at the way he bent and moved his body.

'It figures a white boy never seen no black boy dance before. I bet you don't even know where yous live, do ya?'

I thought about that for a while and had to agree. 'No, I don't. My mom picks me up and takes me home. Without her, I'd be lost.'

'Not me. I was born on the street.'

I thought that must've hurt a lot.

'If you go down that street over yonder,' he said this as he pointed to the far end of the school, 'and go about three blocks and see a white house, that's where I live.'

'Wow.' I nodded in true wonderment. This boy certainly knew his way around the world. 'Can we be friends?'

'Are you color blind or just plain messin with me?'

'I don't think so.'

He slapped his thigh and grinned his beautiful teeth and shot out his arms to both sides of his body as in some final dance gesture.

'Sure, we can be friends, but you gots to learn somethin right this now. I'm black and yous white.'

'Why does that matter?'

The little boy laughed and wiped his forehead free from sweat. 'You white cracker don't know the world very much, do ya? I bets you color blind and all.'

'Can you teach me?'

'I'm black and yous white, you see, and a long time ago in a land far, far away your white kinds caught my black kinds and put heavy chains on them and bringed them to this land and made them slaves and dos all the work so yous white kinds can sit in the shade and drink icy tea.'

'I like iced tea,' I said.

'Yous see. Slaves of the black by the whites.'

'Crap,' I said, using the only profane word I knew. I shook my head and added, 'That's not very fair.'

'So yous see why it's difficult for a black and a white to be friends.'

'I don't care about that. Don't you want to be my friend?'

'Ha! Look at this crazy white boy.' He patted my shoulder. 'I like you. Sure, we can be friends.' He held out his hand and we shook and I had made my first friend all by myself.

'Can you teach me to spin on my head?'

'I can try but it's hard for whites to dance breaking like me.'

'I see.' I tried and he taught me all about breakdancing and different dance moves he had seen on television. Then he said he had to run, his mama was calling him and I waved goodbye to him and told him I'd see him later alligator, but I never met my friend again and for years after I thought this had something to do with the color of *my* skin. But now I stood near the birdbath as the images of my friend dissolved in the front schoolyard. I headed back inside and returned to my morning class.

The teacher asked if I'd been to see the principal. I lied and said I had. What did he tell me? Not to do it again. I don't believe you're telling the truth. You should be crying and giving me an apology. Why would I be crying? You didn't go to see the principal, did you Cody? No, I didn't and I'm not going now. I don't want to cry.

She grabbed me hard by the shoulder and walked me right out the classroom while wide-eyed students gripped their pencils and crayons and sat stunned at the rare sight of a little kid arguing with an adult, and not just any adult: the adult was the teacher, who was all-powerful and all-supreme. Then the teacher made her last mistake, or her first mistake, with me. She reached down and with both hands picked me up off the floor. 'You're going.'

'No, I'm not.'

I then proceeded to unleash kick after kick after kick after kick into her shinbones until she dropped me back to the floor and bent over to grab her legs in pain. The pain would not have been so bad if I'd been wearing sneakers like all the rest of the students, but I was a Texan, true and through, and like loyal Texans my family had bought me cowboy boots for my first pair of shoes — more for the additional support for my clubfoot.

After kicking my teacher's shins with my boots, I was suspended for a week from pre-preschool while the teacher informed the principal who told my mother I wasn't allowed to return to school wearing cowboy boots — somehow my boots had become lethal and changed the way the game was played, and that suited me just fine — but I could return to pre-preschool only wearing sneakers like all the other students. I needed to conform or else. Then I'm fine with not going back to school, I told my mother, I hated it there anyway.

But my mother and I went to Payless and bought me a brand new pair of sneakers with Velcro-straps — which I thought my boots were far easier to slip on and wear — and that was how I came to own my first pair of sneakers and how I continued to learn to sing,

And crown thy good with brotherhood.

I don't need to turn to look back over the arm of the sofa because I can hear the rain growing louder against the windows, but I do lean up and slip off my boots and recline back to the sofa as I cross my legs and wool socks and settle in.

What're you thinking about, you say.

Everything. And nothing.

Can you be more specific?

I'm thinking about the rain and how it sounded when I first woke that Saturday at six to attend the Fun Run.

By the time — which was about eight in the morning — I got to Howard Payne University and parked my car in the lot next to the music hall, the rain had moved in to an October drizzle and we had to have the introductory meeting inside Mims Auditorium — next to Grace Chapel with its classic white steeple — and where just outside a massive gate had been erected earlier that year to close off city traffic from entering the university grounds. Now Wilson Gate was open and marked the beginning and end to the five-kilometer (or three-mile) Fun Run.

Inside Mims, where the university held mandatory chapel each Monday and Wednesday mornings, the organizers instructed the runners on the route, which most townies knew by heart: we would leave the gate, go about twenty yards to Austin Avenue, take a left, go straight for about a mile, take a second left on the old road called Cordell Street that headed away from downtown and towards the State School, a prison for unruly teens, take another left and take the curving road called Coleman Street to the overpass. If we were to take a right on Coleman Street instead of a left, we'd hit Bluffview Drive, where Northwest Elementary School sat near

Trigg Park and in the shadow of Big Hill, where West Highway 67 connected Bangs to Brownwood.

At the bottom of Big Hill — more a small mountain than a hill — and at the end of Bluffview Drive, some years later the city would build the new Brown County Jail on an empty plot of land and dedicated the private street out front as W.C. 'Jack' Fuston Lane, named after one of my many great ancestors who as a twenty-eight-year-old police officer was shot and killed in the line of duty on February 3, 1939 while attempting to apprehend an escaped fugitive. To this day, Officer Fuston remains one of the brave officers who gave 'the last full measure' for the city of Brownwood, a city he served that had once long ago been called a settlement.

The Settlement of Brownwood was first legally established on the east side of the Pecan Bayou on February 5, 1858. In 1860, there were 244 people. By 1870, the population had risen 123% according to the U.S. Census to roughly 544 citizens. Ten years later in 1880, the population had exploded by 1,446% to 8,414 souls. But I wasn't thinking of Brownwood or Jack or his sacrifice, though I found it odd I was twenty-one, some years younger than he, as I attended that Fun Run on Howard Payne's homecoming weekend.

On Coleman Street, like I said before, we were to take a left and follow the curving road beneath the overpass and turn our final left on Clark Street, which was the road closed to public access and led to Wilson Gate near the three bell towers, which rang every hour on the hour as I made my way to class or sat in the classroom and when I heard the bells sound, I'd think: who do the bells ring for? They toll for thee.

Coming out of Mims Auditorium off to my left in the drizzle of rain were the three bell towers in the open courtyard, where I'd often rest between classes staring up into the trees and spring sun, but at that time in the rain were two freshmen with mallets banging a large, iron barrel as tradition demanded they do from midnight to the end of Saturday's homecoming football game, which the Yellow Jackets hoped to win. But the boom of the barrel in the rain sounded more like the call to join a funeral march through the city streets.

The runners gathered behind the open gate on Clark Street and that was when I saw Gianna, the wife of a friend I'd known since elementary school, with her mother — may she rest in peace — and Gianna's sister Nicolette, whose husband was a practiced runner and who often participated in mini-marathons. Gianna told me his name was Saul or something like that. I looked around to find him but remembered I didn't know what Nicolette's husband looked like. The race was about to start and I told Gianna to tell Dylan, my best friend and her husband, hi for me and she wished me luck. I said I didn't need luck but thanked her anyway and joined the pack of runners ready to start the race.

An organizer at the head of the pack fired a toy pistol and the runners lurched forward trying not to step on one another's heels. When the pack turned left on Austin Avenue and crossed the intersection that had been blocked for our safe passing, the pack began to spread out and I charged forward keeping a more-than-comfortable pace near the front. A fourteen-year-old boy, a seasoned track star from one of the local high schools, shot ahead of the pack and vanished as he turned left on Cordell Street. I heard later he finished under twelve minutes.

By the time I took the left on Cordell, I'd found my rhythm and decided to push harder, after all it was a race and I wanted to punish myself. You see, back then I'd been through some hard times — not like in *An American Tragedy* by Theodore Dreiser, but hard enough to break me nonetheless. I remember feeling lost, without any direction or star to guide me, and so I started going to the university gym where I worked out five times a week, and running at my top speed on an inclined treadmill balanced me to some degree: I may not have known where I was headed, but I was going there fast and in excellent shape. At the time I toyed with the fantasy of trying out for a Major League Soccer team in Dallas, but being born with a clubfoot put me at a disadvantage and having indifferent parents put me at a greater disadvantage. But I loved to run and be at my best physically, and that was how I came to enjoy exercise, hard-core workouts, as its own reward.

By the time I reached Coleman Street near the State School and turned left the rain was falling so heavily that my shirt, shorts and shoes were completely soaked, and my wet hair reminded me of another time in the rain I didn't care to think about. Instead, I pushed harder into the downpour and down the street.

At about that time I thought of Natasha who I dated with a half-heart, not so much from her pretty looks and intellect: black-curly hair, plump cheeks, thick arms, large thighs and nice-rounded breasts; but more from not wanting to play with any more hearts. When girls fell in love with me, I had a tendency to break their hearts, and I just didn't want to do that anymore. In *A Time to Love in Tehran* I published a few years back, Tom Bremer asks his friend and CIA officer John Lockwood if John was becoming 'a good guy.' I suppose back then with Natasha I was becoming a good guy, and just couldn't bring myself to commit to another relationship doomed to failure.

I remember one night after studying, I met Natasha and we walked between the red-bricked buildings half-covered in ivies, and stopped beneath the new tower the university had erected in 2001 in honor of a building that had been built in 1890 and burned to the ground — yes, I remember seeing Old Main Hall once or twice as a child before it burned down in 1984.

Old Main Hall was never rebuilt, but limestone or granite or something from the old building was used to help build Old Main Tower near that spot, and that was where I either kissed Natasha or didn't kiss her — my memory serves both possible outcomes, but as I dig deeper and draw closer to my closed shutters and open them to fresh air and sunshine falling on the remembrance of things past, I can see her bundled in her coat, the cold air thick around us, her curls on her shoulders, the way she wanted to be kissed, wanted to be taken and how we kissed a simple kiss that offered no further promises.

Years after graduation, I'd speak to her over the phone for a final time. She was living in Austin, I in San Angelo. When I came home from a long, dull day at American Capital Bank, I had a message from Natasha on my answering machine. I wrestled with calling her, not calling her, and after lying in bed for over an hour unable to sleep, I called her after eleven and we spoke politely for ten or twenty minutes. I lay in bed in the dark and listened as she said she was on a cellphone, out with friends, and my heart just wasn't into dating or even faking emotions I knew had long before died — with her or with anyone.

I ran harder. I ran until my side began hurting, and pushed beyond the pain into a free ecstasy I knew could never last.

At Clark Street, the final leg of the race, much of the pack lagged behind me as I turned left and decided to sprint the last one hundred yards — give it all I had to give — and I pumped my arms and legs and seemed to fly from my troubles and the scars on my body and on my soul, even the scars yet to come.

As I passed the first of the two gates, I could hear the freshmen beating the oil barrel beneath the Memorial Bell Towers: BOOM! BOOM! BOOM! BOOM! BOOM! and the echo spread out across the university in the rain as I ran faster, harder, attempting to break the worst and best parts of myself, attempting to lose my soul in the beating of the drum, attempting to destroy my destiny and all the seeds of depression which hid in me and waited. I ran ever faster.

Out of the corner of my eye I could see the two freshmen like shamans lifting their large mallets and banging the hammers down upon the iron barrel and the BOOMS rising to meet the three silent bell towers to my left and Thomas Taylor Hall across the way to my right. I ran faster to meet with dignity each drop of rain that fell from the gray clouds above. I pushed harder, I pushed the memories of rain and sadness deeper, I pushed until I could push no more and the gate marking the finish line accepted my miserable sacrifice. The end.

I bent down to hold my knees, unable to catch a breath, and remembered to lean up and place my hands on my wet head, gasping for air. Someone out of the crowd brought me a dry towel and a bottle of water. I thanked them. Gianna and Nicolette came over beneath umbrellas to my side and to cover me from the rain. I figured I came in far behind Saul, but as the two sisters stood next to me, they looked from me and back down the road I had just come and I knew then Saul was somewhere far behind me still running his race.

'What's my time?' I asked someone, anyone.

'A few seconds over eighteen minutes,' Gianna said.

I nodded and left them to re-enter Mims to dry and warm up a bit. I burst through the antechamber and into the auditorium out of breath, soaked from head to toenails, tugged my wet shirt off to reveal my six-pack abs to the world, and on stage a group of students stopped rehearsing to turn and stare at me as I came dripping down the aisle. My eyes, still blurry from the sweat and rain, could not clearly see the identity of the girl who ran down the steps from the stage and up the aisle to the back of the auditorium where I attempted to calm myself. When I turned back from seeing another runner come through the double-doors behind me, I saw Natasha standing next to me.

'My god, Cody,' Natasha said. 'Are you all right? What happened?'

'I'm fine,' I said, between breaths. 'Better than fine.'

I wanted to tell Natasha everything that had just happened but I could not find the words to tell her so.

I know I can never go back and I also know I can never change what's happened. What is, is. What was, was. I suppose what I'm trying to do is make peace with what happened to my family, and also with what happened to my America. Both used to be great. But now — we both know how that turned out. Like I said, I'm forty years old and I find myself making the same mistakes my father made, and I'm not even sure he knew what he was doing, but I do and that says something about who I've become.

No, you're right, he wasn't always bad and derelict, and after the divorce when my father was about the age I am now, he attempted to reconcile leaving by taking me to an overnight camping trip so we could be alone and talk about what happened. We got a chance to be alone but I'm not sure we talked openly about what we were both feeling at the time. Maybe he tried. I honestly don't know.

On a Friday I came home to an empty house after school and started packing. From my cousin Brighton I'd been given an old army bag and in this I added some fresh socks, jeans, two T-shirts, a compass, a Swiss army knife, and a combat knife, dull to the tip, identical to the one Rambo carried. Inside the hollow handle of the knife — I'd paid fifteen dollars for the knife a few years before — I pulled out a small plastic bag and spread its contents out on my bed to count the waterproof matches, about thirteen of them, a plastic toothpick, tweezers, fishing line and hooks, a sharp wire for cutting, and a pair of water cleansing tablets. I wrapped everything back up and tucked it back inside the knife and screwed the top with its own compass back on before storing the knife in the army bag.

Next, I moved to the kitchen and searched the pantry for food. I grabbed two cans of pinto beans and four bananas and added to these two cans of Coke. I placed my bag, ready and set, on the kitchen table by the back door and waited for my father to come. I expected he'd arrive at around half-past six, but he surprised me and arrived early at a little after five. He'd gotten off work at four-thirty so we could make camp before sunset.

'Ready?'

'Yes, sir.'

We filed into his gray truck he'd had for a few years and headed out of town. My father was never good at small talk but he could answer any question you put at him, and with a good sense of humor. I think growing up in the house of a reverend and an organ player in the church, among the spirit of the Lord, least of all three sisters — Patricia Carole, Judy Cloise and Treva Dean, who died one August, may she rest in peace. I bet that was hard on my father but I never asked. My whole life I'd tried to put him and my mother at a safe distance, far enough away that they'd never hurt me or the ones I love again, and I suppose I succeeded in the end.

On the ride out I asked where we were going — a friend of his had a place on the outskirts of Early and he'd let us camp — for how long — just a night — that was all — you'll see that'll be long enough. He'd been right about that. I could only take sleeping on the ground for one night.

We drove for about an hour and ended up parking down a dirt road in the middle of nowhere, and I remember how excited I'd been to be lost with my father at the edge of a wilderness as we grabbed the gear and marched into the bush wary of rattlesnakes.

'Any coyotes?' I asked.

'Some,' he answered. I followed behind him and watched as he carried a red ice chest cooler by one hand and a long box with our tent inside beneath his other arm. 'But don't worry,' he added. 'We'll have a fire and they'll stay clear enough away.'

After a good twenty minutes, we found a clearing beneath five trees in a crooked circle and I set the fishing poles and tackle box and my army bag down on the ground. He unpacked the tent with the ten thousand poles and I laughed and told him he'd never get the tent done before dinner, and he remarked how we'd better or the coyotes would have us for the taking. He set to work on the tent and I set to work scrounging for large rocks to make a fire pit and a couple of seats for us to sit on. My father was hard at work on that double-tent but he had some ways to go as I treaded off to collect enough firewood for the night.

With camp fully established — the tent erect, the fire pit stocked, the ground cleared — my father and I headed with the fishing gear over to a nearby ridge where a stock tank was hidden from view. If we were lucky, we might catch some Guadalupe bass.

In almost complete silence in that last hour of daylight, my father and I strung the fishing poles, baited the hooks, moved to separate spots along the edge of the still water and fished without catching a single thing. I never liked to fish to begin with — all those wasted hours of waiting and hoping and waiting and half-expecting feels too much like real life for me, and the failure when I didn't catch anything was clear and evident, poignant and lasting, like a slap in the face — but I was old enough back then to know I didn't care about any damn fish. I was there to make a memory, what few of them I'd have with my father after the divorce. As I cast my line far out into the sunset reflecting in the water, I watched a mirror image of my father do the same. I was glad we were both there, together. After fishing my father and I trekked back to the truck in the dark with a flashlight to grab the sleeping bags and pillows and a box of cooking supplies for dinner.

I got a chance to use my waterproof matches from my Rambo survival knife but the matches had been sitting for far too long and I gave up after my fifth failed attempt. My father reached into the box of supplies and used a lighter he had brought for that purpose alone, and in no time, we had a healthy fire going as the darkness further stole in around us and the stars beckoned us to look up and away. We had hot dogs and chips and neither one of us had a can opener — my Swiss army knife was no use — and so we forfeited the pinto beans, but not the Cokes, for another night.

My father never drank coffee in his life — not that I ever saw before or after — but after dinner in a tin pot he boiled coffee and poured us some in two tin cups. He offered a box of cubed sugar and I added two to my hot coffee and lay on the dirt beside the fire with my arm on the rock I'd planned to use as a seat. My father sat opposite the fire on his own rock.

'How's school?'

'Fine.'

'Heard you got into some trouble.'

'Nothing I couldn't handle.' I felt then my father must've noticed and recognized himself in the way I spoke. 'I heard you and mom got some trouble.'

He grunted and that seemed to signal the close of the door on the subject of both our troubles; we were bred, born, bled Texan and we handled our business with a profound silence that could flatten a mountain, but never us.

'Life can be hard, son.'

'I know it can, but I don't see why it can't be fun.'

I thought he said, 'I can't remember what that's like,' but I could be mistaken; regardless, I sensed an unsettled sadness for the way things soured with my mother, his wife, his life in general.

'Did you have fun?'

'Yes, sir, I did,' I said, taking a sip of my bitter coffee. 'We should do this more often.'

'I agree.'

I looked up at the stars above us, above the trees, above a few wisps of scattered clouds floating in the night sky like ghosts over an abandoned graveyard or lost eagles in search of a home.

'Who do you think made those,' I said, speaking of the stars.

'You mean God?'

'I don't know. What do you think?'

'I suppose He had a hand in it at some point.'

'I suppose so.'

In my life I've seen my father read only two books his entire life: the *Holy Bible* and the *Reader's Digest*; but I was thankful he read at all.

'I'll tell you something, son.'

'What's that?'

We both were looking at the stars now, the fire between us.

'In all my years, which I'd be the first one to admit isn't a whole helluva a lot, but in all those years I've never heard or seen anything, not one thing, to prove to me that there's *not* a God out there somewhere looking down at us as we're looking up at Him.'

'I suppose not,' I said, unsure of what I was saying or wanted to say.

We stayed up late into the night speaking of our memories as though they were legends from another place, another time — and in a way, I suppose they were. Later that night we splashed water on the dying embers and watched the last lineaments of the fire go out before we went into the tent and slept a restless sleep over rocks and dirt that grew colder and harder as the night wore on.

The next morning, we fished at dawn, caught nothing, joked about our failures, had a bite of scrambled eggs, packed up camp, and made our way to the truck having nothing more to say to one another than what had already been said.

They say a man is what he thinks about all day long. And so, I wonder why I'm telling you any of this, a story of my life, the beginning to a long life lived not so well. I also cannot explain to you the reasons why in high school my feelings were so intense that my one-sided love for Nora became locked away in a tumultuous chasm within me, as though it were too fragile for me to give away or to even show her or anyone else.

In a green notebook I wrote poetry for Nora: poems about her, to her, for her, all as I saw her and felt for her. The poems — my very first attempts at writing creatively for a transcendental release into something like art — were the sappy lines of a typical high school kid dealing with an unrequited love. Classic Romeo stuff. I showed no one these poems. Told no one about how my heart as love for Nora was a sparrow flitting through a raging storm without a single branch to land upon. Oh! How I wanted her to be that branch. Never to be. If I was what I thought about all day long, I would've been Nora.

I drifted a lot back then, around town after school — which ended at noon my senior year — driving each street to set to memory because deep down I told myself I was never coming back to that black hole we teens had nicknamed 'Deadwood.' The town would suck you in and you would never be able to escape its grip. At odd times I found myself just sitting at stop signs with no traffic in sight. I asked myself where I should go next. Left? Right? Straight? Turn around and go back? After almost two decades of living in the same small town, I knew the results of each decision no matter which way I decided to turn and drive. But all the choices I could have made still left me in my hometown. It didn't take me long, less than a week I think, to drive every single street in Brownwood, even the side-connecting ones, even the one in downtown near the Drag that the locals always said had once won the Guinness Book's world record for the shortest street — from stop sign to stop sign. I once looked it up and found that it was true. At least I had been there, I told myself, and I didn't intend to ever go back. I drifted and drifted like a Bob Dylan song. Drifting still, you might say, against the rat's race, the hamster's wheel, the corporate slogging of mind-numbing, soul-killing monotony. Drifting over lands and through time and loving every minute. Drifting as though on a river in someone else's dream.

On such occasions when I'd be stopped on the side of a neighborhood street cloaked by large oak and pecan trees, maybe the streets of Vine or Vincent looking at my childhood homes, both yellow and occupied by strangers, Nora's voice and face would appear and she would whisper to me from the passenger seat of my car, or so I thought, and I'd get the idea to drive all the way across town to Early where she worked in Heartland Mall at the Corny Dog Shack, right next to JC Penny, the very same department store where my father and I bought my mother the red polka-dotted dress for Valentine's Day one year long ago now lost to me now.

I never parked outside JC Penny or the main entrance to the mall — both would've been a more direct route and faster. I would park my car, instead, near the entrance to the movie theatre, which was located just outside the mall and much farther away from where Nora worked in the Corny Dog Shack.

I'd stand looking at the showtimes for that month in April, the coming and now playing: *City of Angels*; *Tarzan and the Lost City*; *The Object of My Affection*. I'd stand and quietly mull over each movie with its corresponding times and know I wouldn't be watching any of them because I didn't have any money, or if I did, I'd have to save it for fuel for my car. You might not believe it, since I love movies — a real cinephile like my wife Axton — but I didn't develop a habit for watching movies at the cinema until after high school. As a university student, my favorite times to watch a movie — and even now — would be on Tuesday mornings when the cost for a ticket was cheaper, often half price, and more often than not on those Tuesdays, I'd find myself as an audience of one. One time during Denzel Washington's Oscar-winning performance in *Training Day* my girlfriend at the time and I found ourselves at the back of the theatre alone as she unzipped my jeans and gave me an Oscar-worthy blowjob.

Even now I'm not sure why I hesitated to see Nora, even after driving as far as I did — you'd think I'd be in a rush — but I'd stand for thirty minutes or more outside the movie theatre, sometimes pacing back and forth, sometimes returning to my car to listen to *Pearl Jam* before I'd enter the mall and make my march to Nora and the Corny Dog Shack. On the walk there, I'd even convince myself she wouldn't be working that evening or her boyfriend Dan Martin would be there and everything would become awkward and I'd have to lie and tell Dan I was looking for him instead. I hated to lie.

Most often, though, Nora would be working and when she looked my way with a reserved joy in her eyes, I'd be happy I came to see her. She'd be behind the glass partition frying corn dogs and waffle fries for a couple seated at the back of the open seating area which had three booths by the wall and three sets of tables with a chair on either side. On the weekends, if the seating area was full, customers would carry their food tens paces or so to the fountain, which marked the center of the mall, and sit on the side circling around the fountain as a bench and eat their funnel cake topped with powdered sugar and drink their iced lemonades, freshly squeezed.

I pause and turn from the window to see you sitting at your desk taking a few notes on your yellow legal pad. I tell you those parts about Nora were the parts of my life I never told anyone. The parts about Nora, though, never felt to me like secrets. Secrets involve hiding something from someone. My school-boy crush lasted only as long as high school did. Once the summer of 1998 came, I found myself at the brink of a high cliff, down below darkness and uncertainty, and all I had to do, all the world — as in society and culture, parents and elders — wanted me to do — the very thing I refused to do for months — was to jump. By the end of that year, I jumped. Since then I've been profoundly alone, as I suppose a novelist should be. But then again, I don't know how novelists should be.

The last semester before high school graduation seemed to me a ticking clock, or sand dripping down an hourglass. I watched the grains of sand trickle down the hourglass and it never occurred to me at the time that once all the sand reached the bottom I could, would have to, reach over and turn the hourglass over. Life would start a new chapter and that, too, would one day come to an end. Seasons in a man's life, as much as a woman's, needed to be respected and allowed to change, and through each of these seasons growth would emerge.

As I got older, now almost forty, I lost track of the sand grains trickling and often found the hourglass standing idle. When I did, I thought nothing much of it. I'd reach over to turn the hourglass over and start a new cycle and go about my business. I imagine one day I'll forget about the hourglass and cycles and chapters, so that life will become one moment after the next. That's all life is anyway: one moment after the next. *Mindfulness*.

With Nora in high school she never once gave me a sign or hint that she was interested in being anything more than friends, and for the life of me I couldn't contemplate as to why. As I grew older and far too mature with women — the young and the old, the virgins and the experienced — the tiniest signal — a turning and tilting of the head to display her fanning hair; a look down in timid embarrassment; a casual bending over to reveal her breasts through the opening in her blouse; a bright, white spark in the widening of her eyes; a playful wag of her butt as she walked in front of me; a few seconds off and behind in the conversation to show her nervousness; a double-edged remark that hid its meaning well to the passerby or the faithless unobservant — Nora never once signaled her interest in me, and perhaps that was my sign.

When we spoke at the Corny Dog Shack or on drives in the countryside smoking blunts (seedless marijuana tightly wrapped in cigar paper), she'd stare out and away from me — to the fountain in the center of the mall or out the car window — for long, silent moments, and when I saw her become contemplative — something she never once did with her boyfriend Dan Martin or our other friends — I fooled myself into believing that deep inside she was a lot like me, and we both had so much of everything boiling down beneath the surface and how we could never, not for a single careless second, show our peers. We knew if someone were to confess their true emotions aloud, ridicule would certainly follow. Such was the high school life as a teenager.

Back then I told myself Nora's silence was the truest part of who she was and she was showing her true self only to me. I'd ask her what she was thinking about and she'd often reply with two words: the future.

When I stared out into that void alongside Nora, I'd grow silent and forget about my lusts for her and all the churning uncertainty ahead didn't feel like it was for me or for her. The hourglass was approaching its end and I wanted nothing more than to share an afternoon in bed with Nora where our naked bodies as lovers depleted themselves against one other. The songs of our souls would sing and we'd be as one. What a sentimental fool I had been.

Over the years, I've found the less time and energy a man spent thinking about a woman the more the woman was attracted to the man. The man, for certain, must make advances in her royal presence, but once she's out of sight she should also be out of mind for the man to be able to function and perform as a man. This is the main reason why playboys (men who date multiple women) attract so many women to their side. With Nora I hadn't learned this lesson yet — perhaps she was the one who taught me.

Stephen Dedalus, of James Joyce's *Ulysses* and *A Portrait of the Artist as a Young Man*, once remarked that history was a nightmare from which he was trying to awake, and my old mentor, Dr. Roark at Howard Payne University, once told me a man was what he thought about all day long. Two decades it took for me to bind those two philosophical statements into one around my heart and soul, and I'm the better for doing so.

A week or so before the actual high school graduation ceremony, my parents waited for me at the commencement ceremony in the stifling auditorium in the old Coggin Avenue Baptist Church on Coggin Street just as I had done with them years before when we watched Chadwick and, a few years later, Cassandra perform the ceremony of sitting for hours and listening to dull, obvious advice on how to proceed into the undetermined future. Coggin Avenue Baptist Church and Coggin Street were named after the Coggin Brothers, ranchers and developers who helped build and grow Brownwood. Moses J. (Mody) Coggin, born in 1824 in North Carolina, and his brother Samuel Richardson Coggin, born also in North Carolina in 1831, were two of nine children who finally made their way to Brown County in 1857. In 1862, both brothers joined the Confederate Army during the Civil War. Later, Mody and Sam Coggin joined the state militia to fight against the Comanches. At the time, when I was graduating high school, I knew none of this history about the Coggin Brothers.

Most of the ceremony consisted of sitting in that cramped church for two hours on a Saturday morning as speakers drawled on about how these young minds could go about 'achieving one's full potential' and 'make the most out of an uncertain future,' and then to watch all the hopeful graduates proceed outside to toss their hats into the air out on the front lawn across the street from Dairy Maid, which years later was demolished and turned into an empty parking lot for the Coggin Avenue Baptist Church.

My father Henry would become furious when he found out, after sitting for hours in that church on his precious day off, that I had no intention of ever going and I had spent all that morning by the pool with Nora. I ended up telling my father I had no interest in long-standing, cultural traditions where it was put upon me to blindly follow an invisible, unspoken order. He and I argued, as fathers and sons do, and perhaps that moment for us was the beginning to an end he and I could not prolong nor avoid.

I'm not sure if I regret disappointing my father and mother that day — regret seems to be biased and consists mostly of hindsight. Knowing what I know now, would I still have gone to a friend's house and the pool with Nora? Probably. But knowing what I know now, I might've had sex with her by the pool, in the pool, and inside one of the many bedrooms, or all of them. Or maybe not. I might've avoided her entirely and gone to the church that day. Because, truth be told, unknown to everyone, perhaps even to Nora, on that day in the month of May, Nora's pregnancy was in its first trimester.

Even without showing, Nora carried Dan Martin's child just as Karolina carried my child. But hindsight can tell you these kinds of things: like when a seventeen-year-old you have a crush on was a month or two with child by the pool on a day where people who loved you waited for you in an old, stuffy church, and also in that church that day, graduating a year early as a junior, was Karolina, who still had told no one — not even me — of her pregnancy, also in its early stages. My mother later told me she had seen and spoken with Karolina, and how she'd been 'so very beautiful.'

I'd neglected tradition, custom, my parents, the mother of my child, and my unborn child — even if I didn't know it at the time. And for what? To chase after someone who I knew deep down headed down a different path than the one I knew I was on. But I had. I was a mawkish fool. I know it now.

The only thing I can tell you for sure that I don't regret about Nora was when I drove to her house near Heartland Mall in Early and collected the green notebook of poems I'd given her to read. Nora told me she cherished the poems about her and how she wanted to keep the green notebook. I couldn't see anything because of all the pain in my eyes.

She never kissed me. She never returned my love — other than to be my close friend. She had done nothing to warrant my affection as a lover. I told her the poetry was mine and I'd only intended for her to read the poems for a few days. Her eyes widened. She clutched the green notebook to her swelling breasts, the same I often day-dreamed about. She must've known she was pregnant by then and the path before her and the choices she'd have to make in the months ahead. Her silence must've been a blessing to me. Even if we didn't know what we were doing.

With the green notebook sitting in the passenger seat next to me, I drove back across town and to my home at the Pine Creek Ranch. I'd driven to Nora's early in the morning, around seven, and back at my father's house the mid-morning sun found me in my father's tool shed looking for lighter fuel and matches. Out behind the tool shed, in an old oil drum used for burning nonsense and non-essentials, I dropped the green notebook and poured the lighter fluid empty and tossed in the plastic bottle. The match sparked and lit the green notebook on fire, and I convinced myself in front of the flames that love betrays even the kindest and most faithful of hearts.

My brother Chadwick and I still shared bunkbeds for a time in the yellow house on Vincent — before we'd fight too much and have to be split, and my parents had to put me in one corner of a large den we had next to the living room, and I didn't mind so much because next to my bed a desk and shelves had been fashioned into the wall and, also, I'd never had my own bedroom before, even if it was one without a door — but there's this one time I woke on a Saturday morning in the bottom bunk and I'd felt my hair and it was all wet and I thought I was dying, bleeding to death out of my skull. Then I patted my midsection and disbelieved the proof — there was no way I had wet the bed again. My last episode had been months before and I had gone to the toilet several times before bed, so there was no way I could've 'pissed my breaches' as my father would say, but regardless, my pajamas and bed were soaked — that is until I noticed that my head wasn't bleeding, no, not blood at all, but in fact it was barbecue sauce, and as I tossed my pajamas in the corner and washed up I couldn't figure out exactly how a boy goes to bed all peaceful one night and wakes up all in hell the next morning, but my brother, finally, in his own suffering turmoil of ketchup and wet bed confessed to me: idiot, it was Cassandra. For the life of me, a small boy, the *how* baffled me and I couldn't figure out the *whys*: why would she waste perfectly good barbecue sauce? why would she go and pretend and make me think I wet my own bed? why would she torture me so?

For months after I failed to give myself, or get from my sister Cassandra, a definitive answer to my questions, and with no recourse left to me, a young boy of seven or eight, I slowly, methodically, painstakingly plotted my revenge. A time and chance would come one day and I'd be ready.

Months slipped by and Cassandra held more sleepover parties with a few of her closest friends: Brandy, Meleri, Natalie or Nicole. Chadwick and I had to endure peanut butter in our ears and hair, and wet beds that did not feel or smell like water. Years later, Cassandra would tell me she and her friends peed in a large bowl and then poured its contents into our beds; had to be authentic, she'd say, otherwise, what's the point? I had to hand it to her: she was an artist and in her own weird way she was a perfectionist, like me, but that admission would come when we had grown older and closer and forgiven each other for the follies of our mischievous childhood. One Saturday my revenge would come when we least expected tragedy to strike; but isn't that what usually happens?

My brother and I tossed a football out in the front yard of the great yellow house that claimed dog after dog from what my father said was Parvo, and my target rode happily up and down the street on her pink bicycle.

I ordered Chadwick to come help me and he resisted only until he discovered my evil plan to enact justice on our dreaded roommate who had crossed more boundaries than either he or I would like to admit. Chadwick grabbed a shovel out of the back garage near my mother's garden and we headed back out front to get to work — and later I'd marvel how despite the openness to our activities, all done in the sight of Cassandra, she'd trust me enough to do as I asked; either she loved me or she was incredibly stupid.

At the end of the sidewalk, which ran in front of our house and along the street, a section of dirt and grass divided the sidewalk from the pavement, and it was in this spot of land I gave direction to Chadwick to start digging a hole. He refused at first but I told him it was all part of the plan since Cassandra would never expect him to betray her. She knew I was out for blood and for this plan to work she couldn't suspect me. I had to distance myself as much as possible.

Chadwick finished the hole, two or three feet deep, and said, 'Now what?'

'Now we lay the trap.'

We covered the hole with twigs and grass I had ripped up from the front yard and placed a false covering atop the hole at the end of the sidewalk.

'Now what?'

'Now we wait.' We waited for half an hour as we tossed the football and watched to see if our prey suspected anything.

Many times Cassandra rode down the sidewalk, towards the hole, then at the last second she'd turn off to the side and circle around to peddle back up the street. Just as she was about to give up her afternoon of cycling, I stepped in. I told my sister I needed her help, and told her I needed her to ride down the sidewalk and over the grass and into the street.

'I'm not stupid,' she said. 'I saw you and Chadwick dig a hole.'

'You're right,' I said. 'You're absolutely right. But we filled it up and now we need to make sure it's safe. In case other children might ride down this street.'

She seemed to weigh my answer as I pointed to the end of the sidewalk.

'Just once.'

'Only once.'

Cassandra peddled hard down the sidewalk toward the covered hole and at the last second turned off to the side and circled back around.

'No, no, no.' I marched to the end of the sidewalk and she pulled up behind me. I pointed at the covered hole which looked like a normal spot on the ground. 'I need you to ride right here.'

She hesitated and looked from me to the ground.

I knew I had to do something to convince her the trap was safe, like spreading a little peanut butter on a piece of cheese on a mousetrap. I lifted my foot and acted like I was jamming the dirt down deeper into the hole. 'See,' I said. 'I just want you to ride right here to make sure we filled it all in.'

'One more time,' she said, as if testing my trust, my resolve to revenge all the crimes she committed against me.

'One more time,' I said.

'Last time,' she said.

'Last time,' I said, 'but do it right here.'

Cassandra rode off to the side, circled back down the street, turned and entered the sidewalk at our driveway, and peddled faster down the sidewalk than I had expected. My brother held the football as we watched from the front yard.

At full speed, to my delight and horror, Cassandra peddled faster and faster to the end of the sidewalk, did *not* turn safely at the last second, but positioned her bike to cross directly over the center of the covered hole. I believe that she might have thought the speed would carry her across, like flying, safely to the other side.

The speed, however, did not work to her advantage. The front wheel of her bicycle hit the hole and stuck solid, the bike flipped. Cassandra flipped forward with it and landed face first on the pavement, which, thankfully, was empty of traffic. The bike toppled over my sister and smacked her in the back of the head, and the entire scene seemed to take five minutes in slow motion.

When time sped up again and the bike came to rest in the middle of the street, both tires still spinning, Cassandra held the side of her face and bawled a great terrible cry of regret, pain, betrayal, suffering and anger while Chadwick and I rejoiced. My brother and I danced a jig.

'Rad,' Chadwick said.

'Yeah,' I said. 'Rad.'

I tossed the football high into the air. Chadwick and I raised our hands above our heads as if we'd scored a touchdown in a championship game and shouted cries of victory, revenge fulfilled, and delight satisfied. I ran furiously ten or more times around the front yard in a blind fever of hysterical mania: after all this time, I'd finally got my sister back, and it had been a brilliant strategy on my part, not by my brother. I had done the impossible.

Then reality flooded back and I realized the horror of what I had done. I had personally attacked the greatest monster I'd ever known. I had unknowingly opened the door to all future reprisals while I slept foolishly and unguarded. I had, as I would later learn, become the mad scientist Victor Frankenstein. I would be the one to bear the responsibility for my creation. As Cassandra cried and Chadwick helped her out of the street, I did not see a wounded little girl in pigtails; I saw a monster that, once calmed and settled, would plot her own revenge when I least expected it. I had opened Pandora's Box. I had invited war on an opponent that vastly overpowered me in cunning and wit and devilry, and I was too young, too ill-prepared and too frightened to the open possibilities of a sister's revenge. And so, I ran for my life. Ran, ran, and ran — until I no longer remember the rest of that day.

I'd like to add one more memory about my sister and her bike — after all I can't end on that sad image of her crying in defeat. The time was a few months or a year after my enacted cruelty and I had grown to love my sister in new ways, and she had ceased her midnight sneak attacks upon my brother and me. But something unsettling deeply troubled my sister and for a time I'd beg her to play pranks on me.

She'd respond, 'Why don't you grow up, Cody.'

I suppose that hurt me most. Compared to all her other crazy antics.

I do remember, however, one Friday night my father refused to let Cassandra spend the night at her best friend Meleri's house. Meleri's parents, according to Chadwick who was in the know, were away and there was going to be a party with boys and *MTV*.

Cassandra stormed out of the house, and as I was about to park my blue bike in the garage, I watched her peddle out of the driveway and down the side street next to our neighbor Mr. T's house.

I hopped back on my bike and followed the street which ran down a small hill to Vine Street. Since a large vacant lot occupied about two city blocks to my right, I could tell Cassandra hadn't gone in that direction.

I turned left and peddled as fast as I could, until about three blocks later I eased alongside her. My memory failed me earlier and Cassandra wasn't on her bike then. She was just walking, but with a stern determination and an angry dissatisfaction with the world I've never seen her have before that time.

'Leave me alone. Go away.'

I peddled my bike in circles around her. She stormed on.

'I'm your little brother. I can't leave you all alone.'

We continued on in that way for another block or two.

'Where ya' going?'

'None of your business.'

'I'll just follow you then.'

She thought about this and stopped walking.

'I want you to go back and tell mom and dad I'm going to stay the night with Meleri, okay?'

She had me and she knew it.

'I'll follow you so I'll know where Meleri lives. Then I'll go back.'

Night began to settle in the early stages of an unwanted dusk.

'Do what the hell you like.' Cassandra marched down the road and farther away from our house.

At the end part of Vine Street, before the city changed the layout and built an overpass because of heavy flooding, the road dipped down into a tunnel that ran under railroad tracks. On the other side of the tunnel the road split in opposite directions.

'The tunnel will be the farthest I've been alone away from home,' I said, speaking more to myself than to her. The night, betraying me, sank deeper into darkness. What was I to do? Follow or return?

'Go back,' Cassandra said. 'Tell mom I'm fine.'

I feared she'd be kidnapped, stolen by a lunatic in a black van if I left her and I'd be the one to blame for my sister's disappearance, her death. When she crossed into the tunnel, down the side walkway and out of sight, I knew I couldn't follow her. I'd have to return home. I couldn't see her but I called out anyway, 'I'll do that. I'll go back and tell mom.' I hesitated, then added, 'Because I love you.' I'd never told my sister that before, and I listened for a reply for about two minutes before I turned my bike around, looked once more into the void of the tunnel, and peddled home.

Believe it or not I've told you some pretty happy memories, and those moments suspended in time will be among the final images flashing across my mind when the Dark Angel decides it's time for me to go and leave all this nonsense behind. But there's something twisted in human nature and people secretly want to hear about the deaths in the family, the train wrecks and the billion other possibilities of misfortune that could happen to us but we hope don't.

My friend Whalen could've easily been me. I mean we were born in the same local hospital, we both grew up a block away from one another in the same crummy town in the same crappy county in the same beautiful state of Texas, so don't tell me it's survivor's guilt when I feel horrible about Whalen's death at such a young age.

You want to know all about it and since we have our time together let's get this part of the day over with as quickly, or as easily, as possible, okay?

What really blows my mind is how Whalen and I could be born fifteen days apart — he on October 2 and I'd come fifteen days later — live the first five years within a single block from one another, both growing up in yellow houses, both our families ripped in half by divorce.

Whalen would die, though, at the age of twenty-nine in the same hometown he was born in while I'd gotten out of Texas, seen Korea and Guam, and found myself teaching university in old Saigon. I could speculate day and night about the causes and effects, about the actions and inactions which set our doomed hero on the path over the cliff and onto the tongues speaking of lost destinies and ghosts as if graves could be unburied and ruined lives lived again, but we both know I'd be wasting my time, and your time, so I won't go there. What I'll tell you instead is about the day I traveled the farthest from home and the tragic, fearful world shattered — no, dissolved — beneath each step I braved to take as a toddler.

Whalen Allen and I, both Libras like I said, could've been switched at birth and no one would've known, except for my clubfoot that is. He had blond hair. I had blond hair. He had an older brother and older sister. I had an older brother and older sister. We were both the babies of our families. And though we grew to become vastly different beings, there's a sliver of me who still remembers the joy that came, as a two-year-old boy, when I hugged and squeezed my best friend Whalen, and at the time I had hoped we'd stay like that for the rest of our lives. But when my family and I moved across town to the yellow house on Vincent Street, Whalen and I, best friends since birth, vanished, for the most part, from one another's lives. Perhaps my family moving to a new yellow house to a new neighborhood across town would be the single deciding factor that altered my life-course from Whalen's and thereby sent me to a long and happy life and him to an early death on April Fool's Day, 2009. His wife Angela, survived by Sylvia and Philip, followed Whalen in death two months later.

I once told you I grew up in a yellow house on Vine Street, but that can't be. No, the house I'm thinking about — where my Grand-Mommy chased me five times around the house because I failed to get a long, thin switch so she could spank me with it, and the same yellow house right across from Mrs. Beaman's old, white one — now that yellow house must've been on Avenue C or D or E or one of those letters and like I told you from the beginning: I can't be trusted. Memory locks what it locks and spills what it spills; who are we to judge?

At the time going across the street to check on Mrs. Beaman to make sure she hadn't died during the night had been the longest journey I'd taken alone and I thought myself proud and brave for being able to cross the deadly street without the company of an adult or older sibling.

One day I told my mother that I wanted to go play with Whalen, my best friend, and how I hadn't seen him in a while, in such a long time I couldn't remember when. My mother shocked me when she said for me to go on alone and to check to see if Whalen was at home and if he wasn't then I'd better come on back; there was no point for her to go with me if Whalen wasn't home, because I'd just have to come back anyway. And if Whalen was indeed home then I didn't need my mother there for me and Whalen to play.

Stumped by the adult logic of it all, I had to admit she had me. Though the adult reasoning seemed sound to my little ears, I kept fearing the worst. The one word which stuck out in my mind was also the one word which unraveled even the most sensible logic, and that word exaggerated the fear as I imagined the headlines: KIDNAPPED!

'But Mom,' I pleaded.

'You're a big boy. Go on then.'

With no choice but to go — after all the sound logic had been my mother's and I was a big boy — I opened the front door, stepped onto the porch, reached up and closed the door solid, and turned to face Mrs. Beaman's house. I wanted to wave to her but didn't think she'd be at home, or she could've been dead on her sofa in the living room waiting for me to find her. In the end I waved to her in case she was watching me walking into kidnapped history out her windows and I hopped down the three steps from our porch, walked down the walkway in our front yard, turned left and proceeded down the sidewalk.

The day, cloudy and calm, reminded me — I'm not sure why — of an empty ship at sea. No traffic stirred in our cozy neighborhood. No adults trimmed their hedges or mowed their yards. The lone figure taking an afternoon stroll — if you were to go back in time to watch — would be an adorable three-year-old blind to the dangers of the world.

At the end of the sidewalk I had to cross the street to the other side since the sidewalk stopped at our house and didn't continue any farther. Walking in the street now, a vacant lot with brown weeds taller than me on my right, my fear doubled and bound itself tighter around my neck and chest, and every two or three steps I turned back to see whether or not a black van wasn't in fact creeping a few yards behind me.

Making the edge of the corner lot became the farthest distance I'd been away from home — a mere half-block — and turning the corner and going another two blocks to Whalen's yellow house — why were all the houses yellow back then? — meant I'd have to walk without having my home in my field of vision or line of sight. I'd be far enough away where I could no longer see my house and far enough for any of my screams for help to fall well short of the stop sign at the corner of our front yard. But I detested fear even at that early age and have always decided to do the exact opposite of what fear told me to do.

When I was around ten or eleven, I climbed to the highest diving platform — the kind the Olympic divers use — a good three stories high, enough to break your back or neck if you hit wrong. At the top, I saw children swimming over in the far corner of the pool, in the shallow end, and they appeared as tiny dolls. I thought myself crazy, suicidal for wanting to jump from such an incredible height, especially when no one was watching. I started down the ladder, shaking my head, and half-way down I froze, clung to the ladder from an even greater fear than the one that kept me from jumping.

'Cody,' I said to myself, 'If you don't jump today, you'll go the rest of your life afraid of heights.' I believed what I told myself, so much so I started back up the ladder and found myself once more at the edge of the Olympic diving platform peering over the edge to the deep end of the pool stretching down another twenty feet below the surface. There would be one way for me to do this, and that was for me to jump off the edge. Don't look. Don't think. Don't hesitate. Just run and jump.

I calmly and coolly collected myself as I walked to the back of the platform, turned and without another second to sway my decision, I ran full-speed and lifted five feet higher than the platform, spread my arms like a bird, felt myself arch and descend. My body straightened, head down, and at the last second, I brought my arms and hands forward into a single point and entered the water in the best swan dive I've ever done since.

The speed with which I traveled carried me down deep, deeper than I had ever previously gone before, and I kicked off the bottom, shooting myself up and out of the water, my face in pain from the impact.

I swam on my back, looking at the height from where I'd jumped, fallen, soared moments before and thought myself lucky to be alive, uninjured, and I told myself I wasn't going to tempt fate twice; I wasn't going to try that again.

I climbed the poolside ladder and shook my legs a bit and stared at the Olympic diving platform to my left and to the oblivious children swimming and splashing to my right. I didn't quite know how to act or feel at doing a remarkable thing while having no one to see it and share in the accomplishment. In the end, I joined my cousins at the shallow end of the pool and never said a word about where I'd been or what I'd done. It wouldn't have mattered.

Now back to that three-year-old we left by the corner near the vacant lot: he's still there looking up the road to Whalen's house in the near distance, some two blocks, and back to his home, a mere half-block, and our dawdling adventurer decides its best to cross the street to travel on the sidewalk near the row of houses on his left, and then to cross back over the street to get to Whalen's house on his right, and as he walks along the row of houses he begins to consider, for the first time in his life, a world greater than himself: who were these people living in all these houses? did they have little boys like Whalen? or little girls like Kim, Whalen's older sister? or were these invisible strangers old like Mrs. Beaman? were these silent houses, each and every one, filled with dead people? waiting for a friend or loved one to come along — like someone would do one day years later for Whalen — and find them dead?

I shook the thought and questions out of my head and ran the rest of the way to Whalen's house. He would not be at home. A sturdy door to a child's knock would be my only reward for having traveled so far so alone.

On my way back I walked down the sidewalk next to the houses filled with the silent or the dead, but instead of crossing the street by the vacant lot and return the half-block home, I decided to explore the world while I was at it, and I turned right at the corner and walked a half-block in the opposite direction of my house.

For thirty minutes or less, I roamed a large empty parking lot across the street from a church, and I remember thinking how I'd never known I lived so close to a church — roughly one or two blocks away — and that was how I discovered that the edges to my reality, to my world, could dissolve and give way to greater boundaries, more unexplored lands, to places I'd never been before but was willing to go — if only I chose to do so.

I returned safely home and kept thinking of how if all these houses were filled with the dead, then that was all right all right all right, all fine by me because at least there'd be a church nearby to bury them and see them on their way to heaven or to hell. Or perhaps they would remain as ghosts.

I had hoped Whalen and I could live to be old men, fathers together. Why not? I thought. If I could travel to his house all alone, then anything was possible and everything eternal.

You were right when you said that some people end before they have a beginning, and I'm not sure what I have to say about that. Doesn't sound very fair to me. I'd really like to get up there to heaven and ask God who was the one canceling all the clocks ahead of schedule, and I'd smack the angel in charge and tell him to have a heart.

I lift myself from the sofa and hesitate when I see my boots off to the side and I flashback, just for a second, of the time I lost my first pair of boots to a teacher with weak shinbones, and I decide to let my boots remain where they are beside the sofa and I turn to check the clock on the wall.

'Ten o'clock,' I say. 'That's it?'

'Did you expect to be finished by now?'

'I'm not sure what I expected. It feels a helluva lot more than two hours.'

'No need to hurry, is there? You booked the whole day, didn't you?'

I don't answer but instead go to the bar in the corner of the office and pour myself a glass of Fiji water. There's no scotch or gin.

'I almost went to Fiji,' I say. 'Did I tell you about that?'

'No, you didn't. Would you like to tell me about Fiji?'

I've grown accustomed to the intrusive questions so I drink the water down and place the glass back on the counter. From behind me I can still hear the rain pounding the windows and the low lamp lights make the office lie in heavy afternoon-like shadows.

'Still raining?' I say.

'Did you expect for the weather to be clear by now? Do you have another appointment to keep? Plans you'd like to tell me about?'

'In fact, yes.'

I walk to the windows and find the city sinking in fog, mist, and an endless streaming of computational codes in the ancient dialect of rain. I return to the sofa and begin by telling you of my father's twenty-fifth birthday.

One Wednesday night, my Grand-Daddy, Reverend CG, preached a sermon from the pulpit with a fiery zest I'm sure he believed he was forever altering the life-courses of the men, women and children seated in pew after pew, row upon row in the congregation at the Assembly of God church I told you about. The energy buzzed the room into 'Amen' after 'Hallelujah' and Reverend CG's face grew redder and more intense as he neared the climax of his sermon when my father, who was not my father at the time but still just a boy himself, burst through the doors at the back of the assembly hall filled with the spirit — cognac, rye, whiskey, vodka, take your pick — and the spirit filled Henry so he shouted above all to hear,

'Praise be to God! Praise the Lord! Hall-a-loooo-yah! God bless our beautiful America!' Henry ran down the center aisle waving his arms above his head. 'Amen, Amen, Amen! Praise the Jesus! Praise the sweet Jesus!'

One need not imagine the Reverend gripping his Holy Bible in a half-instinct to hurl the testament down upon Henry's head from on high, much the way Moses did to the wayward peoples of his time, but before Reverend CG could hurl that Great Book at his son, two laymen had Henry by the arms and dragged him up the aisle and out of view and earshot of the wide-eyed believers whispering and giggling and snickering and the men slapping their thighs in jest with their Bibles and the mothers uncovering their babies' ears and the almighty Reverend saying, 'Now, where were we?'

I've always associated myself with my father's parents, the Reverend and the Organist, and I recall fondly of vacations at Grand-Mommy and Grand-Daddy's lake house in Breckenridge, once home to a little more than five thousand souls.

To drive there from Brownwood took about an hour, and my father would drive north alone with his three children to deposit us at the doorstep of the lake house for the weekend and immediately get back in the car and drive back to spend Friday night and the days that would follow with his wife alone.

Sometimes Chadwick, Cassandra and I stayed at the lake house for a week playing outside in large sand pits we built into underground forts, but that'd end when Chadwick would jump on the roof of my cave in hopes of burying me alive; or we'd fish with Grand-Daddy out on a thin strip of land that jutted out into the lake from morning to noon, and then we'd pack up the tackle and net and take the fish, maybe two or three trout, back to the house to be cleaned and prepared for supper. We'd play hide-and-seek, a game I didn't like too much none because Cassandra and Chadwick would leave me to hiding in a stuffy closet for an hour to go play outside or watch television. When I came out, they'd say they couldn't find me, that I had won the game, and I'd fuss and tell them I didn't care too much for winning, but what I did care for was that we'd have time to play together because one day we'd all grow up, grow old, and grow to become different people all together. That didn't seem to bother them none.

What I loved most about the lake house were the times Grand-Daddy would take Chadwick and Cassandra into town and I'd have the whole house with Grand-Mommy, the one I told you used to read to me about Louis Pasteur.

Grand-Mommy and I would have the whole house, quiet and calm, together and she seemed to enjoy my company as much as I enjoyed hers. She, old but still beautiful, made me a peanut butter sandwich with a glass of cold milk and I'd sit on a high stool at the counter in the middle of the kitchen. She would stand across from me and lean on the counter, and I'd look to my left and see the bay windows reveal the body of the lake forty yards downhill, and she'd tell me over lunch of how Chadwick cried when he was a baby and Cassandra, in a time before my birth, would sleepwalk at night around the lake house and pee in a random corner behind some door. Milk would spill out my nose and she'd help me get cleaned up, and I loved her more for the time and attention and care she gave me. We were friends and we knew it.

I'd eat my lunch listening to her stories and looking out at the lake and I'd think this was the most perfect day of my rather short life. Then Grand-Mommy would speak to me of sacred omens and signs that taught men and women and even boys like me which was the correct path to go, and she'd tell me of the legendary Big Bird — not small like a wren or kingfisher, but great and big like a wood stork — but I was young and I kept thinking of *Sesame Street* and how a giant yellow bird would somehow dance in the middle of the lake, and she'd tell me how we couldn't see Big Bird now, at lunch, because he'd come at dawn or dusk, but if I were lucky enough to wake early to watch the sunrise, as she often did, I just might catch a glimpse of the magical bird right out yonder, and then, like her, I'd know I was going to have a great day.

One morning shortly after that lunch, I woke before dawn to a cold, dark house to go pee, and after finding the house frozen in time, a stillness to the lake house that seemed to age me by decades into an old man like my Grand-Daddy, I rubbed my eyes, yawned, scratched my butt and remembered my Grand-Mommy's story about the enchanted bird in the lake waters.

I crept into the giant kitchen, a bit grayer than the rest of the sleeping house, and I hoped to steal upon my Grand-Mommy by the bay windows to hold her hand and look for the Big Bird, but she wasn't there.

The bottom of the bay windows came down to my stomach and I adjusted my eyes to the landscape of land and water, searching for a yellow bird from *Sesame Street* flapping its crazy wings.

The lake, empty and still like the house behind me, carried the coming dawn gently with each wave sloshing to shore; and then there in the low light of a new day, barely visible near the trees half in and half out of the water, standing on one leg in the shallows, a white wood stork turned its head back towards the lake house and looked directly at me. Big Bird and I locked eyes, our souls sharing secrets, and I could hear its thoughts and I believed it heard mine, but the majestic wood stork seemed to speak to me of my future — not just the day ahead but a long life filled with wonders still strange to me then. A minute or two must've passed, no more than five, in this way — bird and boy together in a shared instance of immortality — when the sun eased high enough to cast its light onto Big Bird standing in the lake. The wood stork twisted its head away from me, seemed to turn its face to the sun, spread its great wings wide and flew low over the water at first and then with a few mighty flaps Big Bird ascended and flew off, away over the lake, leaving me in the lake house watching my first sunrise alone.

Matthew 7:24-27: where were we?

That's right. I grew up loving nature and the outdoors more than a classroom and an office. Being next to a lake appealed to me, and I'd often skip university classes on a Tuesday or a Thursday and drive out to Lake Brownwood near the spillway, a massive dam you could drive across or get out and look to one side a beautiful still lake and on the other side a gushing and rushing of water-jets feeding to rocks below. On the left there used to be a parking area where you could get out and walk down to the water's edge or do like I would do and head off into the trees along the shore and down winding trails which split and forked into high and low paths, but as long as you kept the water off to your right and in sight you'd be fine.

In high school some of my closest friends — Karolina, Nora, Dan Martin, Joseph Gardner — and I would go smoke marijuana out on a boulder, like a giant's toe, that rose out of the water and remained a bit hidden from the trail. Sometimes we'd strip in the heat and jump off that giant rock into the icy-chill of the lake.

In university I stopped getting high, stopped smoking marijuana; God knows I had smoked enough — my party days and nights ended with the toll of the high school graduation bell — and I'd come out to the rock on a clear day when I should be in a university literature class studying Coleridge or Shelley or Wordsworth and I'd strip, leave behind those British poets, and sunbathe in the cool of the morning hours.

I'd sit on that rock looking at Brownwood Lake for hours and I'd think of my grandparents' lake house and the white wood stork and my Grand-Mommy, who died in the summer of my eighth-grade year and how I visited her in one of Abilene's hospitals for the last time and how the hospital room smelled of raw death and that was how I knew my Grand-Mommy was going to die and even sitting on that rock I couldn't hold back the tears. I'd sit and think of my mother's ring when I'd turn and see the spillway off to my right, and I'd have to relive that rainy day all over again until I'd grow a bit angry about the ring and the eventual divorce and turn my back to the spillway and face the open body of water sporting an occasional boat or two out for a mid-morning jaunt.

I'd think of Alexandra Earp, a girl I'd briefly dated in my eighth-grade year, and how we fell in love, quietly and innocently and shyly as young teens can, and how she moved away that same summer before we could have sex, before she could have been my first. My friends said she moved down to Austin, but back then without the internet, she could've moved to China for all I knew. Alexandra Earp was gone just like that. Before I could overcome my shyness, overcome my fear of being physically attracted to her, she was gone. Gone was the first young girl I had ever wanted as my true girlfriend, to kiss and to hold and to talk to. But her mother got a job and left Brownwood. I'd find out years later, when I was forty, that Alexandra moved with her mother to Abilene and how Alexandra would graduate as a junior and then move to Beaumont when she was twenty-one. In the eighth grade, though, I knew none of that. Alexandra was the one I wanted as my girlfriend, and she sincerely loved me back because she could be herself around me. But just like that, the Universe dealt me blow after blow. My Grand-Mommy was gone. Alexandra was gone.

Out there on the lake on that rock, if I got too angry, I'd try to recall John Keats and my favorite poem — 'When I have fears that I may cease to be' — and other poets like Frost, Hughes, Billy Collins, Auden, Eliot, Emily Dickinson, Whitman and oh so many more. The poets would calm me beside the lake, and at times I knew that days like that one was far better and more rewarding than any other day spent in a classroom.

The rock would grow warm beneath me and I'd sit and think of my sister who I nearly lost once or twice and I'd worry about the time — if it ever did come — when the world would become too much for my big sister Cassandra and I'd lose her for good.

I'd often sit out on that rock by the lake thinking of Karolina, my high school sweetheart I'd lost a few years before, and our daughter Alicen Beth, who wasn't even a year old yet, and how she'd never know that her mother and father really did love and care for one another once. How my daughter would grow and I'd only ever be just a shadow of a memory of a thought about a young man her grandparents had known for a brief time. I'd sit and dream about what kind of woman she'd be in twenty years and where'd I'd be and if we'd know one another. Evelyn Romig, one of my literature professors, asked the class once what our most perfect day would be like, and I had lied and made up some bullshit but I kept thinking about the days I spent alone on that rock by the lake and I couldn't think of a better day than that.

I'd sit on that rock by the lake and think about all my high school friends I'd lost — some to the facts of life: we grew apart; some to university moves: we moved apart; and some to death: we just — well, we just.

I'd imagine my cousin Brighton Cambridge, the one I told you about who died too young, and I'd imagine he sat beside me there on that rock next to the lake. We'd speak of loved ones; he'd ask after Chadwick and Cassandra, and I'd tell him they were both fine but he'd need to watch over Cassandra, she needed more help than most. Then Brighton would ask about me and how I was doing and I'd try to change the subject by reminding him of how I used to love to play football with him and Cassandra and Chadwick on Thanksgiving Day out on the top hill overlooking Papaw and Mamaw's cabin in Monroe, Louisiana, and how we'd get cold and have to come in away from the pine trees to a cozy home smelling of hot turkey and sweet potatoes, or I'd tell Brighton, who loved Superman above all other heroes, of all the new movies about the comic book heroes we grew up reading, and he'd shake his head at me and ask me again about how I was doing and why I was all alone on a rock by a lake. I didn't have an answer for him then and I still don't. I'd already be quiet on the outside but I'd say aloud, 'I don't know, Bright. I just don't know.' Internally I'd grow silent, staring out over the lake, and any imaginings or dreamings would cease and I'd become even more still and solid, like the great Buddha must've been beneath the Bodhi tree, and I'd try not to think of anything or anyone and for a time I'd succeed. I'd be at peace with myself and the world.

I'd continue, though, to sit for a while longer on that rock by the lake and wonder if my dreams of becoming a novelist would come true, become realized, and I'd wonder if I was ever going to ever get out of that crummy little town — which I later grew to love — but at that time I'd spent my whole life, some twenty years, in Brownwood and the city felt like a black hole that kept sucking and pulling and devouring the best parts of my soul until I had no choice but to give up and to give in and quit my dreams and become the 'model' citizen.

I hated that crummy little city in that crummy county that was first measured in 1846 by William Wallace, a deputy surveyor for the Bexar Land District. By 1856, Welcome W. Chandler, Israel Clements and James H. Fowler, the first cattleman in the area, settled in Brown County, established on August 27, 1856 by the

Texas State Legislature and so named for Henry Stevenson Brown, commander at the Battle of Velasco. I imagined I'd end up like these men, forgotten and buried and stuck in this crummy county and crummy town.

'Bullshit!' I'd say aloud. I'd shake my head, look between my legs at the rock that was growing hotter, and think to myself how I could never be someone who quit and gave up so easily on anything, especially my childhood dreams; I mean, that was all I had, a huge chunk of my soul, my very existence and if I didn't have that, then what did I have?

I'd think about how damn hard it was to live in this world, but how much harder my life would be if I had no dream to cling to, to work towards, to achieve, and that was how I came to dedicate myself to being a writer, as a novelist, and how I told myself I'd never-never-never give up on my dream, and that no matter what I'd get there in the end.

The sun would be good and hot by then and I'd stand and have one last look out over the lake, my nude body exposed to the freedoms of the world, bordered by the edges of my reality, and then I'd take my time and dress and hike back up the trail to my car where I'd parked it.

I'd look one last time at the spillway and say, 'never-never-never,' and then I'd turn back to the lake to add, 'for you, Grand-Mommy,' and turn my car around and drive back to town listening to the wind rushing in through the car windows and feel how good it felt to have the wind rustle my hair and to still be so fucking young.

I forgot to mention the dream I had last night. I was twenty again and I discovered Karolina had written a book for children and, more shockingly, aborted our baby and buried the body far out in the countryside. My brother Chadwick, acting as some sort of guide, appeared alongside Karolina in the dream and the more his presence entered the dream the angrier I became. Karolina led us to a place near the unmarked grave of my unborn daughter but she became lost and couldn't remember exactly where she was going or where she needed to go. 'How could you not know?' I remember saying, but like in most dreams I couldn't hear my voice. Then Chadwick defended her and by that time my tolerance for that smug bastard extinguished and I wrapped my hands around his throat, as my father had done to me once, and began choking Chadwick as hard as I could. I believe fear crossed my mind telling me that I would kill him if I continued, but as I told you earlier, I often do the exact opposite of fear and so I squeezed harder. Then I woke up, relieved I was not killing my brother. I've never had that dream before and I'm not sure why I had it last night.

Tell me about the time your father choked you, you say.

Christ, where does one begin?

It must've been early 2000 or 2001, I can't be certain, but I'd place my money on the latter, because shortly after the incident with my father, I spent the summer of 2001 in the lake house out on Lake Brownwood writing my first book, a novella called *A Father's Son*, and I remember that time well because my sister would often visit me during that summer to drink Corona and swim in the lake, and when Cassandra wasn't there I was either working as a roofer under John Ferryman, working on my book, or making love to my girlfriend Juliet — I had been her first lover — and my fair, green-eyed Juliet had been the factor which ignited a chain of events no one foresaw when we woke one Sunday morning.

I still lived with my father out on Pine Creek Ranch in the early part of 2001 and my relationship with Juliet had been new but I was ready enough to introduce her to my parents, so I arranged a Sunday lunch at Underwood's Cafeteria, a barbecue and steak house, for my mother and father to meet Juliet. But like most women in my life back then, I would soon be disappointed and should've known not to trust her.

After I'd been working all night, my father woke me early Sunday morning to remind me about the lunch date and I rolled over in bed and said yes, we'd be there around noon. I had planned to drive and pick Juliet up but less than an hour later — my parents already on their way to church — Juliet called and left a message on the answering machine, which I heard activate from the bedroom, and she basically said she wouldn't be able to make it to lunch.

'Shit,' I said and rubbed my face trying to make sense of what was happening out of my control. I called my mother's house but she didn't have an answering machine and there was no point because she wasn't there anyway. I had no honest way to contact my parents, being before the popularity and commonplaceness of cellphones and smartphones, and I thought I could just shower and meet them for lunch anyway, but to tell you the truth I became extremely bummed out about not meeting Juliet, depressed even, and didn't feel like my parents should have to waste money on me. So, I went back to bed and slept a soundless sleep; after all, I figured my parents would wait then eat and come home and I'd be able to explain everything and they'd act as reasonable adults and would understand the occasion had been out of my control.

Sometime later, for me that is, my father banged open the door to my bedroom, burst in shouting, 'Get up. Get up, you lazy sonuvabitch!'

'What?' I rolled over and up to my elbows to try and determine if the house had caught fire or what could be the big deal.

In my boxer shorts I came into the living room with my mother calmly sitting on the sofa by the windows and my father, obviously pissed off, pacing the room with red puffed-out cheeks like a bull angered in a Spanish coliseum, and I thought 'shit,' not only had my day started off badly it was about to get a whole lot worse.

'Where were you?!'

'In bed, obviously.' My father didn't appreciate my answer. 'Where were you?' I asked. In my family, for some masochistic subversion, we tended to ask one another the same question, repeating each other, in an argument in order to create equal footing for control — not a method I'd recommend.

'We were waiting for you, Cody,' my mother said.

'For over two hours,' my father added.

'Why did you do that?' I remember thinking it quite absurd for anyone to wait two hours. I'd wait thirty minutes tops, then I'd enjoy a little barbecue for lunch and be on my merry way.

'We were waiting for you,' my father said. 'And your *little* girlfriend.' His tone made his intent clear.

'Henry,' my mother said.

'Juliet canceled at the last minute. It wasn't my fault.'

'Why didn't you tell us?'

'How?' I let out a laugh at the sheer impossibility of his request and the absurdity of the argument. By this time, I was still half-asleep and not taking the conversation too seriously.

'You could have called Underwood's.'

'The restaurant? You've got to be kidding.'

'You think I'm kidding?'

'Henry.'

'What, Gwendolen? Your son left us sitting outside in the parking lot for over two hours. This is his fault.'

'It's no one's fault,' my mother said, but Henry didn't want reasoning.

'Why didn't you just eat without me?'

My father turned to me with a tremor finding his jaw and spite in his eyes.

I can't be sure when or how the discussion soured but the beast escaped its cage of restraint and proper etiquette and the argument heated and more subversion followed and at some point my father said he was taking away my car keys, his last bit of control over me.

Once, years later, Henry would interrupt a pleasant dinner I was having with my mother and her then boyfriend, Vincent, at the man's house on Vincent Street, which I found ironic because his home was just a few blocks away from my childhood home where Cassandra fell out of the back of the truck and cracked her skull in the driveway. Regarding my father, the police had to be called because no matter how civil Vincent and I spoke to Henry, he'd become irate and more unreasonable — so no one can blame me for leaving Texas and my family behind. Henry even told the police officer he wanted to take half my car because he had cosigned the purchase, and for several minutes he attempted to steal the battery in front of us until he found the car door locked and the police officer said he'd have to leave the premises or he'd be arrested. 'Yeah, arrest him,' I remember saying. 'The man's crazy. Fucking insane.' And when my father became angry, that's exactly what he was: crazy.

On the Sunday I was supposed to meet Juliet, Henry grabbed my car keys, much to my mother's protest, because he said I didn't deserve the responsibility of a car if I didn't know how to be responsible and meet him for lunch like I said I was going to do.

By this time we were both good and angry and I ended up breaking his ugly, old brown recliner and a small glass table next to it — both I'd later replace out of my own money — but he lurched out at me and we wrestled for a few seconds until I realized how small and weak my father had become and I tossed him to the side and onto the floor. He got up and attacked me again and I grabbed him by the upper-part of the arms and threw him as hard and as far as I could. He landed with a thud against a wall.

'Stop fighting,' my mother screamed.

I didn't hesitate the second time and I straddled my father by sitting on his stomach and holding his shoulders to the ground. I had him pinned, defeated, and he knew it. He should've just given up.

'Stop fighting,' I said. 'I don't want to fight you. So just —'

I noticed then I was unable to speak and instantly attempted to draw a breath, but failing, I could not breathe. My father had his hands around my throat squeezing to save his life, squeezing to take mine.

'Stop it, Henry!' my mother screamed. 'You're hurting him.'

For an instant, complete violence swept my mind and I knew if I were to escape, I'd have to bash my father's brains into the carpet, but I couldn't bring myself to do it. Another second passed and his hands released my throat.

I gasped for air as I stood off to the side clutching my throat, oxygen slowly returning.

'What are you trying to do?' my mother said. 'Kill your son?'

'God, Gwendolen. He started it.'

'Yeah, Henry,' and I'd always call him by his first name after that day, 'are you crazy? Are you fucking insane?'

'Watch your mouth in front of your mother.'

'Fuck you,' I said. 'Go fuck yourself.'

'I'm getting my shotgun,' Henry said. 'I want you outta here.'

'Henry, just stop it,' my mother pleaded. 'Just stop it.'

'Get your fucking gun you fucking pussy. I'm outta here.'

I went to my bedroom and threw on a T-shirt and jeans and my shoes and walked out the front door and down the steps. I stumbled and one of my shoes came off but by this time Henry had opened the front door and I could see the twelve-gauge in his hands.

'Get off my property!'

I had already made about twenty yards down the gravel road — not running, not walking too quickly, just walking in a rage — and I turned back, shouted, 'Shoot me,' and with both hands flipped Henry the middle fingers and yelled, 'Go fuck yourself!'

I limped down the gravel road with one shoe and didn't look back when I heard the shotgun blast. By that time, I didn't give a shit. The day had gone beyond repair, beyond human decency. As I walked to the end of the gravel road where the mailboxes signaled the paved road leading back to town, I thought — as I placed the remaining shoe in the mailbox — how I could never live with either Henry or Gwendolen ever again. I didn't belong to them anymore and I could no longer relate to the people they'd become or to who they'd always been. Henry and Gwendolen had become strangers to me and in their physical presence I saw the failings of human endeavor, smelt the stench from the gross absurdities found in the undereducated. The impoverished souls stained with too much anger stemming from an excess of too much regret was the driving force to keep me walking, barefooted, down the pavement, mile after fucking mile into town and to Dylan's house some fifteen miles away, without ever once looking back — and for much of my life, I've done just that. And no one could ever walk a mile in my shoes, I was thinking then, because I had none.

On another ordinary day in the lives of men and women, the night of October 17 found me celebrating my twenty-fourth birthday alone over a shot of tequila, a margarita with rocks and some fajitas at a Mexican restaurant down the road from my apartment. As a kid, my parents would take our family to Mexican restaurants for our birthday parties. At first, when I was younger, we always went to Pulido's, and years later when we were teenagers, we'd have a quiet lunch or dinner at Gomez's. To compare those two Mexican restaurants, Pulido's was nicer and cleaner but didn't have as good as hot sauce (salsa) and chips as Gomez's restaurant. I'm not sure if Gomez's is still there or not, but Pulido's would close down for good in 2006, the same year I left Texas for South Korea.

As a young man, I had not minded eating alone. I had often gone out to eat alone since I was eighteen because I disliked having roommates, but on the night that triggered a change within which would lead me to jump out of a perfectly good airplane, I sat alone on my birthday and listened to the waiters and waitresses sing 'Happy Birthday' to someone in a group seated at a table opposite mine. What were the odds?

Back then I kept telling myself I hadn't found the perfect person for me and I didn't mind waiting for the one to complete me, make me whole, to become my better half. I'm not trying to sound mawkish; I just want to set the context on the depressing night I had, which would not have been so bad were it not for the birthday party at the table next to mine. What were the odds?

At that point in my life I had lived alone for two years, worked at American Capital by day, Monday to Friday, eight to six, while studying for a master's in literature in the evening, feeling braindead most nights, working on a short story collection I'd later call *The New America*, which would end up a finalist in the 2008 Indie Excellence Awards — for what it's worth — and on top of all that I had little to no time to visit my family, especially my daughter who would be five that December, and minus time spent for going to the gym and chores, I'd attempt to relax by reading Hemingway's *For Whom the Bell Tolls* for the first time by the fire in my apartment, so you can see why I didn't have many friends and why I enjoyed a quiet dinner alone on my twenty-fourth birthday. I'd be forty years old by the time I'd re-read Hemingway's book.

Still, something profound and eternal troubled me all through my solitary birthday dinner when I looked into the eyes of a wooden statue in the likeness of a Native American war chief (why they had that statue at a Mexican restaurant. I'll never know). I drove home to sit for an hour or two out on the balcony smoking cherry tobacco from my pipe, and that 'something' would be the deciding vote to propel me forward a following month to go skydiving.

How I chanced on the idea I'm still not sure, but I did some research online and found a company, which I discovered to be professional and affordable, an hour or two away in West Texas, in the middle of the wilderness.

I'd be lying to you if I told you I wanted to jump out of the plane for adventure, to create a bold new experience. No. The reason for my jumping had been a bit more sinister and twisted than a thrill junkie's desire to meet with the possibility of death.

No. It had been none of that. My reason was a test. I'd grown tired of the routine — working, studying, writing, studying, writing, working, writing, working, studying — all backed by rejection after rejection after rejection after rejection after rejection. Other factors included a lack of forward progress, stunted momentum and stagnation. Meanwhile the Universe remained removed and silent to my struggles and dreams of becoming a novelist. The harder I worked at achieving some semblance of success the more the world seemed to shit on me, and I couldn't keep circling in the hamster cage without a sliver of justification, a sign from above.

The test was simple. If I jumped and died, I'd know — or not, because that would've been all she wrote — that the Universe no longer could lie to me, telling me I was someone extraordinary when in fact I had become a pile of mashed bones and muscle because of a failed parachute. But if I jumped and did survive, the Universe would be telling me that I was worth a whole helluva a lot and for me to continue, to persist, on the path set before me and to know the future could be a beautiful mystery. In plain speech, I was ready to die — not in a morbid wish to end my existence, but in a desire to confirm myself to the world, to the Universe, to God.

The drive out I left the stereo off and listened to the wind rush free through my car, watched the world for one last time — if I died, I died, but if I lived, I knew I'd be different — and I spoke softly to the Universe about not having any regrets and about the confirmation regarding my Personal Legend I needed for my survival, for my sanity, for peace to find my love.

Training for a solo jump from five thousand feet, after signing the necessary forms and release waivers, could not have been simpler and lasted just under three hours. The training coordinator spoke gently but firmly and covered each piece of equipment and the steps to get me from the ground to the plane and back to the ground safely.

When he hooked me to a simulator — a mock parachute suspended a few feet off the ground — I was stunned to discover how common 'twist lines' were and how easy twisted lines could kill the skydiver. Much like how the playground swings and their chains can become twisted after spinning in a circle, the twist lines could easily be untwisted by doing three things: pull, kick, twist. First, I'd have to pull the lines on the parachute apart, kick out strongly to create a spin, and the lines would twist out and become free. Then I'd have to tug the chords to extend the parachute to full inflation. All that would be left would be to manage the descent by pulling either the left or right chords to guide me in a wide spiral down-down-down, like water winding down a drain.

Suited up, the training coordinator clipped on my helmet with the video camera attached and we marched to the Cessna out on the hot tarmac. Getting into the plane was one kind of emotion — like part of an expected routine — but jumping out of the plane when there's nothing wrong with it was a whole new set of emotions — like confusion wrapped in quitting and the acceptance one needs to have to honorably face death. The training coordinator had told me that once the plane crossed into the drop zone the door would open and I'd need to jump. Hesitation, of any sort, could not be tolerated. The small plane had been louder than I'd expected and the training coordinator had to yell for me to hear him.

'Nearing the DZ,' he said as the plane climbed to five thousand feet where the air cooled and time slowed. 'Get ready.'

I gave a thumbs up, as I'd been instructed to do for any kind of communication, and nodded my consent.

The training coordinator leaned over, pulled on a latch and the door instantly shot open. Down below the airfield and hangers appeared like lines and squares drawn on a piece of paper. If I had once known what it was like to be incredibly small, a Thumbling to the world, I understood then what it was like to be a great giant in any one of the fables and fairytales of old.

Cars inched along like lazy ants, and I thought, 'shit, that's far.'

For a few seconds a cold fear gripped my muscles and I thought back to that same fear that had once possessed me on an Olympic diving board high above a swimming pool, and I became aware of my earlier training then as a child to overcome a fear which controls far too many people in this world.

'Go,' the training coordinator shouted. 'Go, go, go.'

My knees failed me but I didn't need them. I crawled to the open door where the training coordinator hooked my chute to the outside of the plane, setting a rip line to automatically open my chute, and I continued crawling outside the plane into air flying by at incredible speeds.

I stepped onto a tiny platform for one foot to position itself as I held tight to the wing of the plane and eased myself farther out. While holding fast to the wing, I removed my foot from the platform and for several moments I hung off the wing, flying one with the plane. As instructed, I turned to my left to check the signal, saw the thumbs up, the all clear to release, and I let go of the plane.

The wind velocity pushed me back and I separated from the plane, from everything I'd ever known in this world. For two or three seconds I felt like I hadn't moved at all, that the plane had continued zooming forward but I had stopped, stayed in the same place, locked in a time and space far beyond any boundaries I had ever known, and I kept thinking how the world continued onward in that plane and now I was heading in a different direction.

Then I spun facing the ground, the chute opened and thrust me upward in a hard jerk. Instinctually I looked up, saw the lines twisted — my death knocking and the door cracking open — and I pulled, kicked, spun. The lines untwisted and when I yanked the chords, the chute opened wide and full and slowed my momentum.

On the radio attached to my chest I heard the ground coordinator guiding me left, then right, in a wide circle, easing a gradual descent for the next twenty minutes or so.

At first, I freaked. The ground thousands of feet below me haunted me like the dark depths of an ocean beneath my floating legs. I attempted to keep me from falling, but I soon realized there was nothing above me but the chute and that alone I would have to trust, and that I did.

Instead of looking down, I looked up and far over the countryside, to the small mountains and smaller hills, and for the first time in my life I saw and felt the way eagles and falcons see and feel. Like drops of rain sliding down a window so did the cars trudge along the highway. The man-made world revealed its greatest lie to me then and it showed me how truly miniscule and insignificant human civilization really was when compared and set against the natural wonders of the known world high above. I flew as birds fly. I breathed air unknown to most other mortals. I drank in the Universe one millisecond at a time. Time and Space ceased for me as I shifted left as though a hawk leans to its side and enjoys the new rush of wind on its feathers. That *something* I had discovered on my birthday to be so profound and terrible and eternal broke its chains from me and I became free, ever since.

Soon the ground would rush up to meet me — though I wanted to stay high in the air, live there if I could and be no longer attached to a world that held more problems than solutions.

My ecstasy would see me safely to the ground, which met me with a bump to my butt, and such immortal delights from my flight would find me in my car driving back in silence, a buzzing in my ears, in my heart, while the videotape of my experience sat as the only passenger in the seat next to me, a crude witness to my glory, and the endless calm of being up there with my head in the clouds would follow me back to my empty apartment that Sunday evening in San Angelo.

Years later the visions I had while being suspended between heaven and earth would be my guide as I boarded the plane at DFW international airport to leave Texas and my American past behind for an international one and to help the world and its people become a bit better, more united, less dependent on fear, and to become more open to experiences which share and teach us to cherish love. But I knew one thing for sure: America was far more country than city.

There's something very instinctual about not wanting to show people you're injured or hurt, not wanting to show people your injuries, your pain, your scars, your broken parts.

My mother, God bless her soul, would shut the door to her bedroom more times than I could count and cry into her hands or a pillow. I had to live with those sobs for a good five years after the divorce and at the time, foolish as it may have been, I despised her sorrow, because she was crying as a result of her mistakes, her loneliness, and I doubted at the time that any pain could be attributed to a regret for her actions which led to an infidelity and then to a divorce, breaking to pieces the family she nurtured. She'd cry for hours and my knocks would go unanswered and after a time she'd come out and refresh herself in the bathroom and put on airs as though she needed no one.

The instinctual part of hiding our pain, our wounds, must've come from a time when the tribe, the clan, the community demanded peak performance in a kill-or-be-killed attitude, and even the Spartans adopted the anachronistic disgust of disfavoring the weak by tossing to their deaths any newborn babe found to be flawed, unfit, and as I consider my clubfoot I know I would've been one of the uncountable infants ordered to an early grave. But who is strong enough to fight human nature?

Just this morning, on my way to your office I saw a young man limping from an injured left knee and the young man attempted to conceal his injury by wearing trekking boots and using a hiking staff for support. He could have been hurt on an early climb but I don't think so. An understanding of human nature and a little common sense — okay, a lot of common sense — can be combined to better perceive the conditions of a person's mind. As long as I had known John Ferryman, a true friend when you needed one, he had been all laughs and all smiles. In the summer of 2001, with gas prices steadily rising, I rented a lake house and began a summer job, which I loathed, as a roofer under John Ferryman, whose father owned the company.

I'd wake at six, right about the time a silver dawn yawned and stretched itself over the rolling lake, shower and have a few cups of coffee while I did my morning reading — I was reading either

The Sun Also Rises, *Death in the Afternoon*, or Steinbeck's *To a God Unknown* — and by seven I'd drive into town taking Highway 279 then take a left on East Commerce Street which I'd follow into Early and to the roofing project at Heartland Mall.

Now that it comes to me: Riverside Park had been off East Commerce next to the Pecan Bayou and not near the ballfields across town by 3M. Festival Park had been near Gordon Wood Stadium and the baseball complex I told you about. I haven't been back in almost twenty years, and the mind certainly does begin to play tricks, doesn't it?

Heartland Mall, just off of Highway 183 where that church with the peach tree I told you about was located in my childhood, but now as a summer roofer, twenty-one years old and in what I thought to be my prime, I'd drive into the empty parking lot to Heartland Mall, that reminds me now of a scene out of Cormac's *The Road*, silent and void of existence, and I'd drive around back and park a good ways away from the building. Sometimes I'd be early and I'd roll the windows down, recline, and listen to *Pearl Jam*'s 'Yellow Ledbetter' or 'Black' and wait for John and the others to show.

The heavy equipment, like the boiler, we'd lock and leave overnight. When the others started to arrive in the company trucks, which I had to do at first until I told John the inconvenience and gas money would be too much to bear he laughed and said why not, as long as I showed up on time he was fine with it, but it did run against custom. That was all right, I remember saying, I like going against custom; uncontested traditions have always bothered me, made me feel uneasy, and I'm not at all sure why.

When the team arrived, I popped the trunk, rolled up the windows and locked the doors. In the trunk I kept the roofing company's long-sleeved tan shirt covered in spots of tar, a grimy cap and work gloves. After grabbing these I'd slam the trunk lid shut and head to the side of the building where John, the team leader, organized the others, and every day he gave pretty much the same speech:

'Drink lots of fluid,' he'd say. 'It's free and today's going over a hundred.'

'No rain?' I'd joke, because if it rained, work would be canceled. We'd laugh and John would quip,

'If it rains, we don't get paid.'

José and Miguel and Anselmo would tease me. José, the oldest, would give me a playful punch on the arm as we waited to climb the ladder to the roof and he'd say, '*Pobrecito*,' meaning 'poor little thing,' and he'd use this word '*pobrecito*' at every break, once in the morning and once in the afternoon, and at every lunch, at around eleven. I'd hear nothing but *pobrecito* as a response to anything I said and for the longest time I had no idea what the word meant, but as the days grew hotter, filled with the buckets of our sweat, I grew to love José and his brotherly affection. José meant well and meant no harm, and we'd tease one another all day any way.

In the morning I didn't need to climb the ladder but I'd do it anyway, wanting to scout out the lay of the previous day's work and compare this mental image with the one from the end of the day. John would fuss and tell me to get back down and start heating the boiler.

'In a minute,' I'd say. 'Give me a minute.'

José would turn to Miguel and Anselmo and say, '*Pobrecito* misses us,' and John, Miguel and the others would laugh and I'd grin.

We'd begin by eight every morning, break at ten and two and be done by five, and the job was hard-dirty labor, but at that age I enjoyed the outdoor work and the sore muscles that came with it. I'd climb back down the ladder and start the boiler and every twenty minutes or so I'd drop in a log of solid tar to melt and pump up to the rooftop where Miguel would fill a wheelbarrow with the scalding, liquid tar and wheel the load over to John, José, Anselmo and two others who'd be laying the stuff down with mops and shoveling bits of gravel into the mix.

I'd sit in the shade for twenty minutes, reload another log to keep the flow high and strong, monitor the temperature and return to drink from my personal cooler off in the shade of the building, and I'd think how people do this kind of work for a living, day in and day out for fifty years or more, all across the country, all across the world, and how they were paid shitty wages, and I'd known then how important university was to me and how much I enjoyed working with my mind more than my hands, something very different from my father.

At lunch I rarely ate and yet I'd climb up to check on the others and mentally record how much we'd been able to do that morning and how far we had to go. One by one we'd climb down and sit on the grass, laying bits of cardboard down first, beneath the shade of a few trees and I'd watch them eat their lunch. José and Miguel and Anselmo would bring Mexican dishes from their home — usually homemade tortillas with meat — John would have chips and a sandwich.

I'd drink the iced Gatorade and dream of the cold water at the lake with Juliet in my arms, and the roofers would laugh during the teasing jests we'd pass our simple meals with. Then we'd slip our caps down over our faces and try to get a bit of rest before starting back at high noon, and I always felt good resting alongside those men because we were men doing men's work and no matter how bad or how hot things got, we could laugh at our circumstances and who we were. There was a certain quality, a realness, an authenticity in all of that.

One afternoon, sometime after three when the day seemed to become paper thin and most unbearable and I'd want to collapse, Miguel slipped on the roof and fell onto the liquid tar. From the ground I heard his screams and John leaned over the edge of the roof and yelled for me to call an ambulance, and I held out my gloves and said, 'How? With what?'

I ran around the side of the building and into the department store and looked around for an employee. One sales assistant, some girl no more than sixteen or seventeen, asked me if I needed help and I told her to call an ambulance and did my best to explain the current situation and ran back outside to see John's truck whizzing by the boiler and out the parking lot of Heartland Mall.

I climbed the ladder and found from José that Miguel slipped in the liquid tar and had half his lower back and legs and arms covered in the stuff that when it cools it dries quick and stays attached to anything it touches, including flesh. José explained how

John had been the one to set Miguel down off the roof and into the truck and drive the young boy to the hospital where I'd been born across town. We shook our heads, said *pobrecito*, and examined the scene with Anselmo acting out the part of Miguel and we'd shake our heads even more, have a smoke and say our well-wishes, we'd hope he'd be okay. We really did hope he'd be fine, but we knew better. We knew what life was really like. *Scars and pain*.

In the end I never saw or heard of Miguel again. John said Miguel would have to take a break for a while and heal up, and John told me things had been pretty bad, bad enough you just didn't want to talk about our even joke about it. Miguel's accident shook me up and one day I climbed to the roof and told John I couldn't go on doing what I was doing, how this job wasn't really me, who I was as a person — which must've looked silly at the sight of me in a tar-covered shirt and pants, an old sweaty cap and sunglasses — and he had laughed when José said, '*Pobrecito*,' but John told me to go on and take the day off and have a nice cold beer or six and to get some sleep and come back tomorrow.

The next morning John called and left message after message for me to wake up and get my butt out of bed and get back to work, but in my heart I'd made my decision and nothing could ever take me back.

Even now, I find it strange to think of Heartland Mall, where on a fall morning in 1998, a few months before my first daughter's birth, I had walked into a Marine's recruitment office and the Marine behind the desk told me that once I signed on the dotted line I'd be given four to six weeks to say my goodbyes and I'd be out of this crummy little town — and he must've used that line a hundred or a thousand times, then and since, because he almost sold me on it. I told him I'd need some time to think about it and walked out of his office, out of Heartland Mall, and when I did the sun slipped out behind some clouds and I stopped walking just to close my eyes and feel the warmth on my face, and I knew then the Universe had different plans for me. I enrolled in Howard Payne University in January of 1999 and a few years later America would go to war with terror and most of the Middle East.

The feeling I got the day I walked out of the Marine's office and into the sunshine almost copied itself when I turned back on the roof seeing John and José and Anselmo and the others, but not Miguel, hard at work and how I knew I could never fully belong to their beautifully-cruel world as a roofer, and when I climbed down the ladder and off the roof at Heartland Mall, my heart free, the sun once again warmed my face as it had done almost three years before, and I'd known then I'd made the right choice for my life and for my soul.

I'd continue to see John, my sister's old high school friend and confidant, over the years for drinks at the Crazy Lemon or beers at his house, but I never saw him again after I left the States, and a part of me regrets that decision.

Last year my fourth book, *A Time to Love in Tehran*, was published on April 2, a day after Whalen's memorial, and I'd posted online a marketing excerpt from the book for purely promotional reasons, and the passage went something like this: 'And as she stared out the taxi window at a beggar frozen in the snow, I yearned to have her look at me. The passion was not in any one part of Leila. It was everything made whole, unified by prominent forbearance of her ancestry and future. She was a timeless aggregate, provocative and world changing. Children would become her blessing, one day, and I wanted to share in that dream. Her stare often moved me into speechlessness, captivated me into forgetfulness, and I longed to know what she was thinking without her ever having to say a single word. But I knew such things were impossible for me.'

About a week later I'd learn that my old friend John Ferryman, at the age of thirty-nine, would put a gun in his mouth much like Hemingway and end the life we all so dearly loved. I do feel partly to blame because I'm reminded of what I posted on that April 2 and how the voice, that last line, must've sounded a lot like John's: 'But I knew such things were impossible for me.'

God have mercy on your soul, dear brother, and may the angels comfort your children, Louisa May and James Fenimore, in their times of need.

My whole life I've been too ambitious, never stopping to feel the loss, the pain and never taking a pause to look back at my life until now, and I'm not sure how I feel about that.

We know in our hearts time slips by too quickly, but yet we wake each morning to do our best to get ourselves to the next level, the next month for some, and the years roll by and we find the best parts of our routine were the faces and voices across from us, the very ones we wanted to help but in the end alienated.

We are all outcasts, I hear you say; are we not?

Even as I speak to you now the Universe erases my life away from the very beginning of who I was, who I am. Several years ago, my mother's house caught fire with my sister still asleep inside — Cassandra thought it might've been her cigarette that started the blaze. No one had been there but Cassandra and Lazarus, a cat I'd found on a street outside a church as a kitten. My father and I, along with a team, had helped that same church put a roof on a new assembly hall the summer I found Lazarus, who had been all black with white paws and a white mustache. I keep thinking about what would've happened to Cassandra that night of the fire if I hadn't scooped up Lazarus and brought him home.

Lazarus, somewhere under the bed, meowed and sounded an alarm, waking Cassandra and saving her life. Regrettably, though, Lazarus perished a hero inside my mother's house, which burned to the ground — my sister stunned in grief to watch the orange-blue flames lick the night — and in the ruins would be our childhood photographs and videotapes; ashes to ashes, dust to dust.

The day we buried Grand-Mommy in the cemetery out in Early had been cold and the faces standing around her coffin had been strange to me. The pastor said his prayers and my father bowed his head as his sisters, my aunts, wept. I cried quietly in my seat in the front row. The loss of someone so pure and caring, of a wise woman who taught me how to pick blackberries and how to be a gentleman by holding doors open for women and the elderly, of a woman who ministered to the sick, of a woman who loved so easily and who had been so easily loved in return, the loss of such a person made me want to love more deeply and to value the time still afforded me with the ones I loved.

At my Grand-Mommy's funeral, however, I had wanted to read the bedtime book about Louis Pasteur that Grand-Mommy had so often read to me to help me take a breath, rest comfortably, close my eyes, and to find a sleep so peaceful you'd believe it was eternal. My Aunt Treva — may she rest in peace — said there'd be no time for me to read a children's book at the funeral. I clutched the book against my chest and said I'd wait and read the book to Grand-Mommy once everyone left. Aunt Treva said there'd be no time; we were leaving soon. I remained quiet but angry throughout the rest of the service because I could not read to Grand-Mommy to help her find that everlasting sleep which comes to all living beings without discrimination or prejudice.

With the casket exposed six feet in the ground below me I made a silent promise to Grand-Mommy that I'd return one day, when I could drive, and sit beside her grave under that tree and, with my own child possibly beside me, I'd read to her the story about a man who *never never never* gave up and, as a result, lived a remarkable life.

I'm forty years old and I've never been back to read that bedtime story to Grand-Mommy. Once, when I was sixteen or seventeen, I drove out to look for her grave and spent an hour without success. A few years after that I drove out once more hoping to find her grave, but I failed again.

Both times wouldn't have mattered anyway. I didn't even have the book anymore, nor did I know where to buy a copy (this was before the internet and Amazon becoming daily rituals). I had gone in empty handed and had wanted to check up on her and say a few words and to see if she had anything she still wanted to say to me.

I remember becoming frustrated at being lost in the cemetery, unsure of which tree she had been buried beside, and after thirty minutes I found a stone bench near where I thought she'd be and sat down to say a few things my heart needed to say, and what little I do remember includes tears and an outpouring of grief. Grand-Mommy had been one of the truest people I had ever known, an angel in a time of need, and when I needed her most, she wasn't around. If I ever felt too down, she'd remind me how special life could be and how God was silent but ever watchful. She had a way with people, with me, and that's one of the things I miss most about her. I suppose I'll be back one day to read that story or I'll regret it if I never do.

I stand and go over to the window. The rain over New York City breaks and seems to be slowing and I curl my toes inside the wool socks I'd gotten for my birthday. The socks keep a snug warmth over me as I place my right hand, my writing hand, flat against the windowpane cool and moist to the touch; then I think of Axton, my Chinese wife who had once been a model and an entrepreneur, and our Sunday lunches in Hong Kong at the Café de Paris, where we'd lose ourselves to old English songs from the eighties and nineties and drift away in casual conversation lovers so often do in that modest duplicate of a Parisian restaurant on Elgin Street over double espressos, hot English Breakfast tea with milk, and set lunches with fresh loaves melting butter to start.

Perhaps the lack of aristocratic blood in my veins helped me to enjoy the simpler things in life: like how when I was younger my favorite combination of food and drink had been bread and water. My mother would bake fresh loaves of bread filling the white house on Durham Street with a sensation of a peasant's hut in a field under bloom in spring, and I'd wash down chunks of hot bread with large glasses of water. My second favorite food-drink combination had been a nice, cold Mountain Dew with Frito-Lay corn chips while on road trips to Louisiana or Kansas or Chicago.

In my younger years, still do I imagine, I enjoyed long drives through the vast Texas countryside as much as I enjoyed long strolls, often without company, in parks or alongside lakes. I'd drive far into the empty land and think of how old Texas was and how the name came from the Spanish pronunciation of an even older Caddo Indian word '*Tejas*' meaning 'allies' or 'friendship' or 'friends.' That's what Texas was: the Friendship State. The state's motto: Friendship. Home to the rodeo, the horny toad (actually, a horned lizard) and the prickly pear cactus. So much history, and I wanted none of it back then.

Several times when I lived alone in San Angelo, I'd hop into my car late at night and drive out of town listening to the radio and become lost to friends, family, the world, and when I believed no one knew where I was at, I'd turn around and head home only to fall asleep in a self-loathing about having to wake the next morning to work at the American Capital Bank where customers ritually complained daily with such anger and frustration that I knew most people were having a hard time in their wonderful fairytale lives.

I've spent my whole life doing things I hated or doing what others had wanted me to do, and in the process, I struggled in the background with trying to get to a place in my life where I could do what I love and get paid well-enough for it. But the world is just like the Sahara and dreams fulfilled are like oases few and far between. And here I am in New York City telling my life story to you, and I'm not even sure you believe any of it. Are you paying attention? Listening? Why would you listen to me? Why would anyone? Why would you?

These are but a few of the memories and dreams at the beginning of a long string of thoughts, puzzled pictures and photographs, voices and smells, emotions and moods, and film clips haunting me — as I once haunted empty houses — reminding me of the ones I loved and lost; beautiful snapshots of a life most people have already forgotten or chosen to ignore.

Let me tell you about my birth. I'd be lying to you if I told you I didn't remember anything about my time in my mother's womb and the birth which followed. The emotions, the waves of moods, new sensations — delight, fear, irritation, calm, sleep, discomfort and comfort — are what I recall most about being in the womb, a warm jelly of floating isolation. I distinctly recall pain as I tried to kick the hurt away the more my foot ached and I'd clinch my tiny fists in absolute agony. I hear all the time about the debate between Pro-Life and Pro-Choice, and although I believe in free will and a person's right to choose as he or she pleases, I'll tell you this much: if awareness qualifies as a characteristic of life, then I was both within my mother's womb.

Most of the time I slept and dreamed of the faces belonging to the alien voices out there — out there in the world I felt must've been far stranger and more complex than the cozy bubble I occupied, and somehow I also sensed my residence inside my mother could not last; each day I could feel myself growing, stretching my boundaries, and the occupation of my beloved hostess had to end, for my sake I'd have to move on — a trait, the habit of evolving, I'd adopt throughout my life.

When the birth came I faintly hold a sensation of being squeezed out of my 'home,' my mother, all along my skin and a great white light, much the same kind the revenant claim to see at the end of a long dark tunnel; yes, to die must be to experience another kind of birth, and speculation attempts to explain what exists on the other side of that blinding white. For me it had been pain from the twisted clubfoot and I screamed my first breath to make clear to the world I'd entered as a fragile, dependent creature that I was broken and I needed help getting fixed — and maybe that's why I'm talking to you today — the doctor on duty in 1979 forgot to weigh me before rushing me to surgery and not to my mother's arms.

For the next few years I'd have more surgeries, more severe throbbing-mind-numbing pain, more casts than I can count as my clubfoot eventually straightened out and healed — and in South Korea, Vietnam or China when I saw old men or young women limping because of a clubfoot like mine, I felt fortunate and lucky to have been born to my parents in Texas.

I learned to roll over with my cast — the first real accomplishment I can remember — and I felt overjoyed at the achievement until I found that once I rolled onto my stomach I couldn't lift my head up; my neck was just too weak, and I'd lie with my face in the living room's shag carpet each day until I grew strong enough to lift my head up to see the world in front of me. After I tired of relishing in and perfecting my second greatest achievement, I found moving impossible. At first, I believed the cast, a heavy weight on my right foot, held me back, but in reality, my arms would have been too weak. Before long, I learned to crawl by grabbing tiny fists full of shag carpet and I'd spend as much time allotted to me by grabbing carpet and pulling myself forward a half-yard at a time, usually across the living room to the television left playing to allow the cheering voices to soothe me and to keep me company. When I reached the television, I would hold up my hand to the screen only for my mother to come and move me back to the far side of the room again. Even as an infant, fictional characters had been my friends, my companions.

Over time, a small eternity to my infant mind and body, I'd learn to stand with my cast and the steel pin sticking through my heel since birth. When I learned to walk, I did so with the aid of two wooden crutches — aluminum would not be in vogue for a decade or more — and with these same beloved crutches, an extension of my physical body, I could move quickly — a sort of three-legged scooting-run — across short distances. In my clubfoot with its scars, the pain dissolved into a constant. I grew up believing all people in the world lived daily with such extreme anguish that I chose to never complain about my ailments or limitations. Maybe that little boy I used to be thirty-plus years ago had been right. Maybe we're all living with pain hidden from others, but we just keep silent.

My Grand-Mommy and mother would take the wrought-iron scissors, place me in warm water pooled inside the kitchen sink and, despite my thrashing and throat-hoarsening screams, my Grand-Mommy would hold my hand and lift my neck out of the water, and my mother would take the iron scissors to my leg and cut the old cast off my clubfoot. Before they'd finish, I'd collapse, my feverish mind imploding into exhaustive calm, and they'd carefully wash and dry the fresh scars on my clubfoot, slip on a special protective sock which allowed my toes to breathe, and they'd wrap new wet layers of bandages up and down my right leg. The wet plaster, which would dry and harden hours later, when applied felt cool and secure and I'd fall asleep in my Grand-Mommy's arms as I listened to her voice — which I sometimes still hear — saying, 'Don't worry, Cody. You're going to be all right. Just you wait and see.'

Unrecapturabilities: that's what life is all about, and I'm just cozening myself into thinking that Time and Space are not linear nor forward moving and how the subjunctive mood doesn't even exist anymore when you think about it. An absence in the totality of consciousness predominates.

Modern man, the modern woman — if you so kindly prefer — and why not throw in all of modernity while we're at it — all of which are a fragmented illusion to the precepts of survivability, but in this case to survive means to stay afloat long enough until the sharks come. The modern individual is a fragmented concept: splintered by dual psychologies, the anachronistic and the novel, at war between being a slave and being unique, being dependent or being independent, but either way the result is lose-lose because the costs will either include your community or your soul. You're damned if you do and you're damned if you don't: welcome to the civilization of YOU. If God-Allah is the almighty, the universal 'I AM!', human beings must be the reverse opposite, the mirror image question 'AM I?' of their creator. You'll either be connected to humanity and disconnected from God or connected to God and disconnected from humanity. There's no two ways about this enigma. One way or another you'll have to go all in, make a choice, and evolve if you will.

I remember I'd been four or five, when the age still held fresh memories of being an infant babe suckling my mother's breast for warm milk, at the time of my first major disconnect, like a slap in the face I could not ignore. Like I said, I'd been four or five years old because my family and I were living in that yellow house on Vincent Street I've told you about. My father must've had Chadwick and Cassandra out for the day because my mother wanted to take a nap and she sat me down alone in front of the television to watch cartoons. When I was a kid, television amused me only for so long and I'd get up and roam around the house — inside and out — to explore and to see where everybody'd gone.

Once when my mother dropped me off at a babysitter, an older couple retired with children grown into adults, Reba would set me down alone in front of the television to watch the same gray tomcat chase the same brown mouse, and after about ten minutes of such nonsense I got up and went in search of my babysitter. I found, instead, an empty house breathing in simple afternoon shadows. The bedrooms and each closet spoke to me of lives I'd never known nor would ever come to fully understand.

Methodically, from room to room, I'd go in search of community — a friendly hug, a greeting hand — but discovered rooms in silhouette, casting faint light from the windows onto black-and-white photographs, and I'd think then, as I'd stare at an empty chair, how I must've somehow walked through a mirror into a delineated universe of exact opposites: one held rooms full of people in light and laughter, and the other held rooms void of people, emptiness in shadows and silence; and I'd look in a mirror at my self-image who must've been the one lucky enough to live in the peopled world while I was doomed to haunt empty houses.

After exhausting my search of the house for Reba, I'd open the screen door to the porch and step outside. With hands on hips, I'd turn my head from one side of the porch to the other, but no sign of my babysitter. I stole beside the ample bushes posted alongside the house. Still nothing.

No sign of people. There'd be a robin or hummingbird or a stray cat idle in the flowerbeds or a ladybug or a roly-poly on a leaf, but the grounds proved to be abandoned. I opened the back wooden gate and stepped inside an overgrown garden, *la bonne vaux*, and smelled, one by one, the roses, sunflowers, orchids, daises and the rest but still found no sign of humanity in that secret garden. As far as I knew, I was the last boy alive on Earth.

Feeling fearful I'd be trapped in this Mirrorworld forever, I hurried back to the front of the house, up the front porch, into the house and back into the bedroom with the wall mirror. I touched the identical hand, made connection with my doppelganger, stepped slowly forward until I believed myself passing to the other side. I turned back to a familiar room to the one I'd just left and not wanting to jinx my hypothesis, I dropped back down in front of the television still playing the same brown mouse and gray tomcat I'd left in the beginning.

To my amazement, however, my fears also confirmed, Reba the babysitter trotted in calmly less than five minutes later and asked if I wanted anything to eat, but I don't remember replying because I kept thinking about how I'd found a portal to a gray world without people and that explained the disappearance of my babysitter and Mrs. Beaman, my old neighbor.

So, when my mother deposited me onto the carpet in front of the television, I'd have to test whether or not I remained in the world which held my family, because even a glimpse into a mirror could teleport me to the other side. After fifteen or twenty minutes of tomcat chasing mouse, mouse chasing tomcat, and after however long it took to grow bored of the television — and maybe this, too, is one reason why I enjoy reading so much — I began my exploration of the house. All the front rooms — the living room, kitchen, dining room, den, my sister's room at the front of the house — all lay empty and eerie, waiting for people to occupy and fill them with energy, emotions, voices, movement. I crept down the back hallway — my brother's room to the right, my parent's room to the left — and centimeter by centimeter I cracked open my brother's door. But this room, too, spoke of things that had been and were possibly to come.

At my parent's door, I peeked through a slit no larger than an eye's width and my heart leapt to discover I had not been abandoned, had not entered after all the Mirrorworld, because my mother lay on her bed. But what was she doing? She didn't sleep, but instead made soft, appealing noises I'd never heard a woman, or anyone, make before.

And I remember this well. My mother wore light-pink, silk lingerie lifted around the folds of her thighs and belly, her legs bent at her extended knees as she lay facing the ceiling, eyes closed.

I quietly shut the door and returned to the world of cartoons but such a childish activity never interested me much, and deep within my psyche I fought the images I had seen in my mother's bedroom; had I seen anything at all? What did I see? What was my mother doing to herself? Had I been mistaken? Imagined it all? Investigation was needed. I crept back down the hall and inched open the door to my mother's room once more.

She lay as she did before, her feet nearest the door. Her legs spread wide and I could see her pubic bush and the wet, pink spot she rubbed with her right hand as she grabbed and massaged her left breast with her left hand, and she appeared to be enjoying herself immensely. Her hips and butt would lift slightly off the bed as her hand circled a pink area that resembled a mouth beckoning a kiss from another mouth. The more I watched her breast evoking its sweet reminder to me of a nipple, light and round, which had fed me out of infancy, I longed to suck once more my mother's breast.

I leaned down and crawled alongside the edge of the bed to go unnoticed. My mother's sounds stirred in me an echo of a call I'd long forgotten, and I desired to be fed, to be made full. I sprang like a cat onto the side of the bed and placed my mouth over my mother's left breast she lifted up and exposed with her left hand, as though she held to make ready, and I began suckling and sucking.

She responded in what I know now to be pleasurable, accepting tones and she must've believed her wild fantasy, her imagined lover, had come true. I sucked and enjoyed the feeling of the nipple once again in my mouth, and my left eye widened when I saw my mother playing with herself for a few moments longer than I'd expected — but then again, I'm not sure what I expected.

Then my mother's eyes shot open, realization flooding her senses as her body stiffened and became hard. She slapped me across the face with such a mighty blow I fell back off the bed and started to cry.

'What are you doing here, Cody?'

A palm to the left side of my face where she hit me with her right hand that had only moments before been a pleasing agent.

'I live here.' I cried.

'No,' she said as she slipped her nightie back over her breasts and down around her waist. 'What are you doing sucking my breast?'

After being slapped, I'd known that what I had done as a baby could no longer be welcomed from me as a small boy: I was too old to be suckling and sucking my mother's breasts, and the Universe seemed to agree.

Palm still to face I said, 'I'm hungry. I wanted milk.'

'Oh, baby,' my mother said. 'Why didn't you say so?'

'I saw you there.' I pointed a tiny finger to the place where she had been on the bed, on the same bed where many years later I'd lose my virginity to Karolina the day before my eighteenth birthday. 'I thought you wanted to feed me. Give me milk.'

She knelt beside me and caressed my hair and the slap mark on my cheek.

'Baby,' she cooed. 'You're a big boy. You drink milk from a glass now.'

'I didn't know.' I sniffed to hold back the gobs of snot in my nostrils. I wiped my runny nose with the back of my hand, but I couldn't stop the tears. 'I didn't know I was a big boy. Chadwick calls me a baby.'

'I'll have to talk to your brother,' she said and took me by the hand, leading me to the kitchen. 'But first, let's get you something. What do you want?'

'I don't know.'

'Do you want some warm milk?'

'Mmhuh.'

I can still see my young mother in that soft pink nightie boiling me milk and both of us doing our best to forget about what happened between us; but that was how I came to know that I was no longer a baby but a big boy, and how I came to know, somewhere deep within my being, a longing had been awakened for women and their delicious breasts.

Two years before I jumped out of an airplane, I had several lovers who would enter my life as easily and quickly as they entered my apartment with the fireplace in San Angelo, and would leave my life as slowly and methodically as they exited that apartment.

At twenty-two years old, I had just begun to form the life of a serious novelist. While other writers were getting advanced degrees and kissing ass up in New York with proven experts in the fields of literature often found in historical universities or contemporary mediums like literary magazines or newspapers, I was writing in Texas at my rolltop desk and typing late into the night, all alone and separated from the rest of the world (this was around the time I was working on the collection of fiction for *The New America* I would publish three years later), and I'd welcome nightly visitors to appease my more earthly, sexual cravings by the fire.

Also at that time, I'd been too naïve to comprehend that most writers, especially in New York, spent their twenties at writing conferences or in fellowships, basically networking with other struggling writers, and few of them spent their twenties cut off from society, unknown to Facebook and Twitter and other social media (which eventually in my thirties I was forced to resign myself to as well) and these writers spent far less time than I did over the last few decades developing and honing their craft and polishing their writing as an art form (this is proven by the observable fact of the remarkable number of writers who quit while still in their twenties or who find no financial value to their efforts and give up in their early thirties, even despite their small successes in publishing and in academia), but these writers, unlike me, spent their time developing a network of social contacts who were also writers, writing instructors and editors — many times a writer will eventually evolve (or become distracted) through these three stages of seeking financial reward for their efforts in the fields of creative writing and literature.

The truth was people couldn't judge another person's talent, but what they could do was judge another person's personality (whether by their limited cultural standards the personality of the writer was likeable or unlikeable, malleable or unmalleable, agreeable or disagreeable): if an editor or literary agent didn't like your personality or your social upbringing or your personal history (very little of this is relevant to the kind of art a person can produce), you'd never be published or accepted by that particular editor or literary agent. New York writers had learned this lesson long before I did: publishing one's work came from friendships, personal relationships, guanxi, connections and not from a writer's ability (the latter, however, actually determines a writer's 'permanence in literature'). So goes the paradox: spend time building relationships and kissing ass (known to New Yorkers and others as 'the Scene') and attempt a sudden, unexpected rise in fame through favoritism from fellow friends and colleagues in the writing and publishing industry, or spend countless hours, days, years, decades alone (as Salinger did in New Hampshire and as I did back then in Texas) devoting one's self to the purity found in the nature of writing and literature as an art form and become intimate with the craft that becomes a part of your daily thoughts and desires and hopes and dreams.

So not of New York and not of New England, there I was in Texas oblivious to what it takes to excel as a writer in the real world (guanxi), and because of that ignorance, or the lacking in desire to know, I'm most thankful. I might've given up years ago. Who knows? What I do know was that I would not be the writer I am — a writer more concerned with fiction as a form of art. To think otherwise, for me, would be sacrilege, a disgrace. Over the lonely years while working on my craft, my devotion would become absolute. So, there I was in Texas, thousands of miles removed from 'the Scene' writing day in and day out, caring only for my work, for my craft. By doing so, by becoming immersed in my creation of literature, I shunned the world (this is a necessary understanding for you to have of my time in my early twenties).

For years I had no desire for a phone. When one of my grandmothers (Mamaw) died, my mother called me at my office (I was too poor to even attend the funeral — the costs of fuel and lost wages would've been too severe). Without a phone, a landline as they once called it, young women and old women simply started showing up — no strings attached — and arrangements for the next visit would be made before each woman left. The routine, for me, was ideal. In my free time I spent reading and studying the classics, writing my short stories and novels, and making love to women by the fire — though little 'love' was involved. Looking back, I cannot complain. Life was peaceful and casual, and I got a lot of writing done.

By post, I'd send stories off to literary journals and magazines and query letters to agents and publishers only to receive rejections back (once I received a rejection in a child's handwriting, my first clue that the publishing industry was not completely professional) or I'd hear silence, a void of nothingness so deep I became comfortable in its abyss, a second home for me, a necessary mood a successful writer must become accustomed to if fame is ever to be managed.

I wrote on, even when good sense should've made me stop (but fame and fortune did not drive me forward — no, a stronger angel compelled me to continue with my writing).

And so, I made love to women to ease the sting and pain of rejection I was constantly receiving from the literary world up in New York and New England. We'd often be by the fire in my living room, a woman's nude body in my arms, and I'd look over to see the flames, and I'd think of the flames that burned to ashes the green notebook filled with poems I'd written for Nora in high school. I'd tell myself then the greatest rejection a writer could suffer would be one of oblivion, and the fire and ashes would win if I were to simply quit (for years I fought myself over this, but something deep within me was stronger and won out each time). For me, burning my own literature, compelling myself — as a writer — to hide my written work from the world would be the greatest form of rejection I'd ever receive. When a notice of rejection came in the mail, I'd start the fire and drop the letter into the flames, receive the woman at the door, pour the drinks, and caress her and lick her ten times more gently by the fire and consider the flames until we both lay on our sweaty backs exhausted and out of breath.

On many nights by candlelight, I'd work on scenes to go in a novel I'd been writing since I was nineteen years old (my first semester at Howard Payne University found me often in the great halls of its library, a holy place for me back then, when a ray of sunshine struck me one afternoon and inspiration tore through me to last decades — it has — and the name of the novel rose to the surface of my consciousness: *The Endless Endeavor of Excellence*, and I'd be working on and off for the next twenty years developing this novel), when Adrianna, a seventeen-year-old Hispanic virgin, would knock on my front door and I'd have to stop working on *The Endless Endeavor of Excellence* to let her in.

I often didn't need to speak and I'd calm her by taking her into my bedroom, where my rolltop desk covered in notebooks and my leather chair waited for me, and remove her clothes as I kissed the exposed flesh which surfaced. Her brown skin, tender to the touch of my lips, weakened and relaxed. Fully in the nude I'd slip off my rosary and place it around her neck where the beads and cross hung between her womanly breasts and dark nipples. As virgins often do, she'd lie on the bed waiting and watching me undress. When my boxer-briefs came off, I would let her eyes grow large and wide at the sight of me fully exposed and growing. Then I'd slip down alongside her in the bed. With the candlelight soft on our bodies as one, we'd play and play and play.

Before the clock struck midnight, Adrianna would leave, sometimes having drank me dry and satisfied with more love for me. I'd bolt the door and return to my rolltop desk in the bedroom shrouded in candlelight. I'd fall heavy and shirtless into my leather chair and rub the beads on my rosary that faintly smelled of Adrianna. I'd be forty years old before I learned that in 1948 Hemingway, who was forty-nine, fell in love with an eighteen-year-old woman named Adriana Ivancich in Venice. But I didn't know that then.

I'd continue writing a scene in *The Endless Endeavor of Excellence* where one of the protagonists, David Chiron, has a vision of a young man sitting at a rolltop desk wearing nothing but a rosary. David Chiron would look over the young man's shoulder to see a Corona typewriter and the young man writing the very life David was living. Or I'd work on a scene with another protagonist by the name of Brighton Cambridge, who was in love with a young woman who happened to be the daughter of a wealthy plantation owner in South Carolina a few months before the beginning of America's Civil War. Brighton, a lowly field hand, labors in the barn tossing hay when the virginal Adrianna knocks at the barn door. Such was my life as a writer at twenty-two years old.

Kierkegaard's Leveling: you can't be at all sure where I'm going with this but I suppose you'll know the end when we get there, and that must be the most precise analogy for people struggling for equal opportunity and financial freedom out there in New York City, Boston, Chicago, Kansas City, Oklahoma City, Dallas, or even in Cody, Wyoming or in a small southern town like Brownwood, Texas.

My mother had always told me that anything was possible as long as I put my mind to it, but she never spoke of the hard work I'd have to put in, and I told her this a few years before I left the States and when I did, she fell to her knees crying from the weight of too much — too much truth, too much reality, too much remembering.

My mother also never mentioned how cronyism, nepotism, guanxi or 'connections and networking' as the establishment coined this moniker, and how terribly important community and heritage, even ancestry, were to the success of my life, and for most people out there in middle-class America and out there in the world like me, social mobility — or the lack thereof since recent studies have discovered that the United States was one of the worst countries in the categories of social mobility and financial equality — was far-fetched and outlandish as say winning the lottery or going all in on Red 33 or Black 40 and hitting the jackpot, but then again the casino would eventually come over and explain how a mistake in the machine caused you to win and how they were sympathetic to your complaints but how your victory would be forfeited on account of the technical malfunction, and how bullshit really wasn't a polite response to such a serious issue, security please show this person to the door, throw her-him-they out where trash belongs. I went all in for that 'hard work' and 'land of dreams' and 'the sky's the limit' and 'you're special' nonsense early on. I mean my mother meant well but she was likely feeding me that same proletarian garbage the underprivileged and labor classes have been vomiting to their offspring for years, like birds of a feather.

There's this British documentary started in the fifties — I forget who created or produced the thing — called *Seven Up!* or the *Up Series* — not like the soft drink — about how a dozen or more children, starting at the age of seven, were interviewed every ten years until these kids reached their sixties. The whole half-century study had been inspired by Francis Xavier when he said: 'Give me a child until he is seven and I will give you the man.' The result was as many proles might expect: the wealth of the parents dictated social mobility and the eventual outcome of wealth of these seven-year-olds.

I remember this one cute seven-year-old boy who grew up on a farm and had high ambitions, wanting to be an astronaut or something like that, but by the age of seventeen his prospects of getting off his family's farm and making something of himself were limited, and he knew it. His father had made it clear the best choice for his son was to carry on in the tradition, and there's one scene — if you ever get a chance to watch this ethnography — of the seventeen-year-old boy with his little blond-haired brother skipping stones by a river in the countryside. The little brother, oblivious to the world or the camera stationed on the opposite bank, happily tosses in a pebble, but his older brother, fully aware of his own fate, angrily grabs rock after rock, head constantly down, and chunks the rocks, one after another in steady assault, into the river without looking, and one could see delight, the fire of life, vacate the teenager. I believe that boy had every right to be angry because no amount of dreaming or planning or hard work was ever going to change the path life had put him on.

The hardest part of something like that, for me, was learning how *not* to become bitter. Jesus showed anger in the temple as he knocked over animal cages and whipped the merchants from His Father's house, but bitterness was a different monster and could not be tolerated. I didn't mind becoming angry at my circumstances, like that teenager by the river, but I could never allow myself to become bitter and cynical; that would have been a much worse and more permanent defeat to me than any kind of failure, which was usually temporary.

I remember when I was ten or eleven Bob Moffat, somewhat of a superstar in the English soccer leagues, organized a tryout for his soccer camp held far, far away in England, and on a Saturday morning the 1979 Eagles and I met at the soccer complex with the Brownwood Regional Hospital, where I was born, nearby on the overlooking southern hill, and we exhibited our dribbling, passing, juggling and shooting skills for the benefit of the Moffat crew and after practice our coaches, Mr. Stark and Richard, handed out the brochure and the camp costs listing the daily activities and outline, etcetera, and my teammates and I — I found out later we had all been selected despite our level of abilities — had about two weeks to confirm back to our coaches. The cost of the soccer camp ranged slightly above five hundred dollars but did not include air travel.

My mother said she'd think about it — a phrase I came to learn adults use to buy time and hope the issue magically vanishes on its own. Two weeks passed and I afforded my mother space and time to make her decision. After one soccer practice — where'd we been given a final warning and reminder to make a choice about Bob Moffat's soccer camp or forfeit the experience to next year or to never — I asked my mother about her decision. With a bit of sincerity and honesty mixed with empathy which stung me, she said that she couldn't afford the costs.

'Even if it meant my future as a professional soccer player?'

'Even if it means your future as a soccer player,' she replied. 'I can't afford it. Maybe next year, okay honey?'

I turned away from her and looked to an old warehouse that had been recently converted to an automobile repair shop and I answered her like any mature adult, void of childish delusions,

'There won't be a next time and you know it.'

I had been right and there was never a next time, but in retrospect my mother had told me indirectly I couldn't do something, breaking her axiom of how *can't* wasn't in the dictionary and how the word *can*, holy and resolute, should be spoken with absolute certainty and authority about one's prospects.

I remember the day my mother marched in to Mrs. Ragsdill's office — the fifth-grade principal I told you about — because Mrs. Ragsdill had sat me down to discuss my issue with fighting and I'd told her that once I reached the sixth grade I wouldn't fight anymore because I didn't want to get in trouble on account of how the sixth grade started flag football after school, and I continued by telling her how my ultimate dream was to play professional football with the Chicago Bears, despite my clubfoot I could be a kicker or a quarterback — and back then no one had even heard of Troy Aikman and how he would one day lead the Dallas Cowboys to Super Bowl after Super Bowl with his clubfoot.

Mrs. Ragsdill answered with her adult reasoning and said such dreams weren't logical or rational and for me to think of the mass number of young boys, all healthy, all around America who shared in that same dream and stood a far better chance at success than a boy with a clubfoot. I just couldn't do it, you understand? Life isn't easy. It's difficult, don't you see?

That had been on a Friday before the end of the school day and my mother marched me into Mrs. Ragsdill's office on Monday morning, bright and early, and all three of us sat down and my mother, God love her, pointed a finger at Mrs. Ragsdill and said, 'How dare you tell my child, any child, they can't do something? You should be ashamed of yourself. *Can't* isn't even in the dictionary, only *can* and *cannot* and my child *is* going to grow up knowing he *can* do something, anything, just so long as he works hard for it. This is America, land of opportunity, of our father's pride, and I'm honestly disgusted. You should apologize to my son right now.'

I had never seen firsthand my mother come to my defense like that before, and Mrs. Ragsdill, the cowardly administrator she was, turned to me and offered her 'most sincere regrets for having misspoken' and how I should 'listen to your mother' and how she had 'never meant to imply I couldn't achieve my dreams.'

I'll admit it felt like a small victory to see Mrs. Ragsdill, my prime enemy at East Elementary School, like Bart Simpson and Principal Skinner, dropped down a peg or two. But for the first time, the blinding scales had been removed from my eyes, like washing mud from your face, and I could see as adults truly see and not as children see.

'Thank you,' I said, 'but I can't accept your apology. Mother, the principal's right. I don't stand a chance at playing for the Chicago Bears. I mean, I have a clubfoot and I live in Texas and Chicago is way up there. It's not logical for some crippled boy like me to achieve his dreams in the NFL. They're just too big and I'm just too small and crippled, and this has nothing to do with can or can't; it has to do with life and what's real, what's how. Now, before either of you say anything, I've heard enough and I'm tired. I'm going to go outside now and be alone to think and leave you two to finish up. Please don't be mad. I'm not angry, not really, and neither should you. I'm going now.' I slid from the chair and left the principal's office, waved to the secretary who must've heard the whole conversation and I stepped into the supply closet I told you about to lay my head on the desk prepared for me and my ever-growing isolation.

Now years later, as a teenager riding in a car next to my mother after soccer practice, I stared at the automobile repair shop in the warehouse and thought back to the fifth grade and to how my mother had defended my right to a dream, to my pursuit of happiness, only for her, years later, to tell me to my face that something wasn't possible and it wasn't possible because of money, which we didn't have.

'Talk to me,' she said. I had been silent for a while and she, like most women I know, sensed something was heavy on my mind. 'Tell me what you're thinking. I want to know.'

I faced her as she drove and said, 'I'm thinking how my future has already been determined by the past. The sins of the father passed down to the son. That's what I'm thinking.'

I turned my face away from her to look out the car window and for the first time in my life I had spoken my unfiltered thoughts to an adult and my mother became stunned as she acknowledged the sheer immensity the truth brought to our lives. We remained silent for the remainder of the ride home and I'm not even sure I spoke to her later that night.

One way or another, my future had been decided — not by me but by a nameless, invisible, external force I would come to know very well as I ventured out into a life that seemed to belong to someone else.

Living abroad in Asia, American holidays didn't mean quite as much as they did in the States: Christmas wasn't as colorful nor merry and passersby didn't spread cheer by randomly shouting to one another 'Merry Christmas!' If one ever heard the expression at all it usually needed a lengthy explanation because most Asians and non-Americans were more familiar with 'Happy Holidays' and nothing about 'Feliz Navidad,' and that would be about the time when I was sucked into a literal discussion on all matters Christmas and by then the cheer melted, transmogrified into an apathetic balm.

In Vietnam, and in some places in South Korea, many locals had a hard time wrapping their minds around Christmas Day being on the twenty-fifth of December, while many more companies and grandmamas believed with unshakeable faith that the twenty-fourth, Christmas Eve, qualified as enough Christmas for them. Sure, that's a broad generalization to make but year after year, I'd find that my generalizations became a standard to gage social behavior by, like the North Star, and I began to learn how top government officials lazily viewed the masses.

Thanksgiving was a separate matter altogether, and if I was lucky enough I'd spend a pleasant evening at an upscale hotel or restaurant with strangers, an eclectic medley of expatriates from Australia to Great Britain with a few of the locals mixed in, and it felt to me like the few locals quietly joined the dinner party to try a little turkey and to observe the 'foreign devils' in their natural habitat.

At this hodgepodge gathering there'd be the prized turkey photographed several times over, rarely a smoked ham, possibly freshly made cranberry sauce — if I were lucky the chefs in back knew what it was — and on one or two occasions, if the price was right, I'd find myself eating hot pecan and pumpkin pie with vanilla ice cream, but that wasn't often the case in Asia.

Thanksgiving abroad never held up to the ones back in the States where I'd have a day or two to recover — when I was a kid we had about five or six days — to celebrate and to visit family, to help clean the ancestors' gravesites with my mother in charge of the operation and I'd look down at the mélange of names written in stone and ask myself who these people had been and what had they done with their time while they had it. Were they like me? Were they remembered? I thought not.

Somewhere in the background on Thanksgiving Day there'd be a local or national parade, my favorite being Macy's in New York, and a few movie marathons playing *James Bond*, *Rocky*, *Star Wars* or *Star Trek*. Don't exclude the Chicago Bears or the Dallas

Cowboys on a given day in the ages gone by, both possibly battling for the famed 'turducken' in the frozen tundra as I'd watch from a cozy living room in my Papaw's house in Monroe, Louisiana.

Papaw and Mamaw — long stresses on the vowels — may eternity accept them with open arms — were my mother's parents. Papaw had been an oil man out in West Texas for a time before moving to Monroe — an hour or so east of Shreveport, if you know where that's at. Papaw and Mamaw, like most of my Rawls relatives, lived in the dense woods where we'd race four-wheelers down back trails, curving and dipping into muddy terrain and leading my cousins, Shane and Micah, deeper into the wild where they often hunted bucks and turkeys for sport and for sustenance.

In the eighties, as a child, I'd sleep out on Papaw and Mamaw's screened porch, the dark woods inviting me to come and relieve myself. In the middle of the night, I'd stand barefoot just inside the tree line hoping to see Bigfoot watching me, and once or twice I thought I had. I'd be listening to the crickets and the hush of the wind and imagine who I'd be in twenty or thirty years and whether or not my own children would be fortunate enough to sleep out there as I did, and if they'd wake before dawn to watch the darkness retreat into a mild gray that appeared to slip from the grass and pines.

In front of Papaw and Mamaw's house we played touch-football on a large hill. Chadwick and I would ally ourselves for the day and play against Brighton and Cassandra, or as my other cousins grew older, Nathan and Daniel — the latter being a diehard Aggies fan. Brighton had cystic fibrosis but he'd play an hour out in the cold with us so he'd have a day of normalcy. I found out years later he'd spend the next few weeks after Thanksgiving house-ridden hooked to breathing machines to help facilitate his lungs, but at the time he and I trotted down the hill tossing one another the football and he'd come in the overly warm house coughing up a storm, well, I thought people coughed and how that was normal, and I'd been a fool for thinking he'd grow to be an old man with me.

My cousins and I piled our plates with hot turkey, smoked ham with rings of cooked pineapples, dressing smothered in brown gravy, sweet potatoes hidden beneath melted marshmallows, and huge spoonfuls of cranberry sauce. For dessert we'd have choices of pecan, pumpkin, sweet potato, chocolate, vanilla, apple or coconut pies. A plate at a time I'd eat outside in the cold listening to my father, Uncle Gerard, Uncle Shorty and Papaw, my mother's father who smoked nothing but Marlboro well into his eighties, chat about politics and how the federal government stuck its goddamned nose into other people's business, or about family and how well my Uncle Desmond's Christmas tree farm was doing that year. We weren't rich, but we sure felt like we were.

Uncle Desmond and his wife Bedelia lived a half-mile down the road from Papaw and Mamaw's, and alongside Uncle Desmond's cabin a good chunk of land had been cultivated to growing and selling Christmas trees at his small business called Precious Memories. Most Thanksgivings, while strange families came and scouted out their favorite holiday tree, I'd play hide-and-seek with Cassandra and Chadwick and my other cousins, running in and out of row after row of Christmas trees waiting for those families to come and cut them down and take them home, much the way we'd do — carrying a twelve-footer fastened on top of the van from Louisiana back to Texas, a good eight-hour road trip. Uncle Desmond, like an off-duty Santa, would lead me and Chadwick, like faithful elves, to his Christmas tree lab stationed at the bottom of a hill behind his cabin and he'd show us the hybrids he often tested and attempted to perfect. 'They'll be something one day,' he'd say. 'Just wait and see.'

Each Thanksgiving, as an early morning fog rolled in among the pines and Uncle Desmond drank his coffee like the most contented man in the world out on his covered porch, he'd tell us children of our ancestors, of Leopha America and how strong such a woman was back then in the early days of our great nation, or he'd tell us children of a time when he used to work for the postal service driving a big rig, and how on a foggy day, much like this one today, he had been doing damn-near eighty down the highway and the white fog collapsed the road visibility to a ten yard stretch or less, and how he slowed and then braked hard when he saw another rig's tail lights spark bright-alarming red. Uncle

Desmond's rig slid and screeched safely to a stop and found a dozen or more cars and trucks piled up in a mass collision; he lit flares and warned the coming traffic to a halt.

When he returned through the fog, however, he found the rig in front of his truck to have busted tail lights and there was no way in hell, not on this earth anyways, those back signals were working to warn him in time. He was this close — and he'd hold his two fingers an inch apart — from slamming into the back of that truck and being killed. To this day, something or someone was watching out for him, but, God as his witness, there's no way those tail lights had been working; something saved his life that day. Uncle Desmond would drink his coffee, slowly growing quiet, and I could see him looking out to the fog covering his front yard and him imagining a distant highway.

For a proper Thanksgiving lunch, my family and I would congregate at Uncle Desmond's and he'd have a wooden table with side benches some ten or more yards long out on the uncovered porch at the side of his home. The men and boys would be seated first. Once my sister sat beside me and Uncle Desmond scolded her and complained to my mother how he'd never seen such defiance from a girl before and he told Cassandra to get the hell in the kitchen with the rest of the womenfolk and to serve her brothers.

'Yeah, Cassandra,' I had said. 'Go serve me. I'm hungry. And don't forget to put sugar in my coffee.' I didn't drink coffee then but I liked saying it.

'I'll serve you,' she said, 'with spit in your food.'

'On second thought, I'll serve myself.'

But my mother would bring my food and apologize to her brother and get Cassandra into the house until the men and boys had eaten their pie and had their coffee. Over time as I grew into a man, I'd gradually watch this custom of men dining before women eventually change and become dated, but there was still a hidden sense that each knew their proper places, which my sister still contests even to this day.

In life, I'm not sure how most people get to where they're going anymore, and maybe that's the consensus shared by most

Americans and billions of others all across the world: how does one *become*?

I've long held empathy for those souls who lose their way and commit suicide, but the truly depressing thing, if you really want to know, is that about a few months ago I finally came to a clear understanding of why individuals end their lives, and I'm not pleased about this sort of knowledge either.

I strongly believe why most people are unsettled when they speak to me or are near me is because I break down illusions — not only in my life but in all that I see — and illusions are what people need to make it through another grueling day. Culture rests on a foundation of shared illusions, so does a society; there were people I came across who were afraid of me, afraid of what I might show others, which must've been the truths behind the illusions. But what bothers me — and I'm not entirely alone on this — was how, from the level of the individual on up to the highest corporate and governmental positions, corruption rested comfortably and uncontested in the folds of the shared illusions by the communities at the lower levels in society.

But greater fears exist, and some of those include the total collapse of the system — whatever system that might be — and the disintegration of the communal structure binding individuals to one another; after all, most individuals are afraid to be separated from the group and the herd mentality rests easy with them; they are most afraid, after finding their dreams dashed and failure complete, of living a lonely life. Hemingway, though, understood all of this when he proclaimed that being a writer was a lonely existence, because he knew the illusions as well as I do and he knew that artists, true artists, could never belong to the masses. Now you see me, he said, and now you don't.

I can still remember the first time I was abandoned as a child. My immediate family and I had traveled to Tennessee or Mississippi, and I faintly recall my mother pleading to go see Graceland, once home to Elvis, and my father sternly refusing, too far out of the way, and how my mother bowed her head and said there'd never be a next time.

We traveled in Old Blue — that worn-blue station wagon I told you about — and the farthest back seats had been laid flat to accommodate blankets and pillows for Chadwick and I to sleep out the journey. Cassandra slept in her own blankets in the row directly behind the driver and passenger seats.

My father had been driving for most of the day and he wanted to make Texas by dark but my mother had to pee. Grudgingly, my father pulled to a rest stop in the middle of the woods and my mother rushed out. When I heard the door slam shut, I peeked out the back windows to see her running inside. I wanted to be with her — much more than I needed to pee — and so I slinked over the back seat behind the driver's seat where my father waited listening to the radio, Cassandra and Chadwick completely wiped, and I stealthily opened and eased the door closed and hurried around the back of the station wagon and into the store.

The attendant, an older man who must've been in his forties, pointed to the back where the toilets would be. I ducked in to the little boy's room and took a little extra longer than normal because, to be quite honest, I wanted to test my family and to see if they really loved me by knowing I was missing. I washed my hands twice more and dried them with paper towels and confidently came out of the restroom. When the attendant saw me coming up the back aisle, he froze, turned to me to the parking area and back to me, and I knew then what my answer would be.

'Were you with them?'

'Yes.'

'They just left.'

I stepped to the entrance and peered out into an empty lot. No Old Blue. No family. My heart sank, and there's no point in trying to describe the feeling I had then as a toddler being forgotten by his family because there's nothing to compare it to.

I opened the door and kicked at the gravel in the spot my family had been moments before and held my hands on my hips and looked down a long road which bent and vanished in the vast woods that surrounded the gas station.

Back inside the store, stools lined the bar where the attendant served drinks and hamburgers, and I remember wanting a dill pickle because there was a huge glass jar of them on the bar next to a second jar of equal size filled with brown eggs.

'Want a coke?'

I did but I had no money and I told the attendant so.

'That's okay. It's on the house.' He hesitated, then added, 'It's free.'

By then I became afraid I might be poisoned and kidnapped by this stranger and I declined anything free to eat or drink.

'No, thank you, sir.'

'Where you from?'

'Texas.'

'That's far.' He wiped a wet glass dry with a white dish towel. 'Do you know which city?'

I thought about that because it was such a good question and I should've known the answer. I felt a bit disgruntled at my parents for not having taught me.

'Nope.'

'Do you remember your phone number?'

Again, a very good question I had no answer to.

'No, sir.'

Ten minutes passed and I thought I needed to say something to make the man feel at ease because he seemed to be more worried than I was and that made me nervous.

'I think I'll have that coke now. My mom can pay when she comes.'

'You sure?' He might've been asking me if I was certain my mother would be coming back for me and I sat puzzled for a moment. 'What kind of coke would you like?'

'Coke is fine.'

He popped the top off the glass bottle and the Coke had been ice-cold just the way I liked it. 'Don't worry,' I said. 'It's okay. My folks always forget me.'

'They do?' He stopped wiping the counter and looked back to the empty gravel lot and the gas pumps outside. 'Should I call someone? The police?'

To this day I'm not sure why he was asking a kid who had just been forgotten that kind of question, but that really worried me and

I knew calling the police would open a can of worms and cause a mess of things and I'd be sure to get in trouble then.

'I wouldn't,' I said as confidently as I could manage, despite having never been on my own without my family before. 'They'll come back. They always do.'

'Well, okay.' He retreated into his work and I attempted to chat about the weather but as the minutes slowed to a grind, the more agitated he became with the possibility of a little kid being forgotten and left in his store and the manhunt which would likely follow. I calmly sipped my Coke and after about thirty or forty more minutes — the detour and delay must've pissed my father off — my mother came rushing back into the store.

'You see,' I told the attendant.

As they say, my mother was a nervous wreck and tears poured down her face. I tried to calm her down and explain the situation and have her pay for the Coke but the attendant said I was a delight and I was fine, a good boy really, the Coke was on the house, and my mother thanked him profusely for watching her baby. She whisked me up into her arms, where I'd stay until we made it home to Texas, and I fell asleep with my mother promising me that she would never, never ever leave me again.

When I was seven or eight, several years later, my mother left me again. My father had a gray truck by then and he rented a camper for the week to place over the truck bed in back. In Andrews, out in West Texas that smells of oil money, we picked up Uncle Gerard and his family and also Uncle Smiley with his wife Samarah and their son Brighton Cambridge, who I've told you about. All the children filed into the back of the truck beneath the camper filled with sleeping bags, blankets and pillows on an old mattress while the adults snuggled into the front cab as we made our way north to Santa Fe, New Mexico for a ski trip. For hours the children chatted and slept through the night until the cold became freezing and unbearable and we begged to have the adults open the back window to allow heat to flow in to the back camper. Soon the frostbite lifted to a snug sensation easing the children back into complacency and back to sleep. We had left Andrews in the middle of the night having been awoken from warm, safe beds to pile into the back of the truck to sleep the rest of the night away, and by morning I stepped through the back camper window and over the tailgate to a snowy, wintry wonderland, and I felt I had left one dream and entered another.

As I stood holding myself, I looked to the three-storied log cabin we'd be staying in and a stir from what must've been another life, either in my past or in my yet to come, rippled through my legs and arms as I longed to live in a cabin covered and surrounded by snow. I begged my parents to leave me for the day to be in that cabin all alone so I could wander its rooms and staircases and feel at home again partly because I cared little for skiing; in the end we pulled on our ski suits and drove to the resort where my family would spend the day on the powdery slopes. My mother left my brother and sister in charge of me and right away I knew there'd be trouble. For thirty minutes Chadwick, Cassandra, Brighton and I hopped on and off the practice lift until they grew bored of the ride-around, and of me.

Faster and faster they skied ahead and away in their honest eagerness to absently leave me behind and to become separated so they could go on and enjoy their day on the beginner's slopes. To this day, I expected better from my older brother Chadwick. I would never leave my son nor my young brother, if I had one, the way Chadwick left me that day. As I said, I became separated, cut off, and the day just got colder until I believed I'd freeze to death if I didn't find a house, a car, a cave, a shelter, a blanket, a cardboard box, anything, to protect me from the biting wind, from the cruel elements.

My instincts kicked in and warned me to get out of the cold. I skied to a café nearby and stood outside for a time watching skiers deposit their skis against the wall, and then it occurred to me that I had no money. But I didn't care. I needed to get warm or I would die. When I walked in, feeling more alone than I'd ever felt, I welcomed the warmth from the kitchen, from the coffee, and from the noise of idle banter. I half-expected to see my family gathered at a table laughing when they saw me and yell to me to come join them, and ask me what took me so long, and welcome me like a lost hero returned. But a strange family, not mine, gathered at that banquet table, and that was when I saw my future by the window.

Where shadows of skiers passed by the frosted windows as if in a dream, a man and woman sat across from one another and I half-believed the brown-haired man was me in a distant time still unknown and unexperienced. He wore a vanilla-colored sweater with a black coat hanging down the back of his chair, and his coffee steamed up before him. A brunette sat opposite the man and she wore a gray, wool sweater that came up to her chin and she tucked a curl behind one ear as the man made her laugh. The rest of the world zoomed out and all that was left was that couple by the window.

Even the restaurant silenced as I considered the sight of these lovers to be the most beautiful vision I'd ever seen in my life, and then the spark of a writer ignited within and I desired to tell their story as only I could. A moment later the noise drowned me while time rushed quickly forward as I remained standing in the center of the restaurant. I loathed returning to the snow, away from bliss, but I had to find my family and I wouldn't do it there. Outside, I skied to the practice lift where I'd wait another hour or more with my tears freezing to my cheeks, and finally a lone figure stretched out her arms through a blur of tears and sight and held me close and said she'd never, never ever leave me again.

There's so much I haven't told you and there's so much more beyond that I'm not even sure I can. I do remember, though, one morning in Discovery Bay, Hong Kong when I was on my way to write this book I'm telling you about.

Next to the ferry station where I drop my wife off so she can go into Central for her daily commute to work, there's a promenade that runs along the bay all the way to the beach. One particular morning, about 8:15, I happened to see a red, plastic shovel — the kind kids use to dig in the sand — floating near the rocks below the promenade where I looked over the railing. A momentary, abject sadness gripped me in its sudden embrace until I noticed hundreds of white jelly fish swimming near the surface of the water, and for some strange reason I thought of how weather to describe emotions in a short story or novel wasn't true to the reality or nature of things, because lovers could meet in a coffee shop on a rainy day or a fifteen-year marriage could end on a perfect, sunny afternoon over cocktails. Like the jellyfish, which can be a portent for thunderstorms in the days to come, moments and key events in life prelude even bigger events and memorable moments — even if they turn out to be unfavorable.

On the promenade I watched the jellyfish swim in their close-knit community and I believed I spotted a pair of lovers swimming side by side, keeping close to one another so as not to be separated, and at other times I followed a toddler jellyfish playfully darting between mother and father and its elders. For the jellyfish, harmony depended simply on them being together.

I'd walk the length of the beach, which takes ten to fifteen minutes, before I would head back to the clubhouse, which I passed on my way to the beach, and sit and write in the corner of the clubhouse's reading room. During my morning walk, I'd have time to look over the railing as long as I wanted and watch the floating community of jellyfish. Each jellyfish I saw reminded me of someone from my past: ghosts swimming in the murky depths of a bay called Discovery.

I tried to piece back the timeline of my life and the life of my family, and I found the individual pieces allusive and bound by all the other pieces in no particular order, swimming not through a maze of memories but in a sea of them.

After the night my parents sat us children down in the living room to speak of their divorce and their mutual parting of ways, my father must've moved out of the house and into Camelot Apartments across from the city's high school. In my head, when my sister moved out of the house shortly after, I believed Cassandra joined our father out on Pine Creek Ranch, where my father did eventually end up years later.

I'd lie awake at night thinking of them out on the ranch beneath the grand kaleidoscope of stars, and in truth my sister moved to Camelot because there was a swimming pool outside the back door of my father's two-story apartment. For a decade or more I don't know why I didn't put the pieces of the puzzle in the correct spots and order, because I do recall clearly staying with my father on the weekends in Camelot, and how Chadwick and Cassandra would throw me about in the pool to try and drown me. Chadwick would place his hand on top of my head and hold me under, and no matter how much I fought, he'd fight harder. It was only when I learned to stop fighting, hold my breath to wait patiently and calmly at the bottom, did Chadwick lose interest in torturing me. Cassandra often did nothing or laughed and enjoyed the play, a teen who suntanned by putting Crisco cooking grease on her skin so she'd get that perfect brown all the girls wanted in the 1980s.

I remember clearly my father's motorcycle parked outside his apartment and how my mother would drop me off and I'd hesitate every time, afraid of that strange door and what lay beyond. After that summer, Chadwick moved to Kansas to begin university, where he'd meet and begin dating his wife. Cassandra lived with Henry in Camelot and would walk to high school located across the street. I moved into Chadwick's old room and set up my own little world for the next several years fit with a small bed, a pullout sofa, an entertainment center with a twenty-inch television, a VCR, and a seven-disk stereo system I'd listen to for hours. I'd put on recorded thunderstorms to play all night while I slept dreaming of a young girl in China who was waiting for me.

At times, I'd pull shut the blackout curtains, pop in a CD of rainforest sounds in a spring rain, and sleep a day or night away, endless hours of dreaming. Once I slept eighteen hours straight, and when I awoke, I still felt tired.

Even that timeline can't be true and I've learned long ago not to trust myself, not to trust my memories. (I know now some of those memories could've been fabricated from my imagination.) But for most of my life that was how the timeline fits, or doesn't fit, and that was how I made sense of things.

In truth, or fact, Chadwick's first year in university would have left Cassandra starting as a junior in high school and me starting the seventh grade, because when Cassandra moved to Dallas to attend university as a freshman, I started high school as a freshman and missed being in high school with my elder sister by one year. The trouble with the facts was that it didn't fit my version and narrative of events, because I also knew for a fact my parents divorced, or officially separated, when I was in the fifth grade, by the sixth grade things were cemented, and I believe that was the last year I lived with Chadwick; meaning, if this version holds true, because Chadwick sometimes dropped me off in his little Volkswagen Beetle-Bug, the one we nicknamed Herbie, I was in the middle of the fifth grade (I'd walk myself to school a year later). Cassandra was in high school as a freshman when Chadwick was a senior, and somehow both versions, my truth and the hard facts, turn out to be the same in many ways, even though to me both seem disconnected and fractured from one another and the whole of my floating memories. The timeline fits but I can't bring myself to trust any of it. The jellyfish float and I think back. They were trying to tell me something.

I think and look back to when I was a freshman in university studying seventeen course credit hours while working full-time at fifty plus hours a week to pay for my car and a one-room shack in the woods at the edge of the city limits, exhausted out of my mind the whole time, unable to afford a proper meal, buying eighty-nine cent burritos from Taco Bell to stay fed, trying to make time for Alicen, a toddler by this point, and then I met Juliet one night on the Drag with Sawyer and Dylan, when they were still friends.

Juliet had green eyes, long black hair and freckles I so adored on her cheeks and arms. We made love for the first time in that one-room shack, and in the summer of 2001, when the world still made sense to us, we made love over and over in the lake house I rented to finish writing my first book, *A Father's Son*. Juliet and I saw the first *Fast and the Furious* film together one sunny afternoon and I truly felt I loved her. Even so, the knowledge of my future held no place for her and it pained me to see a life without her. But I had a choice: follow my destiny or stay with her. I chose my destiny. That was also the same summer I worked as a roofer with John Ferryman and his father's company. (How the pieces do seem to fit at times and make perfect sense.) The jellyfish float and I still think back.

I think and look back to when I was in my last year of university, 2002, and how I met Natalie at the Crazy Lemon one night and we ended up making love in her bedroom that had a view of Lake Brownwood. She had a tattoo of an Irish Circle, a Celtic knot, above her left breast and how her voice haunted me for years with memories of our brief night together — one night, that was all we ever had together, though I had wanted more time with her — and before we exhausted ourselves in her sheets, we had walked down to the docks on the lake and I had foolishly dove head first and scraped my head on the bottom — so damn lucky not to have broken my neck — and how Natalie led me up the grassy slope at three in the morning to her bathroom where she applied rubbing alcohol with a cotton ball to the wound bleeding from my forehead as I sat on the counter. She looked soft to me then, even though she was two years older, and I kissed her and we didn't stop kissing.

What I didn't tell you, or anyone for that matter, was that I did see Natalie again — one more time towards the end of that summer before she moved back to Houston, Texas. In my own twisted way, I loved her but I was young and I enjoyed having sex with as many women as would have me. Needless to say, Natalie found out my true nature and we fell out of favor with one another. But that's embellishment — you must know it is — and I'm here to tell you the truth.

One night, before I was to meet Natalie for the second time, I did lots of cocaine with Matson, a mind-numbing amount of cocaine, and I wasn't right in my head when I went to a bar, the Roadhouse, to meet Natalie. I walked into the bar high and excited to be meeting Natalie but when I first saw her sitting alone at the end of the bar my mind twisted upon itself and I didn't recognize her. And if it was her, I couldn't just go up to talk to her. My mind started playing games with me, and I questioned reality: the real felt unreal and the unreal felt real.

I spoke to friends and watched the young woman I believed to be Natalie at the end of the bar and tricked myself into believing it wasn't really her, and if I did go and talk to this young woman who looked to me like it was Natalie, this doppelganger, then the real Natalie would walk in and catch me in the act, and then I'd be busted and I didn't want that at all.

For a time, after about an hour, I sat alone drinking a Corona when Natalie came up to me and said, 'I've been sitting alone at the end of the bar for an hour waiting for you to talk to me.' And that's exactly what she said because I'll never forget those words.

My brain, however, translated it differently under its cocaine fueled delusions. I turned to her, my mind weirded out by way too much cocaine and Corona, and I honestly didn't recognize Natalie; my mind was incapable of putting the memory of her from the weekend before to the face, the facts, standing right next to me. My twisted mind made me honestly believe that this woman was not my Natalie and she only resembled her in appearance. I didn't say a word to her. I got up and walked away. She must've left because I didn't see her for the rest of the night.

And what did I do?

I picked up a kindergarten teacher, a hot blonde with well-manicured nails, and we stayed up until five in the morning having hard, rough sex, and not once did we make love.

Over the next week I sent special blue roses to Natalie and tried to see her. I called and she had every right to refuse my calls. And that was when I decided to never do cocaine or any hard drugs again. Mind altering was right. To be honest, that young man has kept his promise, because no number of apologies can ever take away the pain that I caused Natalie. I'll never blame the drugs, but that's what hard drugs can do to the mind and to people's lives. But that wasn't the last time I saw Natalie either.

The last time I saw Natalie was a month or so later. I had met this guy Tucker and we'd started to hop bars together. One night in the Roadhouse we met a bachelor party, or that's what they called it, which consisted of a group of seven or eight rich kids down from Texas Tech in Lubbock to celebrate their pal's upcoming wedding. Tucker and I drank with them at the bar and foolishly we followed them out to a lake house owned by the groom-to-be's father. Over the course of the night, Tucker tried to persuade me to leave and I refused. I'd just learned to follow the Universe and I was set on seeing where this particular night would lead. I should have known better.

Tucker left. Me and these frat guys found ourselves in the kitchen at three in the morning playing 'Slaps' or 'Who Can Take the Most,' a slapping game I'm now sure they probably invented just for me, but the game was simple: slap your opponent as hard as possible on his bare chest (we had to remove our T-shirts) and he'd return with his best slap, and the first one too weak or too cowardly to handle the pain lost the game of Slaps. I actually enjoyed the pain back then. I worked from one nameless guy to the next, and eventually won the contest. No guy had wanted to match me in slaps, and I believe now that their plan to get rid of me or test my resolve had failed.

Shortly after, one by one, the guys headed upstairs to crash. At nearly five in the morning, the early light creeping out across the still waters of the lake, I found myself alone downstairs sitting in a chair wide awake. Back then alcohol acted as a stimulant and I could stay awake all night just by drinking beer. Unable to sleep, I decided to play some billiards and in the middle of my solo game, one of the guys came downstairs to raise hell and to tell me to go to sleep. I politely refused. I wasn't the least bit sleepy. He and some other guys started to shove me out of the billiards room and out of the two-story house by the lake.

My first thought was one of surprise: how bright the night had become. With that thought a fist cracked my lower lip and jaw. I stumbled backwards and touched my lip and found blood on my fingertips, and I remembered the knife in my pocket. I carried this knife, a gift from my father, with me each night that summer. The knife was a collector's edition to celebrate Christopher Columbus discovering the Americas, and on its side were the three ships Columbus was best known for. The Columbus knife, silver and extremely sharp, waited in my front, right pocket of my jeans.

I backed up to regain my balance on the front sidewalk and faced three guys I'd spent the night drinking with and slapping as hard as I could. I knew in a second of sobriety that if I did fight back someone would die, and I couldn't bring myself to kill anyone.

So, I cursed them. I yelled. I flipped them off. I walked away. They let me walk away. After all, that was all they really wanted: for me to be gone.

I never carried the Columbus knife with me again, but on my lower lip, on my right side, there's still a small scar to remind me of that Sunday morning when I walked down the highway with my T-shirt removed and pressed against my mouth to stop the bleeding.

The first truck to stop and offer me a ride was one of the frat guys who belonged to the bachelor party. He'd been the designated driver and I'd been waiting for him to return to give me a ride back into town, some thirty miles away. Even though he was kind and sincere, the thought of him being friends with the guys who had cracked my lip revolted me and I refused his help. He gave up and drove on to the lake house.

The second and last truck to stop to offer me a ride was a stranger in his thirties. I'd been walking the isolated country road for thirty or forty minutes — I never wore a watch in those days so I had no idea how long I had actually been walking — when he pulled up alongside me and asked if I'd been in an accident. The thought never occurred to me but it would look that way to a passerby. I thanked him for his kindness and honest concern, said there'd been a fight but he should see the other guy, and that I really just wanted to walk. He understood, eventually gave up as well, left me alone and drove away.

I walked for what seemed another twenty minutes or so, maybe longer, when out of nowhere I came to a side road that led to Natalie's lake house, and how the hell that happened I'll never know. I'll also never know how I recognized that road in the first place. But I had.

I followed the smaller road and walked to one house I thought could have been Natalie's, but either way I was depleted. After the night I had, I couldn't keep walking. I lay down against the trunk of a tree next to the driveway and sat with my T-shirt pressed to my face, blood down my bruised chest and on my jeans, and I just sat looking at the lake house thinking to myself that I had followed the Universe, step by step over the course of the night, to this house, to this spot against that specific tree, and I didn't even know the reason why. When the thought finished, my eyes heavy with sleep and too many burdens, Natalie appeared with her dog around a corner from the back of the house and she didn't see me there in the shade. I reclined against the tree, unable to move, and I watched her. I told myself I could still walk away and she'd never know I'd been there. Then her dog, a great chocolate Labrador, lifted its head in my direction and I knew I'd been spotted. I dragged myself up off the side of the tree, walked into the bright sunlight with my left hand in the air as if to surrender and hoarsely called out, 'Natalie! It's me. Cody.' She didn't respond. She stared at me as though I were a ghost damned to wander the earth for an eternity. 'Natalie. I'm hurt. I need you.' Her hatred and anguish for me didn't abate nor vanish from her eyes even when her voice came out gentle and said,

'Are you okay? What happened? Were you in an accident?'

I understood then that's how it might've looked: a drunk driver slamming into a fence and somehow walking away.

'It's a long story, Natalie.'

We stood face-to-face, her Labrador sniffing the blood on my jeans.

'I had a fight with some frat guys down the road and I need a ride into town. Could you help? I can call someone to pick me up. Please?'

She didn't want to help but she did.

'Wait here,' Natalie said. 'I don't want you getting blood all over the house. I'll drive you into town.'

'Thank you,' I said, and I watched her lead her dog to the back of her house. I followed and waited for Natalie by her bedroom which had a sliding glass door for entry, and I stood there on the grassy slope which led down to the docks, facing the waters on the lake glittering with flecks of shimmering white beneath the Sunday morning sun, resembling the light of a thousand souls dancing in a rainbow formation upon the surface of the lake. I stood there and felt shame and remorse for who I had become and for what I had done, and this no one ever saw, but that shame and remorse grew and sank within me as I looked out over the lake that now-lost morning.

During the drive into town, I tried to explain things to Natalie, to make things right, but she turned to me and said,

'I can give you a ride into town but I don't have to talk to you. I don't want to talk to you and I don't want to listen to you talk.'

She faced forward and never said another word to me in her life.

'That's fair,' I said, 'but please let me say this one last thing before you never speak to me again: for what it's worth, and it's not worth very much now, because I hurt you, and for that one night we had together, I did love you, and for everything I've done to you since, I am truly and deeply sorry.'

We sat in silence as she drove me to my car outside Tucker's apartment.

'Thank you for your kindness, Natalie,' I said. 'I am sorry.'

She didn't look at me when I said those last words to her nor did she look at me when I closed the door to her truck. I doubt she looked at me when she turned the corner and drove out of the parking lot and out of my life forever.

The Universe, though, wasn't done with me just yet.

I attempted to start my car and found the battery dead. I banged on Tucker's door to try and wake him so he could give my car a jump. Tucker didn't answer the door and I didn't blame him after the night of heavy drinking we had done. I hoped my car would start again but it didn't. I sat there thinking of walking to Pine Creek Ranch, which would've taken me another two hours, at least. Then I thought of an old school friend, a young woman, who lived in an apartment a few doors down from Tucker. I knocked on her door and she seemed to me wide awake and alert.

'Could you give me a ride home?'

'What happened to you?' she asked. 'Did you have an accident?'

'No. It's a long story.' I must've looked pretty bad, I told myself. 'I just need a ride home.'

She drove me home to Pine Creek Ranch, and I never said a word, not even when she asked dozens of questions. I was too exhausted and ashamed.

I did say, however, when she dropped me off in front of my house, the only words I could manage out of all that shame burying me. 'Thank you,' I said. 'Honestly. Thank you.'

That same Sunday, my mother offered to take me to get stitches so my cut would heal properly and not leave a mark, but I told her I wanted the scar as a reminder.

'A reminder of what?' she asked.

'Of everything,' I said, and I had meant it.

That Sunday night my father rented the film *Vanilla Sky* with Tom Cruise and Penelope Cruz. My mom had given me some pretty strong painkillers — codeine, I think — and I lay on the sofa half numb to the world and thinking to myself as I watched the movie how I couldn't be sure if what had happened by the lake that morning with Natalie actually, in fact, had happened. Had she given me a ride? I'd like to think so. I'd like to think I had a chance to apologize to her, to show her how messed up my life was and how she'd be better off without me.

The last twenty-four hours didn't seem real to me, but I still have a scar to remind me of that night, even if I can't be sure, not a hundred percent certain, that I did see Natalie by the lake one last time, even if I had to pay the heavy price of shame. But I'd like to think it happened the way I told you.

The jellyfish were still floating in Discovery Bay and appeared at ease with one another as I walked away. I passed the clubhouse and headed to the beach and I did so without a word spoken. I kept thinking of Einstein and what he had said, 'I have realized that the past and future are real illusions, that they exist in the present, which is what there is and all there is.' I kept looking at the bay because I was seeing the water shimmering white and I couldn't help but to remember what I've long tried to forget.

Anytime I speak on the topic of identity, fear seems to be lurking in the background. Social systems of control stem from fear on all sides of that two-faced coin of threats and derisive manipulation. In the agricultural age you spoke earlier of, village elders feared total collapse of the community, either through a plague, a war or a devastatingly horrid harvest, which led to instigating fear into the masses. But the masses care less for the whole and much more for individual concerns. The village elders, therefore, had to institute laws and customs and ordinances, much like the dreaded *Prima*

Nocta, in order to subjugate individuals, in effect the masses as a whole of individuals controlled by and through the individualistic fears of any given family unit or individual. Can you imagine bowing and submitting to the *droit du seigneur*?

Humanity has evolved since Edward's decree to breed out the Scots, so when I speak of identity, to me, there's a clear pushing back, a systemic rejection of external forces manipulating an illusion of fear into one's life. In order for the individual to create and become an identity the person needs to reject any fears which may bind him-her-them to any shared illusions within the community. The masses, in forms of society, government, or tradition will ultimately seek greater control through stronger forces using fear as the main weapon of attack. Again, illusions attempting to dispel the individual anomaly in twisted hopes of saving, again out of fear, the community — much like the village elders and kings did centuries ago during the agricultural age you mentioned.

Out of this struggle of Self against Self and Community against Self comes the Hero's Journey made famous in the twentieth century by Joseph Campbell, a mentor of mine in a way. Campbell dispelled the illusions and broke down the communal walls built over the centuries with bricks and bones of ignorance and fear. In the Hero's Journey, the hero sets out on a quest to save the village, the community — which seems to me a romantic ideal to begin with — and in the process of doing so, the young hero destroys in the cave of his soul the infantile ego and becomes the individual, separate from the community, in order to save the community from a terrible disease or a ferocious dragon, as he-she-they were meant to do.

The idea and ideal of the hero-heroine is the mythic dream of the individual and rarely do communities work together to shape, not the individual, the identity of the community as a whole, and rarely did the masses evolve beyond the control of elders, mostly made monarchial and maniacal by the illusory power the elders believed they wielded over the masses.

A model clash of these two opposing forces I found upon arrival in Hong Kong in June of 2014. A few days into my stay I met with famed photographer Jeff Widener, who captured a lone man with a white grocery bag standing directly in the path of a row of army tanks on June 4, 1989 in Tiananmen Square, China. I arrived in Hong Kong on June 1, in time for candle ceremonies and Widener's exhibition and speech to the public at the university. By September the Occupy Central protests, or the Umbrella Movement, began, lasting seventy-nine days.

Nathan Road, a major artery on the Kowloon and Mong Kok side of Hong Kong, would be shut down and filled with protestors living in tents and hastily constructed shelters used for meetings and study quarters. Central and Admiralty, districts of a kind on the island side of Hong Kong, would come to a standstill and crippled the financial district, hosting City Hall and the Legislative Council Complex, turning the city into a ghost town overnight.

While walking down the carless roads in Hong Kong's city center and listening to the multiple individuals giving speeches in Cantonese to the masses, a collection of mostly university students numbering in the tens of thousands all across the city, I thought to myself then how the Umbrella Movement was a beautiful demonstration of non-violent protests for a noble cause by a collective opposing the invisible, often silent, elders who desired Communism.

Hongkongers stormed out of buildings and flooded the streets to show Beijing that true, ultimate power rested in the common person and for a time Hongkongers were filled with joyful determination. Winter, however, came. The protests dwindled. The people returned home having made no real difference, having made no significant change to the way the system worked, because as long as the community or the individual entertained and participated in the illusion, the system would never be broken. Only when the illusion becomes abandoned would real change occur. Even Catalonia attempted in October of 2017 to dispel the illusion and break free from Madrid's control in Spain.

In Hong Kong in the fall of 2014, on an overpass built like a valve in the heart of one of the world's most recognizable finance centers, I sat on the cement divider between the lanes and looked down the sloping road marked with graffiti and over all the varied-colored tents, like being in 1969's Woodstock, the uncountable signs demanding democracy, the Mockingjay symbol spray-painted on the pavement and on columns supporting bridges, near the LegCo the Lennon Wall asking for peace and for, what I believe to be, predetermination, their right to choose their own destiny and their own identity. Hongkongers desired Hong Kong to be excluded from China and to be allowed to fulfil its own personal legend. For China, that was never going to happen.

Even a year after the failed protests — a few weeks after a radio interview I gave stating in open-minded, perhaps too simplistic, terms that 'Hong Kong *is* China' — at the Hong Kong versus China World Cup qualifying match, Hongkongers held for the television-viewing audiences signs which stated 'Boo' in open defiance of China's plea to FIFA to stop its citizens from booing the Chinese national anthem — and more signs with the phrase 'Hong Kong is *not* China' stated the city's intent on not being associated with the mainland.

In Barcelona, hundreds held signs stating 'Catalonia is *not* Spain.' My heart dropped when I read about these signs and these incidents in the *South China Morning Post*, and again when I read that similar signs popped up at one university I had previously worked at as a Visiting Fellow, because I understood what it was like to search for an identity, to struggle and to fight to have that identity recognized and accepted by others, and for the pain the quest causes to all parties involved. It shouldn't be that way but it is.

In the end, Hong Kong became just another territory of China, and the bridges built connecting Hong Kong to mainland China prove this to be true as well. The spirit of what Hong Kong used to be and its death gasps, I witnessed in October of 2014 and later in 2019 — sentencing to a single footnote how Hong Kong became just another Chinese city like Beijing or Shanghai one reads about in the media. The international global icon Hong Kong used to be once long ago in a time far, far away will become less than a memory; the city's British identity and culture shall become history.

Some of the best times I spent as a writer was when no one even knew I was writing. Once, Dylan's wife Gianna, commented on the fact at how shocked she had been to discover how much I'd written for my second book, *The New America*. I had written most of the stories while living in San Angelo — I'd later finish the collection of fiction when I moved to South Korea to write full-time.

In San Angelo, though, I lived in a cozy one-bedroom apartment with a walk-in closet and a fireplace in the living room where I could spend quiet evenings reading by a modest fire. In the dining room I had one desk and computer stationed below a poster of Albert Einstein and his quote: 'Great spirits have always encountered violent opposition from mediocre minds,' and to the right of the desk a bookshelf fashioned into the wall, much like I had as a child, accommodated a dozen or so books I needed for my master's courses in literature at Angelo State, and some three hundred more books in a bookshelf to the left of my desk. In the bedroom I exercised my body on a professional gym workout bench with free weights, and exercised my mind while excising demons at an antique rolltop desk my mother had given me.

At the famous rolltop, my favorite desk to have ever written on, I sat in one of the most comfortable leather swivel chairs I've ever used. I'd spend whole weekends in that chair writing stories no one would read, and my favorite story out of the inspiration of that desk and room had been a story loosely based on Hemingway as a gray-haired man working alone on a novel in his home. The story was called 'The New America,' which later became the title of the collection, and the subtitle had been a question: at what price do we suffer greatness?

After all the trials I've had as a writer and as an international author, I can see why Jerome Salinger locked himself away in a cabin somewhere lost in the New Hampshire wilderness and mountains; Salinger captured the purity in his art, and, to him, publishing tainted the writer. The author of *The Catcher in the Rye* would eventually slip into legend after abandoning the communal illusions while the expectant masses, always wanting, dreamed of having one more book by the author. Give us more, they said. More!

Little Hometown, America

There was a time in the early 2000s at American Capital Bank when a young woman kept calling up on a Jerome David Salinger's credit card account. Jerome Salinger's account listed him as a male living in Cornish, New Hampshire and his birthdate as January 1, 1919. The young woman sounded nothing like an old man, and I kept asking the woman to let me speak to the primary card holder, Jerome, just in case it might be the legendary writer and recluse. She always refused. I imagined that was his daughter taking care of his account. She and I spoke on multiple occasions and she'd always get upset and demand a manager to handle her requests. I never did get to speak with Jerome Salinger.

To think of it, Hong Kong ranks third behind Russia and Turkey in wealth disparity while the United States and Great Britain proved to be two of the worst countries for income equality and social mobility. Finland, the Netherlands, Sweden — who want to avoid bringing attention to themselves and do an incredible job at remaining low-key — much like Jerome Salinger if I think of it — are some of the wealthiest nations that also allow for social mobility and lower levels of income inequality. So as I consider these facts and the deck stacked against millions of Americans, and billions more worldwide like in Hong Kong, I believe myself lucky to have been able to close the door to that apartment in Texas, light a few logs in the fireplace, brew a fresh pot of coffee — hazelnut if I could afford it back then — and open a journal to a blank page with pen in hand to enact the sacred ritual performed by the individual alone.

You were right when you said, once, that I didn't belong to this world. I don't, you know. From where I'm standing the world grows greedier and more corrupt and the masses take it up the ass. Look what happened to those princes in Saudi Arabia around the time Catalonia's quest for independence. Look it up.

I don't mean to sound so pessimistic, because I'm really an optimistic kind of guy. But sometimes the truth needs to be said and when the truth comes out it often doesn't sound very good, but that doesn't mean the truth should be silenced either. I guess that's why the prophets of old lived outside the city gates. On one hand the individual has the government whipping the peons in one direction, and on the other hand the individual has the prophets and priests and pastors pulling them in another direction, and while everyone's distracted in this little righteous game the corruption and greed continue to become worse while honest men and women suffer. Does that sound fair to you? No, of course it doesn't, but I've been all around the world and lived in some memorable and historic cities, such as Saigon, and I've seen the problems and the corruption you speak of in America and I've seen the use of fear as a systemic control in every place I've been and lived, and that tells me more about humanity than I could ever tell you.

You were right. I don't belong in the world. People, the masses, have no desire to hear the breaking of their crystal illusions with diamonds of truth.

One such illusion, since you asked for an example, is how corruption is not the norm but honesty and truthfulness are. The masses, the people, have it backwards: corruption and greed, that's your normalcy, that's the normal state of human activity in the world today. The moment honesty and truthfulness shine through, like a sunray between storm clouds overhead, the people stand in awe and murmur to one another how such wonderful ideals still exist in the mire of the human condition, but the storm clouds collapse once again shutting out the flash of light so briefly held for another day, another time when it may be needed most. I mean, look at what happened in Hollywood after Harry 'Gangbanger' Dickstein and all those #MeToo scandals. That's the world we live in. Guanxi through sex and intimidation. That's going to be world changing stuff right there. As it goes, the masses celebrate good-heartedness and integrity because those traits are so rare, and condemn corruption because it is so widespread. What do you imagine, then, the world would be like if such things could be flipped and the illusion turned? Can you imagine? Can you imagine a world where truth and honesty are widespread and corruption so rare? Can you?

We began this conversation because you asked me about identity. Who are you? you asked. Who are you really?

Who am I? I am a person without fear. In my own private ways, I fear God, but I do not fear other men and women. I do not fear governments nor do I fear threats made against my free will, because I always have a choice. I am free to speak equally to all, whether to a garbage man on the street or to a president of a university or a nation. I am free to be true to myself, free to carefully consider traditions and customs with open eyes and an open mind, and if even a single mustard seed of fear existed in my soul, I would be unable to be true to myself, to live to my full potential.

Erich Fromm once said that 'man's main task in life is to give birth to himself, to become who he potentially is,' and that 'the most important product of his effort is his own personality.'

I am free to be who I am because fear does not exist within me. Because fear does not exist, it remains powerless and useless and becomes its true nature: fear becomes vile and crude, a silly little thing used by weak people who seek to control others. Since I am free, my thoughts are my own, my actions are my own, my life is my own to live, and my character, which establishes my personality, is my own. And if Erich Fromm was right, then I have achieved my greatest success.

At times when I reclined in that leather chair next to my rolltop desk in that modest apartment in Texas I told you about, the one with the fireplace and all the women, I'd try to imagine a time and place, a world if you would allow my freedoms of expressions, organized and governed by elders who were unafraid and free — unlike those officials and cadres in the French government who you heard had confessed their fears — and normal citizens would also be unafraid. I'd imagine what the world could one day look like and be like. I'd imagine the world, the cities, free from fear and the manipulations of its controls used by the weak and insecure to conquer the masses. I'd imagine the world looking back at itself — some one or two hundred years from now — and teaching its follies to the next generation free to evolve, to become, and to be whatever identity it wishes itself to be. Can you imagine? I can.

There was this dream I had once about two young lovers called George and Elizabeth. For some reason Elizabeth died in her innocent prime, let's say seventeen. The dream started with

George, years later, out hunting in the fields for rabbits. George became an excellent hunter, the whole village admired him, because he learned to call Elizabeth's name while out hunting and the rabbits would hop out of their hiding places to seek out the source of the name only for George to find the bunnies with a bullet. George never shouted his former lover's name but whispered 'Elizabeth' long and slow out into the wind and the rabbits would jerk their heads, perk their ears and pounce in the direction from which the name came.

'Eee-lizz-aa-beth. Eee-lizz-aa-beth.'

Then POW!

I could see George in the morning light crossing a hill with his rifle in one hand and two or three rabbits hanging by their ears in the other.

Now aged and in his thirties, George vacationed out in the Caribbean, where he enjoyed snorkeling and diving deep into the heart of the shadowy blue. One morning, swimming alone — he never married — George dove deep to reach the bottom in search of a blue starfish.

Rising to the top, one prized starfish in hand, he heard his name being called. It was so unexpected and so close, he thought someone was behind him; he turned, dropped the blue starfish and found the ocean empty.

He dove thrice more, each time hearing his name.

'GG-ooo-rrr-gge. GG-ooo-rrr-gge.'

George swam underwater fifteen meters at a time, following the source of the name, coming from a cavern of a sunken ship solidified by patient corral over hundreds of years.

He gasped a mighty breath, dove to the ship, where he believed gold awaited him, heard his name beckoning him under the ship, into a hole and into the arms of a giant octopus that hungrily wrapped its massive tentacles around George, who struggled and fought, but the octopus refused to let George go.

I find myself in an awkward position with my feet flopped over the top of the sofa, my back against the seat cushions and my head dangling with an upside-down view of your office, and all the while I'm thinking what a strange and simple word 'upside-down' is and how much the words 'upside' and 'down' contradict each other. I right myself and once again lie normally on the sofa. My Omega watch reads eleven; one more hour before we can call an intermission for lunch, and the weather's clearing, so that's good too.

Let me tell you about trumpets, I say, since we have a little time to kill.

Whenever I hear a trumpet playing, I think of a life I've lived in heaven, paradise valley, before this life I find myself in now, as though the trumpet's melody hints to my psyche that I did not begin in this life nor will I end here.

I know about the Biblical revelations since I've read the King James Bible from cover to cover and how the four trumpets will mark the sky, the earth, the sea, and the springs to welcome the calamities which begin the obliteration of life as we know it, and how the fifth trumpet signals the star to fall, making way for the last two trumpets. The first four wake the world, so at least we see the end coming, and that's a good thing, I suppose.

Trumpets do hold for most people odious and foreboding portents in their music, but for me I'm stirred to attention, like when I'm walking down the street in a crowd and I come across a man playing a trumpet for pocket change on the corner or over in an artificial alcove, and I find myself stopping and forgetting my errands and I think to myself: yeah, I know this song.

The sound of a trumpet lets me know simultaneously that time's running out and there's still time, and I can't explain how those two opposing thoughts merge into an emotion of heavenly calm. If I hear a trumpet, no matter where or when, I have to pause and reflect on who I am, what I've done with my life, and where my life is headed, and I can't be sure if I'm alone on this adventure and that such phenomena don't happen to other sane individuals.

In the key of C, I might consider Duke Ellington on piano and Cat Anderson playing his trumpet and I'm thinking to myself how I should've learned to play a musical instrument, because words in language hidden in books appeal to a single reader at any given time whereas music is immediate and can instantly affect millions. Writing lacks this immediacy and the trumpeter playing on the street corner taunts me to shame, and the trumpet seems to sing, 'Look at what I can do,' and I look back, because I must walk away telling myself to pay no mind to such delusions of grandeur, but there were Louis Armstrong and Miles Davis and they were grand.

One last thing I think about when I hear a trumpet is an idea I have lodged in my being that plays once more in my mind's eye this scenario: I've lived a long life and arrive, finally, at the Pearly Gates, where God Himself steps out between the golden gates and immediately I kneel in the light of His brilliance and how transformational His energy consumes me. Deep down I know I've been here before and I'm secretly hoping — which is pointless because He knows ALL anyway — that God won't ask me that dreaded question, but I also know He will and He does ask the question I've heard a hundred times or more: 'You've lived a long, full life, Cody, and you may enter My kingdom and live out your eternity in holy, remarkable peace, but before you do —'

— here it comes —

'— would you go back, for me, and live your life all over again, from beginning to end, from birth unto death, in a selfless hope and striving in bringing at least one more soul home; would you do that for Me?'

I know I don't ever want to go back and wish each time He doesn't ask that same question, but He does and I must answer the Creator of All. If I say no like I want, I could enter heaven and never have to go back, but in doing so I'll feel guilty for eternity at having rejected God and there's no way I'd be able to face the archangels after such disgrace.

Would you do that for me? The question echoes through me and the selfless side wins and I nod my consent, saying, 'yes, I'll do that for you,' and God reaches down to touch me on the head, saying, 'I have faith, Cody, that you will return to Me with love in your heart,' and that's when my mistake, my human folly, hits me, but God has touched me and I'm back in my mother's womb trying to punch and kick my way out, to no avail because I'm good and trapped, and the memory of my life to come slips into a void of unknowing until I can no longer remember my name as I close my eyes to sleep in hope of evoking the peace I briefly felt in heaven.

When the trumpet stops playing and becomes silent, the spell's broken and I go on my merry way up the street, and all the while I'm trying to recall what it was I was thinking about.

I've been told, as you've also told me once upon a time, that this book by normal standards was too long and unusual for a manuscript. Agent after agent, publisher after publisher, several hundred, enjoyed finding one reason after another to reject this book, to reject me, and for a time I believed their reasoning was valid.

As time passed, though, I reflected on the issues agents and editors had with me and my book. I would find myself alone at the edge of a wide beach in Discovery Bay telling myself that this book was long because life was long. Life also does not have any clearly indicated chapters. The book, for me, had become a representation of life in all its randomness and in all its infinite and finite winding ways. Life was long, too long at times with no chapters, no place to stop and rest, until you get to the end and you want it to never stop or you wish to start all over again. Life, as linear as it may seem to us, holds more randomness than we'd like to believe. The book, like life, developed and grew of its own accord, and through each seemingly random event a story began to form into a complex whole. I'd like to sit here in your office and tell you that I had control of the process the entire time, but you'd know I'd be lying because that's not completely true. The book, like life, seemed to take control and know where it wanted to go next. I had to simply follow along. Many times, I did not feel present as I put words to page; I often felt lost in another universe. I'd awake two hours later still sitting in the chair, pen in hand, Moleskine notebook in lap, and I'd find I'd written fifty-five pages as though in a single breath with a solitary swipe of the hand. I couldn't explain it any better and clearer than that. The book had become what it needed to become to live. We'd like to tell ourselves, comfort ourselves really, that we have complete control over our lives and in the power of a single heartbeat. We'd like to sit back and convince ourselves that we've mapped out our lives to such an orderly degree that we can become bold about tomorrow and, therefore, we'd be able 'to go confidently in the direction of our dreams,' as Thoreau so nicely phrased it. We'd like to believe we have power over the end just as we'd like to believe we have power over the whole of our lives. We'd like to believe, believe, believe in something, anything, so long as our beliefs comfort us and confide in us a strength to walk the paths that we secretly know will always lead us into the unknown fog which has no name and lies directly ahead no matter which way we choose to turn. We could despair, but we'd rather grow brave and build a little more dignity than what we had before with each step forward. There's real courage in choosing to live when all the world seems against you, and in that courage can be found dignity. Let no one convince you otherwise.

Like this book, I won't be able to tell you what's going to happen next or how it's going to end. You'll just have to take the journey like everyone else. In doing so, however, you'll know your solitude was an illusion because you did not take the journey alone; with each step, like with each page you turn, you'll have figured out that you're on this adventure with everyone who came before, with everyone who'll come ever after, and with everyone, right now, who'll be by your side every step of the way.

Genesis 4:1-6: when I began this conversation with you, I never intended to talk about so many other people, but as you stated in the beginning it's certainly unavoidable. We are all connected.

Much of my life has been twisted and wound up in numerous other lives I'm uncertain as to where I end and others begin, like an ouroboros, snake eating snake, until there's no question about it: we were all products of one another; there's no denying that now.

Only now do I think of my brother Chadwick, and though I've done my best to leave him out of it, I find there's no way to tell my story without involving him. Chadwick was and will always be the Golden Child, the firstborn male heir, of the family. Unlike Cassandra, I happened to be born male and presented an immediate conflict to Chadwick's rights, though I've never given much of a damn about such trifles — which seemed to aggravate Chadwick all the more — and so he distanced himself from me at the very beginning, unlike my elder sister who cradled me as her own son once upon a midnight's dream. Even Cassandra's adoration of me threatened Chadwick's sense of destiny and intensified his insecurities at being the prized offspring my parents long awaited.

Chadwick, five years my senior, acted superior by regulating any interaction with him to limited conversations and minimal direct contact. What I recall of Chadwick in my childhood is a blurry image of my big brother on the outskirts of a bubble I could never breach, could never quite reach beyond a fog-boundary because as I grew a year older so did Chadwick and the border between us would also move slightly, until I gave up altogether at any attempt to pierce into the legend that was my brother's world.

Once, Chadwick had been left in charge of me and we jumped on the trampoline together in the back yard. Every few minutes he'd leave to run inside the house for a few minutes and return to push me down and conquer the trampoline I'd so freely given if he would have only asked. At one point I would have given my life for my brother but that time has long passed into a fable of its own history. Now Chadwick's a stranger to me, but then he was my big brother and I wanted to be like him, to follow him over the far seas and to the ends of the Earth.

He bounced off the trampoline and landed in the grass and disappeared into the house. Ten minutes passed. Then twenty. I knocked on the back door because I found it locked. No answer. I returned to the trampoline and resumed jumping for a few more minutes in a solo delight. Then I began to imagine the worst: my brother lying dead on the floor of the kitchen as I enjoyed the trampoline all to myself. How horrid a brother was I?

I knocked frantically on the back door. Chadwick cracked the door a smidge while the chain barred my entry. I pleaded for him to let me in. He refused and shut the door in my face. I knocked and knocked until he cracked the door once more. I leaned my face to the opening begging for my brother not to lock me out of my own house. Chadwick's brotherly response was to squirt a liquid chemical into my eyes.

Instantly my eyes began to burn and I screamed out in holy terror; I actually thought Chadwick had sprayed fire into my eyes and I kept asking myself how the hell was it even possible, but my eyes burned nonetheless. My sight emptied into total darkness where flashes of white beams shot through the darkness one after the other. I had been blinded and before me all I could see was a universe of stars exploding through a dark void.

I pounded on the door in a desperate plea to be let in to wash my eyes and face but Chadwick squirted a second dose. I stumbled back in sheer frustration and bedlam caused by the burning blindness, and I remember thinking to myself how I was going to go blind and how my days of sight ended before I'd even seen the world or a woman's breasts or my own fist born son.

I tumbled off the porch and tossed myself over the ground in search of the hydrant my father used to water the back yard. My hands fumbled along the wall and I must've been way off because I couldn't find the knob or the hose. I used my shirt to wipe my face but my eyes burned more fiercely. Somewhere and somehow, I found the dog's water bowl to splash my face but the bowl lay empty. By this time Chadwick came to my side and I asked what in God's name had he squirted me with.

'Windex,' he said.

'Who in God's name,' I said, 'does that to his little brother?'

Chadwick led me by the arm up the porch steps and through the back door and into the kitchen where he washed the chemicals out of my eyes.

Sitting on the floor of the kitchen, I dried my still-partially-blind eyes with a dishtowel and felt pity, of all things, for my brother, and in a low voice I said,

'I hate you, Chadwick.'

'I'm sorry, I didn't mean —'

'Yes, you did.'

'You're right. I'm sorry. Can you forgive me? Can we not tell mom and dad about this?'

'I could've gone blind, of course I'm going to tell them, you asshole.'

'You're right. It's my fault. Please don't hate me. I'm truly sorry.'

Chadwick stood over me with his hands on his knees as I attempted to see through blurry images of a stove, of a cabinet, of my brother's face.

'No,' I said, 'I don't think you understand. I hate you. I can't love someone who would blind another human being for pleasure. I don't know what kind of person you are.'

'Be that way then.'

'Exactly what I thought.' I said, 'Today you've shown your true colors.'

Years later after soccer practice out in Early, Chadwick had been instructed by our parents to give me a ride home into Brownwood. Both our teams had scrimmaged at the same complex that evening, but Chadwick out right refused logic and reasoning and made it clear in no uncertain terms was *he* going to give *me* a ride home.

'But why? I'm your brother and we're going in the same direction.'

'I'm not going home,' he said. 'Find your own way, punk.'

'What did I ever do to you?' I asked, my soccer bag hanging from my shoulder. One by one cars drove out of the gravel parking lot with the sun quickly descending. I feared I'd be abandoned again.

'Nothing,' my brother replied.

'Then why won't you give me a ride home tonight?'

'Because I don't have to.'

With that Chadwick slammed the door to his beat-up, light-blue Volkswagen Beetle and waited for his friend and teammate Michael to join him off on their merry adventure, wherever that might be.

I waved down a passing truck with a few of my teammates in the back and asked for a ride home. They were more than happy to assist.

As I climbed into the back of the truck, Chadwick peeled his beetle-bug through the gravel lot. The back tires spun the heavy butt of the Beetle-Bug wildly from side to side. Chadwick accelerated as he began to lose control, and he over-corrected his position, swerving from one side of the street to the other in a frantic attempt to regain command of his car. Just as soon as he had left me to fend for myself, Chadwick and Michael slammed into a five-foot ditch on the far side of the street, where my ride soon slowed next to my brother's car accident.

Chadwick and Michael emerged from the beetle-bug shaking their heads and lucky to be alive and unhurt. A back tire was blown and I knew Chadwick didn't have a spare.

The driver asked Chadwick, 'Do you need any help?'

I leaned to the front window and said, 'Don't help him. He's ungrateful. He didn't even want to give me a ride home.'

The driver said, 'Really?'

'Shut up,' Chadwick said. 'What did I ever do to you?'

'Nothing,' I said, smirking at the turn of phrase and of events.

'Why won't you help me?' My brother pleaded. 'I don't even have a jack.'

'Because I don't have to.' To the driver I said, 'Leave him. He's a big boy.' I turned to Chadwick and added, 'The punk can find his own way home.'

The truck drove away with my teammates and I laughing and waving goodbye to Chadwick and Michael stranded in the failing light.

That old trampoline of ours had seen better days, like the time Chadwick's friend Darcy came over to the house on Vincent. Chadwick shut himself in his room to listen to vinyl records while Darcy and I jumped and played on the trampoline.

At some point during the fun, I wagered Darcy, who rose to a good three feet above me, that I could knock him to the ground in one punch. He contested the idea of how such a small boy could bring down a giant like him. I mentioned, quite ironically, the story of David versus Goliath.

'There's no way,' he said. 'It can't be done.'

'Then what's the harm in trying? Or are you chicken?' I pounced around the trampoline flapping my arms and moving my head like a chicken.

After much teasing, Darcy agreed to the duel. 'Only one punch,' he said.

'All I need is one,' I said.

'Then give me your best shot.' He held his hands behind his back and lifted his jaw for the fatal blow that never came.

'Ready?' I said.

Darcy puffed out his chest. 'Come on, squirt, let me see what you've got.'

'You asked for it.'

In the center of the trampoline, I dropped to one knee and punched, as hard as I could, Darcy right smack in the balls. The giant imploded. Darcy's hands emerged from behind his back and he held his crown jewels as he slunk to his knees and dropped over on his side, where he remained for a good thirty minutes. Being small and having the advantage of a surprise attack, I didn't hesitate to run like hell off the trampoline and behind one corner of the house, where I gulped my fear down and peered around the edge to see if I'd waken a sleeping bear. But five minutes passed, then ten minutes, and I slowly walked to the border of the trampoline to check on Darcy. 'You okay, man?' A groan followed another groan. Darcy held his privates in a fetal position in the center of the trampoline. Never speak ill of me. I was just a boy who didn't understand this crazy world and its crazy ways.

Unable to move myself, I watched him for another five minutes because I couldn't be sure if he was playing possum to try and trap me. I climbed on to the trampoline and placed my hand on his shoulder, much the same way I would do in a few years with Cassandra, and asked Darcy if he needed to go to the hospital.

'Get Chadwick.'

Without thinking things through — after all Darcy was on the brink of death and who was I to refuse a man's dying wish — I ran and pulled Chadwick outside, where he looked to his fallen friend and asked, 'What the hell happened?'

Darcy groaned and squirmed, unable to lift himself, and added, 'Cody.'

Chadwick turned to me with an anger I had only seen in my father's face,

'What did you do?'

'I hit him.'

'You hit him?'

'He hit me in the cock and balls.'

'Yes,' I said. 'I hit him in the cock and balls.'

'In the balls?' Chadwick knelt alongside his friend. 'Does it hurt?'

'My balls,' Darcy managed to say. 'My precious balls.'

'Yes.' I said, 'In the balls.'

'Why did you do that?' Chadwick asked. 'Why?'

Darcy groaned and writhed. 'My balls,' he said between moans. 'Why? Why? Why?'

'Because he bet me that I couldn't knock him down with a single punch.'

'You did that with one hit?' Chadwick knelt beside Darcy and placed a hand on his friend's shoulder. 'Only one?'

'Why? Why? Why?' Darcy twisted. 'My balls. My balls. My balls.'

'Yes,' I said to Chadwick. Then I turned to Darcy and concluded, 'That should teach you to never underestimate the little guy and to never make bets. You're a Christian and you shouldn't be making bets, especially with your body. Consider this a lesson learned and be done with it.'

Although Darcy eventually managed to crawl off the trampoline and into Chadwick's Volkswagen Beetle-Bug, and despite being able to forgive me for proving him wrong, Darcy doubtfully never came to forget what I did to him that one afternoon on the trampoline. Years later that same trampoline would meet its own end behind the white house on Durham.

Behind that same Durham house, Chadwick and I erected a small soccer field with a regulation goalpost and net. Chadwick and his best friend Michael had planned to steal the equipment alone until I convinced them that bringing along a squirt like me would make them less suspicious and help them to have less of a chance at getting caught. Chadwick, Michael and I borrowed my father's truck and trailer, and at four in the morning we drove to the Early soccer complex I told you about with a soccer ball, a shovel and a pickaxe.

Chadwick parked truck and trailer along the fence line with the truck facing outward to the exit, and we three musketeers began shoveling an old goalpost out of the cold earth. The digging was awkward and slow at first because every time a car's headlights came down a backroad behind the sports complex, we'd drop the shovel and pickaxe to knock the soccer ball around as though we needed a pre-dawn workout. By the time we got good and going, we warmed up and forgot about traffic and focused more on speed.

Until, that is, we hit cement at the bottom of the first of the two posts, and we nearly gave up because Chadwick and Michael disagreed about what to do. Chadwick wanted to continue, get it done with, while Michael feared being caught and arrested by the police. I had always known Michael was a coward — and a few months later he would go into my bedroom while I was still asleep before school one morning and steal seven dollars (a five and two ones) from my wallet lying on the dresser. I addressed Chadwick in the hallway about the theft, said I'd seen Michael steal from me with my own eyes in the reflection of the mirror, and wanted Chadwick to stick up for me, his little brother, but Chadwick had made his alliances and he shrugged me off and never spoke of the crime again — but as I was saying, I had not known Michael was a thief then but his cowardliness started to shine through that early morning at the soccer complex.

Being the youngest had its disadvantages, but I knew a deciding vote when I saw one. I voted with my brother to stay and get that damn post out of the ground. I told Michael if he wanted to quit, he could go wait in the truck, but Chadwick and me were getting this thing out of the ground and when it came time to play soccer, Michael wouldn't be invited over.

By six, both posts had been freed and lifted out of their cement holes. We three managed to carry the goalpost to the fence and drag it over easily enough. Chadwick and Michael strapped the metal poles to the trailer as I kept lookout. As the sun started to ascend and we drove down the backroads into Brownwood, I realized how this was the first sunrise I'd seen with my big brother.

By the end of the day the goalpost was erected and cemented in our back yard behind the white house on Durham, where the trampoline had to be moved to the space between the house and the garage — a tight fit but a fit nonetheless.

One day several neighborhood kids and I jumped on the trampoline, like we had done several times before without incident — and as the five of us hopped and bounced and rolled and tumbled, I saw in the midst of ten feet a pair of wrought-iron scissors, much like the kind I had known in my years as an infant. I halted the jumping and picked up the scissors and immediately began looking for a puncture, which soon presented itself. I made the four children sit, as I did myself, in a circle.

'Who brought the scissors?' I asked. 'I'm not angry. I just want to know.' I wasn't angry at all but I was disappointed.

No one replied.

'Why would any of you bring scissors onto a trampoline?'

'How do you know it was us?' one of the boys said.

'Don't be stupid,' I said. 'I'm not stupid and since no one wants to admit it, I'll say that I know one of you brought the scissors to try and put a hole in the trampoline. Well, you've done just that. You can go home happy, but you've ruined the fun for all of us.' No one spoke and each child listened patiently as I finished. 'Now since no one's claiming the scissors, I'm going to keep them. I'm going inside now and all of you need to go home or I'll call the police and have you removed off the property.'

Children often found it strange when I spoke to them like an adult — and come to think of it, adults find it peculiar when I speak to them like an adult — but either way no child spoke in angered reply or abuse. The illusion surrounding the conspiracy had been shattered and, as often as it does happen, not one of them could deny the bald truth.

'Now go home and think about what you've done. But I never want to see any of you ever again.'

Each of the four began to apologize and blame the boy who had spoken out, but I heard none of it.

'Too late,' I said, waving my hand. 'I gave you all a chance in the beginning to be honest but none of you took it. Now leave me. I don't want to be friends with people like you.'

With scissors in hand, I hopped off the trampoline and went inside my house. Out the back window I saw three of them turn on the boy who had brought the scissors and they argued for a time until I opened the back door and told them to leave now, right this very instant or I was going to call the police. I shut the door and watched out the back window the four of them crawl off the trampoline and, with heads low, walk home in dejected shame. One or two of them would drop by in the weeks to follow, arguing their innocence in the case and wanting to jump on the trampoline, but I would hear none of it and told them to go away and leave me alone. Over time the tiny puncture in the trampoline from that day grew and grew until the thing itself was ruined.

I've never cared much for hospitals, but I've seen my fair share of them. If I could go the rest of my life without seeing another hospital, that'd be just fine. You'd find no complaints here.

A year or two before I left the States in 2006, my mother had neck surgery, and I drove up from San Angelo to Abilene thinking about how much I hated hospitals. When I arrived that Friday evening, I was surprised to see Chadwick wasn't there. In his place, where I suppose it should've been, was my father. Despite my parents having been divorced for more than a decade, my father stayed faithful to my mother, and deep inside me I felt more love and respect for my father.

He and I shook hands and I caught up on my mother's condition: she was resting and the surgery had been a success, but she still felt weak and pain and couldn't swallow. She had her surgery on Thursday and as much as I wanted to be there then I couldn't get away from American Capital Bank, but what worried the doctors was that my mother should've been starting solids but on Friday evening the IV was still stuck in the back of her hand and she had trouble drinking water or chewing ice-chips. My father finished by saying he'd stay a little later but he needed to head back to Brownwood for work at the plant in the morning; he'd been at the hospital for two days and now that I was there, I could watch over Gwendolen, my mother.

'Where's Chadwick?' I said, 'He should be here.'

'He had to work.'

'So did I, but I'm here.'

I'd gone into work early that morning and left around four to drive up, and so I was there when the nurses served dinner to my mother. I held the spoon up to her dry, cracked lips and fed her the chicken broth, but every time she attempted to swallow even a little sip she'd gag and choke and spit the broth back into a rag I had ready. After thirty minutes of gagging and choking on soup and water, my mother lay back exhausted and worn. I told her I'd wash her body with a warm, wet rag later.

'Thank you, son,' she said, and she looked at me with that odd eye I've seen on a few other occasions in a few others who were also suffering. Was this the look of death? Of pain? Of acceptance? Of complete surrender to one's own mortality? Of fear for not wanting to let go but knowing the odds? I had seen that odd eye in the dying before and to be honest — if you really must know — it scared the shit out of me. I didn't want to see my mother in so much pain and I couldn't let her see me cry. I told her I'd be back, to rest, and I went out into the hall to find my father.

'What's Chadwick's number?'

'Why? What's wrong?'

'Just give me your phone. I'm calling Chadwick.'

'I just spoke to him.' My father handed me his cellphone with Chadwick on the line. 'Here,' my father said to Chadwick, 'your brother wants to talk.'

'Where are you?' I said to Chadwick.

'What do you mean? I'm in Oklahoma. How's mom?'

'Don't give me that. Answer my question: where are you?'

'I'm at home. Why? What's wrong?'

'That's right. You're at home snuggled in front of the TV with your beloved wife and kids all the while our mother's dying.'

'What happened? She's dying?'

'She's on her deathbed and all alone with only one of her children to say goodbye. How would you feel?'

'Cody, I can't. I have —'

'Don't give me that bullshit. You're the firstborn, the Golden Boy, the favorite. My whole life I've had to live with that knowledge but I've learned to accept it. Fine. I'm the baby. So what. But our mother is dying and you can't even come say goodbye to her because something's more important. Well, fine. But you'll regret it when she's gone and you have to carry her coffin.' Sure, I oversold it, but you had to do that with Chadwick.

'What happened, Cody?'

'She's not good and she needs you here but you're not; that's what's happened. I expected this from Cassandra but not from you. What the hell's wrong with you?'

'I'm driving down tonight. I'll be there in a few hours.'

'That's what I thought. Now you're acting like the Chosen One.'

'Shut up and put dad on.'

'No, you shut up and listen to me. Mom needs you and you better be here tonight like you say or I'm coming for you. I'll beat the shit out of you, big brother. You better believe it.'

'Okay, okay, I will. Just put dad on.'

'I'm warning you, mister,' I said. I had so often heard that phrase used by my mother I couldn't help but throw it back on Chadwick. 'Here's dad.'

I handed the cellphone back to my father who looked at me stunned because he had never heard me speak like that to Chadwick and my father had never known how I really thought of my big brother before.

'Chadwick will be here tonight,' I said to my father, who didn't know how to respond.

He put the cellphone to his ear, and as I walked back into my mother's room, I heard my father tell Chadwick, 'She's not good, son. You'd better come.'

I held my mother's hand, much the same way I'd do with Axton twelve or more years later when I had to rush my wife to the ER in Hong Kong at two in the morning and the doctors said they found internal bleeding and that my wife was also five weeks pregnant, but the doctors might have to remove one of the ovaries and a fallopian tube. They'd said the pregnancy was ectopic, outside the womb, and how I cried and held Axton's hand — we'd gone from having a child to the doctors telling us they'd have to stop the bleeding by removing affected parts because of a ruptured cyst on one of Axton's ovaries. I cried, fearing I'd lose Axton forever, and held her hand and told her over and over and over again, 'It'll be okay. It'll be okay. It'll be okay,' and I stroked her hair while Axton said, 'My baby, my baby, my baby,' and Axton stared up at the ceiling thinking how she was to become a mother in one minute and not in the next.

I remember that night well, some five years ago, when Axton, all hunched over from the internal bleeding, and I stepped through the automatic doors into Canossa Hospital's lobby and there before us were a hundred moths — or white butterflies, as I'd say later — flittering in a giant ball over the lobby chairs, and I kept thinking how one doesn't see such a sight every day and this night must be special; and it would be because Dr. Eric Lee pulled down his mask and sat beside me to explain that Axton's operation went better than expected, she's recovering, how the cyst was removed, the ovary repaired, and no parts needed to be removed, but how he doubted that she was pregnant, but she'll recover and be better than new in no time.

I held my mother's hand unaware of my own future — the one with Axton and our unborn baby in Hong Kong that would come a decade later — when Chadwick rushed in sometime after nine that Friday night in Abilene.

'Oh, Chadwick,' my mother said, barely able to speak through her sore throat. 'Oh, Chadwick.'

'I'll leave you two alone,' I said. 'I'll be in the lounge.'

'Now that I get here you run away,' Chadwick said. 'I came all this way.'

'I've been here by mom's side all night. You need to see mom. I don't need to see you. I just figured the Golden Son needed a moment with his mother who brought him into this world.'

'Son,' my mother said, and I didn't know which son she meant.

Chadwick remained speechless as he looked from me to our mother, hooked to monitors and machines. She appeared pale to the bone.

'I'll be back in a little while,' I said, and walked down the hall to the lounge to get some free coffee.

By the window, I sipped my coffee and looked out over the city and the land under night with the bright light of the lounge reflected before me in the window. I could also see my own reflection in the window but I refused to look at myself. Instead, I stared far into the night knowing, deep down, that my mother would die one day but tonight she'd be okay now that Chadwick was there, and Cassandra would come the next day to keep me company and bring me some food. But then, by that window, I thought of how I wasn't needed in this world, not really; there was Chadwick, the beloved son, and Cassandra, the cherished daughter, and then that was enough. There was no need for a third and I ended up coming out twisted and broken and filled with pain.

I sipped my coffee and thought of that time when I was just a teenager and my mother and I drove to St. Louis to visit Uncle Smiley and Aunt Samarah because my cousin Brighton had undergone some sort of surgery, a double-lung transplant, I think, but I'm not sure because I want to say that major surgery came much later, but I remember watching Brighton, colorless like ivory, sleeping in the hospital bed with a tube down his throat and a machine breathing for him, and how he didn't even know I was there next to him, and how I prayed for my cousin to get better, to live a long, full life with me as his friend, because Brighton was the best kind of person with the purest kind of character God could've created in a human being. I admired Brighton for maintaining such a positive outlook on life while suffering more than I had ever seen any one person suffer.

Brighton, however, would suffer complications and die on April 22, 2001 — a Sunday I now cannot remember. Even while battling cystic fibrosis, he'd preach in Israel and Singapore. I regret not going to his funeral, but I couldn't bring myself to see him in a coffin. To me, that wasn't him. Never would be again.

I kept thinking how young people like Brighton Cambridge should be one of the lucky ones, the ones who get a better shot out of life than the young man standing with a cup of coffee and a chip on his shoulder in the reflection of the window in front of me.

Othello has long been my favorite of the Shakespearian plays, and although I remained fascinated at the villain Iago's ability to sway poor Othello the Moor, and in the end to escape punishment from his evil devices, I find the play a comprehensive collective of all human emotions. If extraterrestrials landed at my doorstep and asked me to explain human behavior, I'd hand them a copy of *Othello* and tell them to read it and slam the door shut in their green faces.

What I find a bit more interesting is that the play is as applicable and topical today as it was when it was first written and performed in 1604. Iago has his ambition, corruption and greed. Desdemona has her beauty, innocence and love. Othello has his honor, naivety and jealousy. And the play speaks to me of how even the best of friends can seek to ruin you and take all the joy that you have, and that true friendships are hard to come by after high school and university.

When I lived in that yellow house on Vincent Street, the one I told you about, Keven lived directly across the street and although he was my sister's age, a few years younger than Chadwick and a few years older than me, Keven and I became quite close one summer and we had many adventures together. One being the time Mr. T, our neighbor who owned a second house that sat empty next to mine, caught us poking around his additional house one dull summer day.

The vacant house stood to the left of my yellow house without a fence to separate the two. Keven thought it would be an excellent idea to do some exploring in the old barn-like garage behind the vacant house. We parked his Diamondback bike against the sidewall and thought we were safe enough because we entered through the alley, which also had no fence, and concealed Keven and I from the main road, Vincent Street, and a direct line of sight from Mr. T's house on the adjacent corner. What Keven wanted most was to explore the attic of the garage but to get to the loft's window we had to step through a door in the side building that connected to the main structure of the garage. I hoisted Keven and he used my shoulder to step up and before I knew it, Keven vanished through the opening in the attic.

'What do you see?' I asked, my heart pounding in my ears. 'Help me up.'

'Just some old junk.'

'Let's get out of here.'

'Give me a minute,' he shot back. 'I want to have a look around.'

The small side building I stood in had not been used in many years and cobwebs filled every crevice that I saw. A pile of boards lay stacked to one side near the wall and the dirt floor caused more dust to stir in the air than usual. Shafts of light poured in through the back and front passages as I craned my neck up to see what Keven saw.

Then like a raging bull charging from an opened gate, the old man Mr. T barged in through the back door of that little shed. He stepped over the board there at the bottom of the door and his arms stretched out in a lurching fury to clutch his victim as though he were the creature in Mary Shelley's *Frankenstein*.

Upon this sight, I bolted free out the front door and into the back yard, over the chain-link fence, and knowing I might be followed or watched by Mr. T, I didn't run into my back yard off to my right, but instead kept full speed down the driveway next to the vacant house, turned left, away from my house and Keven's and Mr. T's, and sprinted as fast as I could down two blocks, turned the corner behind the supermarket, and hid behind a tree as I put my hands on my knees and tried to catch my breath. After several minutes, I stepped out from behind the tree and out into the street and found I hadn't been followed by Mr. T or by Keven.

I'm not sure how or when Keven and I met up later that day, because I made sure my trail had grown cold before I snuck along the alley behind my house and into my back yard and finally into the back door of my house. Keven would knock on the back door some hours later, and I stepped outside — I'm not sure why but I never liked letting anyone inside — and we hid in a storage building behind my house where my father and mother kept the Christmas and other holiday decorations.

'What the hell happened?' he asked.

'I don't know. You tell me. I got out of there when Mr. T came. Did he catch you? What happened to you?'

'Did you take my bike?'

'Why would I do that? Your bike was out back and I ran out the front.'

'I bet Mr. T has it.'

'I bet he does. Watcha gonna do about it?'

'I don't know. He must have it locked up in his garage.'

'Do you think we could steal it back?'

'I'm not going to steal my own bike when he stole it from me.'

'Maybe we could call the police?'

'And get in trouble for snooping around on Mr. T's place?'

'Say,' I said. 'Where were you? I called for you but you were gone.'

'After Mr. T came in, I hid in the attic until he left. He must've thought you were alone and that my bike was your bike.'

'Good thing I didn't bring *my* bike.'

'Hey! What's that supposed to mean?'

'Nothing. It's just one bike is better than two.'

'That doesn't help me.'

'No. No, it doesn't. I think you should just go talk to Mr. T like an adult and apologize and ask for your bike back.'

'You should come with me. Let's go together now.'

'Then he'll know I was there too.'

'You're not coming?'

'Why? It's not my bike.'

'Some friend.'

'Hey. It wasn't my idea to go trespassing like Tom or Huck. At least I had the good sense to leave my bike at home.'

'You don't understand. My dad's going to kill me. That's a Diamondback; it cost him over five hundred dollars.'

'You better go get it then,' I said. 'I'm going in. It's getting late and dinner's ready.'

Keven broke down that night and told his father who whipped him good and hard with belt and buckle, and then the two walked across the street, Keven all in tears, and apologized to Mr. T for the disturbance, agreed Keven would do some chores at Mr. T's place, and retrieved Keven's precious bike back.

Some weeks later Keven and I played in the storage shed behind my house because we had hoped to clean it up and make a clubhouse. The building was quite large, some fifteen yards long and ten yards wide, but dust and spiders and chronic disuse made it hard to get the place clean.

'This place has a bathroom,' Keven said. 'Does it work?'

'Nope.' I stood at the front door imagining this building being someone's home, maybe a servant's quarters in a time before my birth and arrival to this planet and found the scene odd.

We moved around the boxes, pushing them off to the back or to the side until Keven uncovered several large boxes filled with *Playboys*. We, as teenage boys that summer, had hit the jackpot.

Over the next few hours, and the next few weeks, we scrolled through stacks of nude women from the sixties, seventies and eighties and feasted on the delights of seeing what we believed we'd never see: college girls, mature maidens, exotic lovelies, voluptuous virgins, and oh so many countless more. With each raw curve and bared nipple, I drank in the pleasures of these strange women until my dreams became erotic and wet and embarrassing.

I'd find out much later that my mother had bought these boxes of *Playboys* from her boss, Dr. Bovary, and Keven and I could never figure out why a man would ever part ways with such beautiful denizens eager and ready at the fingertips. But by the time Keven and I found this piece of information out, my father had removed the boxes, burned my mother said, and changed the locks on the back shed, much to Keven's dismay. By the end of that summer, Keven and I would have our greatest falling out — we'd never be the same again nor did we speak much after that — and if I'm to blame myself, then I'll blame jealousy for my actions, much like Othello.

Keven and I had gone to the vacant lot I told you about behind Mr. T's first home many times because of the great bike trails there. Mr. T had often complained but since a dirt alley separated his back yard and the empty lot, he could do very little to stop Keven and I from riding there, even if it was private property.

The dirt alley ran high above the vacant field and from this point one could shoot down a sharp drop some twenty feet high, where the short trails ran through small trees and large rocks. On one occasion I had gone down the hardest trail thirty times and each time I'd hit a large rock protruding from the center of the trail and I'd flip bike over bruised body until I'd lie smashed at the bottom of the trail in the empty field. I'd groan and ache and think no one would find me and I'd die all alone as I stared at the blue sky and white clouds above, all so simple really. I'd re-strengthen my courage to get up, climb the hill, get on my bike and master that trail. The trick, which I did finally learn, was to dodge a tree partly in the trail on my left, then immediately avoid the rock in the trail to my right, weaving an S pattern between the two and sailing on into the vacant field and into victory.

One day, Keven and I were riding the trails when Chadwick came to call me home to supper. Keven made a snide comment and I returned with a quip of my own. I'm not sure what was said but we had been riding all afternoon and we were hot and tired and grumpy. We began arguing and wrestled for a bit before Chadwick stepped between us, which fueled the verbal assaults all the more.

'I'm not going to fight you, Cody,' Keven finally said.

'Everyone needs to calm down and go home,' Chadwick said. 'Cody, mom wants you in now.'

'Yeah,' I said to Keven, 'run home you fucking pussy.'

By this time the insults had been overused and we'd grown sour. Keven and I had wrestled for a bit but now Chadwick stood between us in the middle of the field and no matter how I tried — I was out for blood — Chadwick would not let me by. Keven walked his bike up one of the trails on the hill and started walking down the alley towards his house a block away. At this point Keven was some fifty yards away and Chadwick blocked my every attempt I made to rush around him. Instead, I recalled the story of David who brought down a giant with a stone. I bent down looking for a rock, found one, hurled it and missed. After finding another one, I hit the metal dumpster at the end of the alley, where Keven stopped, some ten yards away from the dumpster, and looked down the hill at me. In what I thought to be a taunt, he began to slowly peddle away.

With each throw Chadwick would stop and watch the rock soar through the air and miss, and as he turned his back to me, I looked for my third rock, which I found to be a good heavy size, and spotting my last chance, I held the rock to my lips and said, 'May your aim be true and hit its mark.' I closed my eyes, breathed and steadied myself. All time slowed. When I opened my eyes, Keven, far away on the hill, appeared close to me, some ten yards or less, as if the Universe had grown smaller in that moment, and I let fly that rock with the anger and frustration and willpower of a fallen angel. Chadwick, as if in a trance, watched the rock crash into Keven's side, causing the boy to topple to the ground with the bike between his legs.

Not missing another chance, I darted around Chadwick, who could not believe his eyes and stayed frozen in the middle of the vacant lot. I climbed the hill in a run and seeing Keven moaning in the dirt and holding his side, I knew I had slain my adversary. I calmly walked over to him and said quite harshly, 'That's what you get.' Then I picked up his bike, carried it to the end of the alley and was about to throw it into the dumpster, but decided to toss the bike into a pit filled with an old tire, piles of dead trees and other rubbish behind the dumpster. As if the Universe fulfilled my every wish that day, a boulder about the size of a bowling ball emerged in the center of my vision down on the ground next to my feet. I lifted the boulder and chunked it into the pit where it smashed, making a noticeable dent, in the frame of Keven's beloved Diamondback. I turned back to see Chadwick stuck in a time lock of shock, still in the center of the vacant lot, and once more I looked to my fallen friend squirming in the dirt of the alley — and it felt like I had all the time in the world — but by then I cared very little, because no matter what I did my friend would turn against me when the time and opportunity came. I walked home fueled by the power of my rage and the pride that overwhelmed me at having hit a target dead on some fifty yards away with a single stone: that had been one miraculous shot.

My whole life I've been looking to swallow the sun or the moon or for someone else who has, but I've never met anyone who ever did. If you try to stick your head up and be spectacular, extraordinary, people will come and chop it off on the quick, which makes no sense to me. Lots of these same executioners lie to themselves and say they're not involved in any groupthink and deep down, without kidding themselves, they know who they really are, and they don't mind dragging down others with their foolish song and dance.

The jungle's dark but full of diamonds. Dark but magnificent. One must go in to fetch a diamond out. There's no question about that, is there?

For whatever reason as for whichever design the stars above divinized for my life, I was born without the ability to bullshit or the tact to kiss ass or bend over and take it up the pucker. Certainly, having a smart mouth and a stubborn heart factored heavily in my Texan upbringing, meaning I didn't back down from a challenge, especially when my opposition deserved little respect in the eyes of the public. To sum, forthwith, I was not born a sheep to be led passively to the slaughter; I was born a lion, and most of my life was spent coming to terms with who I am and with who I needed to be.

For much of my life I've been lucky and fortunate enough to avoid the corporate dogma that belittles and plagues the mind and spirit of so many beautiful individuals. In my early twenties while I studied at night for a master's in literature, I'd work an eight to five job, Monday thru Friday, sometimes Saturday, at American Capital Bank. My most memorable phone call came in one of the last few years of my employment — in 2003 or 2004, I think — when Michelle Obama called several times to speak on her husband's private account. Each time representatives would read the script apologizing for the inconvenience and how she needed to have her husband call so he could add her to his private account, that may or may not exist, and then we'd be delighted and more than happy to assist her. Around the office, like hedgehogs popping up from their holes in the ground, my colleagues would raise their heads out of the cubicles and say, 'Osama Obama's wife called again.'

By ten that morning the call would cycle around and land at my desk, and finally I tossed the script, laid it out straight to her: there was no way anyone was going to risk getting fired by talking to her, regardless of who her husband was.

At this time, I should note, Senator Obama in America was practically unheard of, and the only reason I recall the incident is because the Federal Bureau of Investigation had alerted all banks across the country to red flag any customers that may have suspicious Middle Eastern names and/or purchasing activity that would seem out of the norm. It was then I realized how shabby and unprofessional the FBI was, because it was calling on me, as well as other random individuals to spot on a case-by-case basis terrorist activity. The FBI didn't have a clue what was going on. One can empathize with me, then, that a name like Barack Hussein Obama would draw attention to civilians gripped by a terror from the 9/11 attacks from a few years before.

Eventually I convinced Michelle Obama to conference her husband the Senator in and then I'd be able to verify his information and then get his permission to add her to the account as an authorized user. Michelle was obviously in a hurry and wanted to simply have it her way and contest a late fee charge recently applied to the account, but even then, as I'd explain to Barack, authorized users couldn't request fees to be removed or make changes to an account, only the primary cardholder could do that, and after Bush's Patriot Act, bank employees could no longer add secondary cardholders to an account after activation. I'd need to speak with her husband directly.

Obama came on the line and by that time I was good and pissed off because of Michelle's bitchy attitude. Everyone in the office loathed speaking to her — hence the nickname — but I'd given her the benefit of the doubt — a consistent flaw I keep having: giving people the benefit — but she ended up disappointing me, like everyone else, anyway, and the office at American Capital Bank knew who wore the pants in the progressive Obama household.

After verifying Obama's information — name, address, social security number and telephone number — I gave him the ultimate test:

'Sir,' I said, 'let me *educate* you about our policies.'

This was a trigger phrase that I had perfected over my years at American Capital because it performed the function of my job while pushing the right buttons on about 99% of the callers. They'd blow up and curse and argue and bemoan and tell me exactly how they should be spoken to with respect, mind you, and to remember who was on the other line; 'I know who I'm speaking to,' I'd say, then I'd rattle off all of their personal information and shopping lists. Sometimes they'd ask for a supervisor and end up getting, per policy, another employee who pretended to be the supervisor for such calls, which was fine by me because it gave me a break from talking. But Obama baffled me and I grew to respect the man when he replied, 'Okay, please educate me about your policies so we won't have this problem again.'

Never in my time at American Capital had I heard such emotional intelligence from a man or woman. Obama spoke with such a carefree attitude that I wanted to sit by a fire and have a coffee with the man.

I explained the boring policies involving late penalties, added his wife as an authorized user, explained more about the policies of what she could and could not do on the account, issued a card to her, waved the late fee, explained more policies and informed him that he had been late three times in the past six months, news to him, and that in the future we might not be able to wave any additional fees. No promises.

Obama listened patiently, with restrained wisdom, and acknowledged what I said with direct but practical questions. Then he did something else that customers rarely did; he asked me about myself. I told him I was a graduate student by night in Texas, a long way from Chicago, one of my favorite cities because of Walter Payton and the Bears, and that I was writing a book called *A Father's Son*, and elaborated a bit about Paul who was the orphan in the novella.

'That's interesting,' Obama said, 'because I'm writing a book as well.'

'Really?' I said. 'What's it called?'

'Nothing's official yet,' he said as if I were another friend over the phone, 'but I've been thinking of calling it *The Audacity of Hope*, because like your book, it's about a father and his son, but this happens to be about my father.' Obama elaborated on the topic and on his other book, *Dreams of My Father*, published in 1995, and I jotted down the names of the books. A few years later I'd see Obama on the *Oprah Winfrey Show*, and I said to myself: 'That's him. That's Osama Obama.' What's also interesting to note is that his book about his father was published in 2006, the first year I'd spend overseas.

Over the telephone, Obama and I discussed our books and our future plans, and although the call ended after forty-five minutes, killing my average talk time for that day, I left the conversation feeling a little lighter, a little more grateful and more appreciative of the human race; that is, until the very next call shot through with a temperamental woman demanding she speak to a supervisor. She cursed and screamed and probably foamed at the mouth, and since her account was marked for Collections, I said, 'Just one moment and let me get *you* someone to help *you* handle *your* account,' then I warmed transferred her to an agent in the Collections department so they could get the money she owed.

Most days I'd sit at my desk staring out the window over the empty Texas landscape and dream about being out there and not spending my whole life slaving away for pennies making some corporate Fat Rat richer and greedier. On average I spoke to 250 Americans daily, estimating to about five thousand customers a month, some sixty thousand individuals, if not more, a year, and a majority, if not all, presented themselves to me as a spirit in turmoil and in a kind of purgatory: suffering unfiltered hatred at how much debt they owed and at me for holding them accountable for their mistakes, but I sympathized with them and knew the system was broken.

Even in 2005, we at the bank knew the economy was headed for a crash. The bubble, ever so evident by then, grew and grew and we were told by headquarters in D.C. to keep our mouths shut if any reporters called: we didn't want to cause a panic and collapse the entire system, did we? Instead, defaulting mortgages and other bad loans were sent to Countrywide, which made a fortune by accepting anything on paper in order to resell back to other banks to keep the wheel spinning. A friend once told me how his cousin in California worked for Countrywide and profited over five thousand dollars a month in commissions alone, and the way customers flocked to Countrywide to pass over toxic debts would be much the same to dropping bleeding cattle into a nest of starving crocodiles. On January 6, 2006, I had had enough of Countrywide and American Capital, and I walked out at 10:30 on a Friday morning, said I needed the day off to think about if I really wanted to continue down this path working for a place like American Capital. I never returned. I never looked back.

I've never regretted that decision to quit because over the years while working at American Capital, I recognized a pattern in the average American: most of them had made their decisions centered and focused on money. After January 6, I told myself I'd exempt money from the equation and make choices based solely on this question: regardless of money and profit, does the outcome of this decision make me truly happy?

I would learn to base my decisions on personal and family happiness and not on money, because while working at American Capital I witnessed firsthand the collapse and demise of a nation's morality, ignoring the altruistic gains of happiness. In South Korea two years later, I watched the wheel stop, the banks fail, the system plummet, and I'd shake my head: Wall Street knew it, saw it coming like the iceberg in front of the Titanic, and they didn't give a damn, just plowed ahead. Money, and the pursuit of profit, broke America in my humble opinion and this was based on the assessment of speaking to more than sixty thousand Americans a year for over three years, a total estimate of 180,000 Americans. I'm not proud of this fact.

One phone conversation I do remember fondly, because it didn't want to make me blow my brains out, was the time when I worked overtime on a Saturday afternoon, practically alone in the office. A woman shopping for a wedding dress called because her card was getting declined. She cried honest tears and pleas for how she couldn't believe that this was happening to her on this day of all days and to see if there was anything I could do.

I remember reviewing her account and seeing some late fees that had never been credited. This in itself was usual since most customers never called in to have the fees waived. I did some of my magic, waiving about a hundred, if not more, dollars of fees, lifted the restrictions on her account and after about an hour, the young woman, whose name I sadly do not recall, cried, this time, tears of joy because her card went through, the purchase for her wedding gown accepted, and how lucky she was to get me on the line because she had tried many times to get someone to listen — no problem, I said, glad to help — and she'd say the two words that often escaped most people but moved me to a belief in the graciousness of the human species. She sniffled over the phone, must've wiped her eyes with the backs of her fingers, and said, 'Thank you.'

When the call ended, I logged out of the system, rode the elevator down to the parking lot, and drove home to that empty apartment with the fireplace I told you about.

With Chadwick off to college in Kansas, my mother and I lived alone in the white house on Durham I've told you about.

Most days I'd come home and watch *Star Trek*: *The Next Generation* from four to five or meet Sawyer at Coggin Park to play basketball until evening. Some days I'd just sleep. There were times, as I had done since I was a child, when I'd lose myself in a book.

My mother often arrived home from work after eight or nine to cook a late dinner and we'd part to our separate bedrooms for bedtime. So, you'd be right to say that after the divorce I spent the next twenty or so years alone, living a writer's life I suppose.

When soccer wasn't in season, I'd come home to an empty house and spend an hour on my bed masturbating to nude women, and the erotic fantasies slowed my life to a crawl as I imagined lying in bed with a lover on a quiet afternoon; I would often fulfil these mild daydreams in the years ahead of me, but at the time I was discovering my own body along with my own preferences, which turned out to be the opposite of my mother: Asian, dark hair, bosomy, seductive. At one point in the masturbation trials my self-conscious stunted me with a hard-pressed guilt to the point I'd have to sneak into the bathroom after midnight with a dictionary and encyclopedia to fondle myself as I read the scientific definitions of that very act I performed, until the exercise grew to be more enjoyable and less sinister, and I'd read later how a man should release his sperm every forty-eight hours to maintain a healthy prostate. Even if religion might've been against me when it came to masturbation, science, at least in my mind, was on my side. I chose to ignore the damp religious sound of guilt.

Some of the imagined lovers I had back then still etch a far greater and lasting impression on my mind than many of the some two hundred plus lovers I've had in my lifetime. But to be honest with you — if you must know — as much as I enjoy lovemaking and the raw beauty of fucking, I've never wanted my life to be about sex, and for this reason, among many others, was why I dedicated myself to becoming a polymath and deepened my love and respect for writing. If sex were to be my demise, an education would be my freedom.

My sister had been vacant from much of my life and I suspected she had run away, much like the time I told you about. I thought nothing of it when my mother told me we were going to go visit Cassandra. I often asked little to no questions, more out of my lack of any solid or significant interest than shyness, but when my mother drove out of Brownwood and toward Abilene one Saturday morning I just had to ask,

'Where are we going?'

'I've told you already.'

'Answer my question: where are we going *now*?'

'We're going to visit your sister?'

'She lives in Abilene?'

'You'll see.'

I loathed this statement from my mother — still loathe it to this day — because it simultaneously avoided my question while drawing a finality to the issue. In response I didn't speak to my mother for almost two hours. Instead, we listened to music on the radio.

I'll be honest with you — as you asked me to do in the beginning — I hated my mother when we pulled up to a security guard at the entrance of a mental health correction facility. I read the name on the large white sign out front and immediately knew what had happened to Cassandra, although I didn't know for how long.

As we drove through the checkpoint and into the complex, I felt duped and that I had been the one tricked into being committed to this insane asylum for teens. If that would've been the case, like Cassandra, I would've never spoken to my parents again. I would have never forgiven them. But that's just me.

At the reception desk a nurse handed us name badges, which I found odd and ironic as I placed it over my heart, and visitor passes which hung from lanyards around our necks. Another employee led my mother and me into an outdoor waiting area shaded by trees. From the bench I sat silent, looked down a slope to the barbed wire fencing where a lifeless yellow field lay barren, and waited for my sister to come. All the while I kept thinking: how could parents do this to their child? I had no answer then and I still have no answer. Maybe I'm not supposed to have one.

A doctor came out in his official white lab coat that made me want to puke, and he explained Cassandra's medications, her treatment and reaction to it, her diagnosis, and a possible release date — some six to eight weeks away. I asked the doctor after he queried for questions, 'May I speak to my sister alone?'

My mother spoke instead, 'I don't think that's a good idea, son.'

'I wasn't talking to you,' I said, and I turned to the doctor, 'I'm asking a reasonable question to a professional and I'd like an answer. So, one more time: may I speak to my sister alone?'

The doctor glanced at my mother who nodded consent and I shook my head in disgust.

'I don't see any harm in speaking to your sister,' the doctor finally said. 'Any other questions?'

'No.'

'Thank you, doctor,' my mother said.

'Well then, she'll be right out in five minutes and you'll have an hour.' He left the way he came.

When Cassandra emerged, I almost didn't recognize her as my sister. Dark crescents underscored her eyes and exhaustion permeated defeat throughout her body. My mother attempted to hug her daughter but Cassandra pushed her away and walked down the slope as if taking a stroll through a private orchard, and I felt Cassandra hadn't been outside to enjoy fresh air in many days, possibly weeks. I didn't know.

'I'll speak to my sister now,' I said. 'Alone.'

'I don't think —'

'I wasn't asking for permission.'

I joined Cassandra alone at the bottom of the slope where we could see dead bluebonnets rotting in the sun. I didn't know what to say. I had had no idea of the punishment and torment she'd been suffering, and it was then my heart opened to the whole world, its pain and its suffering. 'I'm sorry they did this to you,' was all I could say. I reached out to hug her and she accepted. We held one another for minutes. Embraced as though twins in a womb. Cassandra clung to me as if she were drowning at sea and I could save her, but I knew I couldn't. I wanted to fly her out of that cage, to have the power to stand against all in my way, to do the impossible and free my sister from her misery, but I would fail. I did fail her in the end.

Instead Cassandra and I walked side by side as she spoke of the mind-numbing medications, the verbal abuse from staff, the lethargic dullness of group talk, the demented patient who had sex with her toy monkey by using its tail as a flaccid penis. There was also the girl interrupted who diced her wrists with shards from a flower vase. The blathering insane. And my sister was one of them.

'If I'm not crazy,' Cassandra whispered to me, 'I will be by the time I leave here.' I remained speechless and nodded.

By the end of her whole story, she had told me everything of her injustices and anguish, and I had only listened. 'No one's ever listened to me, Cody,' Cassandra said. 'Thank you so much for that, little brother.' She hugged me and held me close. 'I love you so much.'

'I love you too,' I said from a place I've never known before, 'but please don't blame God for this. Don't hate Henry and Gwendolen. They don't know what they've done. Blame me because I'm just as guilty for not stopping them — even though I had no idea. But I don't want to lose you, Cassandra. You're my big sister. I had no idea. How could I be so blind?'

'Oh, Cody,' she said. 'Never grow up. This world is shit.'

In a way, I never did.

My big sister Cassandra would never return home and I now knew the real reason behind her absence: a Shakespearian tragedy of epic proportions: parents betraying child: mother sabotaging and destroying daughter — but I suppose that's why folklore and fairytales, like 'The Three Luck-Children' and 'Little Snow-White,' were first spoken then written: to remind us, to warn us of our worst natures and to save us from darker, more sinister selves.

In time Cassandra finished high school while working part time jobs and living on her own. Then in the summer before my freshman year of high school she moved with her friend Meleri to Dallas to start studying at the University of Texas at Arlington — UTA for short.

By the end of my sophomore year of high school, two years as a Brownwood Lion, I had learned very little about the world as it is and although I was a straight A student on a path to achieve enough credits to graduate in three years rather than four, I had the least bit of interest in excelling as a pupil. I'd been given a chance to live and breathe on this good earth and I didn't want to waste my time in any classroom. So when Cassandra, long estranged, invited me to come live with her for the summer — to see the world, as it were — I didn't hesitate, and to this day I'm still uncertain as to how Cassandra managed to convince Henry and Gwendolen into letting me live a summer as a sixteen-year-old in one of the greatest cities in Texas, and that summer would be the one to change me, made me much of the man I am today.

For three months, June to August, I lived without counting days or living by a rigid schedule, and I lived each moment as though I were in my thirties, free as an adult without consequences from flawed parental guidance.

After three weeks, however, my father arrived at the end of June to take me away, probably at the sole behest of a concerned mother who desired firm control over her son, and I was told I had to get a job or to come back to Deadwood for the rest of the summer, to spend the next few months alone in a house by myself.

By Henry's arrival, I was still unemployed, but several applications had been posted to fast-food franchises, including Sonic Drive-In, Jack in the Box, Taco Bell and Taco Bueno. On the last day of my father's stay, he drove me to an interview I had arranged by phone at Taco Bueno a few minutes south from my sister's apartment. I recall making a key mistake — remember I'd never had a job before, nor wanted one — and I had told the manager I only needed a job for the summer, that I'd return to Brownwood in August for school, and how he rejected me on the spot after I pressed him for an answer. He had told me to go home and he'd call with his decision. Coward, I thought. I told him I couldn't wait for a phone call and I later nodded at his rejection, at least he had enough courage to tell me to my face. I thought to myself how honesty to some degree didn't function well out in the real world, and I looked out the window to my father waiting in his truck. I smiled and shook the manager's hand as though I'd just won the offer, made sure my father could see us — because I knew he would flash back to this moment and all would make sense — and returned with my father to my sister's apartment.

I drew Cassandra and Henry into her kitchen — she had a wonderful loft apartment with her bedroom upstairs, where her boyfriend Riordan would also make love to her as I slept downstairs on the pullout sofa — and I told my sister and my father how I had important news with a grim look over my face. Actually, the grimness came more from considering the possibility of having to return to Brownwood than in any deception, but I said, 'Cassandra, I'm afraid I have something to tell you.'

'What is it?' Cassandra answered. 'Did you get the job or not?'

'Pack your bags, son,' Henry said. How I hated him when he said it. 'Gwendolen said —'

Little Hometown, America

'Let me finish.' I said, 'Cassandra, I'm afraid I have to tell you — that I get to stay the rest of the summer with you. I got the job.' A bold lie but I sold it nonetheless. I gave a huge grin which urged my father to challenge me, to call me a liar.

'You did!' Cassandra said.

'You did?' Henry added.

'Sure did.' I released a ton of positive energy at knowing I'd get to stay with my beloved sister, to not have to return to that prison in that white house on Durham, and Henry must've mistook the energy for having won the job in the first place as he checked his memory of me smiling and shaking the manager's hand. It all fit.

I had waited until the hour before Henry was to leave so once the news was out — I was staying, no question about it, I have a job, I'm a working man now — and less than thirty minutes later Henry headed back to Deadwood and was gone out of my life for the next few months and I had the rest of the summer with Cassandra, who had grown more beautiful and more fascinating in the years of her absence from me; she had, after all, been a cheerleader as a senior for the Brownwood Lions football squad, once throwing me a tiny plastic football as a gift that all the cheerleaders threw to the fans in attendance at Gordon Wood Stadium on Friday nights, and because of her extreme beauty and popularity I wasn't dismissed years later at beer parties thrown by her fellow classmates who never left and became townies.

Cassandra and I, with Henry out of the picture, stood in the kitchen again and I said,

'Cassandra, I have to tell you something, I'm afraid.'

'What is it, little brother? You can tell me anything.'

'I didn't get the job.'

'You lied?'

I never lied. 'Sure did.' I had lied.

She hugged me for a minute or three, just so happy we had more time together. 'But why?' she asked.

'Because I wanted to be with you.' That was the God's honest truth.

Then Cassandra and I sat on her sofa and smoked a celebratory joint.

Yes, she had been the one, for the most part, to introduce me to headshops selling wrapping papers, bongs, pipes, Bob Marley and Mary Jane posters and T-shirts and other psychedelia, and she also instructed me on the joys and dangers of marijuana: Mexican Skunk, Red Hair, Purple Haze, Blue Dreams, Sugar Baby, White Widow, Lemon Cush, and tons more. Although I had tried some pot in my sophomore year, I wasn't a heavy smoker, but this bond was what ultimately brought my sister and me together and saved our relationship.

The first time in her apartment she broke out two fat bags of Purple Haze and Blue Dreams with classic veins and I inhaled the dried leaves on the stem, something divine stirred in me and eased me into peaceful delusions of harems and hookahs and ancient stories being told all night long by the Persian queen Scheherazade.

Most nights that summer in Dallas were immortal for me: Cassandra and I smoking from her bong or pipe with the lights out in her living room, *Seinfeld* playing on the tube, and fresh burritos and nachos from Taco Bueno waiting for us on the coffee table. If part of my heaven exists, it is then and there with Cassandra. Try as I might, I cannot transcribe the importance of those emotions I felt with Cassandra, my big sister, the one who ran away that one time I told you about, and on those wonderful summer nights we drifted into fantasy, and I could write for a thousand and one years and still never do those times justice and I'd only fail in the end. But I'll say this: if I could go back to that Dallas summer and relive it all over again, I would in a heartbeat, without question.

I would later find a job at the Sonic Drive-In in walking distance from my sister's apartment, after having lied about having to attend high school down the street later in the fall. I'd flip burgers and clean out grease-deep fryers after closing the restaurant for the next two months, give most of my pay to Cassandra to pay her back for the living costs, but that's not the story I want to tell.

The one I want to tell is locked in a golden age of beer parties, before he moved back to Brownwood, at John Ferryman's apartment in Dallas only a few buildings down from Cassandra's, and a golden Fourth of July at Possum Kingdom Lake, with Meleri, my sister and her colleagues, along with their boyfriends, and some other people I didn't know. With ice-cold Miller and Bud and barbecue and enough Mary Jane to satisfy a small nation, let's say the Vatican or Monaco, we partied like rock stars on the edge of the lake in the bright day of a sun that could do no wrong as *Hootie & the Blowfish* sang 'Let Her Cry' from a portable cd-player.

At one point, Meleri had been swinging in a hammock at the bottom of a slope beneath a tree closer to the water when the hammock broke and she spilled out flat on her ass. The group, drinking and smoking at the top of the slope by the vehicles, turned and looked in silence at Meleri on the ground, then — not my best moment as a human being — I yelled, 'Get up, fat ass!' I had known Meleri since I was a child and blamed her mostly for Cassandra running away that one day, so I can be forgiven a little, but not much more than that. The group, meanwhile, burst out laughing. Cassandra would tell me later that I had said exactly what everyone was thinking but was the only one who had the balls to yell it out — another trait that I'm cursed with: saying what few will say.

After burgers and ribs by the lake, Octavia and Cassandra and me and Kimiko Murakami — a hot Asian-mix I had a major crush on from the moment I saw her and she had told me her name originated from the Japanese words 'ki' for 'valuable' and 'mi' for 'beautiful' — we all four boarded four separate jet skis and raced across the stainless-steel-colored water as though death had happened years ago for us and slipped into a long-ago-now-forgotten memory. At one point, Octavia, Cassandra and I stopped in the center of the lake to rest and smoke a joint. Kimiko, however, remained about ten yards outside our three-pointed triangle and needed to move closer so we could complete a circle. What came next happened in a flash, and in that momentary spark which clings life to death and death to life I witnessed my whole life flashing before my eyes.

You see, Kimiko Murakami, who idled on the water off to my right, drew down hard on the accelerator lurching her jet ski forward like a rocket shooting into space where she then hit a residual wave from a passing speedboat. Her speeding jet ski slammed the wave, propelling Kimiko's 115 pound frame into the air, her legs and arms spread wide as though she intended to take flight as though she were a newly emerged monarch butterfly from her cocoon, but her riderless jet ski continued charging toward me, who waited idle in the water smelling the sweet scent of the burning marijuana against a summer sun. At the last possible moment, I managed to dive from my jet ski and into the water off to my left as Kimiko's riderless jet ski slammed full speed into the seat where I had been sitting a second before. For a minute or two I lay face down in the water checking to make sure nothing was broken and to give the girls a good scare. Hair wet, I surfaced as though I had survived a James Bond stunt.

A few years ago, though, I can't be sure when, Cassandra told me Kimiko had shot herself in the chest, where her heart should be, with her former lover's Glock. My sister had told me Kimiko had problems. Lots and lots of problems.

Ghosts and legends: legends of ghosts haunted the everyday in Brownwood. One of the unsolved mysteries that many households still whisper across clotheslines to one another more out of a warning than anything else involves the unsolved murder of Amanda Goodman, about my sister's age at the time, on May 16, 1989.

Born on May 13, 1976, just ten days before my sister, the thirteen-year-old nicknamed 'Sissy' had set off, according to local lore, from school one day only to be found twelve miles south of Brownwood out on Indian Creek Road, the same road that had my grandfather's church I told you about. Amanda lay dead in the ditch with a single gunshot to the head, her school books scattered beside her as rain soaked the pages. Some rumors whispered the Brownwood Mafia had a hand in the cold-blooded murder, just a few days after the girl's birthday at Coggin Park. About Amanda's unsolved murder, Sheriff Grubbs had worked the case back then and said, like a bad cliché in fiction: 'It's like an albatross that I've carried for all these years.'

A few miles outside of Early, Sawyer and I would take his car out to Staley Cemetery, nicknamed the Blue Light Cemetery, around ten at night in a mocking hope to catch a glimpse of floating lights or traces of the secret satanic meetings, which caused the cemetery to be closed off to the general public. The stories about Blue Light that got passed around schools included a conjured demon set loose and how the fiend still roamed the grounds to this day. The name Blue Light had more to do, however, with airplanes than spirits. Back in the seventies, the regional airport located nearby placed a locator light as a marker near the cemetery and pilots flying overhead stated the light gave off a blue glow.

On Coggin Avenue, an old dated hospital, before the authorities demolished the structure in the 1990s, was said to house the spirits of those who died in its care. The new hospital, Brownwood Regional Medical Center, the one where I was born at in 1979, replaced the abandoned one on Coggin Avenue in 1970; so, for twenty-plus years the old hospital collected tales of goblins and portals to hell, scaring off teens with wild imaginations and strong beliefs in the eerie and supernatural.

Once with Sawyer, near midnight, I ventured into the old hospital. My whole childhood I had looked at the shattered windows and ivy-covered bricked building hidden in an overgrowth of trees as I passed by in a car and I'd feel a desire stir in me to conquer my fears, to see for myself the devil's workshop — if there was one — or to prove the tales false, and I wanted this more than any longing to discover an abandoned hospital's secrets.

As I grew older and more mature, I considered these secrets to be more primitive superstition than actual demonic inhabitation, more to do with vandals and the homeless shooting up heroine or smoking crack, more gravy than grave — as one grump might put it.

The warning signs on the debilitated fence outside the hospital on Coggin Avenue had been altered by black spray paint from 'Do Not Enter' to 'Do ▮ Enter.' Sawyer made ghostly noises while he waved his hands in the air, 'Oooohh. Don't let the boogeyman get ya. Oooohh.' Sawyer was far more practical and down-to-earth than I was and we laughed at our childish fears while we secretly wished to witness a spectacular event: a UFO above the abandoned hospital; an alien behind one of the trees; a cacodemon-ghost creeping from room to room in the old hospital's abandoned cavity.

Before the old Coggin Avenue Hospital was torn down in the 1990s, Sawyer and I got the chance to explore the ground floor of the neglected hospital without flashlights. Legend had it that the Coggin Avenue Hospital was haunted by souls of patients who had died there and perhaps the Coggin Brothers, Mody and Sam. There were stories of children who went inside for a night and never made it out again the next morning. Or so the stories say.

That Friday night inside the haunted hospital was dark, but there was enough light filtering in from the street lamps along the roadside. In the damp light, red and black satanic graffiti showed in random spots across the floor and walls: the pentagram; 666; the Devil is Behind You — that sort of nonsense. Sawyer seemed more hesitant, however, than I had ever seen him to be before, as if something lurked at the touch of his elbow, and that unnerving instability in Sawyer's temperament put me on edge as we treaded down the darkened hall filled with more dirt, shrubs, empty beer bottles and garbage than wayward phantoms. Having investigated the first floor of the old hospital, I whispered back to Sawyer at the foot of the stairs, 'Let's see what's up there.'

'That's where the Satan worshippers hold their midnight meetings.'

'All the more reason to go.' I climbed a few steps leading up to the second floor. 'I doubt anything's up there anyway.'

Sawyer paused, seeing or feeling something. 'All the more reason not to go.' Sawyer turned, spooked by a stray noise from the back of the hospital which must've been a chance possum or cat or rush of wind. 'What the hell was that?'

'Just a breeze,' I said. 'Now come on.'

'I'm going back to the car,' he said. 'It's late.'

'If you go, I go. But they'll tear this place down one day and we'll miss our opportunity to see what this place is really about. It's now or never.'

'Never,' he said. I followed him back down the hall. 'I don't want to end up dead and haunting this shitty building.'

'Don't worry, Sawyer, I'll come visit you, bring you flowers and conjure you back a night or two for beers and women.'

'Better not risk it.'

We stepped out of a window and onto the ground in front of the hospital nearest the street. The last one out of the haunted hospital, I stopped and turned back at the edge of the window and stared for several seconds into the eternal darkness trying to understand how a building could share in so many births and deaths, sicknesses and recoveries, the natural cycles of life, and still receive such a bad reputation — and when I looked for a minute too long, there in the stolid black of the vacant window's void a pair of red eyes glowed and met mine and I half-believed those sinister eyes were a reflection of my own. 'I see you,' I said, 'and I'm unafraid.'

I ran and caught up with Sawyer near his car he had parked down the road in a quiet neighborhood to avoid suspicion. I jumped on his back saying, 'You'll never believe what I saw.'

'The boogeyman,' he said.

'How did you know?'

'Because I'm the boogey-boogeyman.'

Some years later after a high school party, my friends slept in an adjoining room empty of furniture, seven or eight boys sleeping side-by-side on the carpet, while the living room and its comfortable couch remained for the taking. An air con blasted freezing gusts over the couch but after securing a blanket and a pillow I slipped into a much-needed slumber on the couch all alone in the living room.

A few hours later I woke with the blanket at my ankles and shaking from the cold. I had believed that I kicked the blanket off during the night and thought nothing more of it. I pulled the blanket around my shoulders and snuggled back into the couch ready for a deep sleep to come.

Thirty or so minutes passed and the blanket flew off my shoulders and landed around my feet. I opened my eyes at that instant expecting to catch one of my friends laughing at the prank but the dark living room showed vacant. I stood up and walked to the adjoining room and checked each one of my sleeping friends. All lay in alcohol-induced dreams and I doubted any one of them to have enough sobriety to get up in the middle of the night to play games. I checked the connecting hallway and the bathroom. Nothing. All empty. Just my mind playing tricks on me.

I returned to the couch, pulled the blanket to my shoulders, closed my eyes and set the trap by listening for squeaks on the floorboards.

After a minute or two, a creak sounded and I held my position beneath the blanket. Then the second creak sounded closer. I poised myself. A third creak sounded at my side and I felt a hand on the blanket at my shoulder. I popped up and sat upright adjusting my eyes to see in the darkness.

In the doorway of the adjoining room where my friends slept, I saw the distinct shadow of a six-year-old boy looking back at me with one hand on the doorframe. We remained motionless, like hunter and prey in the wild waiting for the other to make the first move. He looked at me and I looked at him, and the shape appeared solid and moved as a small person moves.

'What do you want?' I said. I held my hands over my knees but didn't move. 'I can see you. What do you want?'

Nothing. No reply. The shadow-boy remained watching me.

'I'm trying to sleep,' I said. 'Come here if you want to talk.'

I could sense the shadow-boy wanting to enter the living room but he stopped himself and hesitated.

'Screw it,' I said, jumping up and charging forward, believing the shadow-boy to be more imagination and shades than an apparition.

I distinctly remember, however, seeing the shadow-boy drop his hand from the doorframe, take a step back into the adjoining room and run out of sight and into the hallway where I knew the bathroom to be. I chased him through the house but never spotted another sign of him, and there were no small children in the house at that time.

I returned to the living room, grabbed the pillow and blanket under my arms and found a spot in the adjoining room with my fellow friends who were all content in their idle oblivion. I fell asleep without further incident on the floor.

In the morning I told Jimmy Joyce — who was also seven years my senior and an old friend of Cassandra's — about the visitation in the middle of the night, and all my friends laughed and said now I knew why no one slept on the couch in the living room, despite being the most comfortable place to sleep.

'When I moved in,' Joyce said, 'I found a pair of little tennis shoes in the closet. Left here from another time. The previous owner said a small boy died in the house years ago. Influenza or something. Didn't believe him until things started to happen at night.'

'Why didn't you tell me this before? Before I slept in the living room?'

'Thought you'd sleep with the others.' Joyce handed me a blunt (marijuana wrapped inside cigar paper) and laughed a jolly good laugh before adding, 'I didn't want to spook you.'

I couldn't quite shake off the dread from the preternatural encounter from the night before.

'Relax, brother,' Joyce said to me, 'there's worse things in this world than demons and ghosts.'

'Like what?' I handed back the blunt.

'Like becoming one yourself.'

I had to admit: old Jimmy Joyce did have a point.

'Now get to school and be somebody,' Joyce said. 'You don't want to be late and end up like me, do you?'

'As you wish, Obi Wan. As you wish.'

Looking back is just as important as looking forward, you told me a few years back, but I'm not sure I can trust that, I tell you as you sit back down in the chair beside the sofa. How was lunch?

You should've joined me, you reply. I had a pan-fried barramundi fillet with baby asparagus. Panera and anise cream came as a side; nothing extravagant.

In the reflection of the windows I see you prepare your pen and Moleskine notebook you've used since I first met you and you begin to take notes where we left off about my torrid life.

Have you eaten?

The weather's starting to come around, I answer.

I stand by the windows and see the gray storm clouds like the backs of elephants softening, nothing poetical in that act which has been done a billion times before and will be done a billion times after I'm gone.

I had a hazelnut latte, I add. I wasn't hungry.

Shall we begin? You cross your legs and are ready to listen. I don't think you're telling me what you came here to tell me. Is that true?

Trust is a damn hard thing to come by in this world, isn't it?

Only if you think so. Shall we?

After I moved out of my father's house on Pine Creek Ranch, I stayed with Dylan for a week or two until I got settled. My old soccer coach from high school would later rent me a studio apartment with a carport that was a hundred yards or so down a street behind his house off the main road. The little place sat tucked away in the trees in an isolated neighborhood a dozen or more yards outside the city line. What I do remember most about that time were a number of things, but three stand out the most.

The first: I averaged three hours of sleep a day for a whole year, and while I had to work full-time many of my choices in my spare time were limited to the Big Three: Eating, Sleeping, or Doing Homework. Often I chose my university work over the first two, and that was also the time I began to feel the strains of an unwanted and an undesirable poverty, a difficult time financially but not a joyless one altogether, despite having to work a night shift from ten to seven at a residential hospital for the mentally ill called South Park Development Center, no pun or irony intended in connection to the cartoon.

One night during my shift, Raymond, an old man who lacked all awareness of his motor functions, unexpectedly shook as though a thousand and one volts surged relentlessly through his frail body. It had been two in the morning, because I checked the rooms on my rounds about then, when I found Raymond in an epileptic seizure. I made the mistake of clearing his tongue and throat with my forefinger, but luckily, he must've favored me a bit because he didn't bite down. I ran from the room, down the hall to the nurses' station,

'Call an ambulance!'

I explained Raymond's condition as severe, as a death rattle. I had never seen a human body shake so violently, and I feared his bones would break from all the stress. I left the two staff flipping through telephone directories in the nurses' station and ran back down to Raymond, whose eyes rolled back deeper into his head and I thought his spine would break from all the pressure placed on it from the tension his body collected as his back lifted off the bed.

I leaned down next to him and spoke softly, 'It'll be all right, buddy. Just calm down. We'll get you to the doctor and they'll take care of you. Fix you right up. Stay with me, buddy. It'll be all right.'

After twenty minutes of this, Raymond eased enough for me to leave him and I ran back down the hall to the nurses' station and found the two staff I'd left still searching for the telephone number to call an ambulance.

'Raymond's dying. Where's the ambulance?'

'We can't find the number,' one of the two nurses said.

'Three words.' I yelled at them, 'NINE. ONE. ONE.'

The emergency number dawned on the other staff member and she immediately picked up the telephone and dialed. The paramedics arrived less than ten minutes later with Raymond still lost in his violent seizure, and I knew time was of the essence. I didn't want to see him die.

The paramedics hoisted him onto a gurney and wheeled Raymond out of the room and left me to feel the immense amount of energy being pulled out of me, Raymond's room, everything, sucked into a pit swimming with sorrow and exhaustion. Raymond's life would be spared that night but I'd never see him again. By the time he'd return, a month or so later, I had already quit, the work was too much despair for an artist, or most individuals, to handle. I could find work elsewhere.

The second: what I remember most about that tiny studio apartment is the creative writing course I was taking every Tuesday night from six to nine at Howard Payne University. I'd eventually get an A in the course, not a grand achievement, but the amount of work each week kept me on the brink of a delusional reality, not quite asleep and not quite awake. I lived by Leonardo Da Vinci's quote: 'I'll sleep when I'm dead,' as I had to write one short story a week — without complaint — and read the work of three or four of my peers out of a baker's dozen — with some complaint — but that introduction into creative writing, sitting in a circle discussing one another's stories, was the highlight of my university education at HPU, and the self which governs my being found the object of my fascination, my *raison d'être* and my *modus operandi*. The course was taken in the spring of 2001 and the following summer I moved out of the studio and into a lake house to work on my first book, the novella I told you about called *A Father's Son*. No one imagined what would transpire later that fall in New York. No one could, that is, but evil men.

But that spring, quite literally, would be the spring of my writing existence. The Universe pushing me ever deeper into a story I could not be able to tell you until now, some twenty years later.

My first writing professor, then, actually worked as a librarian for the university but each semester was allowed one course to teach creative writing, his passion. I do not remember his name; he left no permanent impression other than to recite verbatim what I'd go on to hear and find in my own research from other writers discussing their craft of writing: if you really do want to make a contribution to literature, you'd wake at four in the morning, go into the toilet if you have to, find a quiet place, your car in an empty parking lot if necessary, a writing shed if you have the money, anything and anywhere to get you to sit, butt in chair, to write, write, write.

For me this part of the advice sounded more nonsense than sensical and must've worked on many amateurs before and after me; after all, I mean, why couldn't one delegate writing as the most important activity of the day rather than shoving or squeezing it into the fringes of the diurnal routine, like many famed artists had done, and shove television or a social life into the number two or three spots or not at all. Waking at four in the morning sounded to me like writing wasn't the writer's first priority, and I had every intention of making writing my number one activity I'd turn to daily. But you know this, don't you?

Over the days, weeks, years of my habit of placing writing into the forefront of my life, regulating all else, including family and loved ones, into the shadows of non-existence — the great existentialist emerged — and as my writing habits became the center of my chakra's mandala, writing became second nature, an extension of who I was as a person, and to be honest with you, regardless of success, I felt extremely comfortable with my routine focused on writing, and this routine would lead to motivation, leading to direction, then on into ambition, but I'll say this: the entire time I was having fun at playing with words, experimenting with characters, drafting ideas into stories; if that's work, then I'm the luckiest person alive.

The third: another thing I remember about that studio behind my former coach's house on the outskirts of Brownwood would be how much that shack reminded me of a modest cabin in the woods. On cold mornings, usually after an all-nighter at work, I'd stand in my front door, next to my car backed in the carport, and drink coffee as I leaned against the doorframe and look far into the thicket of trees surrounding that tiny place in a city that had once been the largest town west of Fort Worth. The birds would chirp in the blue mist, a heavy dew settling, already fallen, my neighbors farther down the road gently stirring, and I'd think about how I'd been awake all night watching over the sick and dying and mentally ill, and how that wasn't such a bad job, not at all, not really, even if they paid shit wages, you couldn't put a price tag on another person's life.

The coffee would be hot and steaming, and I'd remember the couple in the ski resort long ago in Santa Fe, sigh to myself at wanting to know when my time would come, when I could ease myself into my dream girl, my unicorn, the one meant only for me, to grow old and silly with, and when would the time come for people around the world to read my stories, my novels, when I wouldn't have to work all night and study all day, when sleep would not be so precious but taken for granted, when the world wouldn't be at war with itself, when I wouldn't be at war with myself, when the time would come for me to stop hiding in the shadows of obscurity and become the man the world needed, when my fears would cease to be, I'd recall Keats's poem: I'd stand at the edge of the world and look out, like I stood on the edge of the doorway, not quite in and not quite out, until fame and love to nothingness do sink.

I'd drink my coffee thinking of all these things and more, and I'd tell myself that I had another five minutes to enjoy the start of a new day before I had to grab my books, get in my car and head to English class, and how the Universe with its galactic gifts waited silently in the background of being for me to rise from the ashes of a middle class obfuscated by poverty and to share my gifts with a world that needed them more than I did.

I tell you I haven't slept in the last few nights because of nervous energy, and because last night, in my hotel room, I sat in nothing but a bathrobe on the sofa staring at the blank television screen and the city out in the early morning darkness, and all I could think about was shame, and how like poverty shame could be passed down from one generation to the next, something along the theory of epigenetics.

My mind kept trying to detach itself from the blame, of how everything had gone horribly wrong with my family and with the world, with what happened in New York on 9/11 and in Manchester, England and on London Bridge, and in so many countless other places around the world decade after decade.

Poverty and shame. Shame and poverty. Could these two be irrevocably and inextricably linked? Could they have nothing to do with one another? What do you think? What do you feel? Please tell me. I'm pouring my heart out to you now about how I was as troubled as Brother Lustig and as lucky as a Sunday-child, and from behind your desk you yawn and sip your English Breakfast tea. You tell me to go on. You're listening.

While you're listening, poverty and shame continue to sink deep into the human psyche, past the foundations of ego, lower still beyond memory, finally cementing in and around the cortex of mammalian instinct. Or at least my thoughts on the matter dove to those depths last night so I might resolve, at least for now, the dilemma of how shame and poverty affect the human condition, and how both could possibly have affected me as a child. Am I a product of my parents' choices? Am I unable to escape from the immeasurable weight of their consequences which have grossly altered certain paths for my life? Has the American Dream truly died? Can there be such a notion as Manifest Destiny? Or from my birth, have I been labeled, classified, categorized, shackled by status and tossed aside?

Now you're beginning to know my thoughts from last night in the hotel room as I sat wide awake waiting for the dawn to come so I could shower, breakfast, and come meet you for our little talk. Because if I'm so burdened by these thoughts of poverty and shame, which have an unlimited number of adverse consequences, how much more so a woman, man or child from, say, war-torn Syria, Iraq, Afghanistan, Libya?

Poverty and shame, for me, were like a giant boa constrictor growing stronger and tightening its grip all around me as I struggled and fought to free myself over the years, and the whole time the snake, so named Poverty-Shame, stared at me in the face with its malicious grin.

In my early twenties — you'll be the first to hear of this — I sought, and received for a short time, government assistance for food. For a month or two I was allotted approximately two hundred dollars per month to buy food and essentials, like toilet paper. My girlfriend Rachel, who lived with me at the time, and I would buy our much-needed groceries using the state-issued card, which acted much like a debit card. Relief, I thought. Sweet-fucking relief.

One evening, after loading our cart heavy with food and juices, calculating the expense to the dollar, Rachel and I waited in line for twenty minutes only to find out that the card had been unexpectedly revoked without a single letter or phone call to inform us of the unexpected status on our food card. After several more swipes of the card, rejection still came each time. We had to leave the full shopping cart filled with plastic bags of groceries, our much-needed supplies for the next two weeks.

The next day I left work early and drove thirty minutes across town to the social welfare office, and met with Tammy, the same woman who had approved my initial application. Tammy apologized for the unexpectedness of the card's deactivation and suspension of funds and told me how, logistically, it would be a nightmare to inform each and every single person in case of deactivation.

'A nightmare?' I said. 'Like how you shop for groceries with the woman you love only to be told that out of nowhere the welfare card doesn't work and how you have no money in your bank account to cover the expense and you have to feel the shame of not having any money, let alone enough, to buy food for your family? Like that kind of nightmare?'

'I'm sorry,' Tammy said. 'I'm so very sorry. We should've sent a letter. I should've called you.'

'What can I do with a sorry? Can I eat an apology? How does that taste? How does that help Rachel?'

Tammy fiddled with my file that lay open on her desk.

'What exactly did happen?' I asked, trying to remain calm. 'You, yourself, approved me for six months. Now after two months, I'm left out in the cold.'

Tammy flipped through the pages and determined the reason for my problem. 'It seems that after a review of your initial acceptance, which can be temporary if the review is not satisfactory, the review found you have a ninety-eight Chevrolet listed as one of your assets.'

'Yes,' I said, 'that's correct. My car is also four years old and I still owe the bank about nine thousand dollars on it. So?'

'So,' Tammy said, 'it appears that after reviewing your application, which includes your gross and net incomes along with your listed assets, that the State of Texas determined to suspend your benefits because, in short, you are worth too much money.'

'What?' I said. 'What? How do you get to that conclusion? I'm broke. Flat broke. I owe nine grand on an old car. I have to pay, out of pocket, mind you, graduate school fees on top of student loans. The price for gas is unheard of and I barely make ends meet with a job that pays just over minimum wage, not to mention I'm trying to pay off credit card debt. It's all listed there on my application. Do you understand I have no money?'

'I can see all of that,' Tammy said. 'But the facts remain: your car is seen as an asset and it appears you are worth more than enough to afford basic elements like food and, therefore, the State of Texas has determined to suspend your benefits.'

'You said that already.'

'You're right. I did. How insensitive.'

'It appears,' I said, 'that I still need a little extra money for food. So, what am I left with? What are my options?'

'Well,' Tammy said as she looked down and to her left, 'you can resubmit a new application but this time leave off your car under assets. After a new review, you might be eligible for new benefits.'

'After the review?' I said. 'Another one?'

'After a new review, yes.'

'But if I did what you're suggesting, that would be a lie. You already know I have a car. I'm not going to lie. Are you advising me to lie?'

'I do, yes.'

'And who does this review?'

'The State of Texas.'

'Who in the State of Texas?'

'We have people in this office who review applicants for food assistance.'

'Meaning,' I said, 'you.'

'Yes,' Tammy said. 'Me.'

'I see,' I said.

'Would you like to submit a new application?'

'No,' I said. 'You're asking me to lie, and you're asking me to do so on an official government document. I'd rather starve before I'd consciously ruin my character.'

'That's very noble.'

'Noble? Can I eat nobility?' I said. 'I came here, to you, told the truth, I need help, and then I'm disrespected because no one had the courtesy to inform me my benefits were canceled. So, I leave work, losing money by the hour, to be told, by you, Tammy, that I have no benefits because I'm worth too much, and then you ask me to tarnish my character by giving false information on a government document. That's noble? I'd like to know what the fuck is going on. Am I dreaming?'

'We don't need to use that kind of language.'

'Or the State of Texas would become upset?' I said, 'I came asking for help. I told the truth. I'm then told I should lie because otherwise I'm worth too much in my own stinking poverty. What's going on in this America?'

'Would you like to submit a new application?' Tammy said. 'You might be eligible for more benefits after the review.'

I looked at her with my fists and jaw clenched. 'No,' I said. 'I do not.' I got up and walked out of her office.

Needless to say, after that incident, my relationship with Rachel didn't last much longer. The shame regarding my poverty and how I was incapable of supporting a family made it impossible for me to continue with the relationship because, I concluded, my girlfriend was better off without me. Perhaps the whole world would be better off without me.

That's what kept me up last night, and the sad thing is this happens every single day in America to good people who want to contribute to society, who long to be of importance, but in their own hour of despair, in their most honest and desperate hour, they are told they are wroth too much, even in their poverty, and they should disgrace themselves further and lie to get a little extra, to get ahead, and in all of that mess Poverty-Shame gets fed but grows hungrier still, looking with its evilness through its eyes and grin right in the face the ones who must eat or be eaten.

My whole life I've felt like I'm a freight train carrying a mountain's worth of rocks behind me as I trudge, inch by painful inch, up a mountain that has no peaks ahead, only clouds for me to climb into or slide back into the valley below, because the poverty and shame of those who came before us could never ease nor relinquish the poverty and shame of those who must follow. Part of growing up was also learning to let go.

We have all the time in the world until we have no time in the world. That was what I was contemplating as a seventh grader sitting alongside the main building looking out over the courtyard.

Ernest would come and go but for the most part during lunch I'd like to sit off to the side and watch the children play their games.

Gavin Longshot, who would later in life become a weightlifter, along with Owen Daily, who had been an all-star pitcher as a kid for the Tigers, the minor league baseball team I once won a state title with; and later Owen would go on to pitch for his father's team the Giants and, later the state champions, the Yankees, the junior league teams I told you about. Owen Daily had an arm back then and after high school he had been in fact drafted by a semi-pro team owned by the Detroit Tigers.

A few months ago, however, I read online in the *Brownwood Bulletin* that the super-star pitcher I'd known as a child and had high hopes for, that Owen Daily had become a UPS driver and he'd stolen some merchandise he was supposed to deliver. The cops raided his house, found the items in question (some rare coins, a handgun) and also discovered a glass pipe for smoking meth and a couple of ounces of pot, but all of this hadn't happened yet and was a long way from seventh grade — when Gavin Longshot and Owen Daily, along with a few boys brave enough to watch but cowardly enough to stand aside and do nothing, began teasing Lynn Evans.

Now to put this in context: Lynn was the daughter of Mrs. Evans, the popular and well-liked Spanish teacher who had taught my sister and brother in high school, and Lynn once had long, beautiful hair and about a week before this incident something had happened to her, gum in the hair or that sort of thing that happens to kids once in a while, and Lynn had to have her long hair cut short like a boys and all the girls whispered hurtful rumors around school that Lynn was in fact a lesbian and the girls began to call Lynn to her face and behind her back as 'Lynn the Lesbian' or 'Lynn the Lezbo' or 'Lynn the Licker' or 'Lynn the Lezzie,' and the ridicule shamed her so.

During lunch one day, Gavin and Owen and their ragtag gang surrounded poor Lynn in the center of the courtyard right out in front of the school, and with no teachers in sight everyone else played on in oblivion. The group of girls Lynn normally played with had ostracized her and the ruthless boys swarmed her as I watched all of this off to the side, until, that is, I became too sick to bear it anymore. Ernest sat beside me then but I said, 'Wait here.' I got up and walked the twenty or so yards to the gang and listened for just a few seconds to be positive of the content before barging and shoving my way to the middle to wedge myself between Lynn and Gavin.

'Go play,' I told Gavin as I pointed to the basketball courts behind him. 'Leave her alone.'

'Or what?' Gavin said, challenging me. 'Are you in love? Trying to save your little sweetheart?' The gang of boys laughed and mocked me. Typical behavior from adolescents, and I was used to it by then.

'I'm in love with the whole human race.' I looked over my shoulder to see Lynn's frown lift when I began to speak and her eyes held a shimmer of happiness in them. 'I love her enough not to let you do this to her. Why? What makes you so cruel?'

'We're just playing with our friend here,' Gavin said. 'She doesn't mind, do you, Lezzie the Licker?'

'That's right,' Owen added. 'We're getting to know the new boy at school.' The gang laughed. Lynn drew closer to me.

'That's not the least bit funny,' I said. 'Owen, we won a state title with the Tigers together, and I expect better from a champion.' At the memory, his face dropped, instantly saddened, with remorse. Too much truth. The illusions breaking. He stepped back.

'And Gavin,' I said, 'Just a month or two ago you had a car accident where your two front teeth got stuck on the dash and got knocked out and you had to have them replaced. Your front teeth are fake.'

'No, I didn't.'

'Yes, you did. The whole school knew about it and for a while everyone made fun of you, laughed at you, I didn't, but now you think it's cool to pick on someone else. Pay back, right?'

'They did?'

'Yes, they did. And guess what. Her hair's going to grow back and all you managed to do was add pain onto pain in this world.'

'What are you talking about?' Gavin said. 'You're toony-loony.'

'Satan, *get behind me*.' I admit I'd been studying too much of the Bible back then, but I hoped it would work.

'He's nuts,' one boy said. 'Conkers.'

Owen grabbed Gavin's arm and said, 'Let's go.'

'You know what I'm talking about,' I said. I held a fist up to Gavin's face. 'Would you like for me to show your friends, all the school here, your fake teeth or do you want to leave us in peace and enjoy the rest of your break?'

'Let's go,' Owen said again. 'He's a lunatic.'

'Make me,' Gavin said. 'I dare you.'

I turned back to Lynn and said politely but firmly, 'Go.' I pointed. 'Go. I'll make sure they don't follow you. I'll make sure they leave you alone.' She reminded me then of Bambi, innocent and defenseless.

'Are you sure?' Her voice sounded sweet. 'I can stay with you. We can be friends or more than friends. I'll do anything you want me to. Just ask.'

'Go.'

'Are you sure?'

'I'm sure,' I said. 'And if they mess with you again, come talk to me.'

I turned to face Gavin, who watched his mob losing energy. I glanced over my shoulder to see Lynn safe and walking away, looking over her shoulder at me. I smiled and so did she. Lynn looked happy to have been defended. But I can't be sure about that.

'Go and play,' I said strongly to the rest of the boys. 'Go!'

'I'll get you for this,' Gavin said. 'You better watch out.'

'You know where to find me,' I said and I pointed over to the side of the building where I normally sat alone. 'Anytime.'

One by one each boy dropped away from the mob and became an individual again. Gavin was the last to leave me standing alone in the center of the courtyard. I returned to my seat at the side of the building. Ernest had followed and listened to all that had happened and he joined me on the ground.

'That was incredible, Cody.'

'I don't call picking on a girl because of her haircut *incredible*.'

'That's not what I meant.'

'I know it's not, Ernie. I'm just pissed.'

'I still can't believe you stood up to Gavin and Owen at the *same* time. No one's ever done that before.'

'Gavin and Owen are cowards for picking on a helpless girl. I'm not afraid of people like that.'

'What if they had a knife or gun?'

'Then they had a knife or gun, but it doesn't change what I would do.'

'Really?'

'Makes me sick. Anyone who doesn't stand up to those cowards, gun or no gun, are even bigger cowards, and that really disgusts me.'

'I still can't believe it.'

'Well I can.' Then I looked over at Ernest with his eyes lit as though he stared too long into the sun. 'Can I tell you a secret?'

'You're in love with Lynn Evans?'

'Get your mind out of the gutter, Ernie.' I turned to look at the empty courtyard. 'I'd be a lucky man if I did and she loved me in return, but I don't deserve love. But no, I'm not in love with anyone. Not sure I want to be. It's me, Ern-myster. I'm different. I'm strange. I don't fit with the rest of them, these kids, these mindless automatons.'

'I'll say,' Ernest said. 'I never know what you're saying.'

'Go play, Ernie. I'd like to be alone. I'm not mad at you. I just have a lot on my mind.'

Ernest walked along the wall in the direction of the basketball courts and for a time I sat thinking and looking out into the courtyard for any sign of trouble when Lynn came to sit beside me.

'I want to say thank you.' She held her hands in her lap but I didn't need to look at her. 'It was brave of you to do what you did. But why did you do it? You don't know me, not really. We've never really spoken much before today.'

'I couldn't live with myself otherwise, so I don't call that being brave. Besides, short or long hair, you're a beautiful girl, and you shouldn't worry. Gavin and Owen will leave you alone from now on. Trust me on that.'

'Let's not talk about them,' she said. 'I came over to see if you wanted to be my friend. I don't have any now.'

I should've said yes because looking back I realize that she must've lost her friends because of all the rumors and it must've been damn hard for her to come over to me and ask what she asked.

'Lynn,' I said, turning to her, still emotionally firm within which must've made her uncomfortable, put her in a state of unease and caution, 'I'm not the kind of guy who has friends. No one really knows me, and even if they say they do, they don't, not really. I wouldn't make a great friend to you. I know. And I don't want to ever hurt you or disappoint you. Ever.'

'How do you know you will?'

'Can I tell you a secret?'

'Sure,' she leaned in closer. 'You can tell me anything, Cody.'

I was surprised she even knew my name, but it felt good to have her by my side, even if she did look like a boy.

'I can see the future.'

She laughed as I knew she would. She covered her mouth with a petite, well-manicured hand. 'I'm sorry. I didn't mean to —'

'That's all right.'

'Can you tell me *my* future?'

'Why not. You deserve it after the day you've had. It might even cheer you up.' As I spoke, I quested the courtyard with a far-looking gaze, gesticulated to the empty yard in front of us, to all the children playing towards the back near the courts and shade. My hand waved across the empty land. 'What happened to you today is but a quickly passing memory, even now you are forgetting. Gavin, Owen and all the others will soon forget what they did and what has happened here today, and your hair, Lynn, will grow long and beautiful once again.'

'That's not *really* my future, even if it is true.'

'Let me finish. I see you, out there as if it's a movie before my eyes. You'll go away on a journey. An adventure.'

'Where?'

'I don't know. But you look sad. As if you don't want to go away. Which is strange to me. I'd like to go away for a while.'

'I don't want to hear anymore.'

'It gets better. I see it. In time you'll return. Your hair is long now, gorgeous and you've changed your fashion. You're driving a fancy new car.' My mind lived with these future scenes, phantoms of another time and place. I never asked for them. Never wanted them.

'I can't drive a car. I don't even have my license.'

'In time, Gavin and Owen and all the other boys will be chasing you and asking for your phone number.'

'Then what?'

'Then you'll reject them, because you'll have a handsome boyfriend.'

'Is it you?'

'I don't know. I can't see it. That's the trouble with seeing the future: it's hard to see your own fate. But I can say you'll become one of the most beautiful and popular girls in school one day, in all the town, and all this that happened today will be forgotten. Even in time, you'll forget what I've said to you today.'

'I won't ever forget what you've done, Cody.'

'Yes, yes you will. That's the part of the future I can see. Everyone forgets, sooner or later. But that's my curse, my mark to carry: looking back, remembering it all so clearly, as though it were last night. Sometimes the weight gets so heavy I want to die.'

'Can we be friends? You never answered my question.'

'Absolutely. I'm honored. But go play. I'd like to be alone a bit before class. Seeing the future makes me tired, depleted like I got nothing left in me. You can understand, can't you?'

She stood, hesitated, then before she left said, 'I'll never forget you or what you've done for me.'

'I hope that's true.' I waved gently for her to leave. 'Go play and be merry. And forget about your troubles. But know I'm always here for you.'

The very next day, sitting in the exact same spot off to the side, I noticed the same gang of boys huddled around Gavin and Owen and I thought: now what?

They were up to something but I decided to watch to be sure they weren't teasing another poor soul who couldn't defend herself. But the gang circled around Gavin in a conspiratorial air of a

Caesar about to be stabbed by his loyal subjects. Serves him right, I told myself, picking on that poor girl the way he did.

Then a banging of doors from the school's main office off to my left sounded. Out marched Lynn, head down, behind her mother who did not look at all happy. Mrs. Evans steamrolled ahead and through the playing children and somehow found Gavin's group, as if it were meant to be, in almost the exact spot from the day before. Mrs. Evans pointed her finger in Gavin's face and unleashed a verbal onslaught which paused all courtyard activities. I'd never seen a mother so harsh with a strange child before.

'Shit,' I said. 'Here it goes again.' I shook my head and lifted myself from the ground. 'Just when you think there's going to be a little peace.'

In the middle of the courtyard a group huddled around Mrs. Evans and Lynn, obviously embarrassed by the unwanted attention. I barged my way in between Mrs. Evans and Gavin.

'Everyone calm down,' I said. 'Calm down.'

'Are you the one?' Mrs. Evans said, her finger now in my face. 'Are you the ringleader who tortured my baby girl?'

'Momma, no,' Lynn said, grabbing her mother's arm. 'He's not the one.'

'It's all right, Lynn,' I said. 'She doesn't know. I can handle it.'

'Quiet, Lynn,' Mrs. Evans said. 'Let me handle this.' She then poured her hatred and scorn over onto me and I did my best to withstand her wrath with a positive heart. 'You're the one, aren't you? You teased her yesterday, didn't you? You're the guilty one!'

'No mam I did not. That was Gavin and these boys behind me, but I recommend you calm down, keep walking to your car and leave these boys alone. You're a high school teacher and these are seventh graders. They don't have a clue what they did. They have no idea.'

'Yeah,' Gavin said over my shoulder, 'keep walking.'

I turned my rage to face Gavin and the other boys. 'Shut up. You're not helping. You started all this and I'm trying to stop your mess from getting bigger. I'm trying to end this.' My body felt light. My heart true.

I faced Mrs. Evans politely, 'I'm sorry Gavin and Owen hurt your daughter's feelings but they don't deserve to be yelled at by an adult. You're angry. I agree. I would be too. But you should call their parents and settle the matter that way. Now is not the time nor place.'

'Who are you?' Mrs. Evans said angrily. 'Why are you trying to protect these boys? Are they friends of yours?'

Calmly, as best I could, I replied, 'I've known these boys my whole life but no, we are not friends.' The boys behind me grumbled but I ignored their spiteful remarks. 'The reason I'm standing between you, Mrs. Evans, and these stupid boys is because if I watched and did nothing today, then I would be just as guilty as though I were to watch them do what they did to your daughter and did nothing yesterday.' I felt my body become lighter.

Mrs. Evans's face softened. 'My daughter told me about you.' I met eyes with Lynn, such a gentle creature. She had spoken of me. 'So, you're the one.'

'I suppose I am.'

'I'm sorry for yelling at you but why are you siding with these hooligans? You should be careful who you associate with.'

'I don't associate with anyone, mam. These *hooligans* know not what they do, but I am of a sound mind that does. I'm the ransom that must be paid. These boys are innocent because they are ignorant of their actions. You, however, are not. You are an adult. You should know better by now than to yell at a bunch of stupid kids. I'm the ransom that needs to be paid. If you want to yell at someone, then yell at me. I can take it. I'll take it all. If you want to blame someone, then blame me. I'll carry the burden.' By the end of this little monologue, I felt myself levitating, glowing from within.

Mrs. Evans seemed to look up at me as I hovered off the ground. 'Who do you think you are? Do you think you're Jesus? Do you think you're some kind of Christ, a holy messiah, the Son of God?'

Lynn tugged at her mother's arm and looked at me with guilt and pity mixed in the dampness of her eyes. 'Let's go, Momma. Let's just go.'

'Answer me: do you believe you're the one and only Jesus Christ?'

'It is you who say that I am.' I mocked her and she knew it.

Mrs. Evans grew angrier at having wisdom poured onto her.

I quickly added, 'But no. I do not think I'm Jesus, as you imply.' The feeling of my levitation gradually ceased, lowering me slowly back to the ground. 'I can see now that the world isn't ready for salvation. Not by me, but salvation from God. The way everyone treats one another. If I had it my way, things would be different. I'm sad. I'm disappointed in the whole human race. I'm....'

'You're what? Say it.'

'I'm ashamed.' Head down, feet firmly on the ground, I finished, 'I've done all I could do. Go now in peace, the both of you. And Lynn, I'm sorry for everything. You deserve better, so much more than this. And remember....'

'Yes?'

'Remember all I've told you.'

'What did you tell her?'

'I will. I promise.'

'She will not. I'm taking her out of school. She'll forget this nonsense.'

Mrs. Evans reached back and grabbed her daughter's hand and led her through the group, which had grown smaller and more silent. I remember waving to Lynn, who sat in the front seat looking straight ahead, and I'm not sure she saw me still looking as her mother drove away.

Mrs. Evans kept true to her word and removed Lynn from school the following day. She never returned to middle school, and thinking of what could have been, I grew more alone in my solitude.

I'd see Lynn two years later in high school. When she did make her triumphant return, all the boys froze and watched this 'new girl' walk down the hall and into the Lions' Den, a large indoor space walled by glass windows to one side where everyone met in the early mornings or late afternoons or between classes. When I first saw her again, I barely recognized her and it had been her name only that brought back the faint recollection to my memory. Lynn's hair had indeed grown longer, more beautiful down past her shoulders, her breasts had blossomed considerably and became the bedtime desire for each boy she blindly passed in the halls with her back straight, her head held high. Lynn dressed much more like a grown woman in her twenties than a teenager, and, yes, I heard from the grapevine that Gavin and Owen chased after her only to be denied.

Lynn and I would meet in passing at parties and our senior year she came, just as friends, with Joseph Gardner to a party I threw at my mother's house on Durham, but I never mentioned to her about that day in the seventh grade. At the party, I stood at the porch edge with my hands up on the overhang while I leaned my body forward out over the steps. I spoke of how I could see the future and how no one believed me when I said I would become a writer and live far, far away overseas, in Africa or Asia perhaps. I spoke to Lynn and looked into her eyes and wondered if she remembered. I had a notion that she had a crush on me after she broke up with her boyfriend and came with Joseph to my party, but I had a girlfriend as well and I couldn't bring myself to make a move on Lynn, because I knew if I did, and we did hook up and sleep together, which I very much wanted at the time, I'd only disappoint her in the end, becoming no better than Gavin or Owen in her eyes, and I never wanted that to happen. I knew then we didn't have a future together, I could see it clearly, and I restrained myself from taking advantage of her. To me, Lynn Evans would always be that little girl with short hair in the seventh grade.

Several years later I'd meet Lynn once more, a final time before I left the States. After high school, Lynn Evans moved to Lubbock and attended Texas Tech University, and she returned home to Brownwood as a junior on holiday back for a visit. We met in a local bar — I can't remember the name now, but it was across the street from the Crazy Lemon — and she was with an ex-girlfriend of mine named Hannah, I think, both looking for people to come to a party at a hotel. I'd been there and done that whole scene by then and I felt Lynn or Hannah were searching for an excuse or a chance to get me alone, to talk, to remember, or to be. But I just didn't want that.

Lynn and Hannah left but returned an hour later, with me a little bit drunker than when I first saw them, and they still wanted to see if I'd go with them to a party at a hotel.

'I can't,' I said. 'I've got plans.'

'Like what?' Lynn said.

'I'm going abroad soon, Africa maybe, and I can't start anything now.' I wasn't sober but I had a good buzz going and I felt on top of the world. 'I would rather you remember me as a good man.' I placed my Corona on a nearby stand.

'I do remember,' she said. 'I remember everything.'

'What's he talking about?' Hannah said.

'Then good. I'm glad.'

'But why do you have to go tonight? Can't you come? It's not like you're flying away tomorrow.'

'Come to the party,' Hannah said. 'It'll be fun.'

No longer wanting to avoid the real reason I didn't wish to go with them, I locked eyes with Lynn. 'Would you like me to tell you your future?'

'Yes,' she said. 'Tell me everything. I'm ready.'

'What?' Hannah said. 'What's he saying?' The country music, another sad love song in the background, made it difficult to hear so I stepped closer to Lynn.

'I can't tell you everything, but I can tell you that I see a handsome husband in your future.'

'Oh, God,' Hannah said. 'Really? Barf.'

'Go on,' Lynn said, still locking eyes with me. 'Is it you?'

'No, sadly. But you'll meet him in a year or two or you've already met him but you'll become more romantic, more intimate in the time ahead.'

'He's cracking,' Hannah said. 'Or he's drunk. Let's go, Lez.'

'Will I?' Lynn said. 'What about you? About us?'

'Yes, you will.' I leaned in and she let me kiss her on her forehead. 'Goodbye, love. I don't think we'll get a chance to meet again, so please be the one who always thinks of me as a good man.'

'You are a good man,' she said. Her eyes held that same look of grief and pity I had seen long ago from her. How those eyes still haunt me now at night when I'm in bed alone and unable to sleep.

'Thank you,' I said, before walking out of the bar, into the cold, cold night and driving home with the windows down. 'Go with God,' I told her. 'Be one with the Universe, and please remember me.'

Our eyes had been locked the whole time, standing close enough to kiss or to feel each other's vibrations, when she said, 'I do.'

About a year ago — I've never seen Lynn again, in person, by the way — I heard Lynn had in fact married a handsome man and has two beautiful daughters, but whether she remembers me the way I remember her, I doubt that very much.

I read about Alexander Von Humboldt once saying, 'In this great chain of causes and effects, no single fact can be considered in isolation.' I feel that's true for me too. And for my father as well. I can't say I'm extremely proud of my father for the way he chose to live his life, but there were times when I'd stand back and ask myself who was this man so very unlike the day-to-day man I'd known my whole life, because in a good way my father would emerge from some reluctant shell he'd spent his life hiding inside to prove to me, a small boy, that, yes, there were heroes in this world and he was one of them. Maybe that's what sons look for in their father: the ability to rise to an occasion when a situation demands it; I know I looked to my father and expected him to be a hero rather than a slave, but most of the time — regardless of how many dinners and movies he took me to — he'd disappoint me by chasing a woman, albeit my mother, who cuckolded him and this brought out the weaker more submissive side of his nature. But I can't blame him either. Love can do that to a man.

There was, however, this one day which stands out in my mind. I believe my parents were already divorced — and even this fact Cassandra drew suspicion on saying that Henry and Gwendolen never legally divorced but merely separated; but I didn't care, the damage had been done and there was no going back.

Chadwick was spending Thanksgiving that year in Oklahoma City with his college girlfriend Annest — who would later mother his two children, Willa and Stephen — and I'm pretty sure Cassandra was in Dallas because Henry, my mother and I had gone through there to visit her — she'd been busy — and to take her to lunch, but Cassandra dining with my parents never made for a pleasant experience, and in the end I feel that Cassandra blew us off; so there we were — Henry, Gwendolen and myself — driving east from Dallas on I-20 to Shreveport then to my mother's family in Monroe, Louisiana for Thanksgiving.

The interstate that rainy day had been busy but not overly crowded to cause any jams among the holiday travelers, but nonetheless Gwendolen would bicker to Henry about his excessive speed. Henry would bicker back about his superb driving ability, and I'd be quite at ease with this playful banter between my parents, who were at least talking to one another again. Like I said, it had been raining, and fog drifted in patches across I-20 making driving safely a conscious-deliberate-focused act, and so my father had plenty of warning to slow and pull off to the side of the interstate when we came to a collection of cars and trucks stopped for a mile up and down the road.

'What's going on?' my mother said in typical fashion.

'There's been an accident,' my father answered. He leaned over the steering wheel and wiped the windshield clear. 'Stay here,' he said, 'and keep an eye on the truck.'

'Henry, don't —' my mother said, but my father had already slammed the door shut. He checked oncoming traffic and then ran across the macadam and down into the center ditch dividing the east and west bound lanes.

'What do you think happened?' my mother asked me.

'I don't know,' I said, 'but I'm going to go find out.'

'Cody, don't —'

'Stay here,' I said, 'and keep an eye on things.'

I opened the door near the dense woods, opposite roadside, and my right sneaker slipped in the wet grass. From behind our car, I made my way carefully across the interstate, which began to fill with more cars lining up on both sides to see what was happening down below in the drainage ditch that ran between the opposite lanes of the highway. I crossed between two cars wet from a new drizzle that began to fall and walked at a half-trot on the loose gravel which ran along the side of the road and at the top of the ditch. When I came to a good vantage point, I could see down, some twenty yards deep, two cars twisted and banged up pretty good. The cars rested on their sides with the windows cracked and knocked out as a dozen or more men gathered around. One man knelt by a splintered windshield. Another man pointed up the incline to a place I could not see. No ambulances had arrived, but I heard a firetruck's siren blaring behind me and soon they'd be down there with my father, wherever he was, but for now the ordinary men climbed onto one of the two cars trying to get someone out of the wreckage.

From man to man I searched for my father as the drizzle of rain made it harder to see. I checked the opposite side of the interstate where thirty or more bystanders held their arms close to their chests and spoke low to one another. I cast my gaze back to the wreckage into the group of crowded men in the bottom of the ditch and I couldn't find my father in his red-and-black flannel jacket. I turned back to see if he hadn't returned back to our vehicle, but I couldn't see through the wet windows. My hair became soaked and I swiped a hand through it to wipe away the rainwater. Moving along the side to a closer viewing position, I finally spotted my father, who no longer wore his flannel jacket, and that had been the reason I couldn't find him earlier. The red-and-black flannel jacket had been thrown over the side of the shattered passenger's window, now facing the gentle gray-green of coming rain. My father was not standing around on the ground with the other men. He had climbed atop the capsized vehicle and reached his arm down into the cavity of the wreckage. He'd dip half his body in then return to the surface only to dive down again with two men holding him aloft by the back of my father's belt, the same I'm sure he used to whip me with when I was younger.

Much like another time, there I stood with the rain wetting my hair and dripping down over my face — for some reason I've always enjoyed being in the rain — and I watched my father and those men trying everything in their powers to save a man? woman? child? I feared, then, the wreckage would explode, like in the movies, and my father would be killed a hero the day before Thanksgiving. I ducked back between two parked cars and returned to my mother waiting in the car. By then I was good and soaked and energized by all the excitement, and by the sight of a new side to my otherwise dull father.

'Where's your father?' Gwendolen asked.

'He's down in that pit saving people.'

'What? He better not be.'

'He is, and his new flannel jacket is halfway in the wrecked car, which I think could explode any minute.'

I enjoyed exaggerating, still do, but it could've happened.

'Oh, God, Henry,' my mother said then, and she paused to stare out through the rain-covered windshield which was impossible to see through, and I wondered what she was thinking of at that exact moment. Gwendolen and I waited for Henry to come when we saw the firetrucks and ambulances arrive. Fifty or more bystanders watched from the top of the ditch and huddled beneath umbrellas. After about forty-five or so minutes of waiting, with the rain picking up quite heavily outside, my father hopped back into the driver's seat and settled himself, all abuzz with thriving energy, behind the steering wheel.

'Where's your jacket?' my mother said.

'Yeah, dad. What happened?'

Henry started the car and slowly entered traffic to resume our journey. 'I don't know,' he said, 'I guess I left it back there.'

I let out a great laugh. What a grand idiot.

'What?' Gwendolen said. 'Henry, that was a gift. Do you know how much I spent? You don't care about anything, do you?'

'Well, Gwendolen, I had to cover the broken glass with something.'

'Broken glass?' I said. 'What the hell happened back there?'

'A woman got stuck under the steering wheel and she couldn't get out. She was wedged in pretty good, and the glass kept falling down into her face. I put my jacket down to help. They ended up using the Jaws of Life to get her out.'

'What?' Gwendolen said. 'Oh, goodness.'

'Wow,' I said. 'The Jaws of Life. That must've been awesome scary.'

'We'll have to get you a new jacket, Henry.'

'I'm fine. I don't need a new one. I'll just borrow one from Desmond.'

'The Jaws of Life. Who would of thought?' I said, 'Was the lady all right? Did she make it out alive?'

'Yeah, she made it. A bit broken and bruised in places but the paramedics said she'd make it.'

'Wow, dad,' I said, 'you're a hero. A real live hero.'

'Yes,' Gwendolen added, 'Now your father can die happy, contented.'

'I'm not a hero, son,' my father said, and he strained to see the road ahead through the flapping windshield wipers. 'I've never done anything in my life to be called a hero. I just did what any good man would've done. I helped when help was needed. That doesn't make me a hero.'

I sat back in the warm, dry seat and stared out into the rain falling over the woods off to the side of the highway running into forever. I was thinking of another day, another time in the rain as a child, and I thought to myself about my father and said aloud, 'Yes, it does. That's exactly what it makes you.'

The thing is I never know if I'm self-destructing or standing up for my beliefs. I need to lie down. Give me a minute.

Outside, an invisible air current pushes the storm clouds away but a few grayish-blue puffs remain as the afternoon brightens in degrees immeasurable, softly perceptible to the human eye. Your office, however, continues to be as cold and as emotionless as ever and that same longing I get when I find myself too long and too cramped up in an office comes back to me in desires of wanting to be completely naked and in bed with a lover wet from her wanting me.

What was that again? I ask. I was thinking of something.

Whenever you're ready, you say, you can continue.

There was this dream I had only once but it had been so powerful and resilient and so vivid that I never forgot any of it, not a single detail escaped my memory.

At the time of the dream, to put this in context, I'd been working as a night manager at the buffet restaurant Golden Corral, the same one I told you about. Sometimes during my shift I'd be culled from my managerial duties to wash dishes, help stack the food counters, assist on the cash register or even cook.

The dream starts with me in the restaurant's kitchen checking orders on paper slips stuck over the serving window where the plates could be passed to the wait staff. I'm reading each order on the slips when the English language dissolves and the words reappear in the form of strange symbols I've never seen before. Confusion sets in. Gabriel Márquez, one of my childhood friends who worked as a waiter at night, approached me in the dream on my right and I thought it strange for him to be in the kitchen next to me and not on the other side of the serving window where he usually joked while waiting for orders to arrive. But in the dream, Gabriel stepped closer, too close for my comfort, his nose almost touching my cheek, and then as fear slipped through me and gripped me solid, I knew Gabriel was not Gabriel but a disguised demon or the Devil itself using Gabriel's image to get close enough to me before my spiritual defenses could be raised. One of the slips in my hand began to shake as the Devil spoke with a striking anger filled with tremendous energy, 'Death comes to those who follow close behind.'

In bed, the dream broke, I sat upright, my heart pounding in me like a madman's, and those words, a sort of omen meant to be a malison, has stayed sharp and permanent ever since, some seventeen years ago.

Over the next few months, I analyzed the warning and found, for me, that there could be two possible meanings: one, if I followed close behind God, a physical death would certainly come — and that didn't bother me so much as the second interpretation because we all have a death to pay for having lived our lives; two, if I followed close behind the Devil, an everlasting death would find me after my last breath here on Earth. I'm positive the Dark

Angel had meant the first, but somehow my guardian angel wanted me to know that every coin has two sides and to not be so easily dismayed.

With that said, my mother used to have this recurring dream but she said it came from a memory she had of an event when her mother and father left her and her six siblings at home for one Friday night to go dancing. The children were playing hide-and-seek and my mother crept from room to room in search of her brothers and sisters — including, I think, Uncle Desmond, Uncle Gerard, Aunt Samarah, Shorty, Easel, and the others, but I could be wrong, because I want to say some of the older kids were out on the town at that time — and my mother, as a child herself, poked her head in her mother's closet and there in the darkened corner, near her mother's large fur coat, a strange, bearded man, like a bear, looked back at her.

My mother screamed her way out of the house and gathered the children in the front yard and told them of how a large, bearded man had been hiding in the closet, and the children waited outside until the father came home to check thoroughly the house and all its crevices to make sure, quite certain, that no stranger, if there ever was one, remained in the house. My mother still swears that a man had been hiding in her mother's closet, and when I lived with my mother, she'd wake screaming her head off in the pitch-black dark to a figure of a man standing at the foot of her bed. We'd never find anybody though.

When my mother had been in college and I was but an insignificant glimmer reflected in her womb, she used to help the church by passing out gospel pamphlets on the street with her friends and fellow believers — being that Texas is in the Bible Belt didn't make this at all surprising.

In a park late one night, my mother and her friend Deborah stood in the glow of a lamplight and handed out the Christian propaganda for an hour or more when a strange, bearded man tentatively approached, drew back, moved closer, hesitated, made a half-step forward, looked from my mother to her friend and back to my mother on this cold, dark night. After a few minutes, my mother and her friend sighed in relief when the stranger left the way he came, vanishing around a bend in the wooded park. My mother and her friend Deborah returned to the church, then home soon after.

A week or so later, my mother once again returned to pass along the Good News in the same park, but this time she occupied a different spot than the one before and it was a lovely, winter afternoon rather than at night. She believed it had even snowed. My mother, without a companion on this day, tensed when the same strange, bearded man from the previous week approached.

'God bless you,' my mother said; she held out a pamphlet and added, 'Would you like one?'

The stranger accepted her offer and ran a thumb over the face of Jesus printed on the paper she had given him.

'May I ask you something?' the stranger said.

'I don't see why not?' My mother relaxed believing the stranger was simply shy and wanted her telephone number.

'You were here the other night with someone else, no?'

'Many of us for the church come here quite often, so maybe. When did you say?'

'I'm not sure, maybe a week ago, but you and your friend, a girl, had been working at night.'

'That could've been us. Why?'

'I think it was you. I'm quite sure.'

'That's nice of you to remember. Would you like to make a donation?'

'That's not why I came today.' The strange, bearded man's eyes dodged the firm looks my mother gave him. 'I wanted to ask you something. I think it's going to help me more than it will you. I'm not feeling so well these days. But I need to know something, if you don't mind.'

'Okay. What did you want to ask me?'

'That night I spoke of, there were three of you, no? Your friend, the girl I'm sure, but wasn't there someone else with you? A man?'

The sun shot free from a wayward cloud and warmed the scene below. Leaves in the trees rattled from a passing breeze. A small boy kicked a ball to his mother nearby. My mother, however, became concerned for her safety and for the man's sanity.

'Not at all,' my mother said. 'There were only two of us. Me and my friend Deborah. I'm not sure which man you're talking about.'

'Are you sure? Quite sure?'

'Quite. Is there something you want to get off your chest?' As a missionary she had asked this question so often that it came out more as reflex than as general interest.

'Yes,' the stranger said. 'I'm not sure what I saw, but I feel I should tell you something. I need to tell someone and I think it should be you.'

'I'm listening. Take your time.'

'That night I wanted to do you harm, or your friend, I don't know what it was I wanted to do but it wasn't good. The first time I came to the park there were only two of you, but I chickened out and left, but I came back when it was darker, and as I neared, I saw three of you standing in the light. There was a man who hadn't been there before and he was standing between you and your friend, and if it wasn't for him, I would've done something that would've ruined both our lives. I can't explain what's going on inside me, or why I'm telling you this, maybe it's because of that man, but I'm sure there was a man with you that night and I'm also sure that same man looked just like this man.' The stranger held up the pamphlet with the image of Jesus. 'I'm not a believer but I'm not going to hurt you. And I'm sorry if I scared you any at all. If you can, please forgive me and say a prayer for me.'

'I will,' was my mother's answer.

The bearded man nodded, gave an awkward smile revealing crooked teeth, and without another word he turned around and walked away.

To this day my mother can't explain why he'd confess the way he did, but she never returned to the park, day or night, and she never saw the stranger again. She was just too frightened after that encounter to do the Lord's work. My mother, however, swears on her grave that her friend Deborah and she had been alone, that the stranger must've been hallucinating, on drugs and seeing things, as crazy kooks do, because there was never any man, a third, there on that night. My mother would grow silent then as if in afterthought, considering an old Bible verse locked away in her, and whenever she imagined about what could've happened that night, she would be reminded that wherever two or more were gathered in His name, there He would be also.

Look Homeward, Angel: it's true what Thomas Wolfe, one of my literary idols, once wrote about not being able to go home again. Some of my last memories of home was of its provincial indolence — mason jars of iced tea, rocking chairs on the porch, stitched quilts and blankets, pecan trees being harvested in autumn — reminding me of a run-down Grecian urn and a city somewhere to the east of Eden, found beneath a sky smothered in a pinkish ocher with a deliciously warm breeze coming down into a valley I'd spent so many years trying to climb and claw my way out of to eventually succeed and leave behind my home in the heartland somewhere in the heart of Texas.

Even though I managed to crawl my way out, I ended up discovering that home — the place I came from and the people who were as memorable as the buildings and landmarks — was a bigger and far more important part of me than I had ever realized, and that turned out to be a good thing.

When I was twenty-two or twenty-three and living in San Angelo, Dylan and Gianna invited me for a weekend on the Guadalupe River in South Texas. I hitched a ride with them on a hot-summer-Sunday morning and a few hours later we eased our eternal-like bodies, the envy of Adonis, into the cold-brown waters of the Guadalupe and reclined ourselves to the tops of our rented inner tubes, which would be transporting us, along with thousands of others that day, down river-miles winding, stretching some eight to nine hours.

Floating idle, pushed by currents beneath, felt to me as though Nature had engulfed us into its timeless existence, at the dawn of dinosaurs, and while we drifted deeper into a new reality far outside civilization, we joked and drank beers and laughed as we paddled ourselves into the shaded side of the river to avoid getting burned by the sun.

At times I'd pop off the rubbery tube, hot and sticky, and dive into the murky deeps to splash cold water over my friends and over my inner tube to cool the hot rubber. Doing backstrokes alongside Dylan, I'd see his tube attached to a spare securing an ice chest cooler filled with enough beers and sandwiches, and he'd raise his bottle of Shiner Bock to offer me, a fish of the river — you're a merman, Gianna called out — a toast for all of us to have long lives, sweet dreams and tons of wild sex. Years later, who would have guessed, Gianna and Dylan would divorce and find different paths than the one they had planned for twenty years.

Hopping back on top of my tube, I'd sun and let my wet hair dry and recall the summers I spent as a child with my family on the Guadalupe and how nothing had changed around me, not a single tree or riverbend, all the surroundings had stayed the same, but I knew then that I was the one that had changed. In one of these summers as a teen, my tube had washed down whitewater rapids and somehow got sucked back into an undercurrent creating a whirlpooling loop, and me smiling like an idiot enjoying the ride. My tube would be pushed out, then pulled back around and in, the cascading water from the higher rocks above pounding down on top of me and my tube only to push me out and pull me back in again. I was enjoying the ride, oblivious to any danger of an undertow, when a strange woman appeared standing opposite me on the shore shouting, 'Help! Someone help him! He's in trouble! Help!' I looked around to see who the hell was in trouble and who she was pointing at and who 'he' was. Soon I found she was pointing and yelling at me. I was the one in trouble, but I didn't have to think long nor hard about it. I was far too young to drown there in that dirty river, so I slipped casually off my tube, wrapped an arm around the rubber tube and began fighting the current until I broke free and swam safely away. I dipped under the water and entered my tube from beneath the center hole and crawled aboard. When I maneuvered the tube back around to face the falls, I looked to both shores to wave my thanks to the strange woman who had helped me, but I found her gone. No one was there.

That had been a long time ago when I was just a kid. Now, I was a young man on the same river that hadn't changed much with

Dylan and his wife Gianna — at the time, Walt, their son, was just a baby — and somehow we're still together locked in that moment on the Guadalupe — once home to the Karankawa, Tonkawa and Huaco, as in Waco, Indians until the Germans, my ancestors from the Rhineland, came to settle New Braunfels — and while I reminded myself of these things and more on the river so named for Our Lady of Guadalupe, the South American Virgin, the *Nuestra Señora*, I kept telling myself also about how times like these with Dylan and Gianna, oh so young and full of eternal beauty, would never fade; how friendships like the ones I had with them meant more to me than any accomplishments, more than literary accolades, and how on my deathbed, I'd see the three of us in the golden age of our youth floating downriver to a destination we'd know once we arrived, and for the time being our companionship would be enough to conquer time.

On that summer day, kayaks, canoes and rafts skirted by as Dylan reminisced about *Pearl Jam*, his favorite band, and about his tennis days playing against a talented boy named Andy Roddick and how Dylan had the stuff himself to go all the way to Wimbledon, to become legend, if not for a grease fire in his mother's kitchen which burned his hand and wrist and put him out of commission. Gianna would speak of her mother — God rest her soul — and sister, Nicolette, playing Scrabble, they were such dorks, nerds, wordsmiths, on a Friday night rather than going out parking with boys. I'd nod and drink my Corona-in-a-can and listen to their stories about days past as I checked out girls in tight bikinis and thongs singing along with a stereo playing Gwen Stefani's 'Hollaback Girl,' and these teens floating on a raft would wag and shake their butts as they shouted in unison with Gwen, 'B-A-N-A-N-A-S!' over and over again until the raft deposited them out of earshot around a faraway bend in the river.

By late afternoon, still hours to go, I had a nice tan and a good buzz going as I drifted in the middle of the river beneath a bridge with railroad tracks. On the other side a girl floated beside me, and beneath my sunshades I'd been thinking of something distant, something about the rain, something obscure about my childhood when I noticed she had removed the top of her bikini to reveal fat breasts and dark nipples.

I'd been staring in her direction but my thoughts consumed my vision with deep, dark memories that when I came back from a place very far away, I saw, quite unexpectedly, her nipples staring back at me. She winked, stuck her tongue out at me, replaced the bikini over her exposed breasts, and paddled downriver to join her group.

Wanting to tell Dylan what had just happened, I paddled myself around to find him and Gianna coming out underneath the bridge and the railroad tracks. In that instant a low rumbling could be heard from behind the trees.

The energy within me also came to a boil. As my emotions erupted, overjoyed at too much pleasure and pain — a Pan running naked and mad through mythic forests and over enchanted rivers — I cried out at the exact instant a train came hurling across the bridge, and I lifted my arms high shouting, 'I AM —!'

The last word became silenced and lost beneath the thunderous roar from the steam engine sounding its horn for the infinitesimal cheers and applause coming from those, like me, on the river below, and I saw the locomotive's captain wave and pull the horn once more, deafening me and my voice with seismic vibrations.

After that summer, Dylan and Gianna would move their family to Americus, Georgia — near Andersonville and Carter's boyhood home — and a month before I left the States, I visited them in that small town, an exemplar of America with a population no more than twenty thousand in Sumter County.

I'd wake early while the rest of the family lay asleep and the fog hovered low around the Victorian houses and I'd drink my coffee out on the wraparound porch, the age of the South settling down on me, a Texan, and I knew I had to leave everything behind, but like the fog obfuscating and obscuring the trees and the neighborhood houses, I couldn't be sure if my decision was a correct one or what awaited me in the lands outside of America, but I knew one thing: if I ever found what Dylan and Gianna had, I'd never let it go. I'd hold on the way Jacob — the namesake for my baby son, Jacob Thor — wrestled with God, and won.

Little Hometown, America

The people you lose remain a part of you, but I want you to define mercy. I've heard that's the truest and likeliest kind of immortality: living on in the memories other people have of you; but I'm not sold on remaining ever-after in the thoughts of an individual that might've misconstrued a thing I said once over wine or did while I was driving late to work or hated me for having the character and integrity, the moral fiber, he often spoke of to his colleagues in the canteen but could never own himself up to having; no, I like to imagine, whether there will be or not after my death, in my corner of heaven or hell, there'd be a little place by a river up in the mountains with a log cabin and a few horses on it. That'd suit me just fine, come to think of it.

Still, it's a novel idea to me how the dead continue to live by remembrance alone, the kind Proust wrote about, and how I'm reminded of John Ferryman, the roofer I told you about who ended up shooting himself — I still don't know why he did it — and how John and me with Matson, now of Round Rock, planned to spend an afternoon swimming and drinking beer with Phoebe at a dock house on Lake Brownwood.

At this time, I was twenty-one and dating an African American pre-med student named Phoebe who had the phrase *Semper Fi* tattooed over her apple bottom. On that day I brought Phoebe along to meet John and Matson, who were both several years my senior. To get to the dock house across the lake we all boarded John's boat and raced onwards as, disapprovingly so, storm clouds moved closer in the distance. I can still see John at the helm with one hand on the boat's wheel and the other around a can of Keystone Light, and he seemed happy and content as his eyes quested the lake waters before him.

By the time we made it to the dock house, a light rain had begun to fall and we had to resign ourselves to sitting around drinking beer and chatting about the same old shit great friends banter on about. At one point, Phoebe began to massage John's neck as she explained the meaning behind her tattoo on her lower back, and Matson and I agreed the reason for having 'Always Faithful' scrolled on her lower back to be quite a clever one. I grew a bit bored, however, and decided to go for a swim.

'But it's raining,' Phoebe said, as if that meant something.

'Just more water. Shouldn't hurt.'

'Watch out for lightning,' Matson said. 'I heard once about a guy who was swimming in a pool during a storm and a lightning bolt slapped him silly. Bam! Just like that.'

'Oh my God,' Phoebe said. 'Was he killed?'

'I don't think so,' Matson said, 'but I'm pretty sure he left the hospital with a new haircut and a fat birthmark on his ass.'

We laughed at the absurd thought of getting hit in the butt by lightning.

'Well, I'm going in,' I said. 'Anyone game?'

All three of them shook their heads as I stripped down to my swimsuit beneath my jeans.

'You sure?' I said as I stood at the door of the dock house. I can still see the three of them there looking back at me. 'Should be fun.'

Again, the three declined. I stepped outside and let the rain wet my bare body. Then I dove off the dock into a lake that had started to swell from the rising wind coming from the approaching storm.

For a time I swam on my back, watchful of passing boats, and looked at the dark, melancholic clouds dripping drops one-by-one onto my face, and I let myself float there trying to forget my friends in the dock house, trying to disremember my family and my roots, trying to empty myself of all history until the future opened and revealed all its secrets to me. I wouldn't leave the States for another five years, but floating out there alone in the lake under the rain I somehow knew there'd be no other choice but to leave kith and kin behind in America; my destiny — which seemed loth to let me have my way, as if predeterminism became a forbidden concept to the realm of my personal Universe — my destiny, like the time my brother Chadwick picked me up and carried me to the merry-go-round and then placed me in the center only to begin spinning faster and faster, ever round and round, until I cried and begged for mercy, pleading for him to stop and when that horizontal wheel finally ceased its motions, I crawled off and lay in the sand seeing five worlds where there should've been only one — my destiny, whatever I needed my future to be in order to live a fulfilled life, weighed heavy on me while I let the rain and lake cover me whole.

I dove beneath the lake's surface and, as I expected, the plethora of noise immediately vanished, breaking into a calm that soothed my turbulent thoughts. Yes, I angered easily back then at the thoughts of a corrupted system having been created for and by the elites several millennia before my birth and how such a flawed system pre-established and pre-ordained who and what I was going to be. The peons would be peons. The lords would be lords. And who was I?

Then I was reminded of JFK's application to Harvard and the five-sentence-long essay included therein. John, knowing the value of an elite education, had been seventeen years old when he wrote to the prestigious university on April 23, 1935. He said he wanted to be like his father, a 'Harvard Man.' The incredibly short essay had been almost identical to the one he wrote for his application to Princeton. Either way, the young man knew the importance of status and how nepotistic relationships mattered more than any mastery of a higher education. God bless America, I said into the rain.

But I had a problem with such limited and dated and moronic concepts. I didn't have a problem with authority. Not in the least. I had a problem, instead, with immoral imbeciles in the positions of authority. Even then, as a young man I believed society, the invisible construction of organized individuals, needed to re-think and re-plan how souls on this good earth were treated. The antiquated system, needing desperately to be modernized, urged the lower-and-upper classes to evolve, but for the people to evolve the anachronistic system needed modernity to come and dust off the primitive practices held since the agrarian age and to grease the wheels with an idea as simple and as old and as profound as Free Will. But I suppose meritocracy is a curse word in a world fueled by guanxi.

With 'Ode to Joy' playing in my mind, I pounded my arms into the thrashing waves rising higher with every passing minute, and I swam farther from the dock in hopes of killing the rage inside me fighting against the chains of a predeterminism designed by the silver-haired elites, and I blamed God when I should've blamed — as I do now — flawed human beings hidden at the top of an abstract concept establishing a system that doesn't work anymore. A system that cried out against me, 'Death to Equality! Death to Free Will! Death to Peace on Earth! Death to Goodwill towards All!'

The storm intensified around me as the waves lifted me up to rock me back down, and I resisted Nature, God, the Universe, all of Man's Creation, by fighting against the passivity of my soul forged by what others expected me to be or to do in a prefabricated culture, marred with too much discontent. I didn't see myself becoming obedient, and somewhere within me those tumultuous emotions subsided along with the easing rain. The waves didn't go as high, the storm clouds charged blindly on their way, out over lake and land, and I was left flat on my back as I allowed myself to do what I believed impossible; I allowed myself to open my heart and say the words I'd fought my whole life from saying. Floating on my back, my hair wet and wild like seaweed, I rested my hands on my stomach. With a voice soft enough for only the lake to hear, I said,

'I forgive you.'

As I swam back to shore, with John standing on the edge of the dock watching me make my way in, I wasn't sure if the 'you' I had said meant God or the Universe, or if in some cosmic delusion that twisted my words into an infinite jest, that the 'you' had actually meant 'me.'

Either way it didn't matter. The storm raged on and I found myself refreshed and at peace with my surroundings and happy to look upon Phoebe once more and her soft features and plump breasts that would fold beneath my hands and arms in bed as the storm pressed us ever closer despite the opposing colors of our skin. We'd make love, she'd always be faithful, and in our hearts we were one and the same.

My sister Cassandra asked me a good question once and I didn't have an answer for her. We'd been smoking a joint on the swing beneath my father's great oak out on Pine Creek Ranch, before the place ended up as one big hole in the rock quarry I told you about.

Cassandra, high on another plain of awareness, Krishna-like, became lost in thought and when she came back to me, she seemed distant and sad; unsure of what she wanted to say. I said, 'The world isn't as bad as we think it is.' A breeze felt good sitting in the shade of the oak.

Cassandra usually sneered at my optimism, but this time the expression on her face remained unreadable, void of meaning and interpretation. No portent could I tell from her downcast eyes.

'It's getting hard, Cody. Unbearable.'

'I know it is.' I didn't know what she had meant. 'It's damn hard.'

'Not like that. You seem to have life all figured out. But what about me?'

'You'll figure something out. You always do. I'll be there for you. Henry and Gwendolen will be there for you.'

Cassandra did sneer this time at the mention of our parents' names.

'God, Cody. How do you do it? How do you see the best in people?'

'I don't know. I just do. I guess I expect them to do the same.'

'There's times when you're not here, you're in class at university and I have the place all to myself and I'm in the kitchen washing dishes and I look out the window at this big, ugly tree and I swear to God, Cody, I can see myself hanging from that limb over there.'

I knew the limb she spoke of. A strong, thick one.

'I even have the rope. I'll use it when I'm all set. Everything's ready but me. How morbid am I?'

'We all have dark days. Hemingway called them his Black Ass days. Ups and downs, that's all. Very normal. Very human.'

'Okay, professor.'

'I'm not there yet.'

'I have a feeling you will be. Call it a hunch.'

'I can't lose you, Cassandra. I can lose any one of the others but not you. Have some faith. For me?'

'I can't afford faith, little brother.'

You could say everything I've ever done in my career has been done in order to save Cassandra and you wouldn't be too far from the truth. But back then I was in the process of saving myself and I didn't know what to say to her to bring her back from the edge, that same cliff millions of others find themselves running towards in the fields of rye. What could a brother say to his sister, to save her, when he could barely damn-well save himself? I don't know. I still don't know.

'What do you want me to say to that?' I said. 'Faith or no faith, doesn't matter. That doesn't give you the excuse to quit on me. We're in this together.'

'Let me ask something,' she said. 'Did the earth ever move for you?'

'What're you talking about?'

'Did the world open up to your dreams? Did you wake up one day and have it all figured out and things came easier? Did life start making sense? Or better sense? Because I don't have a fucking clue.'

I didn't have an answer for her and I knew enough to be wary of my words or she'd slip deeper into the abyss I've often seen her spiraling down into. I nodded and did my best to listen. She needed an ear, not a counselor. A shoulder, not a judge.

'I think I'm going crazy, Cody. I can't stand Chadwick or Henry, and especially Gwendolen. There're so two-faced, phony. I can't trust them.'

'I know what you mean.'

'I worry they'll lock me up again, and this time they'll lose the key.'

'I won't let that happen.'

'After Gator died, I cry every day. He loved me and I let him down. He looked to me to protect him and I failed him. He was such a great dog, wasn't he? God! I miss him, you know what I mean?'

'The best,' I said. 'Look Cassandra, you're no crazier than I am. You're sad. You miss your dog. He was your best friend. You raised him from a puppy. I'd feel like crap too if Angel died.' My Golden Retriever perked her ears at the mention of her name and she raised up off the ground where she'd been lying and came to my side. I scratched one of Angel's ears. Cassandra then hugged Angel as I patted the dog on her back. I had had Angel since she was a puppy too and she'd become family, and no parent wants to see her child die.

'I'm going for a walk,' I said. 'Do you want to come?'

Cassandra shook her head in the negative. She lit a cigarette, instead, and began smoking.

A creek ran through the middle of my father's land. I walked out of the shade from under the oak and down beside the creek, which led me after a few hundred yards to a grove of trees. I looked back at our little creek on Pine Creek Ranch and reminded myself how in funny ways it repeatedly called to my attention, for some strange reason, the River Rhine. I thought of all the composers but how Schumann stood out as the one most related to me; he was the least understood among his contemporaries and how he was ignored within his own lifetime because he often followed no rules and was believed to have had no true mentor nor teacher. His style, his craft, his art emerged from his passion and his unyielding emotions which seemed to guide him and his talent and his music, even into the River Rhine itself where he drowned. Some said he was haunted by the single musical note A sounding over and over again in his head. What madness drives sane artists to genius? I asked myself this question as I looked back at my sister smoking her cigarette beneath the oak tree.

I turned and entered the grove, one of my favorite places to visit back then. Patches and Jedi snorted at my intrusive presence. After seeing I wasn't going to leave, Patches followed Jedi and both horses trotted out and away from the fortress within the trees.

The creek continued through the grove, but I sat for a time tossing rocks into the running water and enjoyed the sounds the splashes made. I recalled the time when Whalen — God rest his soul — and I had packed an old army bag and planned to spend an entire day out on this land. My brother dropped us off at around nine in the morning and I instructed Chadwick not to return before six in the evening.

Whalen and I climbed over the cattle guard and headed toward the great oak in the distance. I had lost touch with Whalen over the years and this was one of my foolish attempts at trying to turn back the clock and restore our friendship to the days when I had lived a few blocks down from him.

Anyway, Whalen and I hiked to the pond with a puppy from a neighbor's house following at our heels and we decided to name the pup Sam, short for Samantha, and keep her with us until Chadwick returned and we could drop the dog off at the neighbor's house down the road.

Whalen and I climbed through the barbed wire fencing with Sam slipping underneath, and we three marched toward the rock quarry as though we were on a quest in Middle Earth.

'Heard there were landmines,' I said to Whalen. 'Better be careful.'

He lifted his foot carefully off the ground. 'Are you serious?'

'That's what my brother said, but he could've been lying. Regardless, I'd rather not take chances.'

After twenty minutes or so, we came to the warning sign nailed to a tree forbidding trespassing and threatening prosecution to all who ventured forward.

'Pay no mind,' I said. 'It's to scare cowards and we're not yellow.'

'It says there's explosives. Buried landmines.'

'I guess Chadwick wasn't lying after all. Have to be extra careful.'

We continued on through a dry, barren land of rock and skeletal trees until we could go no farther. On a cliff above an artificial sea we stood amazed at the sheer size and depth which unexpectedly appeared and opened up before us. To our left, I scouted a gradual descending slope that curled around to the water.

Fifteen minutes later, while Sam sniffed the gravel shore, Whalen and I stripped down. Slowly we treaded the icy water until it reached our waists. Whalen hesitated and looked to the cliffs a hundred feet above us, and then he turned to the darkness beneath the blue of the water.

'How deep is this?' Whalen asked. 'I'm not sure I want to go in.'

I imagined the pit a mile or two deep or possibly bottomless, like the hole I once saw in New Mexico's Carlsbad Caverns. I dove beneath the surface like the fish I am and swam as deep as my lungs would allow but I couldn't reach the bottom, and strange thoughts possessed me of dead bodies being dumped into the quarry at midnight or undercurrents dragging me down to a never-ending depth.

I surfaced, gasped for a breath, and could see Sam staring at Whalen trudging back to shore. I kicked over onto my back, floated for a time looking at the soft, sunny-blue sky above and let the sun warm my upper half as I waited for a whale to rise from the deep beneath and swallow me whole.

The whale never came and Sam would be killed when Chadwick accidently crushed the puppy's skull with the front tire of his car. He had returned at noon, on my mother's behest, and I hated him for Sam's death. Chadwick didn't even show remorse. Said the puppy should've gotten out of his way. He continued to back up until we reached the highway. He couldn't leave well enough alone, could he?

I stopped throwing rocks into the creek, left the grove and returned to my sister beneath my father's oak where she was still smoking a cigarette.

With a patina of contentment, you close your Moleskine notebook and turn your head to the windows in your office. Either I've said too much or too little, or it makes no difference since you're lost in thought.

My back hurts from lying on the sofa and I stand to roam the office with its neatly organized bookcases with first and second editions of all the classics while I pet the fake weeping figs. The afternoon seems to stand still between us and for a moment I think I see a ghost of a frown with a tear in your eye, but I could be mistaken. The tear could've been a figment of my crude imagination. The frown a broken shadow falling wrong. You appear to be full of thoughts that you cannot say.

Outside, New York City has opened and began to stir beneath cloudless skies and the people have put away their umbrellas. Sunlight can be transformational, especially after a good strong rain.

My mother used to tell me another story, I say.

You open your notebook to begin taking notes as if its second nature, like brushing your teeth in the morning or combing your hair at night.

She'd tell me that once, when she was in high school, Johnnie had asked her to meet him by her locker after school. Whether her crush was just a passing fancy or there had been something passionate lurking beneath, I couldn't honestly tell you. But over the years she'd sigh and gain a far-looking gaze, similar to the one I saw when I had been a toddler, and she'd say to me, 'Who knows what might've happened if I met Johnnie that day.' I don't think she meant it as a question.

'I know.' I'd say, 'I would've never been born. You would've never married dad. And Johnnie probably would've ended up fat and bald.'

My mother wouldn't look at me but she'd answer, 'Right,' and after another minute she'd add, 'You're right, son,' and then whatever spell she had been under would break and she'd return unaware that she had been gone.

In my eighth-grade year, my football season ended without a loss, a perfect 8-0. My seventh-grade year, I had begun the season as starting quarterback for the Gray team, considered to be third string, and I helped my team to a victory. For the next game Coach Valdez bumped me up to first string, and although the A team had lost their opening game, I ended my football season undefeated. But it would be in my sixth-grade year, as I helped my team of misfits to the playoffs, when my mother disappointed me with such a betrayal that I refused to speak to her for several weeks.

In the sixth grade I stayed true to the promise I gave to my fifth-grade principal, Mrs. Ragsdill: I had stopped fighting so I could focus on playing football. After school, we'd practice and play our games and we'd win.

Back then the playbook consisted of a few run and pass plays given to every team to introduce the players to flag football. The first and second place teams that year would develop their own extensive playbooks, likely handed down from coach to son, but when I was given a ragtag motley crew of left-footed kids who could no more understand 'offside,' 'the Statue of Liberty play,' or 'Hail Mary,' than my mother or sister, I consulted myself for two days on my bed before deciding to go out and teach these young boys how to play football, and how to be champions.

First, I assigned positions which wasn't as difficult as it would seem: I put the heavy-set boys as linemen and linebackers, the speedy boys as receivers and cornerbacks, and for running back (which we only had one) I placed Terence, one of the fastest black kids in school, leaving me as the quarterback to keep everything simple.

Next, after the other team kept anticipating our every play, since all the teams had the same copy of the standard playbook, I huddled my team up, the coach counting down the play clock, and instructed them to line up as though we would run left, but Terence, instead, would catch the ball in the backfield and run right, in the opposite direction from our team.

'But he'll be unprotected,' one chubby boy said. 'It's madness.'

'Don't you worry about that,' I said. 'Terence can out run any one on the field, can't you?'

'You better believe it.'

The center hiked me the ball, I pitched the ball back to Terence, and as our team ran left, including me, Terence stole off to the right and sixty-five yards later danced into the end zone for a touchdown. From that point on, we steamrolled our competition, and some weeks later found ourselves in the playoffs playing for third place — a poor rendition of *The Bad News Bears*, al la 1976.

I remember the day and my mistake well. I battled with myself quite a bit in the days leading up to the final game of the season about whether or not I wanted to invite my mother to the big event, which would be played under the lights in the historic Rogan Field Stadium, the original high school playing field in ages gone by. The football field was on Brady Avenue that ran parallel to the train tracks and behind our sixth-grade school. Crazy to think those same train tracks carried Brownwood's first locomotive Engine 37 to the depot on December 31, 1885 by the Gulf Colorado & Santa Fe Railway. The trains just keep going, no matter what's happening in our lives. Just like that train I once took in South Korea, the one I told you about. That one's still going too, I suppose.

But in the sixth grade I wanted my mother to watch me play at least one football game that season. I had always walked the four blocks home to the white house on Durham, changed and then returned to the field with plenty of time to warm up. On that day, however, I'd convinced myself to the point of no return, and I persuaded my mother to pick me up from school and we'd go to the game together. I knew my father couldn't make it, or he'd be late, because he finished work at six and that was when the game kicked off. My mother, in a son-less delusion, returned back to the obstetrics' clinic and then vanished into one of the many back rooms with her boss, Dr. Bovary. I had planned to leave at five with my mother, return home to change into my sports attire then go to the stadium early to prepare. By five-thirty, I'd already begun regretting not packing my change of clothes and my mother still locked herself away somewhere hidden in the clinic in one of the many rooms.

By a quarter to six, fully regretting the invitation to my mother, I was shouting her name down the empty clinic halls and checking each and every room in the obstetrician's office, until I came to one locked door, and my heart sank, hardened, because I knew then I was going to be late, disappoint my team, because Gwendolen was screwing her boss. Granted, my parents were divorced, had been for over a year, but Dr. Bovary was still married, and the whole situation disgusted me until I grabbed my mother's car keys, considered leaving her there and driving myself to the game, and eventually resigned myself on sitting in the parking lot blaring the car horn until she emerged out the back door to see what was wrong.

'My game is at six. Right now,' I yelled out the car window. 'Come on, Gwendolen. Let's go. I'm late and I don't have time for this.'

By the time my mother parked outside the stadium, lit and buzzing with fans, I fumed at Gwendolen's indolent non-motherly behavior — I expected better — for making me twenty minutes late. I had already given up on her, decided she didn't care whether or not she saw my playoff game, but I cared about leading my misfits, my boys, to victory.

With me in blue jeans, a polo-shirt and sneakers I trotted through the front gate, down the back behind the goalpost, and over to my team on the sideline, facing the stadium filled with loyal and hopeful parents.

'You're late,' the coach said. 'The game's started.'

'Tell me something I don't know,' I said. 'Couldn't be helped.'

'You can go in on the next offensive. Terence's at QB right now.'

'How are we doing?'

'Tie game.'

I joined my team who grumbled at my late arrival.

'I'm sorry guys,' I told them. 'It's my fault.'

'No crap,' one of them said. 'We're getting our butts kicked out there. Touchdown Terence can't do *every*thing. Where were you?'

'What's with the clothes?' another boy in a football jersey asked. 'A bit overdressed, are we?'

'Let's just say my mother let me down big time tonight, but I'm not going to let you down. We can do this. There's still time.'

On the next offensive, Terence stepped to the backfield and I took my place at quarterback. The center hiked the ball, jamming my thumb and making my fingernail spurt blood, I ignored the pain and ran to my left, turned back, spotted Terence open to the right and threw him a perfect spiral. Terence leaped in the air, the throw had been a little high, and he came down easily on a tiptoe, did some shaking and baking around the defense and high-stepped fifty-five yards for a touchdown. My team and I cheered, the crowd erupted in applause, and we ran the length of Rogan Field to congratulate Terence. In the end zone, I jumped on Terence and gave him a huge hug as the others celebrated around us.

'Nice throw, Cody,' Terence said. 'Let's do that again.'

Together I ran with the team to set up for the two-point conversion.

'We're back, baby,' I said. 'We. Are. Back.'

I'd like to say we won that game. Like John Elway or Joe Montana or Tom Brady, I came in and led my team to victory, but I can't. Nor can I say we lost. The crowd in the stands would see point matched for point as the ninety-minute limit expired with a tie, both teams claiming bragging rights to third place.

When the coach blew the final whistle, refusing me to let my team have one more shot at breaking the tie, I looked up to the stands and felt a great disappointment for my heritage and my mother, the kind of person she had grown to become. Perhaps if I had not been late, my team and I could've won the game. Regardless, I gathered the team and knelt on the forty-yard line and said this:

'I'm proud of you. Every last one you. We did our best, and although we didn't win, we didn't lose either. So tomorrow, when you come walking down the halls, hold your heads up high. You're all winners tonight.'

In each of their eyes I saw a more confident glow than the one I'd seen after our first loss after our first game. I held the football in my hands and added, 'I'd like to name the MVP. Without him, we would've been sunk. Great job tonight, Terence.' I tossed the game ball over to him and he lifted it high over his head and our team cheered and danced around him.

Walking away, I put an arm over Terence's shoulder, pointed to the stadium full of parents and siblings ready for the championship game soon to start, and said, 'You're a star, Terence. Never forget what we did here tonight.'

The coach asked for the football back, and Terence threw it over to him. 'Don't worry. It's symbolic,' I said to Terence. He looked sad and I told myself the game ball had something to do with it.

'It's not that,' Terence replied, turning his head to the crowd up in the stands. 'I just wished my mom and pops could've been here tonight to see me.'

I squeezed my arm a bit tighter around Terence's neck and said, 'I know exactly what you mean.'

November Rain: as a senior in high school I finished early at noon on account of having crammed as many credits into my first three years, and even then my first class, which I often skipped that year, wasn't a class at all but a position as a helper in the attendance office to assist with collecting role cards in the morning.

In the afternoon I'd come home and on occasion find Dr. Bovary's BMW in the driveway. Sometimes I'd keep driving or park outside and wait, sometimes not. Once I stormed into the kitchen through the back door, Big Mama — the Boston Terrier I told you about — greeted me from her nap, and through a connecting door to my mother's room, which was open, I saw the lower legs of a man and a woman lying on my mother's king-sized bed, and I kept walking through the house, right down the hall, into the living room and out the front door. I had nothing to say to either of those phonies, and no locked room in Dr. Bovary's clinic could hide their sordid affair from me. I drove away angry and thought back to the time in the sixth grade when my mother had made me late to a football game because she wanted to get laid.

With the Zippo Cassandra had given me, I rubbed my thumb over its lucky 8-ball and then lit a cigarette — I smoked Marlboro Reds back then — and thought of how my family had splintered apart, disintegrated through a divorce instituted by infidelity. I didn't hate my father so much then for having left us and I couldn't necessarily blame him for moving out on my mom. I drove over to Jimmy Joyce's to see if he was home — we'd return to the white house on Durham and find the BMW gone — and halfway there I remembered one of my earliest memories of my mother and Dr. Bovary.

I'd been four or five years old and my mother took me downtown to a café that served coffee, sandwiches and side dishes of Southern cooking. At first, I believed she was wanting to spend time with just me, but I became disappointed when Dr. Bovary, another adult, arrived to join us at the table by the front window bathed in sunlight.

Whenever another adult captivated my mother's attention away from me, I'd have to play the part I hated most: the role of oblivious child. My mother ordered a hot bowl of black-eyed peas and for herself she ordered a Lipton's iced tea while Dr. Bovary had coffee; he couldn't stay long, and I liked the sound of that. Be gone so I can be alone with my mother.

I do vividly recall listening intently to the adult conversation between my mother and Dr. Bovary because I knew enough to know that my mother shouldn't be out with another man, and if I put two-and-two together, this could've been my mother's job interview, what would be the beginning to the divorce and the destruction of my family as I once knew it. All through the meeting I'd listen and when my mother turned her attention on me, I'd lift my empty bowl up and say,

'Can I have another one please?'

She'd order another bowl of black-eyed peas and resume the talk with Dr. Bovary. For the most part I had never met the man before, though I found it odd that my mother would be meeting him for lunch, but the content of their dialogue, to my child-brain, sounded innocent enough. Regardless of my age, I remember that particular meeting of two souls for a reason and I'm still unclear as to why. Maybe that's where you can help. Can you?

I do remember eating four or five bowls of the black-eyed peas, which warranted a direct comment from Dr. Bovary, 'He sure can eat.'

I nodded that I could and my mother said something lame about me taking after my father.

The bill was paid by Dr. Bovary and he left. My last glimpse of that moment would be my mother ordering for me one more bowl, which seemed tiny to me even then, and the gaze she held while looking out the window and into the future made me want to hug her all the more.

One evening, a decade or more from that downtown meeting at the café — which I'm sure is no longer there; trust me, I often searched for it after I obtained my driver's license — I peeked out through the blinds on my bedroom window facing the front porch and yard and saw Dr. Bovary's BMW off to the side near a large pecan tree by the sidewalk. The car didn't belong in that spot, ever, but I shrugged it off and returned to the television.

My bedroom in that white house on Durham Avenue had a twin bed shoved in one corner, a sofa along the front wall, and an entertainment center with a twenty-seven inch television set, VCR and a stereo that could change seven compact discs with the touch of a remote; I often lived in that room and considered it more a home than the rest of the house.

I ended up switching off the television. I roamed the house looking for my mother, found her absent, and then stood on the front porch staring at the BMW that shouldn't have been there. I called my mother's name. No answer. I had a heavy suspicion she was trying to *play* Henry and hide from me. But like I said: I prefer to break an illusion than to play along.

I walked down the steps, down the center walkway bordered by two rows of lilyturfs — what my mother called monkey grass — and into the street. I found my mother squatting down by the open driver's side door talking to Dr. Bovary.

'Go back inside, honey,' she said, using her silver tongue, to me. 'I'll be in in a minute.'

I had plenty I wanted to tell her but I didn't. I longed to say that she needed to stop fucking a married man, have some self-respect, a little dignity, to grow up and be a mother to her children, and stop all this nonsense about chasing after a guy who could — and in the end, would — never love her the way she needed to be loved. Instead, I did the culturally acceptable thing to do. 'I'm hungry,' I said. I wasn't at all hungry. I was sick to my stomach of those two phonies. 'When are you going to cook dinner?'

'In a minute,' she said. 'Now go in and I'll be there in a sec.'

'Hurry it up then.'

I retreated back into the house, back into my bedroom to listen to Guns N' Roses' 'Civil War' on their album *Use Your Illusion II*, and every few minutes I'd bend the blinds down to check if my mother had finished yet. 'What we've got here is a failure to communicate; I don't like it any more than you did.'

The death of the sunlight came and with it the finale to my mother's rendezvous. Outside, through the blinds — and I'd find out from her later — my mother wrapped her hand around the seatbelt so Dr. Bovary couldn't drive away and leave her.

'And in my first memories they shot Kennedy; cause you can't trust freedom when it's not in your hands, when everybody's fighting for the Prom-Miss Land.'

Dr. Bovary ended up dragging my mother down the block before her hand came loose from the seatbelt. She skidded and rolled away. By the time I knelt at my mother's side on the street, the BMW was speeding around the corner and I doubt Dr. Bovary ever looked back.

My mother left me at home as she drove herself to the regional hospital where I'd been born and had her sprained wrist and ankle, cuts and bruises to her face, arms and back dressed and cared for. Ignoring my advice, Gwendolen refused to press charges against Dr. Bovary, her employer, and she'd continue to chase and woo the doctor away from his wife and family, but several years later she failed and came to her breaking point. The penultimate moment came when my mother dumped a glass of iced tea over Dr. Bovary's head in the middle of the clinic and in front of patients and staff, followed by her firm and irresolute, 'You bastard! I quit!'

After she ended things with the doctor, as employer and lover, I never told my mother how proud of her I was for doing what she should've done a long, long time ago. Sometimes you have to let parents learn from their own mistakes.

The Sword: I'm reminded of the time I told you about when I'd hop into my car late at night and drive the farm roads outside San Angelo. I'd listen to the commercials playing over the radio, a good-brisk breeze hitting my face, and think of John Updike and how he drove the night roads, also, jotting into his notebook the random advertisements streaming through the radio to Harry Angstrom in one of the scenes you can find in the 1960-novel *Rabbit, Run*. You might also hear the radio playing Gay and Butler's 'Run Rabbit Run' sung by Flanagan and Allen: 'Run rabbit — run rabbit — Run! Run! Run!'

I'd keep driving the miles away in the dark with the headlights stretching only so far ahead, thinking to myself of the afternoons

Grand-Mommy and I would take her favorite wicker basket to the garden and pick fresh blackberries. She and I would return to the kitchen, wash and rinse the blackberries the size of half dollars, those old 50-cent pieces, and at the counter — much like we used to do when I was a small boy visiting her at the lake house — she and I would pour cold milk and sprinkle sugar over the blackberries. We'd eat the blackberries with a spoon from the bowl.

Goldie Orella Dawson — that was her name, born August 16, 1919 in Lake Dallas, Texas to William Johnson Dawson from Texas and Dovie Louella Brooks from Alabama. Goldie would go on to marry Carroll Glen F. (my Grand-Daddy) on May 14, 1939. Goldie O. had the energy of a twenty-year-old as she spoke of her youth and her missionary trips to Mexico, and how she loved playing the organ — a lost art these days. To me, Grand-Mommy smelled of lavender and peach blossoms, and I wished I had known her when she had been a younger woman. I told her so, but she was humbled and thankful we got a chance to know each other at all. We shouldn't complain, she told me once, about the good Lord's plans and blessings; it wasn't for us to decide the when and where and why of things. She loved reading to me and I loved listening to her.

After Goldie's passing on June 12, 1992, Grand-Daddy would remarry. I was fourteen or fifteen when I served as best man at my Grand-Daddy's wedding to his second wife, Josephine. I remember thinking how odd it was for a grandson to be his grandfather's best man, and how I detested the idea of him remarrying, choosing earthly companionship over heavenly memory, and if I had been old enough then to drive, free to make my own choices, I would've driven myself to my Grand-Mommy's grave and spent that ceremonial day with her.

My father, instead, forced me to wear a tie, and I held my hands and looked to the grass at my feet, and stood next to Grand-Daddy as he promised his bonding, binding love 'to death do we part,' and I told myself, yes, how fitting death should so easily relieve us-mortals from our obligations of love.

I pressed down on the accelerator and felt the car beneath me lurch into the steady momentum. I wished I could drive all night and all the next day, and every night thereafter; not running away exactly, but running towards something better, but I see now I had been naïve and foolish, a young man in his twenties unable to rest and be at peace with himself, not until he could find the one key which could unlock the door in front of him, a door, I convinced myself, which would one day lead me to a great success, to a grand manifest destiny, then, and only then, would the barriers and roadblocks fall away, leaving an open road, much like the one I was on, before me in all its curves and bends hidden in the darkness ahead.

I'd imagine being another man then — or at least, the man I should be to the world, the man underneath the layers of what other people saw and heard when he spoke and moved, the man he would become behind the locked door which barred his way. And to him, all the doors, made once upon a time without keys, had been bolted shut long before his birth, and there was nothing he could ever do about it.

I would drive for an hour or two, find a spot to turn around and sit parked on the open-empty road as midnight neared. I wouldn't want to return back to that empty apartment, even if it did have a fireplace and it was my own. To return would be like choosing to accept a cheaper alternative for the more costly original. The books on the shelves, the clothes in the walk-in-closet, the food in the pantries, and the logs next to the fireplace were all mine but not mine. These objects, the material possessions of my binding, limited me to the life I had to live pleasing others versus living the life I wanted to freely live, unrestrained and remarkable. To drive back to that empty apartment would equal a small death, and how many of those did I still have inside myself to give?

Because, little by little, with each tiny death, a piece of my soul would be cut away and fed to the vultures that swallowed lost dreams. How silly all this must sound to those privileged with trust funds and silver forks born in each hand and have never known poverty and shame nor the never-ending trials hardships bring to the new day, like that of Sisyphus and his mountain, but even he was born a king and deserved his punishments.

To return back down the road the young man had just traveled to that empty apartment in San Angelo meant to him something like staring at a boulder by his feet and ordered, once more, to roll the rock up the mountainside only for the damn thing to tumble back to its place at the bottom. The game wasn't chess but slavery. The young-conflicted hero didn't know the direct or proper course of action, nor did he believe one even existed. He knew what he had been taught: if he worked hard (believed in meritocracy, that joke-game people pretend we're all playing) that anything was possible so long as he set his mind to the task; to him, then staring through the headlights falling on the darkened farm road, the axiom handed down from one generation to the next like an old pair of jeans sounded flawed and incomplete, as if he knew a better principle existed out there beyond the headlights but he couldn't find it, couldn't touch it with his own two hands — and he feared he never would. He would be called Mr. Middle America, Mister Townie Come-Home, but what good was that to him? What was the point of living a life where his dreams didn't come true? Where the collected treasure turned out to be fool's gold, garbage? Why would he need to matter when the rest of the world didn't even know his name or his troubles?

The person he knew, believed without doubt, he was wasn't the one who lived in his apartment or worked at his job; out beyond the headlights, though he couldn't find it, something of greater importance awaited him, and he seemed to know it by name, if only the dreams at night would stop haunting him long enough for him to remember what that name was.

Compromises need to be made. But which ones? And when? How? What's the point of having a voice when your voice belongs to the Voiceless Generation? That the ones with the voices and the dollars were the ones behind the wheel of commerce and justice, and where they say we go, we go; but somehow such counterintuitive logic didn't make sense to our tragic hero, nor would it ever. How could it be otherwise? Everyone he had ever spoken to felt marginalized in one way or another. How could it be true? How could this be the land of opportunity? The land of dreams come true? Johnny Boy run home? But to where? To who? How and when?

No cars would come. Why would they so late at night? Out here in the wasteland shrouded? Roads built for one. One to come and one to go.

The young hero lit a cigarette and laughed and was reminded of Joyce's Humphrey Chimpden Earwicker, and of those simpler days in his last years at Howard Payne University. At night our young hero who was not HCE, not in the least, worked as a cashier at a convenience store across the street from the town's only bowling alley, two blocks from the old Rogan Field Stadium that been declared condemned and prepared for demolition, and five blocks from Howard Payne's campus down the road on Austin Avenue.

Sometimes his employer, a chubby middle-aged man likely dependent on too much pornography and onanism, invited our hero to play golf in the morning at a course twenty miles outside the city. The golf course had but nine holes, so playing the same course twice counted as a full eighteen. The last hole, a par five, sunk back, almost invisible, on a sloped island surrounded by lush trees and water. A bridge had to be crossed to reach the last hole of the nine.

With his grandfather's rusted driving wood, nine iron, pitching and sand wedges and a putter, the young-conflicted hero outplayed the onanistic employer through the first eight holes — until, that is, the last one: a par five that called for an eagle.

Coming off the tee, the ball zoomed high and clean, a solid shot landing and bouncing and rolling to the center of the fairway facing the flag barely visible on the island. The employer's shot would lie fifteen to twenty yards behind the young hero's and the employer would strike his ball on the next shot to delicately lay up near the end of the fairway closest to the water hazard, then he'd chip the ball over onto the island to double-putt for a safe, face-saving par.

Standing by his ball, the island to the young hero looked within reach of his second shot, as if he could touch the green and flag with the end of his extended iron. The strike, once more solid and on target, would sail high into the catching wind, the employer yelling, 'Brilliant' and 'You got this,' while the young hero looked on as he carefully eyed his ball as it passed its zenith, arched, descended and splashed into the murky moat surrounding the island.

'I thought you had a chance,' his employer said. 'Why don't you take a drop up there? I'll even give you a mulligan.'

'No,' the young hero said. 'I'll drop from here.'

So, he did.

Another beautiful strike landed on its mark. High and sharp, the ball rose and smacked deep into the green, to bounce some ten feet from the hole, and then the ball would begin rolling, rolling, rolling, splash!

The employer, now standing and waiting on the bridge off to the right, didn't offer a single word this time. The slope on the green had been too pronounced, too steep, but the young hero had reached the green in two shots for a possible eagle. Almost.

Each time the young hero looked to the flag marking the hole in the center of the island, he'd remember the 1996-film *Tin Cup* with Kevin Costner and he'd drop the ball over and over and over from the middle of the fairway. Each time his ball either landed — kerplunk! — in the center of the moat, or skidded back down the green slope and rolled off the ledge, lost to the hazard waters.

Eventually the young hero realized that despite his skill and abilities, the course had been cleverly designed, quite methodically, so that he'd lose, defeat himself in the trying. In his silence a small pride rested in knowing he had reached the island, the ninth and eighteenth holes, in two shots, a risk his employer had been unwilling to take; the young hero would recall with credulity the adage: it's not whether you win or lose, but how you play the game that counts; and he had played the game to the best of his skills and abilities.

The young-conflicted hero, still parked at night along the deserted farm road, would flick the finished cigarette out the window and slowly drive back into town. He'd enter his San Angelo apartment, where no one waited to greet him. Without switching on any of the lights, he'd move to his bedroom, where he'd collapse into the leather chair next to the rolltop desk, the antique I told you about, tug the chain attached to the banker's lamp, and opening one of his many notebooks, the young-conflicted hero would burn the midnight oil by writing for you a story, one you probably have never read.

Sometimes with my father, my mother would drive me in that station wagon we had nicknamed Old Blue, the one I told you about in the beginning, to Dallas for my annual checkup at the Texas Scottish Rite Hospital for Children. In the back of Old Blue, my mother would ceremoniously lay blankets, pillows and several of my stuffed friends. I'd snuggle in the back away from the world and traffic, my crutches off to the side, with Monkey, the sock doll with bright red lips, Daffy Duck, who also had his right leg twisted and bandaged, and Marvin, the Cabbage Patch doll who was my favorite with his curly-brown hair. For the two and a half hours I'd sleep comfortably next to my pals and try not to worry too much about seeing the doctor at the hospital for my clubfoot.

I never minded Scottish Rite so much or the trip I'd have to take for the first twelve years of my life. Once inside, a candy striper offered free bags of hot, salted popcorn or sticks of cotton candy. Often, we'd be an hour or so early for my appointment and I'd get a chance to roam and play in the lobby, where the most spectacular mechanical contraption I'd ever set my eyes upon suspended from the ceiling. Like one big toy factory, I could spend hours examining that piece of clever machinery so well-interconnected that one motion fed into another, round and round, always and forever, never-ending, on and on and on.

Two dummy pilots, one waving a Texas flag, sported leather jackets and goggles as they cycled their blimp-plane. Tennis rackets, like petals to a flower, constructed the front propeller. Four ping-pong paddles rotated as the back propeller. Inside the blimp's skeletal frame, a ladder hung down to the two pilots below, gears and pulleys turning and hoisting anchors and balls and flags while spinning the propellers, creating the effect that the two mannequins were in charge of their aircraft high above the lobby floor.

Bright greens, yellows, oranges and deep blues and violets glistened off the floor tiles and furniture down wide, white hallways well-lit. The striking white of the walls matched the level of cleanliness to a degree that made me stop and wonder if I hadn't in fact stepped into a time machine and into the future. The staff spoke low and with a genuine politeness I've rarely seen outside the Scottish Rite. The temperature, that's one thing I can't forget, would be near freezing, regardless if the heat outside reached unbearable-scorching levels or not; the children's hospital reminded me then of a giant igloo but with far more toys, puzzles and magazines free to handle.

Learning to walk, for me, was easier than learning to walk with wooden crutches as a two-year-old child. I wore a cast on my right foot up to my knee for the first three years of my life, and a steel pin secured my right ankle-bone in place for the first year or so of those first three. I could stand myself up along the sofa early enough, and I'd laugh an impish giggle so beloved by mothers at my accomplishment. To be honest, the pain in my leg and foot consistently remained pronounced and throbbing, an extraordinary level of physical torment melding and rooting itself into a mental agony until both mind and body accepted the suffering as part of my normalcy. And that was how I came to understand my typical condition of existence included suffering, a prerequisite I suppose for being the artist I am.

At the Scottish Rite, though, I witnessed much more tragic and severe injuries and disabilities that over the years, as I shed my crutches and began playing soccer and baseball, I considered myself lucky for being merely crippled, like Tiny Tim or Lord Byron or Troy Aikman, but not crippled enough to require additional assistance or hindered by extraneous impediments. There were children at the Scottish Rite far worse off than I, and my heart saddened, and at times hardened against God and the Universe, to see the young, like me, so very innocent and afflicted.

The doctor, as the years passed, required me to perform one task after he would manhandle my leg and check the healing of my scars. The doctor would always ask me to walk barefoot down the hallway, bright and cold to the toe's touch, and sometimes for fun, and much to the doctor's chagrin, I'd run and run and run through the hospital, not one person telling me to stop or slow down, ever, and after a few minutes of exploring the hospital barefoot, I'd run back to the Kangaroo Room or the Elephant Room, where my mother and the doctor would still be waiting for me to return. One of the first times the doctor asked me to walk down the hall, I still had need of my wooden crutches, and even then, I showed him how fast my three legs could carry me. For me, all of this — the pain, the anguish, the disability, my beloved crutches that grew to become an extension of me, like additional legs — all of this constituted a lifestyle I considered normal, and access to the Scottish Rite Children's Hospital, like tourists venturing through the bowels of Google's headquarters for the first time, felt to me a privileged honor, a chance to enjoy a taste of fairy-esque Adventureland separate from the real world where little boys and girls must grow up and suffer.

When I snuggled in the back of Old Blue with Monkey, Daffy and Marvin to return home, I'd think how fortunate I was to get to see something magical and special that the other more normal kids would never get a chance to see, and most of the time I didn't mean the flashy colors or unlimited toys and gadgets. No. Something else, immaterial, was unique about the Scottish Rite, and the magic wasn't in any one thing. But if I've learned anything in my forty years it's that Librans are equally cursed and blessed.

I eventually learned to run without crutches and found myself, one day many years ago, chasing a harmless squirrel before baseball practice at a field across the street from East Elementary. Three of my teammates had spotted the poor creature out in the open and it didn't take much time before ten of us screamed and chased the poor squirrel running for its life from one sapling to the next, finding each baby tree insufficient for escape. One or two of the boys chunked their baseball gloves but came up short of the animal. A few others scooped up rocks and hurled them at our frantic, frightened prey.

What I did next haunts me to this day. After about the second sapling, I recognized a pattern to the squirrel's flight. The squirrel would scamper to one of the saplings, but never to the nearside, always to the far side, find the trunk too small, the height inadequate, and then flee to the next sapling some ten yards away. From the curb I found a Gatorade bottle empty and gripped the glass projectile tight around the neck with the heavy end down, like a club or mallet. When the squirrel rushed to the far side of the next tree and the boys stopped to huddle around the base, I kept right on running towards the next tree to give myself a head start.

My plan worked. As I shot by the group of stagnant boys and past the thin tree, the squirrel, drawing the mob's attention, darted away from the tree and alongside me, the cool-calculated hunter in pursuit. When the squirrel reached the next tree, just ahead of me, it vanished around the far side once more but I didn't hesitate to scout the leaves above. I figured the squirrel would panic and wouldn't make its way up the slender trunk.

I pressed forward to the far side of the tree, came around all alone and a good ten yards ahead of the other boys. At the far side now, a step or two beyond the tree itself, I cocked the glass bottle behind me and that's when time halted, froze, suspended long enough for me to make eye contact with a black-pearl of an eye from the squirrel's fuzzy face, its nose sniffing the air.

The squirrel's odd eye fixed upon me as its two front paws gripped the bottom of the tree trunk no bigger than the length of the squirrel's outstretched arms. The squirrel asked me to spare him, to leave him be, all with a thought, a shared look, but a new heat burned within me, thrived in my young blood and I sought to take from the creature what I did not deserve.

With a mighty blow even Thor and his hammer would be jealous of, the glass bottle shattered over the squirrel's eye and ear, its head crushed, instantly killing the animal. The squirrel dropped dead to the ground.

Time sped up and resumed. My teammates, I remember well — haunted by such nightmares — lifted the dead squirrel by its tail, a mad victory chant rising out of the mob became unified as each boy, except for one, cheered and hollered around the warm carcass eerily similar to some stolen scene reenacted from Golding's *Lord of the Flies* coming to life on the baseball field before me.

The mob carried away the dead and I remained standing in the exact spot where I had thrown the bottle, where I had done what was unacceptable in the eyes of God and the Universe, where I had killed an innocent creature for no other reason than to test my human powers. I turned away from my shame, the mob toying with their prized trophy, and with a grieved whisper I said, 'What have I done?'

But I did know. I had taken life. Betrayed life by snuffing it out completely, simply because I was capable of doing so. I ran a little too well that day, but I walked back to the field with my head low and in deep reflection: O the foolishness of boyhood and the crimes against the sanctity of life my *imago* would be unable to forget.

Like a composer trying to recall a section of a symphony he had written and lost in another life, I recalled what I had forgotten. God, the Universe, I said to myself, pity that poor squirrel and please have mercy on my soul.

Looking back on these events of my youth, I had first believed, albeit incorrectly, I'd be at odds with my life, angry even. But I see now I come from a long line of failures. Texas, after all, is a failed country with its four presidents and constitution. Hell, Texans, plus one Davy Crockett, lost the Alamo Mission in 1836. A long line of failures, one right after another until Texas joined the United States, and kept right on failing. Maybe that's part of the origins of the curse I carry with me: being a Texan.

Now being a Texan does have its more nobler advantages, like in the Alamo, a Texan draws a line between friend and foe, warrior and coward, fight or flee; there's no worldly confusions, no gray like there is in other states and foreign countries, which is where I'd later learn firsthand that your friends were actually your enemies and the closest ones to you were the ones who'd lie to cheat you to your face, and these non-Texans simply, quite ignorantly, expected the deceit to be played out and to be overlooked as part of a larger continuum of camaraderie. Life is never simple.

Texas and Texans can't work that way. A line is drawn between right and wrong, and we do our best to honor that line, often through a resolute character that can do more harm than good. After all, some three hundred Texans bravely fought the grand Mexican army of five thousand, which ended up being defeated as their fearless leader López de Santa Anna, the Napoleon of the West, napped in his tent surrounded by cries of 'Remember the Alamo!' and gunfire.

'Remember the Alamo' can be accurately translated thus: remember your heritage; remember Texas is God's country; remember Texas; remember all Texans; remember you are a Texan; remember to uphold the Texas legacy; remember Texas is a state of mind; remember Texans have honor and pride and a stubbornness found in immovable mountains; remember the brave who died defending freedoms; remember Texas is a land in the heart of each Texan; remember where you came from; remember who you are.

There's much more to it than that, but that's a good enough summary lesson for today, and I think it proves my point about what I'm telling you. I have traveled the world, been places, seen places, and yet the place I most want to go doesn't exist, hasn't existed for a very long time, like a dislocation of two lands, the river and rain between; and my youth, the childhood home I lost years ago, exists for me only in the mind, and all of my history. My life's story is a broken link in a greater reality I have found behind the illusion you and I have agreed to call Time. We may even come to a point when we look back on all the randomness of our lives and find the events were not random at all, but part of a larger design we can partially understand, like children learning language for the first time.

The last time I saw Grand-Mommy she'd been dead for seven years. On August 8, 1999, I believe it was, my brother Chadwick and Annest, his girlfriend, drove down to Brownwood from Oklahoma City to see me baptized by submersion at the Assembly of God Church I told you about. Before the service, Pastor Hiddleston announced the three or four members of the church who would be baptized that Sunday morning before the sermon, and I was one of them. With a white T-shirt and shorts, I stepped down into the frigid waters of the baptismal tank where Pastor Hiddleston waited.

I remember feeling a sharp buzz come over me — maybe it was from the water or all the general excitement, I don't know — but my senses were all out of place. While the pastor spoke of my conversion and faith and my sacrifices offering body and spirit today, I scanned the congregation, looking for my brother, in a euphoric state, a daze of epiphany, I never had before.

My mind glowed with visions: off to my left in the front pew where she sat after she finished playing the organ, my Grand-Mommy, Goldie Orella, sat with her hands folded in her lap. A golden aura surrounded her, as though she was a Force-ghost in a new *Star Wars* film, and she watched me watching her. With her thoughts she communicated to me how she was proud of all the things I had done and for all the things I still had to do, and how I'd never see her again after that day. I nodded as if I understood, but I didn't. Not really. Too much to process, I guess.

Then I turned to gaze at a thick green mist swirling out over the heads of the congregation, and I felt the fear of God fill me. I turned to Pastor Hiddleston to check if he was seeing what I was seeing, but he labored on in his introductory speech to the dull-eyed congregation as though nothing magnificent were happening in the church that day. The energy of that room thickened and intensified and to this day I've never felt or seen anything like it.

Pastor Hiddleston called me to attention and we performed the baptism: 'In the name of the Father, the Son, and the Holy Spirit.' He leaned my head and body back and I felt the water take me, consuming me within and without, and I felt I had become whole at last. When Pastor Hiddleston lifted me up out of the water, I couldn't see anything clearly out in the congregation so I stepped up the iron staircase and down into an adjoining room hidden from the audience.

Gabriel Márquez — my friend the waiter I told you about — was there to keep me company. I failed at trying to tell him what I saw and felt — just as I am sure I'm failing miserably at it now with you — but he listened, and minute after minute Gabriel Márquez grew more convicted of his sins, his shortcomings, led by some invisible energy persuading him and binding tight to his soul. Gabriel wanted to be baptized but he had no spare clothes. Should that trouble the spirit? No, it should not.

Gabriel Márquez, in his Sunday's best, kicked off his shoes and joined in the pool Pastor Hiddleston, who accepted the surprise graciously and proceeded to dunk Gabriel peacefully into the holy water. A calm flooded my being and I felt Gabriel had drawn closer to the mysteries of the Universe and to God.

I dried myself with a towel, changed into my spare clothes, and stepped out the small door to go and join my family before the sermon started.

But there would be no sermon that Sunday morning — and Pastor Hiddleston couldn't ever quite explain what had happened. He did, however, admit to the enormous amount of energy cycling and vibrating through the room, and the pastor later acknowledged to me in private that when God's hand or spirit enters your church, you step aside and let Him work, and that was the real reason Pastor Hiddleston didn't perform a sermon that morning. I've never seen a pastor cancel a sermon like that before, and I doubt I ever will again.

I stepped out from the backroom and I stood stunned in the corner by what I saw happening to the congregation.

A dozen or more young men and women kneeled and bowed at the altar and each one cried out painfully in loud-open prayers seeking refuge and forgiveness. Many more people in the pews bowed and prayed openly; some raised their hands to the heavens. There was a grieving about the place, and I had never seen it done so outwardly and freely before. Others, at one with their souls, worshipped God with praises and songs at the back of the room.

As the energy multiplied and consumed the congregation over the next two hours — the last few affected members would depart exhausted and satiated after one in the afternoon — I remained off to the side remembering my Grand-Mommy, who was now gone, and the green mist that had filled these believers with a spirit of power, of reckoning, of transformation. But when I finally set eyes upon my brother with his then girlfriend Annest in a middle pew, I saw him looking straight at the pulpit where the pastor should've been preaching Sunday's sermon but wasn't, and my brother's stern face lacked emotion, as if he remained incapable of deciphering the strange sights and pulsing sounds of the believers around him. He looked annoyed. Chadwick waited an hour, took Annest by the hand when he saw there wasn't going to be any sermon, and with an air of distrust, unable to explain the events away, he left the congregation to continue what they were doing.

At the doorway, when he passively looked back at me, still standing silently off to the side in patient observance, I saw Cain look at Abel, I saw Chadwick's look of unrecognition, as if he wanted to un-see what he saw in the church that day, what he saw in me, as if I was seeing my own face in his, as if I had become a stranger, at last, to my own family. Chadwick never spoke of that day and I doubt he understood why.

Author of *The Gilded Age*, *The Innocents Abroad* and *The Mysterious Stranger*, Mark Twain once remarked, 'Broad, wholesome, charitable views of men and things cannot be acquired by vegetating in one little corner of the earth all of one's lifetime.'

Most of my family, in all its myriad and complicated directions, ignored Twain's travel proclamation and chose, rather humbly, to nest in close proximity to where they'd been born, and rarely did my family travel the world or hold the desire to do so.

I pace around your office listing all the places my *fata*, my kismet, had taken me: South Korea, South Africa, Guam, Japan, China, Vietnam, Cambodia, Thailand, Bali, Singapore, India, Mexico, Italy, France, Germany, the United Kingdom, to infinity and beyond.

A few years before I became an American abroad, I'd sit at my desk inside a tight cubicle in an office buzzing with voices in heated conversation on the fourth floor of a building I came to loathe in San Angelo, and all I could do, day after day, was turn my head to the wall of windows and stare out into the vastness of the world and tell myself how I belonged out there. One lifetime would be enough, I told myself, to see the lands, cultures, and peoples of this globe spinning around a sun out in space in one little corner of the vast Universe.

One lifetime might be all I'd ever get — disregarding any additional lifetimes I may have had in the past — and to be honest, even now I feel as I did then when I tell you I have no desire to return to this world; whatever 'reality' this Earth ever offered me had been one of conflict at the micro and macro scales. Wars were fought between countries for the very same reasons families were torn asunder. Take a look at a child's playground — in any country with any culture — and you'll see all of humanity at the micro level. Even the individual found great difficulty in living because of conflicts presented by other individuals who often do more harm than good. The cherished ideal of humanity was a glorious one but the scope of such an ideal rarely transcended beyond the element of the individual. One wished to help the starving in Africa, but Africans still starved. One wished to cease prostitution in Thailand and in Vietnam, but sex tourism still thrived. One wished to stop wars in the Middle East, but the wars still raged on. One longed to fulfil a personal dream, but others stood in the way and posed challenge after challenge or even denied assistance so they could feel a twisted sense of superiority. Such was the humanity I have known in my lifetime. In Germany there's a saying: 'The horse wants to sleep in its own stable.'

One can begin to see the predilection of that 'little corner' Mark Twain spoke vehemently about. To tell you the truth I've often envied people like that, people who found a home early on in life and never let that go; how their dreams came true by falling into their laps because of how friendly and nice they were because they always had a home. If you're thinking that's me, you'd be wrong. I had to start over three times before I found the girl of my dreams and we had a son, Baby Thor, and our family created a home in Discovery Bay, Hong Kong.

Three times I had to give up everything I owned and move to a different country and to a new culture. The first time I left Texas to live in South Korea I practically gave all my possessions away to my family. My car and professional weight bench I gave to Chadwick. My Xbox and DVD collection I gave to Cassandra for her son to have. My blue sofa, with two reclining chairs at each end, I gave to Henry. My collection of over three hundred books I boxed up and put in storage. On and on and on, until I got to the small things, the most cherished I gave to Gwendolyn, my mother.

The first time to uproot myself felt like I was dying, or preparing for a death to come at any hour, and how I'd never see my family again. I told them, repeatedly, I had seen twenty-five years of Texas and America and I wanted to spend the next twenty-five years seeing the rest of the world firsthand. It would be ten years before I saw their faces again. (I've been a mild Luddite since high school and I hold an uneasy aversion for video calls, but I did write and post letters. Letters, like the ones I sent to agents and publishers, would receive only silence in return; my family disliked writing letters; even email failed as a form of constant communication over the years.)

My next big move took me from South Korea to Ho Chi Minh City, Vietnam. I remember posting a large box of clothes back to my sister so she could have my smell (that's what she wanted), but to this day I'm still uncertain if she ever received that box that I sent her all those years ago. For this particular move I was ready for change. South Korea was a closed, tight culture and Koreans wanted to 'Koreanize' me. At one point I told my manager that I was Texan and I did not want to be Korean. Vietnam in the south, was more of an open, loose culture, meaning the South Vietnamese were open to all forms of cultures and behaviors. Living in tropical Vietnam, at many times, felt to me the closest thing to living in paradise — except for all the beggars and thieves and the poor development of soft skills which ruin the country, for me, as a living destination. Regardless, Vietnam remains a beautiful place to visit. While I was in Old Saigon for six years, I wrote and completed three novels. The Middle Eastern scenes in my fourth novel *A Time to Love in Tehran* were heavily based on actual scenes I experienced in Vietnam and Cambodia, and I do not think the novel would have been as authentic as it was if I had not gone and lived for a time in a third-world country.

My third great move, a personal diaspora if you like, took me from Vietnam to Hong Kong. In Old Saigon, I'd had a deep-seeded terror run through my veins and thoughts and into my spirit each night for the previous two years: if I stayed, I'd die; die a stranger in a strange land. Something, the Universe, or my ambition or fate, pulled me out of a pseudo-paradise with my nineteen-year-old lover nicknamed Cherry because I knew deep down if I stayed, I would never fulfil my dreams as a novelist and I'd never be happy; I'd never find the one I would spend my life with.

As the Roman Emperor Marcus Aurelius once said, 'The Universe is change.' I had to change. Change something. Change anything. I, therefore, embraced the change and flung myself to the whims of Chance. My decision to do so was one of the best decisions of my life, and the story of my time in Asia and the World, including all the hard lessons I had to learn must be saved for a later time. If I had to tell you anything, though, before our conversation ends, before we end our rather short time together, I'd tell you it's never too late to change your life, to go and seek out the kind of life you can be proud of; it won't be easy by any means, but it will be worth it, and I'd also recommend to take the risks you're afraid of taking because you'll never regret being so brave.

Rye Walls: from the sofa I lean down and slip on my boots. I'm thinking of a song by *The Doors*. The clock behind you on the wall reads ten after five. It's been a long day and it's almost time for me to go. Time for our rather short conversation to come to an end. But there will be more. I promise you.

Our time is almost up, I say. Time to hit the road.

After you turn and check the clock on the wall above your desk, you reply: We have until six. Please continue.

I'm not sure what you want me to say so I stand and stretch out my legs as I return to the windows. New York City has taken on a fresh new sunlight and for a dislocated instant it feels like I'm looking down on Boston or Chicago or Hong Kong, except I'm not and there's no mistaking New York. Even the park has been renewed by the day's rain and looks grand.

I've lived in four different countries and traveled tons more, very unlike the common man who was my father. Henry never held a passport and I doubt Gwendolen ever had one either. But what I'm trying to tell you is that while living in those different countries, I could've sworn I saw the same people, old friends, but in different forms — their doppelgangers, perhaps. I'm sure genes have something to do with it, and I hope it's not a trick of my mind. Either way you have it, I've seen many doppelgangers out there, walking unawares that they were the copy or that they were the original with a copy living in another country where the originals never knew. I had seen them though.

For effect, I turn back to you and say, I've even seen your eyes in different people. You were walking down Queen's Road Central in Hong Kong, a shopping bag in one hand, a smartphone in the other, and from the back a striking resemblance flicked a memory chord in me, and when you turned, or your copy turned, there were faint traces of you in the chin, around the lips and nose, and in the creases at the edges of your eyes. I've known those eyes, but on another level, I've known my mind to be deceived by prominent similarities, the truth cold and hard before me. By the end of the encounter the logic didn't add up — why would you be in Hong Kong? — and I knew the stranger couldn't be you. After all, you're one of a kind and I could never mistake you.

Even at the age where half my life has been lived, I've met and seen far too many people who I'll never meet or see again, and a great many of those I'm quite content, for one reason or another, at never having to cross paths again; but it's becoming harder to look people in the eyes and know that for as long as I live I may never see them again, or if I do, perchance, happen to meet them *en passant*, they will be a different person in a new form living far, far away in another land.

Since I've had to come to terms with the profundity, the irony, the loss many times over, I've simply grown to accept it like most anything else passing under the sun. I guess age helps you to deal with such things, but age doesn't make anything easier, just less shocking and new.

I think to myself for a minute or two then ask, Did I tell you my original ancestors came from the Rhineland in Germany? After many trials and famines, the Fusts settled in Texas, as I mentioned to you before.

My family's surname derives from the German word 'fust,' meaning 'fist,' a kind of fighter or warrior, or one who works with his hands and fists, and some scholars have said that's where we also get the name Faustus, as in the man who sold his soul to the Mephistopheles in exchange for knowledge and power. The good doctor, I'm half-sure, believed he'd be able one day to cheat death and escape his sorcerous pact.

You may also be happy to know Berlin planted a field of rye all along the Bernauer Strasse as a replacement and physical reminder of the concrete wall that had divided East Germany and West Germany for nearly half a century. Humboldt University students sow and harvest the field of rye, bleeding in to the urban exterior among high-rise rooftops and front yards maintaining vegetable gardens, a hodgepodge memorial to lost farms.

Part of my ancestry, somewhere in the chain and legend of time, a great-great-great grandmother married a Native American man from the Blackfoot tribe, and to this day when I travel across Asia, I'm sometimes mistaken for being Asian, though my family clearly had no direct links to that part of the world. But when I'm complimented, I often thank the speaker, explain my possible Native American connection, and imagine that this must be what it feels like to be a global citizen.

We are all divided in one way or another: me with my past; Berlin with its wall of rye; Hong Kong with its future melding into China; the East with the West, and vice versa.

I don't necessarily burn bridges, but I don't keep them maintained either. I've seen the worst in people in all the places I've been in the world — Guam, Bali, Cambodia, a dozen others — and I've rarely experienced the good.

Except for one time, I suppose. On my last night in East Bali, with the ocean in front of me and behind me in shadows cast by the moon Mount Agung — a still very much active volcano — I sat on the smooth stones of the beach just outside the resort and smoked my last Cuban cigar, a *partagás*. The night wind blew crisply onto shore bringing with it the smell of the old sea. Shooting stars could be seen crossing the great expanse out before me in the wide-open realms of infinite space. The beach lay in a somnolent darkness which allowed the heavenly array of stars to be free to shine more brightly.

After thirty minutes or more of sitting alone, soaking in the last reflections of Bali — I'd leave the next morning — Noman, a young native I had befriended came out to join me on the beach.

Noman worked in the resort's restaurant and though he was but a few years my junior — I was thirty-three at the time — he appeared to be a decade or more younger, and I joked that he was hiding the Fountain of Youth from me. Where could I, like he, find the Water of Life?

As I smoked my cigar, we sat side-by-side in our own silence for a time like close brothers who needed few words and fewer gestures to communicate. He tried some of my cigar but he wasn't a smoker and he found the tobacco too strong. We spoke to one another then about our families, about our childhoods, and lastly about our fates ahead. Where would we be in ten years? Twenty? We didn't know.

I kept thinking what it must be like to live and die on an island near the Java Sea — which these thoughts would ultimately inspire my short story 'The Boy of Eight Summers' — and how Noman was blessed with such endless beauty surrounding him, but how he was also imprisoned by his paradise; unable to escape the island, the aesthetic quality of his environment would grow, if it hadn't already, to become a curse. True. That could happen. But there was his family to consider, and then there was culture and tradition to think about. He cherished each one.

There on that stony beach next to Noman, I listened to my friend's stories and peered through my armored-individualistic ocularium just long enough to see how a collective tribe, at its best, could become an extension of who you were as an individual. Community was Noman and Noman was his community.

Still, there were times when he looked to me as I faced the waves sloshing to shore, and I sensed him imagining what it must be like to be me: a man who travels the world alone and smoked cigars in an easy grace among the company of others. I wanted so much for him to believe that he was better off than I was, and how unhappy the pursuit of my art had made me over the years, chasing a dream that never satiated me or loved me as much in return.

Despite knowing that I was being sincere, Noman seemed not to believe me, and he'd turn his head to face the dark waters that had kept him prisoner since his birth and he'd spend the minutes with me, both of us feeling trapped by a thing we could not name.

He'd speak of the boats anchored offshore or the constellations above. When he saw a falling star, I asked him to make a wish. Quietly, to himself, he did.

'Did you make a wish?' he asked me.

'Yes.'

'What did you wish for?'

'I'm not supposed to say. If I told you, it might not come true. But I don't believe in that.'

'Oh,' he said. 'I see.'

'I'll tell you anyway because I'm not superstitious,' I said. I puffed on the cigar and exhaled, grabbed a stone and threw it into the shallow surf. 'I wished for your dreams to come true, Noman. I hope you end up a happy man.'

'Thank you,' he said. 'I want the same for you.'

Not knowing what else to say, he sat for a time and we chatted about small, unimportant matters, the kind of polite talk so easily forgotten among acquaintances. Noman and I shared a few moments more before he said he had to get back to his work closing the restaurant. He wished me well on my journey. I wished him well on his. Then he left me on the beach to finish my cigar alone.

Most of that time, on the beach with Noman, I felt like I was in a dream playing in another person's mind, someone else's dreams that were not my own.

One of the biggest movies of the 1980s, and one I still recall with the fondness of my childhood, was Michael J. Fox's *Back to the Future* in 1985. As a six-year-old child the idea of Time Travel fascinated me, and still does even now as a professional writer and reader where I can travel in time pretty much all day every day. One reason I loved the movie so much back then was because I was just coming to an age when I could discern the past (before my existence) from the present (now me existing) from the future (after my existence) and even deeper into the discernment between fantasy, reality, illusion, and the tangible world around me.

Unlike five years before as an infant when I had crawled into the television set one night while dreaming, I knew that the film *Back to the Future* was more make-believe than an actual documentary (for several years, old reruns of television shows from the 1960s and the 1970s frightened me because the world I lived in did not mesh with the world from those two previous decades; basically, in its simplicity, my mind, as a toddler, could not conceive how the real world around me could be so dissimilar to the past worlds presented to me through the television set each afternoon).

Back to the Future came, for me, at the most ideal time in my childhood development, and the film's journey — of a young man traveling in time to alter his family's past and, therefore, their future fates or destinies, if you will — captivated me in a profound way, not because of the ability to travel through time, but because of a person's power to save his family, his ability to self-direct and course-correct key events in his ancestral line to produce a harmony in his present life, the future in the film's case.

Imagine that! A high school kid able to determine what did and could happen. Now that seems more fantasy than science fiction any time.

Granted, even as a pre-teen I could not hop into a DeLorean fueled by plutonium and change my mother and father's history — I dare not think of the consequences and, as Doc Brown said so often, the repercussions. What I did understand, however, was that each individual choice I made affected me years to come and also my descendants who will one day follow.

For a time, I feared even making the simplest of choices because the results were too infinite and too numerous for my young mind to calculate the odds let alone fathom the immensity of such control and power over life. The possibilities lay before me as a universe of oceans where I was sure to drown because even inaction weighed me with its endless possibilities. As a result, I concluded that mistakes would be made, would have to be made, and to do my best to limit the mistakes in my life (even now the idealism I had borders the realm of sentimentality). After more mistakes than I'd care to admit, I later learned that mistakes were necessary, in part, to learn and to improve. Trial by error (but I can still shiver at this crude notion of personal evolution). Mistakes were necessary in order to learn from those mistakes.

One aspect of the ending in the film *Back to the Future* that bothered me as a six-year-old (not at all to take away from my enjoyment of the experience) was how Fox's character, Marty McFly (also known as Calvin in 1955) and his personal future did not change very much as a result of all his meddling in the past. Sure, his family has a new house with a tennis court and he has a brand-new truck (materialism without question) but he himself rarely changed — even his girlfriend, Jennifer Parker, didn't change.

Think about it: by the end of the movie you're led to believe Marty McFly has grown in some way, but the intrinsic changes happen to his father George (he changes the most), his mother Lorraine, brother Dave, and sister Linda. Marty wakes to a new world where he has changed very little intrinsically while he reaps the rewards of a perfect family: his father George is now a self-confident, successful science fiction novelist rather than a pathetic nerd; his elder brother Dave goes from living at home and working at a fast food restaurant to being a successful businessman dropping by for breakfast; the elder sister Linda is involved with many male suitors and works at a boutique; and the mother Lorraine has lost weight and is quite the amateur athlete who is no longer an alcoholic; everyone is genuinely happy and full of energy and life.

Certainly, lifting the family out of poverty into a blissful life of luxury and success is a clear indication of the changes made. Lesson: Money makes your life better. And it's true. The less time you have to worry about money the more time you have to focus on your health, your family or your personal development and evolution. But you know this already. In many ways, after my parents' divorce, and even before the disintegration of my childhood family, I dreamed of having a family like the one at the end of the film: a father I could be proud of for his own successes; a mother who loves her husband as much as her children; an elder brother humble enough not to act like a total dick; and, an elder sister successful in her own measures by being a lawyer or a Supreme Court judge.

For years, though, I looked into each one of their eyes as they spoke mundane, trivial things to me and all I could think was: what went so horribly wrong for you to end up the way you did? Choices. There's nothing bigger. It came down to their individual choices, which were also governed and limited by their substantial lack of money — as my life was for so very long. Choices. Just like Director Robert Zemeckis choosing to drop Eric Stoltz from the lead role as Marty McFly in the film *Back to the Future*.

Every time I looked into their eyes I saw how they'd stopped fighting years ago and relinquished themselves to their fates: my father settled for as little as possible (a sure sign of personal decay); my mother lived a loveless life as she was scorned by her lover and could find no other (she'd settle for my father); my brother Chadwick found himself married but fucking a mistress who was the yoga instructor (he'd settle once again for his wife); and my sister (the one I thought I could save) settled into her wild ways the way a storm settles into its own destruction over the lands and peoples of this good, mighty earth. And this is putting it nicely. I'd look into their eyes and see shame, pity, anguish, spite, fear, loss, hopelessness, disease, lethargy, uncertainty, obscurity, and regret — consumed by the weight of their own misfortunes. I saw in all of them failed humanity squashing their human potential and greatness. And they chose to allow this to happen. Oh, the irony!

If I could go back and change their lives (I've no right to do so, but if I did), I'm not sure if their lives would be any better in the new future I wanted for them. Life doesn't happen the way it does in the movies, especially one about Time Travel. I do like to lie awake at night, as I did last night, and imagine the possibility of a multiverse having at least one universe where my family is together again and each one of them (Henry, Gwendolyn, Chadwick, Cassandra) are happy in each of their personal successes. They'd be fit and health conscious, smiling and energetic, active and eager for dialogue. Chadwick and Cassandra would genuinely get along with mutual respect, empowering one another. Gwendolyn and Henry would love one another as though only love matters to them and has only ever mattered.

I'm standing in your office looking out the window but I can see my family, a perfect family, well-dressed and laughing around a kitchen shining in sunlight. Their individual pasts lift them higher and higher. Their spirits seem to me to be floating beneath the surface of their skin. The laughter is profuse and I can see true, honest joy in the sincerity of their eyes. They are on top of the world and each one knows it as they all look to me, more a ghost in the corner than anything else. I'm happy for them, though, and they know this, because I did not save them. No, I did not. I was too busy trying to save myself. I'm happy for them because I can see that they are happy. They are happy because they saved themselves.

My ruminations on small-town America do not neglect my dear thoughts for you and your life in Boston and the Big Apple. Instead, I'm posed with complex questions even physics fail to answer regarding two grand testaments of consciousness: subjectivity and objectivity.

Discoveries in science like the 'Heisenberg Cut' stirred debates about how certain experiments in quantum physics with probability waves forced our consciousness to delve deeper into our own understandings on what was subjective and what was objective and how the two could merge as one. In those experiments, physicists were attempting to observe a probability wave but when they did the physicists noticed a sudden change: a particle suddenly became visible. When they observed a probability wave, a particle would appear as though from nothingness as though the act of observing the probability wave formed creation of the particle into existence. An act of observation leading to the act of creation.

In other words, the subjective act created a physical particle from thin air inside an observable event. Would the particle be created even without a physicist observing a probability wave? Some physicists think not and some physicists think so. Like catching a child sticking her hand into a cookie jar or an electrical outlet, the child would freeze and turn (in effect, react) at the precise moment an adult entered the room to observe the child's secretive behavior. What would happen if the child had not been seen by the adult?

The subjective event of the observer observing an action created an immediate and noticeable change in that specific action.

But what if the subjective event is an observer observing (or remembering) his own past? What changes, then, would occur? Would an 'immediate and noticeable change' occur in the past? In the present? In the future? Even Albert Einstein once said that the past and the future were illusions, and that the present moment was all that ever would be of reality. Truth and illusions, apparently, was what I was left with as I stared deeper and longer into my own past each morning in an effort to write this book for you and to better understand the life I had lived and to reshape my memories, those ever allusive illusions, into an order that would force chaos to make sense to me, and to you. Even as I stand before you at your desk and tell the story I've never told anyone, I'm reminded of Rūmī and the ending of his poem 'The Truth within Us':
What is all the beauty in the world? The image,
Like quivering boughs reflected in a stream,
Of that eternal Orchard which abides
Unwithered in the hearts of Perfect Men.

Many nights I can't sleep, like last night, and I'd think on my father and how I had lived decades with an illusion which shames me to recollect. I'd often thought of my father as a failure, a loser, a sellout (what he sold-out to even I do not pretend to know), and I wanted nothing to do with him. I wanted to grow up and become my own man without influence from him or my family, and that was exactly what I've done.

Now, though, looking back at his life through the eyes of a man who looks at history anew, I see how America in the 1970s and the early 1980s suffered under a severe weight of high gas prices, inflation and unemployment. 'Reaganomics' would not kick in and impact the American economy until the mid-eighties, and by then I'd be five years old, walking and talking and remembering and making up stories.

What amazes me now about my father was how he held a job (one he must've hated many times over) in a cable factory (cable TV was just around the corner and ready to make an appearance in the eighties — but no one, not even my father, could foretell how copper wiring would impact the television and internet industries).

My father held a job in that factory for over twenty-five years (I lasted barely six months) while America dealt with inflation growing, unemployment soaring, and gas prices threatening the fates of the free world. Yes, my father remained steady and held an unwavering commitment to his wife, three children, a dog, two cows, a pair of longhorns, and three horses. For many years he was the sole breadwinner and the burdens he must've endured in his late twenties I dare not imagine. He'd wake at five in the morning and be at the factory across town by six, put in a twelve-hour shift, and come home to play with his kids and give attention to his wife. No easy task. He must've sacrificed parts of his spirit on that pre-dawn drive to work while his three children lay sound asleep in their beds.

My father never graduated college. He never saved a million dollars, nor was he given a fortune from his father. My father, Henry, labored to the tune of sixty hours a week during a time when Wall Street executives, those greedy Fat Rats with families of their own, were putting ropes around their necks and guns to their heads every time the stock market plunged to horrific new lows. My father endured, despite giving away the best parts of himself, and he did so for his wife and children. How could a son not be prouder? So, let me tell you now: I am proud of my father.

We all would like to have the perfect life: endless vacays on yachts speeding off to deserted islands for champagne in the hot tub. We'd like to achieve our childhood dreams without struggles and challenges. We'd like to believe the best in one another and feel the best in ourselves. We'd like not to grow bitter and cynical over the events of our lives. We'd like to take the next step and the next turn and find we've reached the destination we've so longed for in our sleepless nights. We'd like to believe in world peace as we, ourselves, spent our time and energy making the world a better place for our children and grandchildren. We'd like to be the best versions of ourselves and find the world accepts us for who we are and for who we could be. We'd like all of that and more. Wouldn't we?

The truth was, however, all of what we'd like was the illusion. Illusions remain forever locked in the past and future. Untouchable.

Unreachable. The illusions of what we'd like and what we'd want would bring with them more turmoil, more grief, more anguish and more strife. The past cannot be touched nor changed because it exists as an illusion no longer real nor alive. The future cannot be reached nor altered because it, too, exists only as an illusion. The present moment holds the power we were looking for. Being in the moment was all we ever had or will have or could have. Mother Teresa said it best: 'Be happy in the moment, that's enough. Each moment is all we need, not more.' If that's true, destinies exist in the here and now, building on our daily choices and actions creating the next moment from the thin air of nothingness. We are the generators of our own creations and the possibilities out there are numbered more than the protons and electrons in all the galaxies in all the Universe. What came before Time and Space? What came before the Big Bang? What came out from behind the dark veil of nothingness? We did. We are Energy and Light made from the stardust of the known and unknown universes. Beyond that veil of dark-unknowing-timeless nothingness that everyone dreads and fears awaits a presently-immediate moment I have seen and it is bright-everlasting truth and beauty.

I offer you my entire youth.
    It's truly fascinating, you say. Heartbreaking even. But nothing special. Nothing spectacular. Ordinary. That's what I'd call it. Ordinary.
    You're not going to publish it, are you? Any of it.
    In this marketing climate, you search for the right words, some politically correct phrase repeated a hundred thousand times until its significance and meaning has become mundane and lost. The industry's taken a hit in recent years, you say. We can't make any promises, you understand, don't you? It's a work of art but it can't, it won't, it never will be published. Coastal publishers, to be quite frank and blunt, don't really want to publish and promote writers and stories from America's heartland. It's not what the foreign-owned publishers want and are willing to publish here in America. Don't you see? You're not of this time and place. You said it yourself. You don't belong, even in your own land. The foreign-

owned publishers want to shape America in their own images. What more can we tell you that you don't already know for yourself?'

I understand the old trick between the business 'we' and the disconnected 'you' well enough but I hold my tongue.

You wanted my book, I say. Now you have it. I offer it to you, regardless. Because the beauty is in the telling, not in the packaging of a product that can't be marketed and shipped overnight to consumers. You understand, don't you?

We do. Very much so, you say. More than before.

You know as well as I do that when we were young, we believed in the best in ourselves and in the best the world had to offer. Not in second best. Or third best. And certainly not in the way the world turned out to be. We expected the world to be fair. We grew up and learned the world wasn't fair. We tried to come to an understanding of who we were and who we wanted to be in the great big world out there. It wasn't a question of understanding one's own destiny, but attempting to understand the thoughts of the supreme deity and to know what that deity wanted us to do with our lives, and to find the truth that is the truth for each one of us — to find the idea we are willing to live and to die for. And still, when we were young, we falsely imagined our parents to be god-like, but we'd discover they were just as flawed as we were, and that death came for them just as it would do so for us one day. In fact, our illusions broke and fell apart one by one until it seemed the world around us had been filled with people who had long ago decided to quit, to give up fighting for a better world to live in; that the next paycheck and bonus mattered more than the morals we learned as children. It isn't a coincidence that most punishments for adults come in the form of financial penalties, the taking away of money, or the threat thereof, to shape social behavior and cultural norms.

That's still one of the biggest illusions governing the world, isn't it? you say. How money dictates morality, our behaviors, our attitudes.

In a way, yes. It's all about power and control, control and power. People deserve better, don't you think?

I don't wait for you to answer.

What I'm trying to say — and failing miserably at it in the process, be patient with me please, I'm almost done — I'm trying to tell you that illusions are the stitches which connect the patches of our reality into a quilt of being with one another, and this in turn shapes the Universe, or what we'd like to believe is Time and Space. I don't mean to preach but to share, and that's why you asked me here today, wasn't it?

Yes, it was. You've helped us a great deal. We might even be able to use the experiences you mentioned for some of the other more established authors. This is how the game is played. This is how the industry really works, don't you understand? You've shown us the complexity of life, and that's what we needed most: a comparison to consider. Nothing illegal in that. But promise us you'll try and use your past to rebuild the present, like the philosopher Samuel Smiles once suggested. Please do try, Cody.

Ideas, the past, memories, dreams are all like Thor's hammer, I say. They return from where they were thrown. I'm afraid my debt is much larger. I lean my back against the windows. You know what I mean?

I'm afraid I don't. Sorry. You close the Moleskine notebook you've been writing in all day and place your hands in the pockets of your cardigan. But you've remembered a life so much richer than the rest of us.

I'm not so sure about that, I say. We all have a story to tell. We are the authors of our own story, are we not?

I think for a minute then add: I'd like to tell you one more thing. It's about my favorite opera, to close out our day, our time together.

You stand and come join me by the windows. The sun sets in the horizon.

Each time I watch Giacomo Puccini's *Turandot*, I'm moved with a sense of belonging and empathy for the whole of the human race and the lovers it has produced, those known and those unknown. My favorite scene must be Caláf's '*Nessun Dorma*' while he pines away the night in the palace gardens beneath the moonlight. Pavarotti, for me, captures best the pain, misery and longing found in Caláf's love for the princess.

Little Hometown, America

In the aria, Caláf sings to us that nobody shall sleep, nobody, and how even the cold, heartless princess will be unable to sleep while Caláf suffers with a secret hidden within his soul. Let the stars tremble with love and hope. None will know my name. And so, it was with Caláf and Turandot. Vanish, o rain. Vanish, o night. Fade, you memory. Fade, you stars. For there is no new thing under the sun. The earth abides forever. I place my arm around your shoulders and kiss you on the side of your head, near your eyes, and finish by saying: God, forgive me for all the time I've wasted.

An old man stood in the snow. Inside the lobby of the office building where I just left you, where you rejected me and my book about a little hometown in Texas, where you said goodbye to me thirty-three floors up, I stood by the front windows putting my coat and red scarf on and watched the traffic go by and saw how the snow fell piece by piece in ruffled layers that reminded me of the snows as a boy when Smokey came to visit and as a young man in the mountains near the border of North Korea where I spent a Christmas alone all those years ago. But even then, I wasn't as alone as I felt while watching the old man in the snow.

Across the street, the old man had an upturned hat in his hand and he was catching the flakes of the gentle snow newly falling. I wasn't ready to enter the cold or the hustling of New York City, much less the smog and noise pollution, because it might have broken the spell I was under and there was only one thing I really wanted to do before I walked the streets to Central Park and so I stood with my hands in my pockets growing warmer by the minute and tried to forget about how your silence was the loudest noise and rejection of all as you sat there at your desk tapping your Montblanc pen on your nose making a staccato rhythm and hoping I would just leave with my heart sandwiched between my toes, but I couldn't leave and we waited in silence like that old man who caught snow in his upturned hat because he had nothing better to do, and it was then in the lobby and not at your desk that a certain kind of truth covered and devoured me like a light bluish-green lava oozing and cooling around me into a glassy jade tomb resembling the shape of the man I had been. I understood that as a Texan, proud-strong-true, my culture was different to the cultures of those peoples found in Guam, Hawaii, Alaska, California, Illinois, New York and Maine, and that when people wronged me I would walk away without a word as I remained in a turmoil of disbelief because I could never fathom doing that to another human being. People could, inherently and instinctually, be so cruel; and yet, I could not. But in my own silence fueled by a most bitter rejection of the world and its people another self fed by the sweet milk and honey produced by a hubris I could not normally stomach to swallow now empowered me into an anger directed inward; because I could not be so cruel in returning my anger solidified my resolve to become better than the cruelty. Still, my own rejection of the world lay at my feet like a hypocritical gift from a spurned lover in the lobby where I continued to watch the old man catching snow in his upturned fedora across the street.

At times the old man appeared to take pleasure in each snowy shape descending in pendulum-like swings that cut its path ever-so-softly, ever-so-casually onto the under-brim of his worn-out fedora. Even as passersby hesitated with a double-look while on their way to meet good and merry friends for happy hour or while on their way to buy a few groceries for dinner, the old man ignored the jeers, the ridicule, the stares, the passive-aggressive snide remarks and instead focused all his powers, all his sweet attention on the most mundane act of easing his fedora under a coming ice crystal, only for it to instantly melt and cause a feathery water stain.

When a bus passed in front of my view where I stood at the windows in the lobby, an argument erupted behind me at the receptionist's desk by an elderly woman wearing too many pearls around her neck. I turned back to the windows only to find the old man with the upturned hat gone. In an instant he had vanished. With nothing more to keep my attention, I felt my welcome being overstayed. I walked out of the lobby and away from the bickering woman with too many pearls and who reminded me faintly of Miss Havisham. I walked into the cold thinking the old man with the upturned hat had been nothing more than a ghost from my overactive imagination, nothing more than one of my characters from one of my stories I had dreamed up to deal with the sting of your rejection. It didn't matter if he was real or not. The streets would swallow me as they did to millions and billions of souls each day. That was fine. To be faceless among the crowd allowed me to grow ever inward, sinking further and farther away from the rejection I had waited two decades or more to avoid. The faceless crowd, however, comforted me by reminding me of one simple fact: I was no different to anyone else. And so, I walked to Central Park in the growing depth of dusk — as my father had done all those years ago to bury Twilight — without a single solitary word upon my lips as if Time were a river dried empty.

Three blocks down from your office building I passed the Japanese Ramen noodle shop where I had so often met you for lunch and how I would have to wait in line for twenty minutes or more before you'd come join me. But I didn't mind then and I still don't mind now. I'd wait for you even if we had lunch tomorrow.

The thought of eating, though, turned the hairs on my arms and squeezed my stomach dry and it was when I passed the noodle shop and it was behind me that a feeling of a calm I had not known since scuba diving off the coast of East Bali found me again in the streets growing more crowded with diners seeking their early suppers so they could take the long train rides to the island or across state and back to home.

At each intersection I stopped and waited my turn, for the signal to change from red to green so I could be allowed to continue my walk, and as I searched the faces of the men and women across the street — some young, some old, some pretty, some not so pretty — I found not a single, similar spark that lit my dreams in my own eyes; their hollow eyes were like dark crystals leading me down into a labyrinth I dared not enter, and I noticed then, stopped there at the intersection, how I'd been hearing the tick-tick-tick of the crosswalk signals of Hong Kong, and the memory of that mundane sound overpowered the silence because once the tone changed — snapping open with a ping! — I'd be given the chance to cross and continue on my way. But the 'ping' didn't come. Only pedestrians behind me pushing, barging and shoving by me came and this surging crowd stirred me from the temporary trance I'd been under.

The first step I placed off the sidewalk and onto the crosswalk below met with a slick patch of ice and the pavement roared up to smack me on the back of my head. A few bystanders stopped to take photos and selfies with their smartphones while I rubbed the bleeding nob on the back of my head. Someone did finally come to offer assistance after a time. An Arab with ashes between his eyes said his name was Art and he was there to help.

Art held a red umbrella over his head with one hand and offered his other hand to pull me off the pavement. He asked if I were injured, if I needed to go to the emergency room, if I needed help, any at all. My vision was fuzzy and I believed I was looking up at a disciple of Christ beneath the red dome of the Vatican and all I could do between the intense throbbing going on inside my skull was to look the Arab Muhammad Art straight in his eyes and tell him,

'The world just bit the fuck out of me.'

The Arab Muhammad Art shook his head and tried to understand what language it was I was speaking until he gave up and walked the way I had come from your office building. The taxis, like thoroughbreds lined up at the racetrack, honked and impatiently waited for me to finish crossing before motoring up and through the intersection. This time, however, was one of the few times in my life I didn't look back. The back of my head stung but Central Park was only a few blocks ahead and that was all that mattered to me after my fall. To find Central Park, yes, and slink inside to some tunnel beneath some bridge and die.

Later, like one of Titan's hydrocarbon lakes, the lake in Central Park transfixed me with its inky surface reflecting the yellow and white lights from buildings as I stood at the lake's edge and imagined the infinite stars of the Universe shimmering at my feet; all of creation below waited for me to jump in and be swallowed whole in order to become a myth, or to be forgotten. Why not both?

But I didn't want to jump in; not out of some divine purpose, but because I didn't want to get my clothes and shoes wet, and I couldn't bring myself to do it. Like in your office, thirty-three floors high, and all the other times with you on our long walks together, a liquid silence filled the spaces between me and the rest of the world, a protective barrier that did not require me to speak because it knew the language of my heart and the song of my soul. But I could never tell you that. Not in a million, billion years. The lake, though, looked deep and endless and I thought how nice it would feel for you to be here next to me. We could hold hands like the way we used to do every Saturday, those sleepy little afternoons when you'd speak of the planet Titan and its liquid methane and ethane flowing between huge mountains formed of solid ice. Back then you had an eagerness to share in your voice, and it pleased me to think of you by the lake not yet ready to freeze, not yet ready to become something else.

After twenty or thirty minutes or so, I turned my back to the lake because I had a plane to catch in the morning and I should've gone back right then to the hotel and packed, but I wanted to walk a bit more, become lost like Holden for a while longer in the trees that still held shadows from my childhood fears, nightmares not from any sleep but from the living moments I chose to block and ignore and eventually left as a young man in a stubborn hopeless rage of never having to return to that nowhere black hole, my hometown, and as I walked toward a yellow glow in the distant trees, I recalled how you'd constantly remind me of your favorite Latin quote, '*Nullius in verba*,' which, as you explained to me one night over the French cocktail Kir Royale, was also the motto of the Royal Society in London. In the sky above us that night, you sipped your cocktail and spoke of how the stars were the true ghosts of the far Past; stars that died ages ago rushing their light in hopes of being seen next to a full moon a second behind us in our time; the universe surrounding us with the Past, and to us that was beauty and truth; or was it truth and beauty?

But there was no truth nor beauty now; no, John Keats had it wrong, my friend; there was only the cold chilling the bones in my toes and the park descending me into a far greater loneliness than any I had ever known. It was then as I neared a thicket of trees, I saw a fire cracking open limbs and twigs, which three Girl Scouts dropped into the flames.

Dressed in their uniforms, the three young girls also wore knee-high socks and short little skirts which revealed a sliver of thigh on each leg. With official berets cocked to one side of their heads, the three teens looked to be triplets and no more than thirteen, but on closer examination between the bursts of rising flames, the three girls appeared haggard and old and their hair color differed in that one was like a remarkable strawberry, one was like chocolate, and one was like gold, and all three of their smiles twisted upright as I approached, lost, as if I had just chanced upon a paganistic cult performing a ritual orgy at the stroke of midnight and I would be their sacrifice.

It would be then, at that moment, in the faces of the three haunted young girls I remembered the dreams: the dreams of the people I've never met, the lives I've never had, the places I've never been and the pain I've never seen. One such dream saw me wounded and limping around horse and mule carcasses and human corpses after a revolutionary battle in a wintry forest. I could never speak to anyone, let alone myself, of the solitude entire that glued me to the mud and ice of that long forgotten, misplaced battlefield of an era that once knew me by a different name. All of this and more stared back at me from the faces of those three young girls by the fire.

'Gilgamesh,' the redhead in the middle said across from the fire, 'What do you want?'

'Who?' I said. 'What?'

'He's forgotten,' the blonde Girl Scout to my left said. 'Shall we help him remember?'

'Who are you?' I said. 'What're you doing here?'

'He's right,' the blonde-scout said. 'We must tell him.'

'We all shall tell him,' the redhead in the middle said, 'because that's the proper way to proceed.'

'Let me, let me,' the brunette-scout on my right said. 'He knows each of us already but must be reminded. He must remember. Gilgamesh has lost his way.' She paused to point at the redhead. 'Pain must go first.'

'I must've hit my head pretty damn hard,' I said. 'What again?'

The fire between us popped and cracked a bit higher and the shadows of the trees around us loomed longer, stretching as it seemed to infinity.

'She's right,' the redhead said, 'I must go first or none of this will make sense.' She looked straight at me from across the fire. 'I am Pain,' she said. 'Do you *now* remember me, Gilgamesh?'

And, sadly, I did.

I'd been fifteen on a late Tuesday afternoon with my father cutting and trimming the lawn of a large, white house at the end of a winding road at the top of a southern hill.

'Whose house is this?' I asked while taking a break from the weed eater, idling a steady hum from its motor. 'Who lives here?'

My father had gone to the truck to get more fuel for the lawnmower and when I asked my questions, he didn't even stop to consider the implications of what I was asking. He bent inside the bed of the truck and pulled a two-gallon tank of fuel away with one hand like an ancient savage in his ability to wield a rock as a weapon.

'Don't know,' he said. 'Don't care,' he added.

'What do you mean you don't know? You're cutting their lawn? How do you not know?'

'Just don't,' he said.

'Then how will you get paid? How will *I* get paid if you don't even know who hired us?'

'I know,' he said. 'Now get back to work. Let's finish before dark.'

The night, he was right, had started to settle between us and all around that large, white house at the top of the hill in my hometown so long ago, and when I looked from my father to a house he'd never be able to afford, not a day in his life, I felt the pain all sons must feel when they come to know their fathers were not who they wanted to be when they grew up.

'I remember,' I said, and I looked at the flames melting the snow as it hit. 'I remember Pain.'

The three Girl Scouts (the blonde, the red, the brunette) clapped with such temerity and erotic laughter around the shaking fire that

I believed the trees in Central Park shivered in the dark outside the penumbra of light. Or it could've been the wind. Yes. The wind.

'I'm next, I'm next,' the brunette-scout shouted with glee. She hopped on one foot in a circle as she waved her hands over her head. 'I'm next! I'm next!'

'He'll never remember you,' Pain said. 'Never.'

'I'm always last,' the blonde said. 'It's simply not fair that you two get to have all the fun.'

'Oh, shut up,' Pain said. 'You're supposed to go last or none of it will make sense.'

'True,' the brunette said. She looked at me from across the flames, the white light reflecting in her dark eyes. 'He'll remember me. Won't you, Gilgamesh? Because we've met before, haven't we? I am Grace.'

And, gladly, I did.

After Howard Payne University, where I obtained a modest undergraduate degree in English, I was accepted into a master's program in American and British Literature at Angelo State University, some one hundred miles via US-67 South from my hometown.

In Tom Green County, San Angelo — a city so named for a Mexican nun — lay in the Concho Valley with an estimated population of just over one hundred thousand souls; once upon a time the city included award-winning writers like Lucy Snyder, Patrick Dearen and Elmer Kelton, as well as the four-time Cy Young award-wining baseball pitcher Greg Maddox, while 'all right, all right, all right' Matthew McConaughey frequented San Angelo from his ranch outside city limits. At the time, which would've been early 2003, my good friend Dylan, who had worked his way to store manager of a nearby Wal-Mart, offered me a place to stay and a night job until I could get settled from the transition of moving between towns. Some twenty years later, Dylan would quit Wal-Mart and walk away from his career and marriage; at that time, though, we had only faint ideas about where our lives would take us.

I had enrolled in graduate classes, which all turned out to be at night from six to nine once a week but on different days. At the same time, I started working at half-past ten at night and finishing after seven the next morning, which was when Dylan arrived at the store for his shift.

I'd crawl onto a sofa or a cot in a spare room to sleep while Dylan's wife, Gianna, would emerge from her bedroom an hour or so later. Even though Dylan and Gianna had a son, a toddler, they had just welcomed a baby girl into the family a year or so before. But from what I remember, both children were away for a time until I could find a place of my own, which ended up being no more than a month or so.

One day, after a few weeks into my night shift, I woke mid-morning with a tremendous urge to pee. With my penis hard and sticking straight through the slit in my boxers, I rolled from the cot, rubbed my balls and stumbled into the hallway ready for an epic piss when the bathroom door unlocked and opened and out came huge clouds of steam with Gianna inside. She was swaddled in nothing but two towels, one wrapped around her head while the other fixed snugly around her large breasts; the towel around her body ended at her pubic hairs still wet from the bath. As the morning sunlight coalesced with the steam flowing out of the bathroom, Gianna and I froze in our unexpected encounter: she stared at my rock-hard erection and I stared at her exposed flesh. Forgetting about my urgent need to pee, I wanted nothing more than to unravel those towels around Gianna and take her in my arms as we faced one another in the hall surrounded by all that steam and sunshine.

But none of that happened. We stood like that for a solid two or three minutes, alone in the house, knowing our wet urges, our hot desires and further understanding our obligations and responsibilities. Neither one of us moved; it was as though we had accidently stumbled into a mirror and through a portal to another reality where we had been given the most perfect opportunity to be together. Even so, even so, I thought of Dylan, her husband and my friend since elementary school, and all I could do and all I could say was, 'Gianna.' Her head cocked to one side, as if questioning the rejecting but polite tone in my voice, and she replied, 'Cody.' For thirty seconds more we remained standing, looking at one another as if we'd never get another chance in the next fifty plus years of our lives. But in the end, I turned and went back to the spare room to wait on the cot, and I lay there a good twenty minutes with my penis hard and my heart pounding in my chest. When all was quiet, I got back up, took a piss, and fell back to sleep until late afternoon to ready myself for class. But this was not the grace the brunette Girl Scout near the fire in Central Park had spoken of. Not at all. I knew what she meant. Now I'm going to tell you what I've never told anyone. Ever.

Right out of Brownwood High, I found myself lost that summer in 1998 without any future plans and, for me, it was as though I stood at the edge of a cosmic black hole being sucked inward to oblivion. While my spirit collapsed within me and my friends since kindergarten and elementary school readied for their summer vacations to faraway places or prepared for their upcoming college semester in the fall, I had no job and I had not applied to any universities. I suppose, now looking back at things, I expected someone at some point, like Henry or Gwendolen or Chadwick at least, to guide me, to mentor me into my next lifecycle, but no one ever did and I found myself at the height of a gorgeous Texas summer tremendously and unforgivably and unbearably alone. From within, I broke. To this day I'd like to say the fracture which crushed me to dust all those years ago has completely healed but that would be a bold lie. I still see the hurt and pain as deep and as thick as it had been for me that summer right after high school ended. As I told you, already, that summer I visited the recruitment office for the Marines, like millions of young women and men before me, and narrowly escaped certain death in an unexpected and unforeseen war in the Middle East after 2001, just a few years after my high school graduation.

Shortly after the episode with the Marine officer in Heartland Mall, what I didn't tell you is that I drove to my mother's house and found a freshly baked loaf of bread sitting on the kitchen table; for some reason I knew exactly what I should do. I had planned to drive out to Pine Creek Ranch, my father's place, to perform the ceremony or ritual, but as I crossed over the crest of the final curve on the final southern hill, I just kept driving farther and farther away from the city and the ranch which had known me since my birth. For a good twenty or thirty minutes I drove deeper into the countryside in silence and let the windows down so the air hit my face while, wrapped in a towel, the loaf of bread lay on the seat next to me. Down an isolated road with the sun starting to set on the western horizon, I parked the car and grabbed the bread loaf. As I walked into a field, my mind worked in a calm determination, as if I were a machine following order from a higher, more intelligent power. Without a word, I walked. Without a word, I knelt in the dying grass of late summer. Without a word, I extended the bread loaf before me on the ground and unwrapped the towel so the bread loaf looked as though it lay on an altar before the setting sun. Without a word, I retreated a few paces back and knelt once again to bow before my offering to all things and to all powers which have existed before me and which will go on existing after I'm gone, and these things and powers have nothing to do with humanity and beasts other than the spark of life it gives them. I bowed with my face to the ground for over twenty minutes in silence — you might say my offering was to Life. Some might argue my offering was to God or to the Universe, and they, too, would not be wrong. An energy of everlasting enlightenment filled me from the ground through my toes, my hands and my forehead and coursed through my veins, and it spoke to me of my life and the things to come.

Later I rose as the sun sank into the earth and the lethargic gray of evening settled naturally across the land. I left the bread loaf, a gift to all that's unknown and holy and good, lying on the towel in the middle of some stranger's field for the ants, and as I walked back to my car parked on the side of the road a gust of wind unexpectedly barreled across the plains and when the wind reached me I heard it say, 'Peace be yours.'

'I remember,' I said to Grace, who looked at me from across the flames as the snow fell over me in Central Park. 'I remember Grace.'

The three Girl Scouts (the blonde, redhead, and brunette) laughed and clapped with such an unholy reverence I believed the fire shook and I could feel the trees in Central Park out in the darkness unseen by my naked eyes shiver beneath the weight of snow. Or it could've been the wind. Yes. The wind.

'It's me, it's me,' the blonde Girl Scout cheered and shouted. She spun in a tight circle on a single toe and flapped her arms down around her bare knees beneath the miniskirt. 'It's my turn. It's my turn! Finally, it's my turn!'

'He'll never remember you,' Grace said as she crossed her arms over her chest. 'Never.'

'He just might,' the blonde-scout said. 'Won't you, Gilgamesh?'

'Oh, shut up,' Pain said. 'Now hurry up and go on or none of it will make sense. None of it.'

'True,' the blonde-scout said. She looked straight at me from across the flames, the sparks flying in the reflections held in her spooky-green eyes. 'He'll remember me. He must. He must! Because,' and she paused to hold a bony finger directed at me, 'we've met before, haven't we, Gilgamesh? I am Forgotten.'

And, unfortunately, I had no idea, not a freaking clue, what she was talking about. Not an inkling nor a zip of anything. I told myself I must've gone mad. Lost my marbles.

'He's forgotten you!' Pain roared. Traces of laughter followed when she slapped Forgotten on the butt. 'See! No one cares about you. No one.'

Forgotten clinched her teeth and fists and gave me a scowl, two twisted lips filled with almighty disgust. 'You did it again. You've forgotten me, Gilgamesh. How could you? Tell me! How?'

'I'm sorry. I —'

'If he cannot remember us *all*,' said Forgotten, running a finger across her throat, 'this will be the end of him and his silly little story.'

'Let me end him now,' Pain said. 'I've waited oh-so long.'

Forgotten sulked by flopping to the ground. She clutched her knees to her chest and said, 'No one ever remembers me.'

'You know the rules,' Grace said. 'If Gilgamesh wants another chance, he'll have to put his hand in the fire and —'

'What again?' I said. 'Come again? I don't think so. Not —'

'He doesn't believe us,' Forgotten said from her seat on the snow. 'Let's just go ahead and eat and be done with him. I'm starving and it's been too long since our last supper.'

'Grace is right, Gilgamesh,' Pain said. 'Place your hand in the fire and you'll be given a second chance or —'

Turning to go, 'It's been fun,' I said, 'but I must get. It's late and I think I really hurt my head.'

There was just one thing, though, and I doubt you'd believe me if I told you, but I'm telling you now that I couldn't move a muscle, not even an eyebrow. My legs, perhaps from standing too long in one spot in the cold, were stiff, solid and unworkable. I couldn't move.

Then I felt my feet leave an inch or so off the ground, which must've been a trick from the cold. A trick of the senses. The numbing of the nerves.

'He'll never remember me,' Forgotten said. 'Gilgamesh has changed. He didn't even bring us a loaf of bread to eat.'

'He has changed,' Pain said. 'He's not the young man I remember.'

'Give him a chance,' Grace said. 'Gilgamesh has found us for a reason.'

From her seat on the snow beside the fire: 'Will you remember me?' Forgotten said. 'Will you, Gilgamesh?'

'He must try,' Grace said. 'Won't you, Gilgamesh?'

'Do it, Gilgamesh,' Pain said, 'or else.'

For some strange reason, and not of my own cognitive efforts, as if it were a metal controlled by a magnet, my left hand emerged from my coat pocket and extended itself, ever-so-carefully, and to my horror, into the heart of the fire.

'Pain,' I said.

'Yes?' Pain said.

'Grace,' I said.

'Yes?' Grace said.

'I….I….I….'

Forgotten bounced up from her seat on the snow. Once more she pointed a long, bony finger at me and said,

'I am Forgotten. Do you *now* remember me, Gilgamesh?'

And, reluctantly, I did.

In the gravity of my youth, I'd forgotten. I'd forgotten so much of the kindnesses from my mother and the laughter of my father, the quick but silent joys a family could bring to an age long lost to depression, ambition and untouched dreams. I'd forgotten how my mother would sit up with me late into the night and hold a cool, wet rag over my hot forehead as a fever burned me inside a fitful sleep. The way my mother ran her fingers through my hair and sang to ease my pain and suffering. She sang to me songs I'll never hear again.

My mother sang to me of her childhood in East Texas and she sang how children must grow strong to grow up. She sang of Hawaii and how she'd never been and how she would go one day to an island like Peter Pan and Wendy, her favorite bedtime tale. My mother sang to me all the silent wounds a mother suffers from her husband and children and how a mother's love could be infinite and safe as a baby within a mother's belly.

My mother sang and sang and sang, and in her voice, I first learned what it was to love, to dream, to live, to lose, to suffer, to hope, to give and to be forgotten. 'She sang to me,' I said to Forgotten by the fire in Central Park. 'My mother sang such wonderful songs.'

'He's starting to remember,' Forgotten whispered to the others.

And so I did because I'd forgotten the rub of my mother's hand on my back to soothe my boiling thoughts or my burning tears or how she'd turn from a hot stove she'd been slaving at for an hour cooking her children dinner and how she'd settle an argument between Chadwick and Cassandra and how she'd calm us by telling us stories of birth and creation and how so-and-so's baby came out lucky and small because America wasn't Africa and we should ever be so thankful. I'd forgotten how she never really made any sense to me then, but how everything she had once said in my rage of youth, now as I grow older, makes sense of all the world around me, a world no longer infinite and safe but small and lucky. I'd forgotten so much of my mother as I tried to leave woman for woman, her for another, and how back then, as I look back — forced to see into the Past because my hand had been compelled to fire — how deep into the night I'd wake inside the cold, endless space of our house, a broken home to a vacated family, and I could hear a sobbing so sad behind my mother's closed bedroom door. I'd stand listening, debating on my course of action: to go back to bed or to go inside and comfort my mother; but the boy I'd been and the man I was becoming raged war within, as it has done with teenage boys before me and will do so after me.

My mother Gwendolen wept. I listened outside her door to her pain, her brokenness so strange and so deep, so stark in its consistency, the rising and falling of the *whu-whu-whu-whu* mixed with the crescendo of her emotional suffering pouring out into verbal expression in the barely audible form of 'why me' followed by an eerie silence found mostly in older women who must eventually turn their gazes inward at themselves, not by mirrors but by hearts alone, and they see what their mad, overbearing choices have led them to: to an empty bed filled with hollow memories and to a blank future of never being wanted or needed as they had been in the prime of their youth and motherhood.

On nights like these I knew I could never get to sleep again, but something else deep within me, a son's bond to his mother perhaps, would keep me sitting by her door and when the crying became loud and without care to conceal, as if she wanted the world to wake and feel her pain to grieve with her, it would be then I held my hand to the door and kept it there until the frantic crying ceased and my mother slept.

'I had forgotten,' I said into the night air at Central Park as my eyes adjusted away from the memory of my mother Gwendolen and back to reality. But the fire was gone just as the three Girl Scouts were also gone. There wasn't even a trace at my feet of where a fire had and should've been.

As a silence filled me with a trepidation I'd not known since my childhood, the trees shook from the cold wind and the darkness collapsed into more loneliness. Looking at my left hand, unburned and unharmed, I recalled my outstretched hand resting on my mother's door and I said to myself,

'I'm sorry. I'm so sorry. I had forgotten. I had forgotten everything. I'm sorry I had forgotten you, mother.'

Into the trees of Central Park darkened by midnight, I walked humbled by my mother's life and love and by a whole universe of memories within me I'd forgotten.

In the sweet chill of the wind I said to myself what had happened could not have possibly happened, and as I made my way forward through the Arc de Triomphe, out of Washington Square Park — how I ended up there, I'll never know — and into Greenwich Village with its intense thrill of New York City's traffic, the cabs raced past me in a technicolor laser-light show as I turned and trudged in my silence along the edge of the park until the city became one with me in a stretch of night that seemed void of time, and while I searched for signs to lead me to the harbor and to the great statue several minutes passed where, despite the city's snow and ice, I'd half dreamed I was once again lost in the foreign megacities — Seoul, Saigon, Hong Kong, Beijing, Rome — I had once known as intimately as my old hometown. Having grown and rendered my years in America's heartland, the oddities of the multicultural puzzles pieced together in misshapen clusters here and there on each street of these megacities looked to me all the more international, all the more un-American and all the more divisive.

When I arrived at the harbor, the statue looked ordinary and lifeless regardless of how many lights lay upon her on Ellis Island. She had once been a shimmering copper, a spectacle to behold in the morning sun from years now lost to the erosive tides of time. She now appeared more human and sicklier in her oxidizing hue of a deathly green that, upon the trick of light and shadow, could glow white or blue, but never the color she had been created to be.

She had been, with her torch lifted high to bring me a bit of light in this dark night, a symbol of my childhood. I'd always seen her on television looking tall and proud and true, and I told myself she was all of that and more back then, but now, in person, she came off short and arrogant, a bit cocky, and false. She had been an elder sister, in her own way, to me in my childhood. I'd look to her wearing her crown in a photograph of a book or a magazine and say to myself she represented the best and the worst of times in America.

For a time in my early teens, while I'd lay in bed imagining what she'd be like if I ever saw her from the bow of a ship, much the way I'd seen in several twentieth century films and documentaries, Lady Liberty filled me with an understanding of how it would feel to be at home in a nation so much bigger and older than I'd ever be, and how she'd be there even after I'm gone from this earth.

As a child she brought me peace, as naïve and temporary as peace can be. But as an American — bred, born, raised, cultured — and a man who had traveled much of a strange world that betrayed his kindnesses, took advantage of his generosity and hardened him beyond his years, the statue no longer brought peace of mind. She brought with her now a reminder of how in ages long ago a colossus might've been built upon the shore or at the edge of a walled city to warn away strangers in a strange land.

Lady Liberty, likewise, brought with her the knowledge of a culture capable of being devoured, conquered and silenced at the king's table known by all as Globalization, and that thought haunts me as much now as then because I had seen the strange lands the strangers came from and no matter how much these strangers professed to be 'American' once they naturalized and proudly held a piece of paper granting citizenship to a nation that, hopefully, always welcomed them with open hearts, open minds and open arms, I also knew I'd felt and bled on the lands they came from, had lived upon those strange lands as if they were my own — but I was wise enough, experienced enough, to know those lands and cultures would never be mine nor would I ever truly belong to them — and I knew that no matter where I lived, what papers I held, or how much I said a thing, I knew — despite my wanting to at times — I'd always be American, I'd always be Texan, and I'd always be unlike those strangers in those strange lands foreign to all things American.

I said to myself as I stared hard at Lady Liberty that my culture did not shape nor mold my identity — which, for me, was true — but I also knew a truth more profound still: my culture preceded my identity; my culture was before, above, beyond and after my identity; my identity was my culture, and this I'd learned after living a decade and more in those strange lands. Lady Liberty's crown now came off as pompous, too full of pride, as I tried to walk away — and I did a few times only to return — to have her answer my unanswerable questions, to have her look me in the eyes — an American trait — and speak truths into my heart and into my soul.

I struggled to see past the fact that she was mere metal and wires and paint and how she had a twin, a doppelganger, located across the Atlantic Ocean in Paris, New York City's sister who too had grown odd and peculiar in her ways over the years. (We can't all stay the same, can we?)

Lady Liberty and her Parisian twin seemed to me a reflection of an unending dialogue, a discourse in a language I hoped never to be forgotten. I imagined the sisters gossiped about how the coming of a new century had changed things, how 'patriotism' had been a beacon in a blizzard at sea but had now become a Red Alert sparking a fear of a future hidden behind the curtain of all that is Unknown.

These two sisters, one in America and the other in France, would speak of how 'nationalism' had become a 'dirty word' which they too could not speak of between themselves. Of how loyalty to a 'flag' could be seen as 'evil.' Of how the words 'racist' and 'racism' lost their meanings by being misused, misdiagnosed and misrepresented, and how those same 'trigger warnings' lost their effects from being overindulged in and overused. Of how 'rights' and 'privileges' became all confused and jumbled and ended up replacing the other.

These two sisters — one American, one French — might even speak of their children and their stepchildren and the infighting that had seeded twisted roots which when fully grown would come to bear tasteless fruits. These sisters would speak of the bickering as any family would but the bitterness, they knew that lived in their children's hearts and minds, would come to nothing good. These sisters wouldn't laugh as other sisters might laugh after such a heated discussion within the family because they've felt the gravity and force of hate before, and this too, they believed their children had forgotten.

These twin sisters also knew deep down in the shells of what they stood for and represented that to focus on identity and race, if spoken loud and proud by one or by many, immediately became a divisive act, separating humanity by its fleshy differences and leaving unity for the human race fragmented, splintered, cheap. But the children and stepchildren of the twin sisters needed deconstruction to better evaluate and understand themselves and societal pressures, which included identities. Did the twin sisters speak of what it meant to be American? To be French? Liberal? Conservative? Gay? Straight? Binary? Non-binary? Artificial? Real?

While the snow weighted my shoulders and melted upon my cheeks and lips, I was filled with more questions than answers and the pointlessness of it all despaired me.

I might've stayed there in silence all night by the harbor staring at Ellis Island and Lady Liberty if not for a horn blowing from the unseen causing me to stir and slink away into the maze that was New York City. In that moment I told myself I heard in the sweet chill of the wind the goat-man-myth Pan playing a sad melody on his flute just for America.

The Moonlight Café, like most small-sized operations in New York City, had a humble, welcoming glow within.

Seated at the counter of that triangular neon-lit café, windows to my back and to my sides, were the day's estranged hunched over plates of steak, pancakes, club sandwiches and fried pickles. Others, like me, ordered coffee, Americano, and warmed their bare hands over the steam and around the porcelain, what little additional heat the coffee could provide.

Among all my travels over the years in foreign lands that seemed to me then distant dreams of childhood rather than actual places, I'd been in dozens of eateries and cafés like the Paris de Café in Central, Hong Kong which served dishes to residents and tourists alike at the best prices possible to maintain the simplicity of who the eateries and cafés were and what they had. No fancy brands. No flashy decorations. No designer seats and tables. Just a small business attempting to make a living in a corporate world that would take, lawfully or unlawfully, everything they had if it could and then call it 'simply business.' Regardless of the foreign countries, the strange foods being served, or even the multicultural languages at play all around me, I'd often had a sense of being back for those early morning breakfasts at Sissy's Red Wagon in my old hometown — little hometown, nowhere.

Moonlight Café, though, had in its relic booths by the windows and its swivel stools at the counter a feeling of belonging, and the belonging was not of a place but of a time and mood. The coffee with a cube of brown sugar the way I like it was strong and black, and I could not think of an exact time or period or era because for me the belonging was lost, had been lost for so long, and the time I told myself was an exact time on the clock you'd never refuse to remember because the time held some sort of personal significance that you shared with the ones you loved most a long time ago.

Though the diners spoke low between bites you could still discern the gist, or the guts, of their conversations:

'Ain't no jobs no how.'

'Who'll take care of my baby if I'm away?'

'It's those migrants flocking like drunken gulls to the city. That's where my job's at.'

'Little John-boy needs a daddy but his papa done run off. What can I make of that? How can I make anything of it?'

'You heard what the mayor did yesterday? Can't believe it myself.'

'Never were any jobs no how.'

'I'll declare, right now, here, before you and all these fine patrons of this wonderful establishment that eggs *are* alive and should not be aborted for people's sickening pleasure of having a little protein for breakfast. Go ahead. Test me. Just try your luck.'

'And what of little Sally? She'll be two next week?'

'I'd heard those jobs got shipped overseas to China or India or some-such-place where they'll work for a whole week for a buck and without toilet breaks. How can I compete against that?'

'Why don't they just make all the bathrooms unisex anyways?'

'I just....'

'Can't....'

'Take it....'

'Fuck this bullshit....'

'Land of dreams?'

'My ass and cock it is....'

'I'm sorry. I just can't.'

Like God must do at times, I turned my ears silent to the grumblings of the two construction workers down at the end of the counter. I closed myself off to the desperate mother in the far booth speaking into her mobile phone. There's too much noise in the low murmurs even at that hour of night and after the day I had, I felt broken, drained, depleted because I couldn't help them, not a single one; I couldn't help anyone because I couldn't help myself, and that was what tore me up inside. I wanted to help. I did. But even if I did offer what little I could it would be useless to those diners in the Moonlight Café.

All I could offer were words — as a novelist words were the greatest, most valuable assets I possessed — but words didn't add up to a hill of beans anymore. Americans needed real money and real jobs, and sadly, unfortunately, all I could offer them were silly, little words.

A purple-haired waitress in her twenties with a nametag that read 'Kyle' refilled my coffee, scratched her nose, winked and asked,

'Want any food today or just warming the benches for the next fella?'

For some reason when I looked at Kyle, I thought of being a kid again playing baseball beneath those grand American skies you only find in the heartland.

'I couldn't eat if I wanted to, Kyle,' I said.

'You know,' Kyle said, 'there's always someone who wants to listen.' She pointed behind her to a piece of paper taped to the wall.

The paper had a phone number beneath 'Suicide Prevention Hotline' in bold lettering.

When I started laughing at Kyle and at the sign, I hadn't even noticed I was laughing. But she or he or they took it as a slight or as a cruelty or as a madness and walked away to return the coffee pot to the warmer in the corner.

The other diners looked up from their plates and cups and lives for a brief moment but soon returned into that solace we all feel when alone in a crowded restaurant. Besides, they knew even if I were mad and needed help, there wasn't anything anyone could do for me. Then and there, at that moment, was the belonging, and it was one of helplessness and futility.

At a quarter after four I'd heard enough from the diners and their constant grumblings. No warmth could cause me to suffer any more. Kyle thanked me for a tip that matched the price I paid for coffee, and when the door of the Moonlight Café slapped shut behind me, the triangular eatery on that isosceles of a corner appeared to me as a giant slice of warm coconut pie out of all that cold darkness welcoming me once more to the streets with a harsh embrace into its fold.

By that time the streets had quieted to that of a deathly hall upon the hour of mourning where a taxi or two would zoom past every five minutes or so and it would be then, just for a few seconds, I'd be tempted to hail a cab and venture back to my hotel room, to a nice-scalding shower and to crisp-white sheets. But the beam of light called to me, and so I walked on saying to myself this was the path I must follow and how I'd never forget that Tuesday morning in September. I recalled my lethargy awakening to a profound awareness of a greater world than the one I'd known for twenty years, and that brave new world wasn't a kind and friendly one.

I've already told you what I did that day, having worked all night at the halfway house, having driven the orphans to school, and it must've been on the drive back when the radio was off and the sharp bite of the rushing wind burst through the van's windows in a struggle to keep me awake and on the right side of the highway, and how I reminded myself of the boring day I had ahead of me with French class at eleven and a death-like sleep from too much overwork and exhaustion, and how I said to myself that many years still lay ahead of me and a novelist one day I'd become, and how it must've been during that lonely drive back when the first plane hit the first tower, because by the time I walked in with the keys to return the van, the news was on the television showing one of the two towers shedding smoke, and how I told everyone that the reports were all wrong and that this was no sightseeing tourist flying a plane into a building. So much devastation and death would follow. But all we could do then was watch.

As I drew closer to Memorial Park the beam of light, reaching four miles into the night sky, appeared distinctly as two beams stretching heavenward as a reminder of all the loved ones we lost and of all the things we lost within ourselves.

Before me Greenwich Street lay solemn and heavy with the memories of the fallen and I had to choke back the tears. The pain, the anguish, the loss rose up from the concrete, the trees, the names and the water falling, ever falling without end, into the golden lights at the bottom of the memorial fountains where the two towers once stood. The voices and souls of the 2,977 victims, plus the six victims from the '93 bombing — the very one I'd done my eighth-grade oral report on — and how the water falling in the fountains sounded like a holy hymn in my heart asking me to try and be at peace with the past and the world around me, and to try to cherish the hour for we do not know when our time will come and when we'll be called home.

A somber, eerie silence quieted me then. When I looked once more over the tribute, a peaceful respect of a fateful day never to be forgotten, the Freedom Tower in Lower Manhattan and the Empire State Building in Midtown standing over me from afar, I said to myself that even though the memorial fountains continued falling in the wintertime as the night sky above me lay barren and black because the beams I'd seen had been an illusion and were not really there as they had been, because the beams of light rose majestically every September 11, and what I had seen, what had pulled me through the puzzling maze of streets and consciousness to 180 Greenwich Street had been in my head only and could not have possibly have been real. Or so I told myself as I turned the corner to keep on moving forward through the hushed streets of an early New York City morning.

I must've hit my head harder than I thought because I kept seeing things that weren't there, and as the thickest part of a cold night lifted all around me to leave me with a sensation of rising from deep underwater to reach the surface, I found a homeless woman sleeping (or so I believed was asleep) on a heated vent gushing hot air out and up like a Yankee geyser similar to Old Faithful in Yellowstone.

Dirty flaps of rags layered on the homeless woman ascended and descended with each gush of air as though she were a mockingbird trapped, and her gray-tattered hair resembled broken feathers rising and falling like the hands from dozens of children begging for food and pity in South Sudan. The homeless woman did not budge nor did she lift an eyelid when I slipped a fifty note into her money jar alongside her head, and all I could think to myself was the first homeless man I'd seen in my life had been squatting outside the National Archives Building which protected and cherished three of America's most beloved documents: the Constitution, the Bill of Rights, and the Declaration of Independence. Even though I'd long ago answered the 'how' I still couldn't fathom nor comprehend nor digest the 'why': why would we, as Americans, ever allow human degradation to happen? But we did, and we still do. The homeless woman in New York City also reminded me of another poor woman bundled in her ratty blankets on Queen's Road in Hong Kong; she'd cover herself with these huge, nasty blankets that probably hadn't been washed in years and she'd lie down at an intersection in Central between the Gap and the Adidas stores, and every time I passed her by I'd be compelled with an overwhelming sense of grief and pity and shame that I'd drop several dollars of coins faced with the British queen into the old woman's open money bag. There was only so much one person could do (one of my biggest regrets at having lived: I had not the resources to help them all) and I walked on into the

New York City streets, hard as ever, and I prayed for peace and for the dawn to come — not for me, but for us all.

By the time dawn did arrive, I found myself at the southern end of Central Park walking through one of those tunnels where people piss late at night and the smell of urine settles over the old bricks. I was on my way to the carousel but figured it would be closed for winter and so early in the morning. That didn't stop me though.

Even before I exited the tunnel, I could start to hear the sweet calliope music and I said to myself that carousels from all over the world played similar songs and how nice and familiar those cheerful musical notes could be to a person. Over the course of the night the snow had stopped falling but started again as the sun stayed reluctantly low in the east.

I hadn't expected the carousel to be open but I told myself, convinced myself for a time, the carousel in the park — the fourth since 1871 — was in fact open since it was near Christmas. I didn't want to go for a ride on it or anything but after the day and night I had it felt like every action, every choice and decision had led me through some strange labyrinth ending at the foot of a colorful, musical, spinning carousel.

When Cassandra was a little kid, our family would visit Six Flags Over Texas, a 212-acre theme park. She was mad about the carousel they had out there as the first thing you'd see as you entered. Even after an hour, my father and mother couldn't get my sister Cassandra off the stupid thing, and with the whole of Six Flags before us, my mother would have to drag my sister screaming and crying off that giant carousel.

I spoke then and I spoke low to myself, 'I'm too big.' I thought someone would answer me but no one did. Not right away.

After about five more minutes of standing in the snow watching the new sunlight glint off the fifty-seven horses and the eyes and poles that held the horses and seats steadfast to the carousel, I heard a sweet voice answer my own, 'You're never too big, baby brother. Never ever.'

Even now as I'm telling you what I should've told you a very long time ago, you wouldn't have believed me if I had said it as simply as this: my sister Cassandra was little again and she stood next to me holding my hand. Her hand was so small in mine it made me want to cry. I wanted to cry because I never wanted to let her little hand go. I didn't know it then but she was keeping me from going over a cliff. The real reason, though, I didn't want to let her little hand go was because I knew that if I did let her go, she'd have to grow up all over again and I knew what was waiting for her. I forgot all of that when she squeezed my hand. 'You're never too big,' Cassandra said again. Her eyes became hot and moistened with pain or joy, I couldn't be sure which, when she looked up at me. 'Come on. Go with me,' she said. 'It'll be fun.'

There weren't any little kids riding the carousel but it stopped for passengers none the less. A gate in front of us swung open on its own.

'Go on,' my sister said. 'Come with me, please.'

She pulled at my hand trying to move me forward, but I wouldn't budge because I kept telling myself how damned depressing it was when somebody like your sister said 'please' to you, and it depressed the hell out of me.

'Come on, Cody,' she said. 'We could ride this thing together. Together forever. Wouldn't you like that?'

I didn't know what to say. Her blue coat looked sad to me then and when I tried to think of something to say, I just wanted to cry. So, I said nothing. I didn't say anything at all.

'Won't you come with me?' Cassandra asked. Her face had this funny looking expression of finality on it, as though we'd never see one another again. She kept playing with the red scarf I had on and so I uncoiled it from my neck and wrapped it snugly around her throat to keep her warm.

'Maybe next time,' I said. 'For now, just let me watch you have fun.'

Cassandra let go of my hand and gave me a great big hug around my waist with her head resting on my stomach.

'I won't forget you, Cody,' she said. 'Never. Never. Not in a million, billion years. Never.'

I could hear she was sobbing, so I said in French,

'I'll never refuse to remember you either.'

She clung tighter around my waist, and then looked up at me with tears welled deep in her eyes, 'You promise?'

'I promise,' I said. 'Now go on. I'll be right here watching. I promise.'

Cassandra's pigtails flapped around her head when she nodded. I wiped her cheeks dry. My sister looked young again.

Before I could hold on to another second with her, Cassandra turned and darted through the open gate and onto the carousel. She ran around the whole thing five times before she chose her horse, a great unicorn that looked all the more splendid with my sister now atop riding in her blue coat in the early morning sun. The carousel started to spin and I watched her laugh and scream with delight as the carousel picked up speed and trailed the red scarf behind her. I should've been afraid she'd fall but the thing was I wasn't afraid for Cassandra. I was just so damn happy she was happy, and if kids were going to fall, you just had to go ahead and let them fall. Each time she came back around to my side where we could see one another, Cassandra would find me and wave and laugh, and then she'd be gone. She'd leave me alone in the snow like so very long ago and I kept telling myself, among many other things, I wasn't frightened and confused by human behavior, not like I was when I was a child, but deep down, now that I had grown into an adult, I was troubled spiritually and morally, nor did I believe I was the first person to come along and be troubled by humanity, by history, by poetry, by all of such things we take for granted. The carousel stopped and my sister shouted, 'Come ride with me. Just once!'

I held my hand up but didn't wave. I do that sometimes. I just held my hand high so she could see me standing there, alone, in the snow. Like old times.

Then what Cassandra did — it damn near killed me — she held up her hand, just like how I was doing it and said,

'I'm sorry for everything. For all of it.'

'I know,' I said, but I didn't know. Not right then. Not right away.

Cassandra dropped her hand and clung back to the unicorn the way she had done to me earlier. The last thing I heard her say — less to me and more to the ancient Universe — was when the carousel started again and she closed her eyes to say, 'I'm not mad at you anymore.' Cassandra quickly opened her eyes as though she had forgotten something. She waved over to me and I waved back. I could see a golden glow all around her. Then she was gone.

The snow grew heavier and I felt so damn sad all of a sudden. I was damn near crying but it was too cold out to do so. My tears would've come out frozen anyway. I was just so damn sad, if you really want to know the truth, because, I don't know why, I can't explain it, I'd lost my scarf and the carousel wasn't even working. The lights were off. The music, silent. The horses, motionless. The carousel, lifeless. I don't know why I felt so sad all of a sudden. It was just that Cassandra in her blue coat going around and around on her unicorn, which didn't even exist, looked so damn happy. God, I said to myself, I wish she could've *really* been here.

By the time I entered my hotel room it was seven o'clock in the morning — I'd been awake, lost, the whole night — and the bill with the paid receipt for automatic checkout waited on the carpet. I switched on the 'do not disturb' signal and bolted the door, sealing me to a silence most often found in crypts.

My flight was at eleven-thirty and I had enough time to shower and pack and eat — if I'd wanted to — but I didn't do any of that right away, and even now I can't tell you the reasons why I walked down the steps to the sofa in the den, sat down in a careful sort of way, and put my hands to my face.

I stayed like that — with my face in my hands, my head bowed — for a long time because I kept thinking about my sister and the life that I could not save her from. I told myself her mistakes weren't my fault, but somehow and for some reason all the mistakes in the world by all people felt like my mistakes and I was the one to blame. As if I were at fault for each war ever fought, each life ever taken, each person's potential lost and forgotten.

I knew, and kept telling myself, I could not be blamed for the Holocaust, for famine in Somalia and Nigeria, for slavery and racism, for the hatred and greed between men and women. The blame, though, felt all mine because to be a part of the human race, much like belonging to a family, meant accepting and owning all the good *and* all the bad.

The hotel phone rang and I removed my hands from my face and tried to recall who would be trying to reach me at that hour on that day and at that time. After three minutes or so, the buzzing of the phone ceased and the room became quieter than before. A stillness slipped in.

I noticed I hadn't taken my boots off and so I reached down and unfastened the straps on the sides and slipped my feet free to curl over the plush carpet. My toes began to thaw and I felt good to be comfortable and safe in the hotel room. I have always liked to travel, and for many reasons, hotel rooms have often felt to me more like a home. Perhaps because of the stillness. I guess that's why I'd end up living in one for a few years.

Out of the corner of my eye, I noticed the red bulb on the room phone blinking to indicate a message had been left for me, but all I really wanted was to read a book to a very special person — no matter what I'd end up doing with the rest of my life, I had a promise to keep — and I decided at that moment in the hotel room that nothing was going to stand in my way, nothing would stop me from reading that book to her. It had been almost thirty years since I made her the promise and I said to myself there wasn't any point waiting any longer. For some strange reason, keeping that promise meant everything to me.

Slowly, I undressed and showered. The knot on the back of my head was much bigger than I had expected it to be, and the dried blood washed off my scalp and neck into the drain like blackened chunks from charring. The hot water and steam helped to wake me but it also aggravated my injury, causing what had been a slight throb in the base of my skull to spread and intensify to the frontal lobes.

The headache intensified and I had to sit in a wet towel at the edge of the bed, still neatly made. The whole time I sat there I kept thinking about my brother Chadwick and my mother and father and how far we'd grown apart, but that was a natural process to growing up and growing old. At least, that's what I told myself, had been telling myself for twenty years or more.

Then as my headache calmed and receded into the background of my thoughts, a subtle truth I'd lived with since writing the book I told you about hit me and I became aware of what had been there all those times I looked back: the causes no longer mattered to me because I had no power to change them; what mattered were the effects created from each one of those moments I told you about. (Even so. Even so.)

When I checked the time on my Luminox watch, usually ten to fifteen minutes fast, the time read half past eight. I told myself I had enough time to make the flight but also that I was feeling slow, unusually slow. I finished dressing, packed all my possessions in an orderly fashion inside my Montblanc travel case, pulled on — weather be damned — my favorite Scottish-wool cardigan — the one I wore when I wrote the book I told you about — placed the keycard on the dresser, unbolted and opened the door.

On the final look around the room I saw once more the red bulb blinking on the phone. I said to myself the person the caller was trying to reach, trying to find, was no longer here, and in a way — whether you believe me or not — I was telling the truth. Without looking back, I walked out of the room and let the door swing shut behind me. I had a plane to catch and a promise to keep. For the first time in over two decades — not counting two hundred thousand words — I was going home.

As the flight attendant handed me my complimentary Bloody Mary with Aviation American Gin before taxiing to the runway, I noticed his nametag read 'Margarite' and I had to pause before accepting the drink in the plastic cup. I looked from the name to his boyish, almost feminine, face of Spanish ancestry.

'Thank you, Margarite,' I said, then offering an excuse for the alcoholic drink so early in the day, 'I dislike flying.'

'*De nada*,' Margarite returned, and left to bring another first-class passenger an issue of the *Wall Street Journal*.

While I sipped on my gin cocktail and stared out the window next to me at the conveyor belt spilling luggage into the plane's belly down below, I briefly hated myself at having missed an opportunity to eat those delicious tacos and have a classic lime margarita, preferably on the rocks, or two at La Esquina in SoHo where you led me that one time through a kitchen to get to the underground restaurant and bar. I told myself there'd be another time, that maybe I'd return one day to New York City as a victor and then I'd have a chance to take you to Las Iguanas or to lead you through other backways and kitchens, but by then you might have moved on to the next young writer so full of promise and talent but so very blind to the publicity and marketing sides of the publishing industry. You might not even recognize me anymore. You might even have your assistant screen my letters and calls. You might not be the friend I imagined you were in the beginning, before all this madness took hold of us. As if publishing a book could mean so much? So little? I didn't know. I still don't know.

Margarite's boyish face reappeared, said we'd be departing soon, and then collected the empty cup from my hand. I nodded and turned back to the window where the crew outside finished de-icing the plane. There was something to be said for such work, a daily task performed with such precision that one false step could cost the lives of hundreds and affect hundreds more. Down below, however, the crew expressed monotony and little enthusiasm for their heroic functions, albeit miniscule in scale the tedious tasks might have been to them at the time.

All I knew, I said to myself, all I knew were words, and such silly little words could never save a life, hundreds of lives, and I couldn't see how the words I had written, would one day write, could ever mean as much, or more, than a crew who managed an airplane, or a teacher in charge of a classroom, or a soldier on the battlefield, or the garbage collectors who kept the city streets free from waste and disease.

As a wordsmith, what contribution to society, to everyday individuals, did I offer? What did words like 'writer,' 'wordsmith,' and 'novelist' truly mean to contemporary society, to democracy, to capitalism, to communism, or to socialism? What, and why, did it matter? Not to me but to all the others out there, out beyond the window that captured my reflection against a runway racing by to be replaced swiftly and easily with buildings and cars growing ever smaller, ever smaller, until there were only clouds resting on my face. I didn't know. I still don't know. Between my fingers were the prayer beads of the rosary I always wore when I traveled, and since we were safely in the air, I let the rosary go.

At the Dallas-Fort Worth International Airport, there was no fanfare from the paparazzi waiting to blind me with their multitude of bright camera flashes. No surging crowd of fans waiting to wave homemade posters stickered with hearts hovering over my cut-out face (not that I wanted any of that, but what does one expect after having to enter back into the invisible hierarchy of society that airports modestly and willingly expose? Perhaps to reach one's destination safely?). No. There wasn't the mainstream-media reporters and their satellite vans (they'd never be interested in a writer from America's heartland). No. None of that. Despite being a regular joe, I didn't want nor need to wait for any luggage since I had my travel case stashed in the overhead compartment, and since I was the first one off the plane, the airport seemed to me nothing more than another stroll I often took on my daily walks with my baby son Thor around the beach at Discovery Bay in Hong Kong.

I found the queue to Hertz, upon my arrival, was nothing but me, quite sheepishly, zig-zagging back and forth, to and fro, between those flimsy nylon straps set up at every counter in the airport to preserve some semblance of social order and, as always, the path of utmost resistance. Still, it was nice to take the keys and papers from a young man, apparently from the tag pinned to his pink tie, named 'William 3rd.' I didn't ask. I just didn't need to hear another story behind a questionable nametag on someone I knew deep down hated his job and who, on a daily basis, was struggling to manage a shred of self-respect to drag feet and body out of bed, as I once did. Like I told you, I was on a mission, and, besides, I'd been in William 3rd's position once long, long ago. The only difference? I had consciously made an alternative set of completely different choices that led to more complex choices which led to more difficult choices until, finally, I became the man I knew, deep down, I had always been, even as a very young boy.

Like the pull I feel between pen and page, my thoughts on the drive to my hometown pulled me back, ever back, in Time and Space as *Pearl Jam* played 'Nothingman' over the radio. With thoughts I couldn't help but think, I'm pulled back to a time I chose to forget for at least ten years, and even then, on the highways across Texas, I wasn't at all sure why I was pulled back to that night when I was nineteen years old. But some memories for me held greater weight than others. I'd been a fool to fight the Universe back then but I tried, as all young people do at some point in life; I tried so damn hard to change not only my destiny but the destinies of those around me. In the end, I failed. It was an historic and epic failure on my part. At times we fail and at times we succeed. At times we win and at times we lose. That's how the game is played.

The night on Pine Creek Ranch I told you about — which you may have forgotten — I see myself looking through a car window at my infant daughter, Alicen. A slight rain had started and I wiped the back window so I could see a bit better Alicen sitting in her car seat. She had been innocent and oblivious to the world crashing outside. I rested a hand on the wet glass because I wanted to touch her, hold her, kiss her and speak to her one last time before she had to drive away with her mother Karolina.

Even to this day, when I searched through nametag after nametag all across the strange countries that I visited and were not my home, the name 'Karolina' stung me, bit me, and reopened the old wound, if not wounds, I had spent a lifetime trying to forget, then to heal, trying to learn to live with and remember without all the pain. The name 'Karolina' would always summon me back to that night much like a genie being sucked back into its lamp. I must go to that night, to that moment in Time when Karolina stood next to me, her hand may have rested on my shoulder — but I don't remember so — as I looked through the window of the car at my baby who waited for the drive to put her to sleep.

Karolina said something like, 'I have to go,' and I must've replied, quite pathetically, 'Please don't. Please, for the love of God, don't go.'

I had turned to her then and in her eyes I knew she saw the damp emotion and pain in my own eyes; she must've also seen the mistakes made, the regrets, the emptiness, the loss, and how all of it could never be undone, could never be taken back, rewound and then changed. For the second time Karolina saw the real me; she saw me without any illusion or fantasy, without any ego; she saw me stripped bare and broken. *Humiliated and ashamed.*

You must already know the story in detail: of how I asked her to marry me and how she said 'no' and how I persisted — me challenging, contesting the immense power and path of the almighty Universe before and after me — and how Karolina asked me what I'd do with my life, how would I take care of her and our baby, and how, rather foolishly, truly like a grand fool, I told her the truth, the mad truth of foolish young boys who measure themselves against their dreams; I told her how I was writing a book, which would be the first of many, a novella about a father and a son, but Karolina didn't want to hear any of it; she asked, 'What then?'

'Then I'd sell it.' For me, it was that simple. But life is never simple.

'You'll sell it? Where? What publisher?'

Of course, I'd sell it. That was the logical next step after writing a book. Then I could take care of her and our baby Alicen while I started writing my second book, a collection of short fiction, then — but she didn't want to hear any more of it; Karolina knew what I could not come to accept, what would take another decade or more to see for myself and to learn and to understand: that dreams, unfulfilled potential, couldn't buy diapers and formula and vaccinations. Nor could it buy an ounce of respect in a woman's eyes, even in the eyes of a young mother who loves the father of her child. (Don't be fooled by my sentiment. Karolina was right to have left me.)

I did go on to write and write and write and finish my first book, and my second, and then another and another as the Universe pulled me farther and farther away from that night and my old hometown. A second memory would, however, always end the first despite being out of order in Time and Space.

You know what happened at the end of the first memory with Karolina and baby Alicen: Karolina and I were holding one another, crying for the love we once had, crying for what we had lost, crying for what we would have to give up in order to survive and move forward with our young lives. I had whispered to her then, 'I love you. I will always love you.' And she whispered back, 'I love you, too, Cody.' We pulled each other closer and the memory ends.

The next memory I would have connects to that earlier memory with Karolina and I holding each other in the rain out on Pine Creek Ranch. The second memory had been when I was a cashier at Burger King and Karolina came to see me one night. At that time, she was seven or eight months pregnant with Alicen. I'll never be sure why I remember the second event after the one in the rain, but I always did and do.

I'd been working at Burger King for a few months — I know I already told you this, but listen because this time it's different — and I'd worked my way up from the grill to the cash register. I'd just taken an order and turned around to prepare the tray on the counter behind me. I turned back to the cash register to see if another customer had come but no one was there. I was about to look back to face the kitchen when out of the corner of my eye I spotted a lone figure watching me closely from behind a display case across the room near the entrance. I hadn't started wearing glasses then so, for an instant, I had thought the figure, silent and motionless, was part of the display case. As I tried to focus on the silent figure, Karolina stepped out to reveal herself and her well-developed pregnancy, her pride and her shame at such a young age. Karolina looked beautiful to me with her hands supporting her round belly beneath a large white T-shirt. The second memory finishes with that moment we first look at one another.

Karolina seemed lost but happy to see me again after my depressing summer right out of high school, the one I told you about. Karolina and I searched for longing and togetherness. We looked for something we could not find. We looked for love. We looked for answers as to why things had to be the way they were and why we couldn't have the fairytale ending: happily-ever-after and into the sunset and over the rainbow, and the kind of success you believe your dreams will bring if you believe hard enough, word hard enough.

We looked through the possible futures, thousands of them. We looked for something we could not find. We looked for love. We looked for answers as to why things had to be the way they were and why we couldn't change our destinies to fit what we wanted and needed them to be. We looked and looked and couldn't find what we were looking for. We looked at one another with every shred of fantasy and illusion that high school grants you and before our eyes we looked and saw all those fantasies and illusions lost. Karolina saw me as I was: a penniless boy wearing an oversized, ugly hat and a nametag hooked crookedly on a goofy uniform. She saw a boy who could never provide for her and her unborn child, Alicen Beth. Karolina saw me as I was: a failure, a fool, a fraud, a fake, a phony. Karolina saw a peon who must take orders from those above. She saw a difficult future ahead for the boy who would spend a lifetime trying to prove her wrong. She saw hardships for the boy who wasn't even aware such hardships existed. Karolina saw a boy who wasn't yet a man. She saw a boy who wasn't the boy she fell in love with. She saw a boy slipping away from her and her unborn child. She saw and saw and saw the truth. She saw what the boy could not see.

And the boy? What did he see? The boy saw a beautiful woman with his child inside. He saw a woman he loved. He saw a woman who didn't love him. He saw a woman who couldn't love him. He saw a mother. He saw a beautiful young mother all alone in a lousy Burger King at night looking at a poor boy who had nothing to give her, except his heart. He saw a poor boy who had no way to take care of her and their child. But he saw a poor boy who wanted to try. He saw the real and the profound. He saw what high school failed to show him, failed to teach him. He saw the consequences of his actions, of his choices, reverberating throughout Time and Space. He saw now the young girl who once loved him. He saw the things that would never happen. He saw himself holding her hand in the delivery room. He saw himself holding his daughter in his arms. He saw himself a man with a woman who loved him and their child between them on the bed. He saw himself as a celebrated novelist. He saw a poor boy with empty pockets and his empty bank account. He saw his inability to provide for his unborn baby. He saw a woman who was also a frightened young girl and a brave, new mother. He saw she would be without his help because the boy had no money and no means to support her. He saw what he didn't want to see. He saw that he had already failed her and their child. He had failed the whole human race. He had failed the only ones he had ever loved.

That's where the second memory ends: Karolina and I, locked in Time and Space, looking at one another from across the empty Burger King lobby; she was very pregnant and I was very poor. She was becoming a mother and I was still a boy. I wasn't the great Jay Gatsby I had read about in the book, nor was I ever going to be. I wasn't the *great* anything. And for some reason, those two memories, in that precise order, would be with me for all my life.

While driving the 177 miles back to Brownwood after twenty years, I told myself each small town (a dot on a line on a map) resembled my hometown in many ways and in many ways each town did not. The plains lay flat as they did in my childhood. Cattle ranches and petrol stations and mesquite trees, as common to the eye as horses and boots in Texas, remained exactly as each had been so long ago. Once upon a time.

From International Parkway outside DFW international airport to Texas 121 TEXpress — a name I've never heard before — to the final southern descent on I-30W to Weatherford, then to I-20 where I met up with 281S through Morgan Mill to Stephenville — Brownwood High's longstanding rival — then on to 377 to Dublin — home to the original soda made with sugarcane, Dr. Pepper.

Still driving, lost to my thoughts and listening to Springsteen's 1984-hit 'Born in the U.S.A.,' ever southward through Proctor, Comanche and on to Blanket — where the old wooden courthouse and hanging tree, or so they say, still stood in the center of town. Finally, I made it into Early, past the cemetery where my Grand-Mommy and Grand-Daddy were buried, past Heartland Mall and into Brownwood, Texas. Instead of exiting the shortcut to CC Woodson Road, I kept on Early Boulevard which eventually turned into East Commerce Street, which fed into the heart of my old hometown.

So much had changed. So much so I could hardly recognize the places where I'd spent the first twenty years of my life. Many of the buildings remained but with new names and businesses within. Completely new buildings had been constructed in new areas of land I never thought to imagine adding a new street with new shops. I had heard once — after I moved to South Korea — that Brownwood finally, after years and years of waiting and hoping, got a Blockbuster video rental store only for the company to go bankrupt. Like me in some ways, the store had come and gone without the slightest disruption to the growth of the city. Sissy's Red Wagon on North Main Avenue remained to me the most recognizable fixture, and though as a child I'd always thought old men and factory workers ate there, the old restaurant gladdened me to recall all the mornings I'd spent breakfasting there myself. And so, I decided to stop and get some coffee.

Some diners would tell you they'd been eating at Sissy's Red Wagon for over fifty years. Most of them, though, simply looked up at who was coming through the double doors — a bearded Texan who had traveled the world, who had been as far as Bali, and who had returned for nothing more than a hot cup of coffee. I nodded — as is the custom in Texas — and some nodded in return. Others, a few of the old breeds, could smell New York City on me and these men, worn from too much drinking and living, gruffed at my arrival but accepted me like the others because a Texan knows a Texan when they see one.

Smoking's still allowed in the restaurant after all these years but that early in the morning the air hadn't gotten bad yet, so I found a place at the counter, which looked to be my old seat I sat in during my college years. I ordered a cup of coffee from a woman in a dark green uniform who looked to be about my age; her nametag read 'Sarah Dee.'

Sarah Dee said, 'You want the chicken-fry, hon?'

'Maybe tomorrow,' I said and I drank my coffee. I added sugar and stirred. I couldn't remember the last time I had eaten a chicken fried steak with cream gravy.

'Well, doll,' Sarah Dee said, 'What don't you want?' She narrowed her eyes at me with her hands on her hips. In one hand she wiggled a pencil and a pad of green paper. 'I don't got all day, sugar-beans,' Sarah Dee said.

'I'll want another cup of coffee in a minute,' I said.

Two stools down from me, a fellow Texan who ate a steak between drags of his cigarette laughed and caused Sarah Dee to give a gruff of her own. 'He's no Yankee Liberal, is he?' the fellow said to the waitress.

'You know where to find me, sugar,' Sarah Dee said to me.

I nodded and replied, 'And you know where to find me.'

Sarah Dee relaxed her shoulders and welcomed me then. 'I'll just be over here making a fresh pot for ya.'

'That'll do,' I said, and it felt good to slip back into the familiar roles these people played with one another; these roles I had known since birth but without knowing I missed them it felt good to have them back.

'What's your name, son?' The Texan asked with the steak still being chewed and a cigarette burning out the corner of his mouth. He leaned over on one elbow and said, 'I'm Bill, Wild Bill to those who know me, and I only ask your name son cuzz I could tell you're from around these here parts.'

I told him my true name and not my pen name.

'You mean to tell me,' Wild Bill said, 'like the name out there on the street sign in front of the police station?'

'That's the one.'

'You related to him, cowboy?'

'As far as I know.'

'Well I'll be damned. What do you make of that?'

'Still trying,' I said.

'You're all right.' The old boy laughed and squinted and finally relented. 'You're all right in my book.'

'Good to know,' I said. 'I was getting worried there for a minute.' I looked at him then, at his bald head, beady eyes, large glasses and the wild beard smashed across his face.

Smelling of steak and onions, Wild Bill leaned a little closer to me as if to make for the ketchup bottle, but as he did, he said,

'You're one of them old breeds, ain't ya? You know what I'm tawkin about? The kind we cowboys only hear in legends these days?'

'Can't reckon I can say.'

'Either way,' he said as he backed away to his seat. 'Either way, it's good to have ya back.'

Wild Bill nodded and I nodded and that was how we left it. Soon after, Wild Bill paid for his breakfast, dropped a few coins for a tip and left.

I then ordered a free refill of my coffee and that was when it hit me. On my second cup of coffee I realized I'd been moving forward for so long I'd forgotten to take a look back at who I really was and where I came from.

There's something to be said about the banter between fellow Texans and the 'downhome' comradery friendships offer, and I spoke to myself on the nature of friendships, far different than the ones I had in Asia as a stranger and an outsider, or if you prefer, as an expatriate — take your pick because the two words mean the same thing — and as I exited Sissy's Red Wagon and entered my rental, I said to myself that no matter how many new buildings or streets were built in my old hometown it would be the people who stayed the same, and it would be these same people who made a city a city, a town a town. I knew, also, even though I lived in the city my heart and soul would forever be in the country. Meanwhile, I drove down 'the Drag,' a street that ran through the center of downtown from the courthouse to my old university. Countless and now endless Friday and Saturday nights would find streams of cars and trucks moving at a snail's pace as teenage boys hung out the windows attempting to woo the young girls with catcalls or loud music. Teenagers from across eight counties would come to Brownwood just for the Drag.

I slowed my rental and recalled how Dylan had been nicknamed 'the Governor' because he set the slowest pace imaginable for a line of traffic and he led the procession more like a king than a governor. Some nights we'd end up with three or four phone numbers with their corresponding names on each hand. One night on the Drag with Dylan and Sawyer, before their falling out years later — homosexual rumors got passed around as part of the reason, but I never did learn the real reason why their friendship broke apart; each person had his story to tell and I wasn't sure which one to believe — and that was when I met Juliet, a seventeen-year-old virgin, and she helped put me back on the path to love.

At the traffic signal at the end of the Drag, I eased my rental to a stop. Across the intersection Howard Payne University looked back at me as though she were a spurned lover who had forgotten me after all these years. I thought of Natasha and our walk one night through the campus and how we talked beneath the new tower that had just been built. I thought of how the afternoons between classes would find me asleep on the plush grass beneath the bell towers (Bells. Bells. The bells toll for thee). I even thought of the Saturday morning of the Fun Run in the pouring rain and how I ended the five kilometer race, all three miles of it in just over eighteen minutes, because I poured out all my rage, all my anger and hatred and spite, and I crossed the finish line where Gianna and her sister and mother waited beneath the umbrellas for Gianna's sister's husband and not for me (Rage. Rage. Rage against the drums).

The traffic signal switched to green and I turned left to continue on my way to a childhood home on Vincent Street. Where the large yellow house should've been, however, the corner plot lay barren and void of all the memories I'd spent and shared there with my family. Two blocks away on Durham Avenue, the little white house where I'd spent years being alone living with my divorced mother was still there, but the house and pecan trees out front no longer resembled the warm home I'd known in my teenage years. I turned left and drove by the house on Durham and down the six or so blocks to Coggin Park, where I once played basketball with Sawyer after school as a kid.

I turned right and drove around the back end of Coggin Park and on to my old high school, home of the Brownwood Lions, which upon my arrival on Slayden Street had the American and the Lone Star flags waving over the campus. Slowly I drove the road between Brownwood High and Camelot Apartments, where I had lived for a time with the kitten I adopted from the streets — the one

I told you about, remember? I named the homeless little guy Lazarus, and how he had a black face with a white mustache, and how he'd lie above my head on the pillow and how he'd stroke my hair with his little paws to wake me up. How I missed Lazarus then.

I continued driving down side roads and turned left and headed to my father's factory, which the last I heard had been bought by a South Korean corporation in years too far back to recall exactly when. With no traffic behind me, I sat the rental at the end of the road near the factory and looked over at the gray monstrosity and tried to imagine how my father, Henry, could spend so much of his life in such an ugly, vapid place. But he did and he did it for his children and for a wife who left him for her unrequited love with Dr. Bovary (maybe that's why I hated doctors so much and never wanted to be one nor called one). My father, Henry, lived much of his day-to-day life in that factory on the edge of town, and when he left after twenty-five-plus years, I don't think he even got a watch. I don't think he even wanted a watch, to be honest.

A truck behind me honked and I snapped back to where I was and quickly turned left. Down the road, less than a mile or so, my old junior high school remained lofted on a hill and when I recalled the two brief years I spent there going through puberty, I laughed. The junior high school looked the same but there was something about it that made it different, that made it look foreign and unfamiliar, as though I only dreamt of my time there and the buildings had never known my footfalls. I stayed to the right on the road and followed the curve up the hill and away from the junior high school and on to Gordon Wood Stadium, which, for me, seemed just as majestic and epic as the Colosseum, the Flavian Amphitheatre in Rome, where magnificent battles had been waged ages ago and victors had achieved glory and liberty. I kept driving down the paved road that had once been gravel beside the baseball complex and around to the stadium recalling to myself the football and soccer games I'd played and watched inside Gordon Wood Stadium decades ago. A part of me hoped that the stadium, like the Colosseum in Rome, would stand for centuries to come. But I knew, as I drove away, I wouldn't be around to see it happen.

Down a ways, the road led to Brownwood Regional Medical Center, where I'd been born in that hospital there on the southern hill on October 17, 1979. The hospital overlooked the once vast and empty fields where I had practiced baseball with the Tigers and later with the Giants, but those fields now had vanished into a mini-community of clinics and offices constructed of brick and bordered by pavement. I'd seen and been in that hospital on that southern hill more times than I cared to remember, but that hospital was where I began, in some ways, my journey in this world and it was nice to see that it was right where I had left it. I turned another left and headed onwards to Pine Creek Ranch.

By the time I reached the ranch it was well-past noon and I told myself that I shouldn't have come back. I should've stayed away and let the memories shine bright. Instead, a hard-bitter reality began to settle in and it whispered to me of how I could never go home again. Of how I could never go back. Though the fence and gate kept me locked out, I could see in the distance of what used to be Pine Creek Ranch and how the old oak tree still stood in the center near the pond where Pastor Hiddleston shot Twilight all those years ago. I could see the land of my youth. A home that was not my own but a land that belonged to those brave women and men who came before me and those free women and men who would come once I was gone from this good earth. Even so, I could see the land of my youth and I felt young and whole and one with myself again. But the reality before me — not the illusions I wanted to see — was that the rock quarry had come and dynamited the land to carve out more rocks inside. Nothing was as it used to be. Such a bold thing to think. As if anything belonged to me. Even so. Nothing was as it should be. There was just a giant hole in the ground. There was nothing.

Like a child left behind, I wandered around the cemetery where my grandparents were buried years ago. My Grand-Mommy, I told myself, had been laid to rest beneath an old oak similar to the one that used to stand at the center of my father's Pine Creek Ranch, and though I first believed the gravestone would be easy to find, I now knelt on the crest of a small southern hill plucking a few blades of grass and seeing, as if for the first time, many indiscernible oaks standing in the cemetery on the outskirts of Early.

The afternoon cut thick from the heavy heat and the expectation of coming rain, but even then I didn't want to go back to the front of the cemetery to the office to attempt communication with the grounds keeper which would only end in his inability to find the records of Goldie Orella, my Grand-Mommy, and in my frustration and despair be told to leave on account of the approaching storm.

Instead, I walked on with the book my Grand-Mommy had read to me as a bedtime story when I was a boy. A book about a young man who never, never gave up on his dreams and, as a result, he had discovered a cure for rabies despite the mocking jeers and ridicule he suffered at the expense of his fellow neighbors, his brethren, his kin.

Beneath the eighteenth oak tree, I heard nothing — no profound German composer and his immortal symphony, no grand line from a Sumerian or Akkadian poem, no sweet song from the birds above — I felt only the sound of a passing breeze carrying a slight American rain which caused me to hesitate and look back, to look down more closely at the letters on the gray stone of mortality beside my boot. I thought of how Grand-Mommy's grandparents, my great-great-grandparents, were Zollie B. Brooks of Alabama, born in 1873, and Francis Louise Painter also of Alabama, born in 1877. Zollie and his wife Francis would move to Texas, grow old and die. Zollie died in 1938 and Francis in 1956, both being laid to rest together in Old Hall Cemetery in Lewisville, Texas. I touched Grand-Mommy's tombstone and the words there, eternally etched to remind you that yes, you did once live such a glorious and golden life and we do remember you. Yes, we do.

A flat, marble bench had been placed next to the grave and I sat with the book on my lap not really knowing what to say nor how to say it after so many years, years that became immeasurable between the living and the dead. I sat and looked at the cemetery filled with plants, trees and rocks, and someone's beloved. Would I one day be brave enough to join them? I had no choice, I told myself. I would have to be brave, because out of all my experiences and out of all my travels I had witnessed too many times the beauty and the mystery and the enchantment of the unseen. I wiped away tears and spoke, 'There's so much I haven't told you, and there's so much more I don't know where to begin.'

After speaking to you for a long time and not knowing what else to do or say, I began reading the book, the one you had read to lay me down to sleep. There in the rain in front of my Grand-Mommy's grave, the one I'd promised to come so far to see, I saw a memory I shared with my son.

Thor was but nine months old and had just awoken from a mid-morning nap in our Discovery Bay home. I put down the book I'd been reading on the sofa and went to my son in the bedroom where he slept in his Baby Björn crib. I picked Thor up and held him close to my chest, his breath on my breath in the bedroom that was all white. We stayed like that, he and I, for a few minutes more and looked out the great big windows to see Tiger's Head Mountain, with all its trees, sloping down to the beach and on to the open bay overcast in a cold November sky. From the pier, down below, a ferry had departed and was spinning in the water to turn and go.

As my son rubbed his eyes to fully awake and emerge from a dream he'd been having, I kissed him on his cheek, and to the windows that showed the ferry leaving down below in the bay, I said ever-so-softly, 'Goodbye, boat.'

CPSIA information can be obtained
at www.ICGtesting.com
Printed in the USA
LVHW040812120920
665767LV00003B/790